IMMORALITY ACT

IMMORALITY
ACT

BEREND METS

The Book Guild Ltd

First published in Great Britain in 2024 by
The Book Guild Ltd
Unit E2 Airfield Business Park,
Harrison Road, Market Harborough,
Leicestershire. LE16 7UL
Tel: 0116 2792299
www.bookguild.co.uk
Email: info@bookguild.co.uk
Twitter: @bookguild

Typeset in 11pt Minion Pro

ISBN 978 1916668 287

British Library Cataloguing in Publication Data.
A catalogue record for this book is available from the British Library.

For all those who suffered
at the hands of the
Immorality Act.

†

AUTHOR'S NOTE

This is a novel and to construe *Immorality Act* as anything else would be a mistake. The characters and the settings as well as most of the incidents are fictional. A few real people like Nelson Mandela, Philip Kgosana and Hendrik Verwoerd appear briefly and the things said of them are historically accurate, but of course they never intersected with the characters portrayed here — that is the art of historical fiction.

Immorality Act takes place from the 1920s to 1961 and spans Indonesia, Holland and South Africa. Readers will find some of the language used politically incorrect, but they are accurate to the time. The South African Immorality Act of 1927 forbade "illicit carnal intercourse" across the colour line and was punishable by imprisonment. The law was repealed in 1985.

†

†

*We shall become nobody's corpse. We shall fight for our
existence, and we shall survive.*

Hendrik F. Verwoerd, Prime Minister of South Africa,
1960, minutes before he was gunned down at the Rand
Easter Farm Show, Johannesburg.

†

*During my lifetime I have dedicated myself to the
struggle of the African people. I have fought against white
domination, and I have fought against black domination.
I have cherished the ideal of a democratic and free society
in which all persons live together in harmony and with
equal opportunities. It is an ideal which I hope to live for
and to achieve. But if needs be, it is an ideal for which I am
prepared to die.*

Nelson R. Mandela, opening statement at the Rivonia
Trial, Pretoria Supreme Court, 1964.

†

PROLOGUE

Cape Town, October 1960

When I think back, the story started in a small cottage on a steep cobble-stoned street in District Six. It was the home of Promise Madiba, a nurse at Groote Schuur Hospital. She was a stunner if ever I saw one. Wow. She had a gazelle's narrow face but a lion's mane of tawny hair crowning an hourglass figure that spun men's heads. Her smile was a two-edged sword, though. It could be broad and inviting or thin and cutting. You were never quite sure where you stood with Promise Madiba.

Promise had kept the cottage nicely. Freshly painted pastel green, it stood out from its varicoloured neighbours that lined the sharp incline, many faded by the irrepressible African sun. She tended her scarlet bougainvillea with care. Grown wild, almost too big for the clay pot she had placed in a corner of the covered stoep that fronted her cottage, Promise pruned the bush each morning, sweeping its papery leaves into the storm drain that edged the street.

On the evening of October 4, 1960, Dr. Willem Jansen had finished duty at Groote Schuur Hospital and had come over for a visit. He was an odd bod. Lanky, pale and blonde, he loped like a giraffe. He had a long, taut neck, protruding Adam's apple, beaked nose, and blanched eyes set more narrowly in his face than you might have expected. He gave the impression of restraint, ready to explode.

Willem had parked his black Beetle lop-sided — one wheel on the kerb — and had brought two bunches of flowers wrapped in brown paper. Three proteas for Promise and seven yellow carnations for Marja, her favourite colour.

Marja was a Cape Malay prostitute. She was quite nice really, but that is for later. She was petite and olive-skinned and had the black silky hair one associates with Asian women. Her face was roundish, dimpled cheeks slightly puffed, she had a coquette's red smile and moved with the tripling gait of a geisha. She always wore a sarong. Invariably yellow, Marja wrapped it tightly, as high as possible, to cover the scar that marked her chest.

Soon after Willem had surrendered the flowers, the three had settled in their familiar semi-circle on the stoep, Willem in the middle rattan chair with Marja on his right, and, as the sun was well down, the girls had wrapped themselves in grey blankets against the cool mist coming off the dark slopes of Table Mountain: they all had a splendid view over the city and Table Bay below. Marja pointed to each new light that winked on in the harbour.

"Aikona, hau, you can't keep up with those lights, Marja, they are coming too-too fast!" Promise chided, took a slow sip of red wine, pursed her lips and swallowed — her hazel eyes sparkled with pleasure.

The wah-wah of a passing police siren accentuated the drum of traffic that beat down from De Waal Drive, curving around Devil's Peak, dark in the distance.

"Willem, don't you agree with me? You sit there quiet as a goat, why don't you say something?"

"Agh, what is there to say?" He brushed a bougainvillea petal from his black trousers.

"Well, you could say that you fell in love with me at first sight. That first day in theatre when you were shaking like a rattlesnake and had to operate on Mrs. Plumbottom. You looked in my eyes, hungry for love."

"I did not. I did not. I was just adjusting my focus." Willem fingered the black polo neck tight at his throat, a pained smile breaking nevertheless.

"And your trembling hand that I stopped from shaking. What of that? I had to put the scalpel right into your palm to get you started. Didn't *that* make you love me? Hau, hau." Promise shook her head from side to side, sucking in her cheeks to purse her lips again, and loosened the itchy blanket draped across her shoulders.

"Agh, maybe, maybe not. What do you think, Marja?" Willem swivelled his head from left to right and shifted to lean more closely into her.

"Well, it can't be love at *first* sight, because that was with me. I was the first one you kissed, wasn't I? Under the Dago Falls, in Bandung, when we were thirteen," Marja said, in her surprisingly gravelly voice, pulling the blanket up closer, a salty sea breeze rising from below. A wheeling seagull screeched as it rose in front of them.

"You're right, Marja, but is Promise wrong?" Willem laughed and turned back to Promise, his slate eyes narrowed to hold her gaze, the loveliness of her face filling him with tenderness.

†

"Hau! We're in kak," Promise shouted as the thundering throb of a descending police helicopter enveloped the bedroom, its blistering light penetrating the dark cottage in a white blaze. Rousing from under Willem, his stiff neck between her breasts, Promise unwound her encircled thighs to release his legs, desperately aware of the semen staining the sheets. "I'm out of here. You look after Marja." Promise catapulted out of the back window — left open just in case — a black streak fading into the distance up Devil's Peak.

There was a sharp rap at the front door. A shrill police whistle. A barking dog. The whoosh and thud of receding rotors overhead. Marja came in from the adjacent room. "Mijn God, wat nou!" Another rap on the door, now harder and a vicious voice. "This is Warrant Officer Piet Marais. Open the door or we will break it down. Open the door."

Willem got up, pulled on a pair of trousers and added a shirt, loosely knotted. He looked at Marja evenly and said in Malay: "Tidak apa-apa, tidak apa-apa. It is okay. Sit. Sit on the bed." Then, as if in a daze, he rose to his full height and made for the front door, just then splintered by an officer's shoulder — three policemen pushed their determined way into the lounge. Each resplendent in smart blue tunics, braced by belted leather pistol holsters, they had the good grace of removing their caps and tucking them under their arms, filling the small cottage with their heavy presence.

"Mijnheer, I am Warrant Officer Piet Marais. This is Sergeant Viljoen and that is Constable Botha. We have a warrant to search the premises under the Immorality Act." He narrowed his pale blue eyes and squinted at Willem to drive home his point, seeming to sniff the air for any impropriety. Marais looked around to survey the scene, keenly alert to Willem's reaction. Taking in the red-tiled floor, the sisal mats, the intricate beadwork and the artfully hung wooden masks, he tested the comfortable couch, stooping down to gauge its spring. He was startled by Willem's reaction.

"Firstly. I am not a *Mijnheer*. I am *Doctor* Willem Jansen. What is this matter of disturbing us in the middle of the night? You have no right. Get that fetid dog out of here. Now."

Regaining his confidence, Marais bristled. "We have every right. If we have reason to believe that carnal intercourse is being perpetrated across the colour line in contravention of the Immorality Act, we have every right to search the place and look for evidence."

"Show me the warrant."

"Here, Doctor, you can read it for yourself; you can use my torch if you need to: the light is rather dim." Marais passed the foolscap and trained his torch before continuing. "Satisfied…? well, I must start with a few questions. And then we will search the place, high and low… First" — he pointed one finger in the air — "who lives here?"

"This is Promise Madiba's house. She is a nurse at Groote Schuur Hospital, where I work. She is on duty tonight," Willem responded, his gaunt face colouring and his deep-set eyes lowering.

"Are you alone?"

"No, Marja is in the main bedroom. She lives here with Promise."

"What? Are they lesbians or something or are you lying? Call her out."

"That won't be necessary, officer. I know your type," Marja announced as she pushed open the door and sashayed into the lounge, wearing Willem's white pyjamas tightly clasped to her breasts. Dark hair piled tartly over a beatific smile, she curtsied in front of each policeman in turn, and then curled up on the couch, a cat in her den.

"Well I never." Marais couldn't believe his eyes; although Marja looked vaguely familiar, the light was poor. "It's a bloody menagerie. A coloured, a black, and a white — no wonder we were ordered to raid the place." He pointed at Willem. "But what the hell are you doing in this house, Doctor Jansen? In the middle of the night with this vixen? I know this girl; she's one of Plaatjies's prostitutes. I have seen her at the Blue Lagoon. Here in District Six."

Feeling finally cornered, Willem retorted at his caustic best. "Fuck you, officer. That is far too long a story to tell. I have nothing further to say."

"Very well then. Stand aside. Sit down on the couch. Men, search the place. Viljoen, look in both bedrooms. Look at the bed sheets for any signs of sex. I will manage the lounge and kitchen. Botha, you check the stoep and look around the house. Turn over the rubbish bin for rubbers. If we find anything we will arrest these two tonight. Get on with it. I think we have hit pay dirt this time." Marais beckoned Willem to the couch and stepped into the kitchen to rummage around.

Then.

"Kaptein. Come and look here, Kaptein."

"Viljoen, what is it?" Marais had exited the kitchen; he looked at Marja and Willem to reassure himself they were sitting on the couch, and then walked into the bedroom.

"The bed sheet is sticky with spunk. And black curly hairs. Doctor Jansen is blond."

"Very well." Marais walked over to stand in front of the pair, the pitch of his voice sharp with tension. "Dr. Jansen and Miss? Miss…? What is your name again?"

"Marja de Koning."

"Whatever it is. You are both under arrest for contravention of the Immorality Act."

†

ACT 1

CHAPTER 1

**Tape Recording by John Terreblanche,
Cape Town, October 1960:
Sister Promise Madiba**

Au! The first thing I remember?

I was nine and I was to start school. My father and mother on that day walked me to school. Me in the middle. My father was big, very dark, like a bull, and my mother the opposite: a gazelle. He was a giant, a chief, very full of himself, and did not care for little things. He kept people waiting to show that he was important. That day too. I had put on my new uniform and shoes, ready to be on time. And he kept Umama and me waiting, until my mother couldn't take it anymore. She rarely gets angry, but I was her favourite and she was fed up with him. "THABO, YOU WILL COME OUT NOW. NOW! TEMBISA CANNOT BE LATE FOR HER FIRST DAY. YOU HEAR ME?"

He did. My father shuffled out of the hut somewhat cowed. But not much. He grabbed my right hand in his left and started pulling me up the path, splash, right into

3

a puddle. My white sock was completely brown. I cried of shame all the way to school. Umama kept saying: "Aikona, aikona, that is no way to treat your firstborn. Aikona."

I hate it when people row; it makes me upset inside. Like a stomach ache.

Promise?

That is my English name instead of Tembisa, my Xhosa one. My teacher gave it to me that first day at school: Tembisa means *promise* in the Xhosa language.

I was born in 1928 in a village called Mtshiso, in Pondoland. I grew up in a mud hut with a peaked thatched roof. Inside the floor was a flattened ant-heap; we used to keep it compact with a coating of fresh cow dung. Aikona, that smelt to high heaven. There was a fire in the middle of the hut. The smoke would rise up from the hearth, circulate around the hut, bathing us with its stinkhout smell, and then dwell in the peaked thatch roof before escaping outside. It is no wonder our clothes always stunk of smoke. Of course, we didn't wear western clothes. A loincloth and a blanket is what we used until I went to school. The smoky acrid smell of wood fire clung to our coverings no matter what we did. Even if we ducked outside under the low door as the fire started when the smoke was at its worst.

Our village lay in a narrow green valley, threaded by cool streams and overlooked by tawny hills. Our kraal of beehive-shaped huts dotted the countryside: footpaths stretched into the veldt.

Like all Xhosa children, I learnt through watching. I learnt to tend the sheep, run, climb, and on hot days, drink milk from a cow's udder. That is nice by the way, but a

4

bit tricky. I also learnt our customs, rituals, and taboos, and around the cooking pot fire, my mother told us Xhosa legends and fables; my father stories of the great Xhosa warriors. I also learnt I should quietly keep a woman's place in the kraal: fetch water in heavy buckets from the nearby spring, and help Umama tend the fire in the hut.

Did I meet many white people?

Not at first, not in Mtshiso. The local magistrate was white, and the shopkeeper, but that was it. Rarely, a white policeman travelled through our area. I thought these people were from another world and was told to treat them with care and to show respect. But they had no role in my life, and I had little knowledge of our difficult relations with the whites, until much later.

One day — I must have been twelve or so — there was a commotion in the kraal. My father was visiting. I always dreaded his visits. I feared the fighting, turning my stomach to knots. I found him crouched in my mother's hut, on a low chair, coughing and coughing till he coughed up a spat of blood and smeared it in his hanky. Then he just sat there panting. He had come to say goodbye. He must have had some lung disease to cause all that coughing, probably TB, but he still called for a cigarette. Umama refused, but he bellowed with rage, so she gave him one from his tobacco tin. He lit up and puffed away, becoming calmer, and calmer, and then died. Just like that. He slipped away.

I don't recall feeling much grief at his passing, but my life was about to change. I was to leave Mtshiso, to enter the household of my new benefactor, Chief Ziyabonga Dlamini. My father had arranged it; he knew he was sickening.

I do recall the long walk. I put my precious school shoes in my bag and walked barefoot with my mother. Every now and then Umama grabbed my hand and clasped my fingers tightly as we made our way along rocky dirt roads, footpaths, and up and down hills and past many villages. At sunset, we descended from a high hill to a green valley below. I had never seen anything like it. A white stucco church. Three low buildings, and eight rondavels, all white-washed and clean, fresh thatch catching the failing light. We walked down the slope, past herds of cattle and sheep, and on into the village and to the chief's house at its centre. A dazzling white limed building; there was a green, green garden in front of it. Freshly cut. I can still remember the crisp smell as a big car came grumbling to a halt. And a big man, very big, got out of the car wearing a smart suit. Hau. He looked so confident. Like the chief he was. My new guardian and benefactor. He welcomed me: "Tembisa, you must be my new daughter." And to my mother: "Inenekazi, she is just as pretty as her father told me. May he rest in peace." My mother bowed her head.

"We will look after her as if she is one of us," he said. "I will make sure that we continue her education. Perhaps she will become a teacher, to help our people." My benefactor waved his hands about. "Please come into our humble home, my gentle woman. Can we offer you something to eat and drink before you rest? You must be tired after the long journey." He swung off his black cowboy hat and bowed in the direction of the front door.

"Forgive me, my gentleman. I cannot. It is too-too painful to give up my daughter. I must go back now. Now, now." My mother buried her chin in her chest.

"Then go well. We will give you some fruit for your journey."

My mother held me to her heavy bosom. She was slim but substantial. That was the last time. She probably caught the TB from my father. So I remember that time. The comfort of her warm breast against my cheek.

Chief Dlamini brought me inside and introduced me to my new sister and brother. Lindiwe was really pretty. Sipho was short, fat and obnoxious. He thought he was smarter than me. But he really wasn't. Not by a long shot.

I was enrolled into the one classroom school next door to the chief's house. I studied English and history and Xhosa. We did our lessons on black slates with white chalk. I was hardworking and more determined than clever: "Knowledge is power," I read in a book by Sir Francis Bacon. This became my mantra.

The chief's indabas were held in a wide courtyard to the side of the church and were grand events: tribal elders gathered from far-off places to talk, talk and talk. They conferred on national matters, cattle culling, droughts, new policies planned by the local magistrates, or difficult laws brought by the government. Au. Au. It was so impressive.

All Pondos were invited, and many came, often travelling by foot or on horseback to do so. The indaba could run on and on. But every night there were festivities. Fattened goats were slaughtered and put to the fire. Pondo maidens danced in circles around the campfires, and tribal elders celebrated Bantu warriors of the past, telling heroic tales till late into the starry night.

At first, as a teenage girl, I was shushed away from the

indaba. Women of course were never allowed to speak. That was a man's job. But I just persisted, and the chief became accustomed to my presence. In fact, I sensed he welcomed it, although he could not say so. I stole with my eyes and ears.

Here I learnt a lot not found in the history books I had read.

How the white man, the Abelungu, had torn the Bantu asunder. Once the Pondos, Xhosas, Thembus and Zulus were one family; now, since the white man had come from across the sea with guns, the land had been stolen and the Abantu tribes shattered. The white man had seized the land from the black man.

One fiery speaker made me feel cheated of my birthright when — I think this is what he said, don't quote me, Mr. Terreblanche — "We are nothing but sweating slaves on our own soil, pitiful renters of our beautiful country, and foot soldiers for the white man's army. In the land of our birth" — he stamped his foot twice — "we have no power to control our own destiny." That was something to remember.

I must have been nearly fifteen when the chief celebrated my standard five pass by slaughtering a fattened goat. He promised he would support me if I continued to work so hard. The next day he put me in his winged Chevrolet and we drove all the way to Clarkebury Boarding Institute at Engcobo. That was a long way on sandy roads. Down through Port Saint Johns, about two hundred miles. I was very pleased. I was to follow my sister Lindiwe. He told me of the great teacher in charge of the school: the headmaster of the great Thembu College founded on land given by King Ngubengcuka.

The school was a revelation. It was my first contact with the white world. Not only was I now being taught by white teachers who had lived abroad in England or Ireland but I was rubbing shoulders with black teachers who had gone to Fort Hare University to get degrees. That was rarefied air. Yes, I agree that is a good word. So much for learning English. It was all a bit intimidating at first but, if my sister Lindiwe could, well, so could I.

By now, I was a prefect in my final year, and Lindiwe had gone off to Healdtown School, and... even if I say so myself, I was quite a looker. I was lithe and thin and could run as fast as a gazelle. Or almost. At least, I had the antelope's sleek looks and slanted brown eyes and a mane of tawny hair to below my shoulders. I could toss my hair like a lion, although I had a bokkie's narrow face. This seemed to unfasten men's eyes. Or so they told me.

Thando... Xhosa for love... was a cross-country runner like me. I used to run barefoot. He wore fancy white plimsolls. That should have warned me off. But didn't. I was attracted by his smooth talking. "Hey babe." You would know the type, Mr. Terreblanche. But I needed attention.

Well, one night, quite uninvited, he crept into the dormitory and into my bed. If I screamed, we would be found out and dismissed. So, I let him carry on a bit while I decided what to do. He wanted me to lose my virginity there and then. I was having none of it. Aikona. I grasped his stones gingerly in warning, slithered out from under him, and ran down the fire escape to exit the building and hide in the bushes outside. Here I had a long night to think on things, waiting for the school entrance to be opened in the morning. And it may surprise you, from what you know of me now, but I found out that I was not sexually excited by Thando — he reminded me too much of my disgusting father.

The plan had been that I should follow Lindiwe to Fort Beaufort once I got my standard eight certificate. That would have been around 1945, but Healdtown School was expensive and Chief Dlamini did not have the money to support all three of us at the time. So, instead, he suggested that, given my school leaving pass, I earn some extra money as a secretary and save up for the next step. That was good advice and came to determine my direction for the future. I found work in a doctor's private practice clinic — on the Coloured side of the practice, of course. Dr. Ian Smith was A-one. He was from Ireland. He let me help, not just doing secretarial work but with the patients: taking blood pressures and eventually, when the nursing sister was sick, which happened regularly, and he was too-too busy, I gave injections into the patients' fat bottoms — jovas, they called them. Vitamin injections that strengthened the men after they had overdone things with sorghum beer the night before.

I must say, lucky for me, Dr. Smith took a shine to me. Nothing unseemly. Although he was quite attractive, but for his white man's sour smell. Mr. Terreblanche, you white men pong. But Dr. Smith saw my potential. After a little less than a year he offered to help support me at Healdtown on the condition that I took up nursing afterwards. As far as he was concerned, the country needed decent black nurses, as most are white.

So, there I was at Healdtown. The largest African School in the subcontinent, with over one thousand pupils. A completely black school housed in ivy-covered colonial buildings, close to the *very* white town of Fort Beaufort, a former outpost of the frontier wars against the Xhosa.

Saturdays we were free to take the bus into town. *Natives Only* buses, of course, filled with Africans going into Fort Beaufort, from the surrounding township villages, to shop, or sell their wares on the street corners.

My new girlfriend Aphiwe and I set about the serious business of window shopping until a sweaty white man with a red angry face shouted at me.

"K….r go and get my letters from the post office; I must hold on to my dog."

"Please, sir, I am busy," I responded, polite as ever.

"No, you're not. Get my post or I will call the police."

Seeing that I was not about to follow his command, the angry farmer exercised his threat. A constable arrived at the double. And, of course, the policeman made the fatal demand: "Miss, passbook, please." You can imagine my shock when I reached into my handbag and couldn't find my dompass, knowing that it meant instant arrest. I was marched off to the police station, booked, and shoved into a jail cell. I was warned that if Aphiwe did not bring my passbook by the next morning I would spend a second night in jail.

My underground cell was like a panther's cage. A sadistic white officer sat at a desk looking at the black animal inside — me — with a bucket of vomit next to me stinking out the place. Things got worse overnight. Two constables started screaming at me: "Jou k….r meid ons

11

gaan jou opfok." I know I don't need to translate; you being an Afrikaner, I am sure you get the gist. And then: "Princess, jy is 'n Princess, but look at you now. You munt." I curled up in the back of the cell and hid my face in my arms, trying to make myself small and invisible, but I was roaring inside.

The next day, much later, a new constable came down, handed me my stamped passbook, and released me from the jail. I found Aphiwe waiting outside the police station in the bright sunlight.

I am sure you know all about the Day of the Covenant, Mr. Terreblanche. The religious holiday held to thank God for the deliverance of the Afrikaner Boers from Dingaan's Impi. Right up your track, no? The Voortrekkers slaughtered three thousand Zulus at the Battle of Blood River.

Back in 1948, when I was in my final year at Healdtown, the day was still called Dingaan's Day, and the school commemorated the annual holiday by inviting a prominent African to address the assembled students from a stage mounted in our dining hall. That year a well-known Bantu historian had been invited to relate the events that transpired on that historic December day in 1838. We expected a man in a suit with a book. Instead, the historian arrived on the stage, bare-chested, to do battle. He carried a shield and brandished an assegai and sported only a leopard-skin loincloth for modesty. After a brief introduction by the school's principal, he started to tell the story in a slow growl from behind the lectern, but then crouched down and leapt into the air; the assegai struck the copper curtain rod suspended above him, creating a loud clash and causing the crimson curtains to flap. The historian became possessed. He announced that the assegai striking the copper rod represented the flashpoint between Africa and Europe. Between what was African and good, and European and bad. We needed to drive the white man out of this country of ours. Let's start this Dingaan's Day. Amandla, he roared. You know the way we do that, stretching out the DLA, in a powerful yell. He clenched his assegai in his fist and raised his shield high above his head. AMANDLA! Freedom! We rose as one and yelled back, NGWETHU! We have the power!

Mr. Terreblanche, that changed my way of thinking about things. It unlocked my spirit.

After completing my schooling, I travelled back to Pondoland to get my benefactor's counsel. Chief Dlamini offered much advice but no money. He agreed with Dr. Smith's suggestion that I should train to be a nurse to help my people. He asked if I was willing to leave Pondoland. I was willing. More than willing. The chief told me that he had a brother. A man of great influence. He was living in Cape Town. If I was keen, he would write me a letter of introduction. Perhaps his brother could get me into nursing school, given that I had done so very well in my matriculation exam. I remember him closing the envelope and writing on the front. Very carefully, so that the ink did not drip: Mr. Goodwill Dlamini, 17 Horstley Road, District Six, Cape Town.

†

CHAPTER 2

Tape Recording by John Terreblanche, Cape Town, October 1960: Dr. Willem Jansen

Agh. The first thing I remember?

You really want me to answer that?

Under the present circumstances? Verdome... Verdome... but if I must... probably... and this may sound a bit over dramatic... but it was... the touch of death. The feel of it. Japanese planes had bombed the city of Bandung, where I grew up. This would have been early 1942 when I was still fifteen. I was a boy scout and so had volunteered for the Air Raid Precaution Service. Which, by the way, proved totally useless against the Japs. All we heard was the hapless wailing of the air raid sirens, on and on, but there were no longer Dutch planes in the air to protect us. Bandung was defenceless. I remember the casualty lying lifeless in the grassy square, the feel of death when I lifted her into the ambulance.

I was scared and dismayed. The Jap invading force looked puny and unimpressive. Just lines and lines of short men in khakis and black cloth caps. Like a swarm of beetles with bayonets. The officers right in front, carrying samurai swords and pistols. How could our KNIL not have stopped these advancing troops? In case you're wondering, KNIL stands for Koninklijk Nederlands Indies Leger. My father was a captain in the Dutch army, the commander in chief of an armaments factory on the outskirts of Bandung in Indonesia.

The country wasn't called Indonesia at the time; that would come after the war. It was known as the Dutch East Indies. The Dutch, as you know, were avid colonialists — in search of trade routes to the east and west of Holland. Many of my extended family settled in Indie.

But let me rather start at the beginning.

I was born in 1926. On the exact same day as Marja. The only difference was that I was Dutch and she was an Indo, because her father had married an Indiesche girl. I was white and she was brown. Although no one would have been able to tell the difference, I am sure, because we were bundled up tight and put into adjacent bassinettes in the Rumah Sakit. The small hospital that served the military personnel in Bandung. This was just blind luck. Our parents lived next to each other on Banda Street and were firm friends as both our fathers were KNIL military officers. So we grew up together like a brother and sister.

One of the things that I really enjoyed doing with Marja was flying kites. Fighting kites. We must have been six or seven, as I remember it. First, we made the kite frame out of bamboo strips and attached coloured paper with glue. Silk paper was best. Then we prepared the glassan kite string: cutting string covered in hair fine glass stuck with chilli glue.

How did we do that?

We took a dead light bulb and crushed it to a powder, mixed in a little glue with red chilli, and painted the reddened glassan onto the kite string that we had wound between two Kenari trees in the back garden.

We used to fly over the grassy square in front of our houses. Marja and I launched our kites high into the wind, carefully unwinding the glassan string from the wound cooking tin, so as not to cut our fingers and draw blood. Then we would talk and fly and fight with other kites soaring over the square. The trick was to get your kite string underneath someone else's. Pull hard, so that the kite jetted up and cut another's string, setting it free to float away. Then the loose kite was anyone's for the taking, as it fluttered and fell to the ground. That is how I learnt to run, fast. To capture freed kites. I needed to be faster than the Indonesian boys. And often I was. Those were some of the happiest moments I remember, free as a parakeet.

When I was a few years older, my father bought a second-hand Willis Overland 1931 model. It had a canvas top that didn't leak. On Sundays, he took me out with his friends, north into the mountains. Once there we climbed steadily. He didn't talk much, like me, but he had a positive presence that you could feel. Willing you up and on. Of course, he was a military officer; what would you expect? I loved being up there with him, the elevation, the views of Bandung below. I was his only child and I felt very special being with him.

My mother was another matter. A strict disciplinarian, nothing ever seemed to be good enough for her; she always seemed to want to control me. So I often sought Marja's counsel on girl matters and tried to be out of the house as much as possible. That is not to say my mother wasn't kind, but just always busy scouting. She was a Girl Guide leader, an Oehoe, in Malay. You could say we were a scouting family. I enjoyed the field trips and was an avid collector of scouting badges. Not for their own sake as much as the skills and knowledge I needed to gain to achieve them. I was particularly proud of the "camping", "cooking" and "first aid" badges that would put me in good stead in the internment camps.

Meanwhile, Marja became ever more beautiful in my eyes. We must have been teenagers by then, because I remember the two of us riding our bicycles together, out along the Dago Weg, and up to the waterfalls and swimming pool that lay about three kilometres up steep hills. You know how things go. We had grown up together, but now things were different. She couldn't go topless in the swimming pool, and when I asked her to come cycling with me my body felt like liquid, for fear that she'd say no. Well, thankfully, she said yes. So off we went. We parked our bikes at the waterfall's edge, put on our swimming costumes, behind separate rocks, and plunged in.

I knew I had to take this opportunity, but I felt unsure, so I manoeuvred her under the waterfall to gain time. And said something silly about the dark birthmark that covered her upper chest having grown larger as her breasts sprouted, forgetting that the birthmark had been a source of continuous embarrassment. I found it a great attraction.

She pushed me away. But not really. And that was my first kiss. There you have it. Under the Dago waterfall.

Can I fast-forward now? To the family promise, before the war started in earnest in Java with the Japanese invasion. Yes?

Well, I want you to know, that at that stage in my life, I was totally colour-blind. No one cared what colour you were. Not like here in South Africa. We were two Dutch officers' families — Marja was brown because her mother was Indies, and I was white. But everyone was welcome at the festivities held in the Dago Falls Club in honour of my father's promotion from captain to major in 1942. Although the threat of war rumbled, like a distant thunder darkening our future.

Our motherland, Nederland, had been overrun by Germany, but, as the war expanded after the fall of Pearl Harbor, KNIL was preparing for a Japanese invasion of Java. So the celebration at the Dago Club was especially emotional. Many were fearful as radio reports announced that a Japanese attack on nearby Singapore was imminent.

Our two families had concluded a delicious rijsttafel, sitting around an oval table for six, with desserts, cognac and cigars, when both fathers stood up. Imagine how proud we were. Both Major Jansen and Captain de Koning wore khaki military uniforms and a black tie, and had loosened their olive jackets, glinting with decorations. They had tanned faces and thinning blond hair. First my father made a few preliminary remarks, as he raised his glass, and then Marja's took over to propose a toast and deliver a promise in that gravelled voice that seems to run in the family: "No matter what the future might bring," he said raising his glass, "each one of us will promise to look after one, and the other."

"A promise till death do us part," we chorused and then grasped each other's hands to form a circle, repeating it again for good measure:

"A promise till death do us part," the pitch of our voices a register higher that second time.

Not soon after this, I'd say maybe two weeks, the Japanese occupied Bandung, and I saw my first death.

And a few weeks later the Japs started separating families and interning military officers as prisoners of war, sending both our fathers off to Singapore, and then Burma, to construct a railroad to Bangkok.

The women folk were separated from the men. One day the Japs drove a truck onto the grassy square across from Banda Street where we used to fly kites and systematically went from door to door to extract the white and Indo women. Shockingly, Marja too. They left the Indiers like Marja's mother behind, though. The Japanese soldiers put the women and children into the truck with what little belongings they could carry and carted them off to Tjihaput, a section of Bandung they had closed off with barbed wire.

I wasn't at home at the time. I had joined an underground resistance movement headed by Major Hopman van der Veen. Called the Jeugdbende, four of us had been charged with establishing a secret jungle base provisioned with armaments for future raids on the Jap invaders. In other words, gunrunning. Punishable by decapitation. We did this at the dead of night. One cold night, after a long journey into the jungle around Bandung, we dug a deep hole, and buried the cachet of arms and provisions. We marked the depot spot on a trail map and spent a long night waiting for dawn so we could exit the jungle.

Stupidly — I still cannot understand what got into me — I kept a pistol in my pocket when we exited the jungle as the sun was rising. We were apprehended by the Indonesian Police on the way down the mountain trail. They of course were no friends of the Japs but had been deputised to maintain law and order. I think they knew what we were up to though; they told us in Malay that they were going to take us to the Bandjaran prison in a horse-drawn cart but would walk in front of us down the hill, and not look back until we got to the carriage. I jettisoned the pistol and the incriminating map to the jungle forever, and so we could stick to our story that we had been on a scouting trip. I think it saved us from the worst, but there was a lot of bad to come.

Can I have a drink of water before I continue, Mr. Terreblanche? I get very emotional about imprisonment. Jammer. Sorry.

At this point in the interview, Dr. Jansen had to take a break. He covered his blackened eye with trembling fingers and turned away from the microphone I had set on the desk between us. I could see the pulsation of his pale neck reaching above his black pullover. He drank down half a glass in one shot and then kept sipping water throughout the rest of the tape recording.

I received a terrible beating from the Japs on my face and my ankles and elbows, accompanied by frightful screeching — then they threw me into jail.

I woke up the next morning to the sound of a cooing pigeon. It always makes me think of my mother's kindnesses. Few as they were. The pigeon must have been out there somewhere, free, but I was below in a concrete dungeon with a barred skylight. I had, of course, never been confined or hurt like that.

Confinement goes to the heart of one's being: you become undone — disassembling in a cage. I hoped that none of my friends admitted to what we had been doing, because that was a certain death sentence.

That day, all four of us were hauled out of solitary and stuffed in a caged box, about three-quarter-man height, with bamboo slats in front. The wooden crates were backed against each other, like a cross, in the centre of a sandy courtyard.

One of my friends, Jan, tried to speak to me. "Willem moet niets zeggen hoor!" — "Willem, don't say anything" — but was silenced. I could hear a rifle butt cracking into him. The sun beat mercilessly on the wooden top, turning my crate to an oven — and then one by one we were taken to a hellish guardroom off to the side of the courtyard for interrogation.

Here sat a bulbous man, brusque and violent, behind a dark table. A Kempeitai officer's cap covered his bald Japanese head. He rose and started a staccato interrogation. A Malay non-commissioned officer in a khaki outfit provided interpretation, slowly.

"Jansen, you will tell us. Jansen, you will be killed soon." Over and over, I cannot tell you for how long; the Malay seemed as terrified of the Kempeitai as I was.

I held to my story in Malay. "We were on a scouting trip."

"Bohong, lies, who sent you?"

"The scout master."

"Bohong, bohong," the bulbous man screamed, perspiration seeding his cap. "During a war against the great Emperor Hirohito? What for? You will tell us. We will kill you soon."

On and on it went. Every so often, the Kempeitai cracked a truncheon down on my elbow, or my exposed knee, as I had been forced to sit cross-legged on the concrete floor. My mind was a haze of pain.

Then the Kempeitai started questioning me about my family. I told him about my father, the major of KNIL, commander in chief of the armaments factory. That was probably a big mistake. I panicked. I saw the Kempeitai pause and look at the Malay.

"Hai, Belandia, we put you back in cage. See you later."

Such sessions went on twice or three times a day. Once they were finished, they put me back into the merciless crate, and extricated one of my friends for the next interrogation. Jan seemed to be hauled off the most times. We could hear the yelled questions and muffled answers from our thin boxes, through the guardroom door.

At sundown, all stopped. A bugle sounded, followed by ten beats on a drum, as a Jap officer took down the red and white flag fluttering over the courtyard. Then we were taken out of our crates and put back in solitary, back in our cell. Here we got some tea and salty rice balls. I was worried about the salt. I thought it was a trick to dehydrate us into submission.

The days rolled into each other. I cannot really tell you

22

how many there were. One is left with one's thoughts at night and in the heat of the day they all run into each other. You hallucinate, thinking of your father, your family, kites, Marja, mountains, school poems, your friends, always with great anxiety. And pain. And sleeplessness. You know you're going to die and, strangely, that is almost relaxing, until you rage against it.

Why should I die? I want to see Marja again. I'm going to kill these Jap klooten!

And then, one day, Jan was no longer in his box. We heard later that he had committed suicide with his undervest.

Things got worse. The bulbous Kempeitai officer was replaced by a tall thin one. The Japs wanted the names of the men supporting the Jeugdbende and that of Major Hopman van der Veen, the resistance leader.

I was trapped. I could not give up the names. I didn't think I was a hero but I was stubborn. I was not going to give in.

So, day in and day out, the psychological torment continued.

At the worst moments, one's mind becomes completely deranged and discombobulated. One day I mistook a dawn for a dusk: the hated red disc flag was being pulled *up* the mast, instead of *down*.

That day I gave up. I cannot remember it all. My mind closed, but parts I do remember. The Kempeitai put a long bench in the centre of the courtyard, and tied my back against it, my arms and legs tied underneath the bench to restrain me.

"Tell me the names." "Namae o oshiete!"

Then he beat me across the chest with a big stave. I could see it coming. The red and white flag flapping above me. The pain was horrendous. On and on.

"NAMAE O OSHIETE!"

"NAMAE O OSHIETE!"

And then the Kempeitai soldier suddenly stopped hitting me and disappeared. He returned with a hosepipe spurting water and trained that on my mouth. Provoking unimaginable choking, gasping, gagging, flooding my windpipe, he filled my stomach to bursting. It felt like drowning on dry land. I wished I could become unconscious. I dreaded the feeling of water backing up into my throat, but the Jap was too skilled to let death happen, and stopped the flow of water from causing oblivion. He must have continued the half-drownings until I gave them the names they wanted. I remember coming to, still strapped to the bench, as the bugle and drumbeat sounded the furling of the Japanese flag at dusk.

That evening, or perhaps another — I was no longer a reliable recorder of time — I received sweet tea in my cell.

And the next morning the three of us who were left were marched out to the firing range to what we thought was certain death.

We had been told to dress in the new clothes we had been given and be ready at dawn. All the prison inmates knew what was in store for us when the bugle sounded, and we were marched out of the courtyard.

We were put with our backs against a wall and three Jap rifleman lined up to shoot us. They didn't even provide us with blindfolds.

We had heard about such executions. The officer in charge raised his samurai sword. A drum beat to ten. And that was the signal for the officer to bring down his sword, and the executioners to fire.

I didn't want to die, so I concentrated on the Jap's eyes that were focused on me, willing him to drop the shot.

I heard the drum beat counting: nine, ten. And as the samurai's sword fell, he yelled. "HI."

They shot. Over our heads. The rifle report ringing in our ears.

I shat myself. Piss dripping down my legs. Something went dead inside me, even though I had not been killed.

My heart raced, I felt nauseous and I must have fainted, because the next thing I knew I was in the back of a truck, flat on my back, on the way to Pasar Andir Camp.

For years I felt guilty about giving up the names, especially when I heard that van der Veen had been executed. It was only much later that I read that the Japs had the names of the Jeugdbende already; they had raided the scout hut where a list had been kept, and we three had been pardoned by Emperor Hirohito. We were too young to be executed.

Of course, at the time, we knew nothing of this.

All I knew was that I was a P.O.W. and was alive. The oppressive nightmares started soon after but the will to live never left me. In fact, it was even stronger than before. I am sure that you have heard of Russian roulette, Mr. Terreblanche. The players put a pistol to their heads with only one bullet in its chamber. I experienced that once and never again. I resolved to keep my head down and do what it takes to come out alive.

By 1943 I had been transferred to yet another camp on Kebon Jati road. There, on my seventeenth birthday, I last saw Marja's mother.

I was called to the camp commander's office and told to kneel and wait. Fortunately, the office had a tall, barred window facing the camp gate where I witnessed a commotion. A frail-looking Indonesian woman was being roughly pushed aside and screamed at. Hai! Hai! It was Marja's mother. Unmistakable. I couldn't call out. I would have been beaten. So I just waited, my heart contracting, as she tottered away.

Presently, two guards came into the office and put a huge parcel in front of me.

"Aita. Aita." — "Open. Open. Now."

The birthday package would prove a life saver. It contained a bed roll, shoes and clothes, a sewing kit, a toothbrush and a scouting knife, all packed into a school-size suitcase. I had to unpack everything onto the floor to show the guards. They looked carefully over everything, taking a long time to admire the photograph of Marja. Amazingly they let me keep the pen knife, which I used to carve Marja's likeness in banyan wood. I think it was quite a good rendition of her face, and I have kept the carving with me to this day.

†

You know, John — you don't mind if I call you that rather than Mr. Terreblanche? — we are such innocents when we are young. So unaware of the big picture. Let me tell you about events on Konininginne Dag, the Dutch queen's birthday, to explain what I mean. Until that time, I had not understood the hatred some Indonesians felt for Dutch colonialism.

We had a fanatic Indonesian — not Japanese — camp commander at Kebon Jati. He had sided with the Japs, no doubt convinced by their well-oiled propaganda machine. All over the camps posters and loudspeakers blared out half-truths that we were forced to listen to ad nauseum:

Tjahaja ASIA Nippon.
Pelingoeng ASIA Nippon.
Pemipin ASIA Nippon.
Japan is the light.
Japan is the protector.
Japan is the leader of Asia.
Japan has come to set the Indonesian's free from colonial bondage.

The camp commander was called Pemipin, Malay for leader. He was about twenty-five and even taller than me. Straight as an arrow, his knee-high boots polished to a T, he strutted about the camp leaning on his holstered revolver and berated us Belandias, us whites, at every opportunity.

On the queen's birthday, all P.O.W.s were amassed in lines on the sandy square that centred the camp and a roll call was performed while the Pemipin observed the proceedings from a raised platform up front, the Japanese flag on a pole nearby.

Then a drum beat to ten, a raised samurai sword was brought down, and we were forced to bow to the flag.

On this day we didn't. Instead, about eight hundred of us half-turned as one and faced a Dutch flag that had appeared in an upper window of the main camp building and yelled "Koningin Wilhelmina" just once, and then froze completely. We did not move. Many had donned orange sashes around their khakis and one, a tall, wasted man, a red disc on the backside of his khaki shorts. The Pemipin went berserk. He started yelling at the guards, who I could see were getting very nervous. They wanted us to go back to our barracks but no one moved. The wasted man, the red disc still on his rear, was hauled on to the platform, berated, and beaten on the ground, over and over.

The Pemipin screamed, "Belandia wij gaan jou doden." — "Blond Dutchman, we will kill you." Until another man just in front of me yelled:

"We believe it is cowardly to beat such a man." He too was hauled onto the platform and beaten up. Right in front of us. Each blow felt by all as they landed. Then the Pemipin removed his pistol from its holster and trained it on the wasted man's skull, the Japanese flag still visible on his bottom as he knelt.

"Back to barracks, or I will shoot."

Which we mutely did.

The Japs liked to rotate P.O.W.s to different camps to avoid clumps of resistance from forming, so in 1945 I was moved to yet another camp, Barrios 111. Here I found Bartje, a fellow survivor of the mock execution. We had both volunteered in the camp's dysentery ward. Dr. Boudewyn Roelofse oversaw the unit. He had trained at Leiden, in Holland, as an internist but not as a surgeon and had served as a medical officer in the hospital where Marja and I were born. He welcomed our help. Then Bartje became ill. Dr.

Roelofse diagnosed shigella bowel perforation. This needed an emergency operation at the hospital, situated outside the camp. The Jap camp commander refused the transfer. We could not help having no surgeon in the camp. All we could do was watch Bartje suffer a horrible death. I think that defeat made me want to become a surgeon. Dr. Roelofse promised to help me if we got out of the camps alive.

Like many camps, Barios 111 had a hidden radio receiver. In the spring of 1945, we received the good news that the American-led Allied forces were advancing in the Pacific; they had taken Okinawa and were advancing south. Then on August 16 — I will never forget the day — a fully laden horse-drawn cart entered the camp. We couldn't believe it. The cart was chock-a-block with bags of rice, vegetables, fruit, eggs, chicken and even beef. We crowded around and followed its progress to the kitchen, where it stopped and was unloaded.

We started cheering and shouting. This could only mean that the Japs had surrendered and the war was over. That day the camp commander gathered us in the square and announced our freedom.

"It has pleased the Imperial Majesty, the Emperor, to offer our enemy peace with immediate effect." Or words like it. We were free to go but must return to the camp at night to await further instructions.

We were no longer beaten, nor did we have to bow and scrape to the Japs; we cheered and shouted and got drunk. The radio was brought out of hiding, and further news broadcasts updated us on the atom bombs that had devastated Nagasaki and Hiroshima a few days earlier, which had resulted in the Japanese capitulation.

Another radio announcement that day would have a shattering effect on us. Mr. Susno Sukarno read the proclamation of an "Independent Republic of Indonesia." Sukarno had been a freedom fighter against Dutch colonialism and became the country's first president. Independence for the Dutch East Indies and the consequent retaliations by the Indonesians against the Dutch and the Indos would wreak havoc across the nation. Indonesia descended into post-war mayhem. The rape and murder of thousands of whites and Indos followed — just as they were being set free from the concentration camps. Hence many P.O.W.s stayed in the camps for protection, the Japs now becoming their protectors until Dutch troops were brought back into the country to safeguard the internees' passage home.

Independence thus caused a mass exodus from Indonesia. Hundreds of thousands of citizens were repatriated to Holland for their safety. Passenger ships that had been converted to troop ships reverted to carry the Dutch and Indo families from Tanjong Priok harbour in the capital, Batavia, to Amsterdam.

My problem was that, although I was now free to leave the camp, I was not at all sure where my or Marja's family were. Or for that matter whether they were still alive. Nor sure what had happened to my grandparents in Nazi-occupied Holland. They had been asked by my father to support my university education should I choose that path for my future.

I went back to Banda Street. The country was in chaos. Our house had been burnt down. Marja's was still standing but there was no sign of the families there. I found accommodations at the Lyceum and spent the next six months figuring things out. Marja's mother had died but there was no trace of my mother or Marja after their transfer to Tjihaput three years earlier.

I scoured official bulletins of deaths and detentions posted at the police station daily, but we were advised not to travel in search of family members for fear of attack by marauding Indonesian nationalists. Reports from Burma were bad. I heard that many P.O.W.s, like my father, had died there, so I started making plans for my own future.

I volunteered as a deckhand on the M.S. *Johan van Oldenbarnevelt* and set sail for Amsterdam.

†

CHAPTER 3

**Tape Recording by John Terreblanche,
Cape Town, October 1960:
Miss Marja de Koning**

Mmmmn. The first thing I remember?

It was the fire. The kitchen fire. Mam and Pap had gone with the Jansens to the Dago Fall's Club and the amah was cooking dinner. She didn't usually cook but Selamat was ill. He was in the servant's quarters resting. I was around fourteen. It was just after we had made the family promise. I was already flustered. The air raid sirens had gone off. But it was only a practice run. I was reading in my room when I heard a loud bang. I ran to the kitchen. It was filled with smoke. And a great flame was bouncing off the stove to the roof. The maid was burning. I yelled for Selamat. I yelled for Willem next door. I ran to the washing room and got a pail of water and threw it over the amah and stove. Two soldiers, stationed outside, came in and took her to hospital. I was frightened. I thought I was never going to get out of Banda Street alive.

Well, Mr. Terreblanche, I know you have already interviewed Willem, so I don't have to tell you that we were born on the same day.

No?

We grew up as brother and sister, being only children. My mother had tried to have another child, but that was stillborn, and she was sick for a long time afterwards. I think that was what caused her to die young during the war. I didn't see her again after we were separated by the Japs.

Did I get on with my mother?

I adored her. She was of course Indies and a Muslim. Always dressed in beautiful batik sarongs, padding around on bare feet. People told me I looked just like her except that my skin was paler. She was gentle, kind and soft-spoken and always seemed to have time for everything; I wanted to be just like her when I grew up. Grounded, and at one with those around her, and the country of her birth. Ja. Nee, it didn't turn out that way, did it?

Willem liked her too. He spent most of the time with us in our home. He found his mother controlling and his father was always busy in the factory, so my mother brought us up.

It was perhaps surprising that she married my father, a Hollander through and through. He must have swept her off her tiny feet in his military uniform. He had a fine blond moustache but was short and thickset, so I was condemned to remain short. But well proportioned, wouldn't you say?

At first Willem and I seemed to grow at the same rates. But then he took off. He used to tell me I was getting shorter, so I grew my hair instead. I tied it up, with fresh flowers when I wore my kebaya.

What language did we speak?

I went to the same school as Willem. First to the Dutch primary school on Riouw Street, close to our home, and then to the Christelijk Lyceum out on the Dago Weg. So I spoke Dutch there and Malay with my mother and the servants, and of course we studied English in high school.

When did I first develop feelings for him? Do you mean sexual feelings?

Mmmmn, do I have to answer this question?

Ooraait.

Quite early, I would say. I remember because I had just started having my monthlies and was very self-conscious about my breasts. You can see that I have this dark birthmark peeping out of my sarong. It stretches over my breasts and it just seemed to be getting bigger and taking over half of my chest at the time. Willem had invited me to cycle to the Dago Falls. And he first kissed me there. In my swimsuit underneath the falling water. It may sound corny now. But he was my first love. How innocent I was. And how dreadful things became. When the Japs invaded.

One day they parked a truck on the field across from Banda Street. They came for the white women and children. The Belandias. They didn't take my mother, but they took me. I shouted; I screamed that I was not white. But the Jap commander didn't care. I had Dutch blood in me. I had to pack my belongings and was forced into the truck. I was told to sit down next to Willem's mother.

We were first taken to Tjihaput. Then, and not long after, we were transferred to the Struiswijk Camp in

Batavia, the capital. We were told to bring only what we could carry. Some six hundred of us waited on the square outside the railway station on Kebon Kawung Street in the burning heat. Those who fainted were dumped in the gutter. The rest of us were crammed into pitch-dark cattle trucks. The train shook so much that the children never stopped crying for the whole thirty-six-hour journey. Like many others I got dysentery. No food, no water, just terrible stomach cramping that felt like my colon was being ripped out of my body. Diarrhoea provided only passing relief. But you had to do it, standing up. It was verschrikkelijk, terrible. I can't ever face a train again. Even the clank of wheels on rails give me the heebie-jeebies.

Around six in the morning we arrived at a mud flat, surrounded by kampongs and rice paddies that led to a large building compound in the distance. We were shouted out of the sweltering trucks and told to line up at the prison's front gate, beside which were heaps of bread laid out on a long trestle table. I was so hungry, I forgot to bow before taking the food from the camp commandant's hand. He raised his crop to hit me but I looked him straight in the eyes with gratitude and he relented, barking out an order instead: "Find a room. Back is best."

Willem's mother and I did so immediately. We found the last cell in C block, its wall blackened by lice. We could read the names of Dutch prisoners scratched on the stucco. The camp had been converted from a men's to a women and children's camp. The first week we slept on concrete. Our mattresses had been thrown in the mud and needed to dry. There was not much comfort from the ablutions either: one tap, one bucket and one waterhole. By the time it was your turn to clean yourself, the day was done. And, in the next week, another six hundred prisoners arrived.

I became depressed, but Willem's mother was having none of it. She was a gutsy woman. An Oehoe scout leader. She started organising and became a hantjo, an internment camp leader, who advocated for us to the Jap camp commander, Aki Tanaka.

There was of course much to be done in such camps. Much to be coordinated. Food, health, cooking, cleaning and, at least at first, reading, music and entertainments, to keep up the morale of the prisoners. A good hantjo organised affairs. She kept the Japs out of our business as much as possible. And tried to protect the women and girls from their drunken lechery.

At first, I was put to work in the surrounding rice fields. Three times a day — dawn, noon and dusk — we had to stand at attention in the burning sun, bowing to the rising sun flag. I thought the sun would never set on this episode of my life. I was sweet sixteen but felt hopeless. Who knew that we were imprisoned here? Would this be the end of my life?

Every now and then, Aki Tanaka presented a list of requests to the five camp hantjos. This could be for farming, maintenance and cleaning work to be done, and often included the names of women to be taken out of the camps, we suspected, to serve as comfort woman. We knew what that meant. It was kind of verschrikkelijk to think about. So we tried not to.

Usually Willem's mother, as a camp hantjo, executed on the work requested but ignored the submitted names. And hid the women in question when the camp guards came searching. Other women crowded around, banged pots and pans and squawked at the guards, to make them give up the search. One night she told me that my name was at the top of the list. Over the next two weeks her hair turned from brown to white.

Starvation drove us all to desperate measures. As the war progressed, our rations decreased. Aki Tanaka became frustrated. He swung his samurai sword and shrieked at us while we stood at attention. After a long tirade, he ended in Malay and Dutch: "Geen Meisjes. Geen Voedsel" — "No girls. No food." And then, one day, he announced that sixty male prisoners were to be added to the compound without a corresponding increase in rations if we didn't comply.

A week later, we saw the men being marched in. We became even more hungry and thin. The cramping and the nausea was sickening. I thought I was going to die anyway, so I might as well take my chances. I told Willem's mother that I would volunteer.

That decision changed the course of my life.

About two weeks later, twelve of us were marched out of the camp, put into a truck and taken to a military barracks across from the botanical gardens at the city's centre. I couldn't help but notice that all of us were pretty, and half were slight Indos, like myself.

We were told to shower, dress in the blue kimono provided, and prepare for an inspection. We were given food. As much as we wanted. I felt better already. But I was scared. I was still a virgin and knew nothing of sex.

We were told to line up in front of three Japanese officers and three Japanese women in coloured kimonos, their faces painted white with bedak. I knew that make-up — I had used it occasionally for fun. Then we were asked to kneel, one by one, and then sing a song. Any song, until stopped. I thought this was a trick, so I sang a Japanese one I had learnt at school in music class. Then we were told to stay in the kneeling position while the inspectors conferred. What happened next was strangely exhilarating.

The most decorated officer, his white helmet crushing his little ears, stood up from his seat and waved a white gloved hand in our general direction.

"You have all been selected to serve the Emperor."

"You four" — he pointed us out — "will be trained to be geisha if you are untouched." He pivoted. "You eight will become comfort women. All are dismissed."

I honestly didn't know whether to laugh or cry, thank them or what, so I just got up, as gracefully as possible, and bowed.

The next day I started training to be a geisha. They wanted me to be ready in three months. It usually takes years and years in Japan. But they needed geishas to entertain the officers and couldn't wait any longer.

Do you know what a geisha is? No?

Well, we are not prostitutes. Far from it. We are artists. Singers, dancers, delicate, fragrant and enchanting. Not courtesans, not wives, we create a world of beauty, a kind of moving work of art. A true geisha can stop a man in their tracks with a single look. A flick of an eye. I learnt to do that. Have you noticed, Mr. Terreblanche?

The most valued are the dancers. Yes, you must be able to play the shamishen, that twangy-sounding lute, and learn to serve matcha tea and pour beer and sake gracefully, but the best way to win over a Danaa is kabuki. I learnt all the skills to entice Japanese men. Exposing one's neck is erotic, more sensual than bare legs to a European. I offered them my kuroyaki-perfumed throat and a bright kimono, cut low at the nape, so that the first bumps of my spine were visible through the chalk paste used to whiten my face and neck. My lips were rouged, my cheeks tinted, and my black hair, sheened and tightly waxed, was knotted with a red silk band into a split peach up on my head. Seen from behind, the effect was provocative: a black cleft with a splash of red at its centre.

I had excelled at ballet dancing at school, so I took to kabuki easily enough. What was more difficult was all the bowing and kneeling in a close-fitting kimono with a bright obi sash snugged at my centre; the etiquette of the tea house, the nightly rigmarole for the Jap officers' entertainments.

You started as a novice, shadowing a full geisha. They were preparing us for future auction. We were shopped around from tea house to tea house in Batavia's city centre, but one's cave remained untouched until you were sold. We were told to advertise that we were for sale by slipping a crab cake onto the officer's knee under the table. And then given to the highest bidder. A virgin like myself fetched a high price and could secure a Danaa who would be my patron, paying a fee to my minders for my continued sexual services.

My first Danaa was rough. His cock was covered in ballitos, plastic beads sutured — painfully, no doubt — under the skin. And he wouldn't stop. It was unbearable.

Kind of verschrikkelijk. It is degrading to talk about. Even now after all these years… Uh!

I never really got used to any of it. I suppose I survived the war and didn't die of starvation because of my choice. That gives me some consolation. But kind off… not much.

Then — it must have been about a year since I was transferred — the geisha chief summoned me and told me I was to return to the Struiswijk Camp. They had no further use for me.

Here the situation was far worse than when I left. I found out that Willem's mother had died of starvation. I felt miserable and even more abandoned then.

But not soon after there was a glimmer of hope. We heard it coming in the air. Two American aeroplanes came flying over the camp, so low that you could see the pilots, who waved, circled in formation and flew back from where they came.

That evening the camp hantjos called us together and said we were free. The war was over. The Japanese soldiers were gone. For a minute everyone was quiet. Then one or two started singing the *Wilhelmus*, the Dutch national anthem. They gathered voice. But I couldn't. I was overcome. I couldn't sing. I just cried.

The next day, three American officers visited the camp in a jeep. They told us that it was dangerous for anyone to leave the camp without an armed escort. Indonesian resistance fighters were killing the unprotected. We should stay in the camp until a transfer could be arranged. Food and safe passage would be provided.

Four months later we were transferred. There were rumours that Struiswijk Camp was going to be attacked by resistance fighters. It was no longer safe, so armed Gurkhas accompanied us to another camp in Batavia, until much later, in 1946, when, finally, we were put on a passenger train back to Bandung. The accompanying Gurkhas told us to lie on the carriage's floor as resistance fighters were shooting at passengers through the open windows. At one small station we saw the heads of murdered white men impaled on upright spears. Verschrikkelijk. I feared for Willem's life, if he had survived the P.O.W. camps.

I suppose it ended up being about two years that I spent in Bandung sorting out my affairs. I heard that Willem had gone to Holland, and that my sweet mother had died. There was no record of our fathers but reports out of Burma were bad. We were now both motherless and probably fatherless. Just the two of us left tied by our promise. So, as my plans firmed, and after much thinking about it, I wrote to Willem of his mother's death in Struiswijk Camp, and that I was aiming to move to Holland. I couldn't mention my defilement, I was too ashamed. I wasn't sure if I wanted to see him again or he me, but I felt duty-bound to send the letter.

I had made all the arrangements. I would travel the hundred miles from Bandung by train to Batavia, and from there had booked a passage to Amsterdam via the Suez Canal. But the day before I was to leave I was raped, and dumped into the river, and left for dead.

Must I go on, Mr. Terreblanche?

If I want…? Ooraait, ooraait!

What happened was this. I was walking along the kali flowing past our kampong just outside Bandung. It was in flood from the recent rainstorms. I was waylaid. I do not

41

remember a lot. A gang of Indonesians were hunting for whites. I saw them coming; they were shouting "Merdeka" — "Freedom". "Death to the enemy, death to the Dutch." They waved pointed bamboo sticks. So I hid in a cave alongside the river. I held my breath as the whole group passed me by. My memory blurs… I want to forget… but in hindsight one of the Indonesians discovered me. And this man raped and kicked and abused me. I fainted as I have no further memory. He must have thrown me into the river. Because when I woke up it was dusk and there were dead bodies floating around me. I remember thinking "God sy dank dat ik nog leeft" — "God, thank you, I am still alive." In Dutch not Malay. It was verschrikkelijk.

And that is the reason I missed the repatriation ship. I found another one, though, in 1949. It would be a longer trip, via Cape Town, to Amsterdam. I didn't mind that. I wanted to get to Holland. I hoped it would be safer there.

May I take a break, please?

†

CHAPTER 4

Willem, Holland

Having introduced Promise, Willem and Marja to you in their own voice, so to speak, so that you, the reader, can get a first-hand sense of them, I will now continue their stories using a tad less journalistic — and more conventional — narrative technique.

It was a grey cold day when the M.S. *Johan van Oldenbarnevelt* docked in Amsterdam, sending a spray of seagulls aloft, screeching in annoyance.

The long journey from Batavia at an end, Willem gathered his threadbare coat, donned his black cap, picked up his thin valise and made his dissolute way down the unstable gangplank, lost in thought. He had been mighty troubled. Had he done the right thing by leaving Marja behind, not knowing of her fate? Should he have searched for her more, before leaving hurriedly to pursue his plans to study medicine in Holland? He had heard of awful things happening back in Indonesia when the ship had stopped at Suez.

"Keep moving. Sir? Sir? Keep moving."

Willem had stopped on the unsteady walkway. He couldn't help himself. He reached into his valise for reassurance. Feeling Marja's carved figurine, he mustered the strength to continue, was processed through the reception hall, and passed on to the quay beyond.

Comforted by the familiar cobble stones underfoot and the crisp fifty florin that a Dutch landing official had given him now lining his wallet, Willem approached a fishmonger who had parked his cart quayside, the salty smell of fish sharp on the morning air.

"Goede Dag Mijnheer. Kan ik u helpen?"

"Agh. Ja. I would like some herring. I have not had rollmops in years." Willem rested his luggage on the fish cart's counter, pinched his Adam's apple between finger and thumb, and continued. "Could you direct me to Den Haag? That is where my grandparents live. In the Vogelbuurt, near Kijkduin."

"That's easy. But the trip will take a few hours." The fishmonger rolled the herring fillet around a gherkin and handed it over the countertop. "First take a train to Den Haag Centraal Station. And then a tram to the Vogelbuurt. I know it well; I grew up there myself. I loved walking on the beach at Kijkduin. Goeie dag." He wiped his briny fingers, smudging his white apron yellow.

A little more hopeful now, Willem brightened, buoyed by fond memories of spending a year's home leave living in his grandparents' house when his father was studying to be a chemical engineer. He could in his mind's eye picture the house at Leeuwerikplein 3.

But, stepping up to its front door after his journey, he

knew something was amiss. Having knocked, the front door opened to his grandparents' sad reception.

"Welcome, Willem." They embraced him in turn, giving of their frail warmth, before asking whether he had heard the news of his father, their son.

"Nee, nog niet."

"My dear child. He has died." They bowed their heads, unable to comfort each other any longer when facing their son's son. Powerless to bear the loss and console him.

Willem stepped back from the front door, still clutching his bag, and clasped his pale forehead in his right hand, pushing back his hat. He turned and walked the five steps back to the wooden garden gate he had swung open a few minutes ago. Willem had feared the worst, but this was final.

†

The only thing that seemed to keep Willem's head from coming apart was to go running. Ever since his kite-chasing days in Bandung, he had found great joy in jogging. It lifted his spirit when he felt down. It brought out a playfulness he had lost, a chance to feel free and yet in complete control — his body answering his call. Whenever the turmoil set in from the camps, the incessant repetitive thoughts obsessively churning in his head — he would calm them, banish them from his mind, by running.

Willem put on his tennis shoes and ran past the Bosjes van Poot and out to Kijkduin over the dunes. From musty forest to silted beach, he switched from leaf-covered track to watery sand, his plimsolls treading deep as he angled his footfall — he crouched lower at the knees to provide purchase in the silt. He headed up the beach for the red light house at Scheveningen, the Noordzee slapping the cold sand as the gulls cried ahead and he splashed below. Willem returned exhausted — his agitation defeated by the flood of adrenaline stilling his noisy brain.

But he needed to get on with his plans despite the tumult in his head — he must apply to medical school. So, not long after registering in Den Haag as a burger, Willem gathered the necessary testimonials and certificates, enclosed them in his leather satchel, and took the train to Leiden. Here he nervously presented himself to the university admission clerk in the imposing seventeenth-century convent building on the Rapenburg, hoping for immediate acceptance as a medical student.

He was soon disappointed. His Indonesian high school qualifications were insufficient to the task; he needed to take further courses to matriculate and achieve admission. However, provisions had been made to assist aspirant medical students with compressed "speed" courses, folding one year into three months, but had to be completed by September, if Willem were to start medical school in that year of 1946.

He quietened his mind to the goal but found that he couldn't remember things as well as before the war. He found it difficult to focus on his studies. To concentrate. Sometimes he couldn't retain much of what he learnt despite hours of study. Before the torture, his memory was photographic; now, it was hazy like an impressionist painting. He got the general idea but could not memorise the detail. Consequently, Willem only just managed to pass the all-important matriculation examination because the examiner recognised his plight and questioned him on the geography of Java, a subject he knew first-hand.

Another fallout from the torture was that Willem found it difficult to deal with uncertainty, or ambiguity, and was loath to make decisions; he became stubborn and strangely passive.

One problem Willem didn't have was impecuniosity. His father had made over sufficient funds — to a family bank account in The Hague — to pay for medical school, leaving clear instructions in a letter as to their use: he advised that Willem needed to take care of himself, lighten up and "live a little".

Accordingly, Willem had found digs in Leiden matching his father's counsel. A garret on Rijnburger Weg, just along from the Academic Hospital and the Medical Faculty buildings.

Willem set about preparing to become a doctor. He fixed his sights on passing the candidates examination in two years' time, allowing him to qualify for clinical training. Largely theoretical in nature, the main subjects were physiology, pharmacology, pathology, histology and anatomy. But Willem struggled to retain the vast quantity of information required; he failed the written examinations with monotonous regularity.

Dismissal threatening, Willem overruled his conscience. He could not fail and took the considerable risk of cheating. Knowing that every medical student had to turn out their pockets before entering the examination hall, Willem Koki-penned the medical mnemonics he couldn't remember onto the inside of his forearm. He wore a black pullover and felt like a tattooed pirate evading justice. His guilt, however, was not as easily erased as the writing on his skin — Willem wiped that away with a cotton ball soaked in ether.

In contrast to studying theory, anatomical dissection was painless. Willem was brilliant at it. Although the rancid smell of formalin pricked his nostrils, and the rictus mask of the cadaver still occasionally brought back death's dis-ease, Willem loved the process of dissecting out the organs. There was no room for doubt. He practised cutting through vessels now drained of life's blood, strangely elevating his mood. He could see the human body three-dimensionally and didn't have to learn the anatomic relationships off by heart, each new dissection building the picture, like a retinal X-ray, guiding him exactly to pinpoint the next incision.

The anatomical juxtaposition was not the problem; it was all the Latinate names he needed to retain to pass the test. The names of innumerable bones that webbed the feet and hands for example. The cuneiform and the navicular, the capitate and the pisiform. He repeated them over and over to no avail, despairing that he would ever pass the *viva voce* oral examinations essential to progress to the next stage of training.

On the fateful day, the dreaded *viva voce* was held in the anatomy demonstration hall. Two professors sat behind a long wooden table bedecked with floating organs encased in formalin-filled glass containers, separated by an array of whitening bones, some recognisable, others not.

In luck, the first examiner asked Willem only about the heart and lungs, a subject of surpassing interest as

Willem wanted to become a thoracic surgeon. But then the second examiner intervened. He leant in and pushed forward the skeleton of a foot.

"Well, Mr. Jansen, what is this?"

"A foot, professor."

"Ja. Ja. Ja. Name the bones."

A bell rang, signalling the end of the examination.

†

Willem loved everything to do with surgery. Called to stand by at an operation as a medical student, on the first day of his clinical training, in the well of the circled amphitheatre that Leiden's Akademiese Ziekenhuis is famous for, he thrilled to the excitement and drama. His heart pulsed in his ears as his eyes lifted to see the spectators, even though he wasn't allowed to touch the patient lying in front of him. That was the assistant surgeon's job. Willem was just present at the operation to watch the procedure and learn how to practise in the future. Close enough in the field, though, to smell the blood and ether anaesthetic — Willem could hear the suction machine's liquid tones, the beeping of the patient's heartbeat, and the professor's whispered admonishments. The scrub nurse's silent acquiescence and downcast eyes, saying more about the power dynamic in the tense theatre than any words could.

Willem was asked to give a hand; the surgical assistant had stepped aside for a moment, to address an emergency elsewhere. He was hooked. This is what he wanted to do. If there was ever any doubt about the matter, that first time convinced him of his calling.

"Mr. Jansen, cut the suture shorter next time."

"Yes, professor."

Willem felt elated by his first surgical experience. He took off the bloodied gloves, gave them to the nurse, and trailed proudly behind the Prof. He had been invited to take a cup of tea in the surgeon's lounge adjacent to the theatre. Willem strode on home afterwards to find something even more exciting and hoped for. A letter from Marja in Bandung: she was coming to Holland on the next ship.

†

What Willem didn't like — in fact, it depressed him further — was the smallness of it all in Holland: row upon row of three-storeyed houses reached up on narrow cobbled streets in the medieval city, many still damaged from German bombing — the sun only weakly penetrated the grey clouds, bathing it all in a wan light. Never a hill or mountain in sight. The odd windmill and church steeple barely relieved the tedium. The fields and acreage beyond Leiden's streets, green or brown depending on the season, bore only threadbare stick trees that punctuated the distance. Cows lolled in the meadows. The whole picture was soporific, predictable and dispiriting — a far cry from the bright, dusty scuffle of the life in Indonesia he had known growing up.

On top of it the Dutch were a dour bunch. The deprivations of war in the homeland lingered in disparaging comments directed at Willem's colonial background in Indonesia. (They thought he must have had it better there.) He felt a foreigner in his own country. He didn't belong, and he couldn't recapture the easy happiness that he had experienced as a child at his grandparents' house in the Vogelbuurt. Except occasionally. On wintry Sundays, the Rapenburg's clock tower rousing him from a fitful sleep, Willem clamped his wooden skates to his boots, padded his thin body with newspaper, pulled on his only overcoat and headed off along the frozen canals that criss-crossed Leiden. A broad scarf tightly wound around his neck, Willem travelled long distances on the ice that connected the surrounding towns. Since the torture, Willem had become inward-looking. Unwilling to expend emotional energy on all but a few others, he preferred the solitude of nature and the powerful feeling of his own vitality slicing clean grooves on the waterway.

†

The great bi-funnelled ship hove to at dawn, Amsterdam reclaiming the M.S. *Johan van Oldenbarnevelt* as an old friend. Willem waited expectantly quayside for the first sight of Marja de Koning. He pulled out the tattered letter from the bag hanging at his side. He had read it again and again. Yes, this was the ship she would be on. The next ship from Batavia. He stood in a crowd at the foot of the gangplank watching the hundreds of passengers disembarking one by one, their eyes filled with anticipation, weariness, and a little fear at what they might discover. Tall, Willem had the advantage. He could see over the crowd of people as the passengers exited the steel hull, training his eyes hopefully on each new arrival; he had not seen Marja since the Japs' invasion more than seven years ago. Would his heart still lift at the sight of her, like before? It was beating in his throat, drumming his ears, and sweating his palms; he splayed his hand across his forehead, pushing up his black hat to see better — willing her out of the boat.

Marja never stepped off the ship. Willem couldn't believe it. He approached an official standing beside the wobbly stairway resting on the quay.

"Officer, Mijnheer. Is Miss Marja de Koning on the ship's manifest?"

"Let me see… yes, oh yes, she is," replied the officer, paging through his clipboard.

"Well, then, why is she not disembarking with the other passengers?"

"Let me see. It says here. Yes, that's right. She was booked in cabin E23, starboard side, from Batavia. The last passenger is off the ship. Perhaps she got off at Suez. Sometimes… you just don't know about these Indos…" The officer pointed two fingers at his temple, his thumb cocked like a gun.

"Mijn Godt, mijn Godt." Willem went into a spasm, his head contorted up at an angle while his slate eyes struck down to seven o'clock and his thin lips compressed to a sneer — his left hand turned out as if readying to catch a cricket ball at the hip. He froze in position for a moment like a figure from Dante's *Inferno*.

"Mijnheer, mijnheer" — the official had dropped his clipboard and tapped Willem on his shoulder to break the trance — "you need a doctor."

"Nee, nee, nee, I'm fine." Willem shook his head three times and continued. "Are... are you certain Miss de Koning is not still on the ship?"

"Ja, ja, I am sure. I am sorry. This happens sometimes. Can I help you with anything else? Do you need a doctor to look at you? For a moment there I thought you were going to have an epileptic fit." The official had regained his clipboard together with his composure.

Willem shook his head, clapped his face between his fingers, tested the swing of his left arm, shouldered his valise and made his way back to the garret in Leiden. He had prepared an alcove for Marja's arrival and had put her carved figurine on the dressing table beside a freshly made-up bed. A posy of red tulips in a Delft blue vase dwelt alongside. Willem had hoped to rekindle what time had lost. He looked out of the narrow window at the sad landscape beyond. Despairing, he struggled to keep his face in shape and his arm from contorting out of control.

†

The gruelling medical school training finally over, a total of five years under his belt, Willem heard nothing from Marja. Truth be told, that was probably just as well as his emotional life had been ripped out of him by his experience in the camps. He was hard-pressed to enjoy other people's pleasure or sympathise with them, preferring to withdraw and not risk disappointment by a failed attachment. He became cantankerous and easily irritated. Inward-looking, he nevertheless absorbed new experiences like a sponge, but found it very difficult to give of himself emotionally.

He appeared slow and withdrawn, his lank yellow hair gathered at his neck, his beaked nose a counterpoint. He stooped, carrying the weight of his despair for all to see. He developed a strange contortion whenever he was unduly stressed. His neck rotated right, his eyes left and his face became a sneer — his left arm extending, curled outwards. Willem was acutely embarrassed by this and tried to hide the twitch as best he could.

As a salve he engrossed himself in surgery. He moved back to Den Haag to the Suidwal Hospital to start his surgical training as a co-assistant doctor. That kept him going.

He found relish in quoting his favourite line as he made the first cut, his scalpel paring the white skin, splitting it apart, crimson blood trickling either side of the wound under the bright overhead light. "You're never more alive than when you're scared to death."

Ah yes, it was scary. Very scary. A surgeon must develop the confidence that they can make their patient whole again after the plunder. After removing an offending organ, or cobbling an injured one, despite the blood loss robbing the patient's life. But Willem was exceptional at it. Totally dedicated to his patients, he was saving himself and the sickened: the intense concentration required relieved his congested mind. He would work and work; he was indefatigable in his efforts. Consequently, over the next three years of instruction, he developed a reputation as a budding surgeon, but needed to find a job as a specialist trainee and had been called up for national service. So Willem attempted to combine the two: he moved inland to Amersfoort for basic training and applied to the military hospital in nearby Utrecht to complete the required eighteen months of service in its surgical department.

He was invited for an interview.

The surgeon in chief, Colonel Hans Groot, presided. Formidable in his bulging brass-buttoned uniform, red epaulettes cresting at the shoulder, Colonel Groot rose as Willem stood to attention, his ample white moustache bristling as he spoke.

"Dr. Jansen, are you ready for the rigours of surgery? Can you stand at operation for five hours straight? Can you bear the bleeding, and the agony in your bladder?"

"Yes, Colonel. There is nothing I like to do more."

"Good. I have a job for you in thoracics. You start tomorrow."

Willem came to life in his grey fatigues and saluted before turning to go.

"But I must warn you. I take no nonsense here. One problem and you're out!"

"Yes, Colonel."

"And one more thing, Dr. Jansen."

"Yes, Colonel."

"Get a haircut."

†

The first year or so went well, but then the stress and discontent got the better of Willem. He found it hard to abide the military's authoritarianism. He resisted rules stubbornly and, when confronted, regressed. He argued vociferously, revenging himself on the Kempeitai at each encounter, often escalating to a shouting match. Willem broiled with anger that he found impossible to contain. The only way he could avoid hitting someone was by turning around abruptly and striding away, usually, to walk or run off his anger outside — he felt beside himself with nowhere to turn.

But, if he couldn't find relief physically, he had learnt how to pacify himself chemically. Still seething, his hands pressed out like parachutes open at his side, Willem made for the washroom and locked himself into cubicle No.2. He had stashed a bottle of ether in the latrine's cistern. Panting, Willem held his breath to listen whether anyone else was around, and then climbed onto the lidded toilet seat, positioned back the cistern's cover, extracted the brown bottle, dunked the plastic cup he had secreted there half-full with the tank's water and topped the concoction off with a shot of ether before drinking the fiery liquid down in one gulp as if standing at a bar. Tranquillised, he monitored himself to ascertain whether the dose was enough. If not, he took another shot and then returned the paraphernalia to the tank, closed its cover, and pulled the chain at the toilet's side. Willem felt hot shame rising as the water flushed down. He knew that abusing ether was against every tenet of practising as a doctor, quite apart from the fact that he could become addicted and might be impaired during an operation, but he believed he could regulate the dose, and the drug relieved his anxiety. Willem judged he had learnt the right measure to manage any situation — enough to go back calmed to apologise for whatever upset he had caused or start the operation he feared performing.

But he did not always get the apologising part right.

Consequently, it was not surprising that Willem was not promoted to captain and found himself often summoned to Colonel Groot's office.

This time for the last time.

"Dr. Jansen. It has come to my attention that yet again you had a shouting match with a colleague."

"Colonel, I am afraid so."

"And I have heard that you have stolen and abused ether. Is that true?"

"I have used some ether to calm myself when I am upset. You do know that I was interned in the Japanese camps?"

"I did. But I am afraid that it does not excuse you hitting another doctor in anger."

"No, it does not." Willem sighed, his left arm starting to turn outwards and his eyes clocking up.

The colonel rose behind the desk to deliver the final blow.

"You will receive a dishonourable discharge from the army."

Willem bowed his head. A blond wisp fell across his brow, escaped from its middle parting, loosened by the cap he clenched to his chest.

"I suggest that you go and practise medicine in another country. I will ask the Nederland's Medical Council to revoke your licence if you don't. I saw an advertisement for doctors to emigrate to South Africa. That might be a better place for a reprobate like you. Dismissed."

†

CHAPTER 5

The Cape Times Herald
The Paper that Cares.
Jan 3, 1958

Broederskap, Braaivleis, Rugby & Sunny Skies
John Terreblanche

Your correspondent usually writes about crime, punishment and South African politics, but has been asked to "fill in" for this social commentary column of our newspaper. I do so gladly to celebrate the essence of our Afrikanerdom: the joy of Broederskap — the fellowship of Afrikaner brotherliness.

But first I wish to reassure the readership of my bona fides — of my true love for our country, and the erudition that I bring to my writing: I was educated at Paarl Boy's High, Bishop's College, Rondebosch, and Cambridge University in England.

***Broederskap**, if not already present during the Great Trek, was certainly waxed during the Anglo-Boer War, and sealed by the Treaty of Vereeniging of 1902, when our Afrikaans language was born. Broederskap is the essence of our fellowship as Afrikaner brethren. If we must metaphorically*

---

draw the wagons around us to protect the lager from the heathen, from dilution of our blood and religion to maintain our volk and its fellowship, then so be it, God willing.

Braaivleis *fosters our fellowship and is truly African. The control of fire enabled the pre-human* Homo Erectus *to distinguish himself from other primates in the Gauteng cradle, near Johannesburg, so many years ago — the mastery of roasting meat and the consequent improvements in diet not only changed early man's external features but also expanded his brain size, differentiating us from the apes. The Dutch word* Braden *was transformed to the Afrikaans* Braai *by early Boers in the veldt and* vleis *means flesh: braaivleis (roasting meat) became a uniquely South African social tradition, kindling fellowship.*

Rugby *was of course imported from England, from a town of that name, and first organised by my alma mater, Bishop's College, on the Greenpoint Common here in Cape Town in 1862. But what made it a singular Afrikaner sport was the Anglo-Boer war. Many of the 24,000 Boer P.O.W.s learnt to play rugby from the British in the concentration camps of India and Ceylon. Upon returning to the motherland, playing rugby became a symbol of Afrikaner resistance and self-sufficiency. Witness the current Springbok team line-up — only one of the fifteen has a non-Afrikaans surname. And his is Irish: Kirkpatrick!*

*The **sunny skies** of South Africa brings Broederskap together — what can be better than a good game of rugby followed by a braaivleis, and a few beers to create fellowship?*

†

CHAPTER 6

Promise, Cape Town

I do hope you like my social commentary piece from the Herald — I certainly do. But now upwards and onwards.

Whenever I gun my fire-red Porsche south along the N1 motorway from the Terreblanche farm, in Paarl, to Cape Town, the unfolding tableau reminds me of curves. The gale-force southeaster curving a white blanket over Table Mountain, its curved slopes ending in Table Bay's curved coastline as it plumbs the vast depth of the Atlantic Ocean. All three curves point to the great city's throbbing harbour, the core of activity known as the Tavern of the Seas. That is where I like to take my pleasures. A good fish restaurant on the wharf. A few glasses of fine Cape wine and, now that I am divorced, a comely lady of good repute to enjoy the rest of my evening with. White and Afrikaans of course, preferably a senior student from the University of Stellenbosch. But I am afraid I digress from our narrative.

†

Another curve, this time man-made, brings Promise Madiba into view: the coal-fired locomotive labouring to get the packed train to the station on time — the railway line curving across the Cape Flats in the summer heat, having descended from the purple-hued Hottentots Holland Mountains in the distance.

"Hau. Hau. It has been such a long ride. Are we nearly there?"

"Where did you travel from, miss?" the pleasantly rotund conductor puffed.

"From Fort Beaufort. I am tired of living on the train. It has been three days," Promise said, clamping her brown felt hat to her errant hair.

"Not much longer, miss, we are approaching Cape Town Station now."

The train hissed into the cavernous station and came to a final rest at the end of the line. The long journey concluded, the clanking of opening railcar doors replaced the sounds of released steam, unspent.

Promise Madiba must have felt a little unsure of herself as she buttoned her canvas jacket, shouldered her travel bag, made doubly sure that she had the letter of introduction to hand, and jostled her way into the imposing glass and steel construction, swarming with activity. The din and sights overwhelming for a country girl from Pondoland.

Cape Coloureds yelled: ARGIE, ARGIE, selling newspapers. Black and white porters in blue and red uniforms pushed luggage-laden trolleys to and fro. Kids cried for their mothers. Untamed children ran circles. Conductors' whistles blew, shouts of: ALL ABOARD, ALL

ABOARD echoed about. People hustled and hawkers sold their goods from the cool concrete floors, and, above it all, none too quietly as they flapped around, pigeons and the occasional seagull flitted in the sky-lit apices of the Victorian station — its steel and glass roof reflecting the sound and light show rising from below.

"Please, sir," Promise said, picking out a black porter to ask her question, "how do I get to Horstley Street?"

"Let me think, miss. You look worried. That's in District Six."

"Ewe." Promise fanned her face with both hands against the heat.

"Go over there" — he pointed a thick finger — "over the Grand Parade in front of City Hall. Past the castle wall. Ask for Hanover Street. It bisects District Six."

Stepping on to the Parade Promise was thrilled by the industry unpacked before her. Multicoloured motor cars were parked higgledy-piggledy, their boots opened to display their owners' wares. Stalls set alongside, laden with food, were manned by cooks boiling, baking or braaiing tasty treats that filled the air with waves of tantalising smells. Grocery, fish and clothes stalls were being packed up for the day. The magnificent Table Mountain range surrounded it all in splendour.

It seemed to Promise that Table Mountain rose from the Parade, curving to its great height in the distance. Completely flat on top, a wisp of cloud rolled over its edge like a tattered tablecloth. She stopped to have a good look. A bit afraid of standing still amid such bustle, she nevertheless dropped her bag onto the pebbled Parade ground next to a stand still heaped with clothing, tied her jacket around her midriff, and then looked around her to take stock of the engulfing vastness. To her left, across the Parade, between the stalls, she could just see the grey castle wall the porter had spoken of and, above the city sprawl behind it, yet another slate-coloured mountain connected to Table Mountain, cragged rocks rising to its peak. She turned right to see another pointed mountain. Standing apart and three-quarter the height of Table Mountain, it had a rocky outcrop at its helm; a lone tree stood sentinel at the divide between grey stone and khaki-green fynbos. Its slope, after first falling, and then curving like the flank of an enormous animal, rose again to finish in yet another fynbos-covered hill, atop of which colourful flags signalled to the ships out at sea. "That's it. Devil's Peak, Table Mountain, Lion's Head and Signal Hill." Promise pointed at each as she turned from left to right, then looked around to see if anyone had taken notice of her. No one paid her any heed, so she shouldered her bag and made her way through the market to get a better look at the imposing Cape Town City Hall, which dominated the southern length of the Parade. The honey-coloured building was one of the most imposing Promise had ever seen. Fashioned from sand-coloured limestone, the ornate Victorian construction had a turreted clock tower standing some five storeys high. Promise had to arch her head backwards to check the time. The black arms of the white clock just turning vertical, she counted six bell peals — she better keep going. Promise made her way through the crowded market towards the castle wall and passed the Harrington building to enter Hanover Street, careful not to meet anyone's eye.

Arriving at the corner of Horstley Street after the sun had set beyond Table Bay, she turned up the uneven cobbled road, the slope of the darkening mountain ever-present, but a few wan streetlights illuminated the steep pavement. Single- and double-storeyed houses rowed each side of the tight street. Snugly packed, sharing walls between them, they kaleidoscoped up the slope, their faint stoep and balcony lights hinting at their variegate colours. Some dunned and fading, only a few bright and new, most of their owners out on the streets, drinking, smoking, eating, playing music, and partying with their neighbours, fired by the gaiety that lit up District Six on a Saturday night.

So too at Number 17, Mr. Goodwill Dlamini's modest house. Promise stood back to take it all in before venturing an introduction. Covered by a red tile roof, centred by a wood-framed gable, its two storeys had been painted yellow. She noted plentiful washing fluttering in the warm wind over the balustrades and taking this as a hopeful sign, plucked up her courage and rapped on the front door.

A larger-than-life man tugged open the door. He gave the appearance of a wide buffalo swaying in the entrance way. A sheen of perspiration beaded his almost bald pepper-corned forehead; his nostrils flared broadly within his round face. Sweat trickled down the trunk of his huge neck, staining the multihued dashiki shirt that stretched all the way down to his bare feet like a portable tent.

"Sawubona, Promise. I see you. Call me Goodwill. We have been expecting you. Come in, please. We have space in a room made ready for you. Tomorrow, we talk. Tonight, we party."

A youthful twenty-one when she arrived in the Mother City, what thrilled and unsettled Promise most was District Six's jumble of people. Walking around during the next months she encountered here a hijab, there a turban, and further afield a fez — the crumpled Malay slouching against a corner smoking something acrid, quite unlike anything her father had ever smoked in his pipe. Although Promise had met plenty of fellow Africans, a handful of whites and one or two European teachers in the Eastern Cape, she had never met a mix-bred Cape Coloured, nor the scatter of citizens from across the world that frequented Cape Town's harbour and made District Six their home. The Dutch, English, Irish, French and Germans from the West, and the Malays, Indonesians, Japanese, Koreans and Filipinos from the East. Never mind the rainbow of religions. Brought up to be a Christian, Promise had not once met a Jew, Muslim or a Buddhist, and certainly never stepped into a synagogue or one of the mosques that peppered the area formerly known as Kanaladorp. The district's past name a blend itself: Kanala — Malay for helping each other; dorp — Dutch for town. In 1867 Cape Town had been divided into six municipal districts, Kanaladorp the sixth. And so *District Six* had stuck, and the old name long forgotten. Its dwellers were very proud of the melting pot it had become, mixing race and religion, cheek by jowl, and officially designated by the government as a mixed area.

It was thus with some dismay that Promise stopped at the Seven Steps thruway to behold a freshly pasted newspaper poster affixed to the corner wall:

The Cape Times Herald

The Paper that Cares.

July 4, 1949

GOVERNMENT PASSES THE PROHIBITION OF THE MIXED MARRIAGES ACT.

The Seven Steps was a favourite meeting place off bustling Hanover Street where residents of the district loved to socialise, peddle wares, and generally keep up with the latest skinner — the scuttlebutt that often ran to diatribes against the National Party's latest proclamations.

"Dit is nou fokin mooi! That is one step beyond the Immorality Act! Already a black can't sleep with a white. The cops will put you in chookie for five years," the coloured man, his hat aslant on his bald head, hissed through two missing front teeth as he pointed at the new poster.

"What, my braaa! They're not going to catch me neeking with a whitey," shouted a Malay, touching his fez in a mock salute.

"Sies. But now you can't marry her either if she gets preggy. The proof will be there for all to see. Dan is JY in die kak." A shrivelled coloured man piped up.

"This will mean the Group Areas Act will be enforced. Just you wait and see." A tall black, lounging on the steps, pumped the air to make his point.

"Sies, what will that mean for ek and jy?" the bald man asked, pushing his hat straight.

"It will mean, you will be moved out," the tall black

spat. "Jha, nee, my braaa. They will call District Six a slum. A black spot! And bulldoze us out. To Langa Township on the flats. Especially us blacks. They'll move us out first." Spitting into the gutter alongside the steps, he pointed directly at Promise with his middle finger. "Just you wait and see."

Taken aback, Promise grabbed the cast-iron stanchion she had been leaning against with one hand, smoothed back her tawny hair with the other, turned, and took the seven steps down on to the busy pavement, almost colliding with a parked grocery cart.

†

Despite the more-than-gracious welcome and the balconied room on offer, Mr. Goodwill Dlamini's reach did not extend quite as far as billed by her benefactor in Pondoland, and so Promise struggled to find a job, never mind a nursing position. Although family businesses abounded in the district, there being scores of barbers, tailors, haberdashers, butchers, fisheries, herbalists, tattoo-artists and grocers, and more than ample entertainment to be had in the many bars, cinemas and speakeasies that congregated around Hanover and Tenant Streets, there was not much work for newcomers. In fact, District Six was seedy, down at heel, and neglected by the government, lacking in social services and general upkeep. The pavements were uneven, the roads were rarely repaired, and rubbish remained uncollected and blew around the streets. Emaciated horses pulled vegetable carts from grocer to grocer.

The dilapidated cars added to the picture of decay. Parked askew and often broken down, when they did work they weaved their way through the narrow side streets, spewing smoke and petrol fumes, which clung to the foul smell of garbage in the smothering smog that often lay over the city bowl in wintertime. The only relief from the side-street stench was when a gale-force southeaster blew it all away.

Promise felt sorry for the snotty children that played in the gutters and pitied the wasted dogs that slunk about foraging for food. She stayed well clear of the narrow alleyways where the good-for-nothing gang members and pickpockets slouched. The district's economy only just managed to sputter along, lacking adequate municipal subsidies, and so many citizens were unemployed and close to the poverty line.

So, instead of a local job, Promise minded the family's clutch of children, cooked, and cleaned to support her keep, and started looking further afield. And, when she had time, she explored Table Mountain's footpaths that coursed uphill to its flat crevassed top, readily accessible by crossing over the majestic De Waal's Drive that curved along the upper border of District Six, just beyond Mr. Dlamini's house.

In her quest for work, Promise ventured beyond the city bowl, to Victoria Road, Woodstock. Dr. Abraham Ebrahim had hung an advertisement in his surgery window, so small she had walked past it countless times. But on this day the bright sun was just rising over Devil's Peak, and the darkened advertisement came to light as it rose. Promise stopped. It was surely a sign. Dr. Ebrahim needed a medical assistant for his general practice. Maybe he would give her a try — after all, Promise had her reference letter from Dr. Ian Smith in her pocket.

A slight Namaquan girl, her sandy hair wrapped in a bright doek, appeared from behind a counter as Promise nudged open the door. "I'm Debbie; how can I help?" Her lips softened and her sloe-eyes settled in welcome.

Promise faltered, mesmerised by the slant of Debbie's high cheekbones, her delicate eyelashes, the white eyeteeth on her pink tongue. It took all her effort to pull out the letter and offer it to the young woman.

"Yes," she said, in that vulnerable way that Promise could never get enough of, "Dr. Ebrahim has been without a medical assistant for so long, I'm sure you'll do for the time being."

Promise told me that she adapted readily to the duties assigned by Dr. Ebrahim. Drawing on her experience with Dr. Smith, she was soon accompanying him on house visits and to the nearby Woodstock Hospital. She marvelled at the nurses in training, their fresh white uniforms and the red and blue capes shrouding their shoulders, as they prattled prettily on their way to the Woodstock train station after work.

J.T. note: Promise didn't say prattled prettily, but I think it captures the scene.

Promise liked the routine. She'd pick up the double-decker bus on Hanover and take it down to the Doctor's Office on Victoria Road, stealing every opportunity she could to spend time with Debbie. Far from arid, like the Namaquan desert town she had moved from to seek opportunity in the Cape, Promise found in Debbie a font of delight. Friendliness became fondness, finding carnal joy in the tiny bedroom Debbie inhabited on a cul-de-sac nearby — black and tan mixing in the timeless act of love.

†

Meanwhile, the National Party was handily assembling the legislation that would create apartheid: The Population Registration and Immorality Acts of 1950. The government compelled the two Acts' implementation by requiring every citizen to register as one of four defined racial groups: White, Coloured, Black or Asian, and made criminal any carnal knowledge between whites and non-whites. Fittingly, the government enforced the new legislation by launching police raids to catch lovers in the act. Lying about the carnal incident was also cause for prosecution.

However, Promise and Debbie were not at risk. Sexual relations between two non-whites was not classified as criminal. Not that criminalisation of the sexual act would have dissuaded either — Promise was fiercely in love, and Debbie reciprocated. In fact, police enforcement of the Group Areas Act in District Six would aid and abet their romance — tying them ever closer together.

†

Returning to Horstley Street one afternoon after work, Promise came upon her uncle. "Hau, Mr. Dlamini, you look too-too sad."

"Yes, Promise, I am very sad. I have received a heavy blow today. This letter in my hand. It is too hard."

"What is hard? Is it a death?" Promised asked, sitting down on a low stool to show respect for her buffalo-sized uncle.

"No, it is worse. It is an eviction notice. We must pack up the house and move to Langa Township."

"Ewe, that is too-too sad my Umalume." Promise shook her head and sucked in her cheeks. "Shoo, shoo, shoo."

"There is a house there on the flats. I will not go. I will not move our family to that sand pit unless they force me." His pained voice rose as he crushed the letter and threw it down in defeat. Deflating further like a balloon fast losing air, Goodwill crumpled out of the front door, looking up to the mountain for relief from his anguish.

Promise rose and followed him slowly outside. This was a heavy matter. A matter far too weighty for a slight girl. She did not quite know what to do for the punctured man beside her. She put her hand softly on the nape of his bent, sweating neck, and stroked gently, soothing sinews tight under his coarse-coiled hair, bristling like a brush.

Then she headed off to Seven Steps to find out what she could about the matter. Was it only the Blacks or were the Coloureds and Asians to be evicted too? She learnt there of the Freedom Day Strike that had been held in the north of the country. Police had killed eighteen protesting blacks in the violence that had ensued.

Promise told me that it was only then that she fully realised the awful truth. It had been gnawing within her ever since her forced overnight stay in the police station in Fort Beaufort when she couldn't produce her passbook. But now it was terribly clear. She was living in a police state. A country of dubious laws, injustice and cruelty.

†

Promise's next steps appeared almost to be predestined. Occasioned as they were by the bulldozing of Mr. Goodwill Dlamini's home and the extraordinary acceptance — brokered by Dr. Ebrahim — into a nursing training post at Groote Schuur Hospital, Promise needed new lodgings. The nursing school was not willing to room her in its *Whites Only* dormitory, but she needed to find a place close enough to get to the hospital at all hours of day or night. So Debbie and Promise rented a small cottage at the upper reaches of District Six, just below the notorious Hospital Bend of De Waal Drive, the scene of countless motor car accidents that had given the curve in the road its deadly reputation.

†

On her first day, dressed in a cloak covering her brand-new nursing uniform, Promise exited the front door, crossed the street and found a nightwatchman warming his hands over a kettledrum fire at the corner of an open plot of veldt, its low flame competing with the early-morning light.

"Sawubona UMnumzana, I see you, sir." Promise bowed, almost curtsying, in respect.

"Sawubona Usisi."

"What is the way to Groote Schuur Hospital?"

"Sister, do you wish to know the long way or the short way from here?"

"The short way. I am late. It is my first day."

"My sister, go quickly. Go up over De Waal Drive under the Devil's Peak."

"Hau, sir."

"Ewe, sister. You can go in the back entrance. At the nursing school."

"Hau UMnumzana. That is where I wish to be."

"Go well, Usisi."

"Go well, UMnumzana."

Promise started her first day perfectly on time, resplendent in her trim skirt, sensible white shoes and nursing cap; the all-white outfit starkly advertised her gleaming blackness, far too obviously for the hospital authorities concerned. Yes, she could continue her training, for they were perpetually short of sisters, but she was remanded to the non-European side of the hospital. And to the operating theatres. There the patients were colour-blind.

†

Promise was not at all blinded however to the ongoing trauma that was unfurling in the country. Working in Groote Schuur's Casualty Unit, her eyes were opened. Internecine gang warfare was rife in District Six and the Cape Flats beyond. Because of the abject poverty, gangs like the Mongrels and the Scorpions fought to extend their territories for hawking, shebeening and prostitution. Usually with the knife but more recently with pistols, the opposing gang members raped and stabbed and killed. The blood-soaked victims of this carnage were ferried up the hill leading to Groote Schuur in wailing ambulances past the hospital's graveyard to be decanted, hurriedly, into the trauma bays at its entrance, there to meet whatever fate was in store for them: admission to the hospital above, or the cemetery below.

Nor was Promise immunised to the deteriorating political situation in the country. In fact, she was inflamed. She joined the African National Congress Youth League and marched through Cape Town during its Defiance Campaign on April 6, 1952, held specifically to coincide with the historic Jan van Riebeeck's Day. The annual holiday that celebrated the arrival of the young captain in Table Bay, three hundred years earlier, which kick-started Dutch colonisation of the Cape and, eventually, South Africa.

The Defiance Campaign had been launched to combat the ever-worsening apartheid legislation and would prove to be a watershed for the African National Congress, transforming the resistance movement from moderation to militancy. A makeover that would be viciously repressed by the government, now newly armed with the Suppression of Communism Act, a much-feared law that gave the National Party almost unfettered power to prosecute against its adversaries.

Promise thrilled to the vortex of activism encircling her, roused to help her people in the best way she could.

†

CHAPTER 7

Marja, Cape Town

Marja told me she was having a hard time of it. After the rape she had lost her bearings. Whenever I asked about it, I first fortified myself with a hit of strength-giving nicotine. I lit my Peterson's pipe and peered through the smoke to wait for an answer, sucking it out of her so to speak.

Marja's gaze first went to a far-off place and then refocused. She'd say something vague, usually starting in Malay — "Tidak apa-apa" — grab her left wrist with her right hand across her midriff, and then start making sense again.

†

Having missed the M.S. *Johan van Oldenbarnevelt* from Batavia, Marja found the next available ship en route to Amsterdam in early 1949. This one was to go via Cape Town, in South Africa, a place of wonder she had read only a little about in her geography classes in high school in Bandung.

Caring little about much else, Marja confined herself to the below-deck cabin, with just a porthole and sullen sea for cold comfort. She withdrew into herself and curled up on her bed; food delivered outside the berth was left untouched. Her eyes flicked around with fright when she heard approaching footsteps in the clanging corridor, just beyond the cabin door. Even a soft knock was enough to spark pulsing in her chest; Marja feared having to open the door and human contact.

She felt soiled and unclean and started to shower and wash herself obsessively — striving to cleanse the filthy rape from her stained body, the kali water from her skin. She felt worthless and dreadfully alone but couldn't sleep, and lay listening, terrified by any sounds of approach. Men's voices she feared the most as they talked and walked past the cabin, the volume increasing and receding as they moved past. Women's voices were not much better — she didn't have the energy for an interaction — but at least they were soothing.

One day — they must have been far into the Indian Ocean by then — a soft voice would not go away: *Tidak apa-apa... Tidak apa-apa... Tidak apa-apa...* Marja opened the cabin door carefully to stop it.

"Selamat pagi" — "Good morning". A slim, saronged amah with a warped back insinuated herself into the cabin. "Marja? Is that your name? You look unwell. The captain is worried about your well-being. Let me take a good look at you." The amah straightened her twisted back to demonstrate to Marja what she needed to do.

"You must stand up straight and be proud of yourself. But you are far too thin and pasty-faced for your own good. I see you can be beautiful — you must be very hurt, but we must get you well."

"Yes, I am. I have been broken inside. I don't know what to do about it," Marja replied, grabbing her wrist with her right hand.

"By a man?"

"By many men."

"I am so sorry. Inshallah, we'll get you through it. Come, get dressed in your sarong; I'm taking you up onto the deck for a nice walk. I will introduce you to some good people. Are you religious? Do you have a Koran? There is an imam on the ship on his way to Cape Town."

Marja strengthened considerably, in her heart and her mind, from the amah's attentions and the imam's religious guidance — she studied the Koran fervidly for its solace of calm and wisdom and became brave enough to face the ship's deck alone, turning the corner as the boat edged the southernmost tip of Africa, setting course for Table Bay.

The majestic ship approached Cape Town as dawn sharpened the edge of the morning light. The stark table of the mountain yellowed horizontal above a band of sea mist spread like a veil around a brightening face, thinning and then evaporating, as the vessel drew closer to the harbour.

Marja stood near to the imam, both hugging the deck rail as the ship steamed into the Duncan Docks. Feeling the loss of his imminent departure, she listened intently to retain the imam's calming voice as he told her of the great faith that their Cape Malay forebears had brought to the city, and his plans to rejoin his ministry in District Six. He pointed to Signal Hill, looming over to the right, and described the Holy Circle Tombs on its flank, just visible, as they approached the quayside.

The imam then invited Marja to visit the Aspeling Street Mosque, during the seven-day anchorage in the harbour, with a stern warning.

"Marja, come and visit us as often as you like. You are especially welcome for Friday night prayers. But never visit District Six alone. Come by yellow taxi; the place is infested with skollies, ne'er-do-wells, and filled with gangs that are up to no good. I am telling you again. It is dangerous." The imam looked like he was about to spit in opprobrium, but left it at that and bade Marja farewell so he could collect his belongings and leave the ship.

Cape Town harbour in 1949 was quite something when compared to Tanjong Priok in Batavia, where the ship had disembarked some three weeks earlier. Although both cities had been shaped by Dutch colonialists, Batavia was flat and had been bombed, while Cape Town had peaceably seen out the war and was backdropped by multiple mountain ranges. But, more importantly, the Tavern of the Seas was a world-renowned city and bustled at the crossroads of many cultures, representing a polyglot of different nations. For instance, Marja had never seen a Zulu in the flesh: their hugeness and their pride. Nor a Bushman or a Namaquan, smaller and paler but no less prideful. And just like Promise she had never encountered a Cape Coloured, for whom, henceforth, Marja would be mistaken when she summoned enough pluck to step off the boat two days after its arrival.

Compelled by the wish to see the imam's mosque and receive the balm of his belief in her, at least once while at harbour, Marja, now a very anxious twenty-three-year-old, was only somewhat cheered by the fact that, because of her Dutch, she could easily understand the Cape Coloured's lingua franca, Afrikaans, allowing her to mix freely. But she was greatly dispirited by the display of apartheid in the making when she stepped off the gangplank onto the quayside: the onslaught of black and white signposts directing where one could sit, eat, or go to the toilet — depending on the colour of one's skin. Freshly painted signs, in both Afrikaans and English, seemed to be everywhere. It was bewildering and foreign. Taxis and buses and benches were designated either for *Non-Whites* or *Whites*. Similarly, there were separate entrances at the customs house, the police office and the railway station that left her feeling giddy, unwanted and demeaned — not at all enhancing Marja's thread-thin confidence. Before Marja was an *Indo* and now she had to think of herself as *Coloured*. She asked for directions to District Six that first day but turned back when she got to the Victorian-style railway station on Adderley Street, down from the harbour. Skittish, she decided to regroup on board the ship and follow the imam's advice and take a yellow taxi the next day.

Marja was impressed. The Coloured taxi driver proved to be a font of information and a tour guide rolled into one; he never stopped talking, the minute she got comfortable in the back seat of the small sedan.

"Miss, shall I take you up Signal Hill first, so you can have a view of the harbour and then we can double back and take you to the Aspeling Mosque. It is just off Hanover Street, about halfway into District Six. I can point out all the sights for you?"

"Dankie, thank you. That is kind of you, but I just want to go to the mosque. Does it cost much?" Marja reached for her purse, resting on the hot vinyl seat.

"For you madam, someone as pretty as you, it will be my pleasure, half-price, maybe a shilling, one way." He sharpened his fez between three fingers, aligned its tip with his spiky nose, and swivelled both in the direction of travel.

"Where did you get to yesterday on foot? Adderley Street? Here it is. You can look up the street and see Table Mountain in the background. Now we turn left into Darling Street. Lots of traffic. Are you used to this in Indonesia? And all these double-decker buses. They're English. Imported from Great Britain by ship. Now over there on the right is the Caledon Square Police Station as we go into District Six, to Hanover Street. They guard us. Hah, I don't believe any of it. They verneek us Coloureds and beat the blacks. Put us in our place, they say. Ever since the Nationalists got the power last year, we are in trouble, ek sê!" He rolled down the window, spat once, cleared his throat loudly and rolled it back up against a belch of exhaust fumes, all the while driving slowly down the vehicle-clogged street.

"Now over there... on the right, do you see that double-storey building? The one with the turret on top and the balconies?" The cabbie looked up at the rear-view mirror, caught Marja's eye and so continued. "That is the Hanover Building. A beauty. On the second floor is the Blue Lagoon. It's a cabaret/night club kind of place. You will likely not go there since I see you are religious, visiting the mosque and all. It's better that way. Lots of prostitution going on here. Lots of gangs, bad stuff and politics." He looked up again and shook his head. "Not much money here in the district; the Nats spend money in the whites-only suburbs, not in the mixed areas around here." The cabbie rolled down the window again; Marja could smell the petrol in the muggy air.

"And, if you decide to walk to the mosque next time, let me point out a few landmarks. Over there, next to the Hanover Building, is the Westminster Cafe, then the Public Wash House, and, two shops down, the Seven Steps. That's a place. Ek sê. It's a walkway, with iron posts at the top of the steps. The dogs like pissing against them, so watch out for puddles. Look on the right as we go past, you can see right up to Table Mountain from there. I think it's about a mile and you are on its slopes. Now… your final landmark is the fish market on the right. You can smell it already. And here we are… the Aspeling Street Mosque. It is very old and named after Al-Azhar Masjied. I can drop you off right here. You can easily walk back. Just take Hanover Street, on to Darling Street, you will see the castle, and the harbour is just past there. Just don't walk at night and you should be fine."

Marja gathered her yellow sarong about her, paid and thanked the driver for his help, adjusted her black hijab over her bony shoulders, and stepped delicately onto the rubbish-strewn street, looking up at the imposing green-domed turret that rode over the intimidating portal, awaiting her entrance. She hesitated in through the door, pushing it open just a crack to slip into the coolness within and on to the thick crimson carpet that muffled the muezzin's cry just starting overhead. Its high-pitched wail, reaching across District Six, was beckoning her in. She advanced to the imam, standing to the side, dressed completely in white, contrasting his dark face. He smiled, showing gapped teeth, and raised his arms in greeting.

"You have come, my child. Allah be praised. Please kneel over there with the other women. And please return on Friday night, for our special prayers."

Feeling a little better now that she had seen the imam again, Marja settled down to the side of the mosque and followed the midday prayers with rapt devotion. Rising afterwards to leave, entranced by the coolness and peace, Marja emerged from the mosque into the glaring sun, the stench of fish rotting in the gutter overwhelming her as she stepped over the road to the opposite side.

"Sus, jy lyk sleg" — "Sister, you look sick."

"Kom sit hier op die stoel" — "Come and sit down here on the stool."

Marja slumped next to a table of glistening fish displayed for passers-by to choose from. The sour stink and bloodied pavement nauseating her further, she collapsed and was carried into the back of a fish stall to recuperate.

Coming to on a coarse, prickly blanket, Marja found herself in a bedded alcove. A curtain shrouded out the dim light that penetrated the depths of the shop; she heard only muffled shouts in the distance, probably coming from the hawkers yelling in the streets outside. Then a chinked voice came from nearby.

"Are you feeling a little better now? You have been lying there for hours. Let me help you up." The curtain was pulled aside, and a willing but crooked hand extended to

82

reassure her. Marja was steadied, given a cup of fragrant tea and a piece of melktert, and sat down on a rickety chair with a shaky view of the street, now turning to dusk. The old fishmonger, bent and twisted by arthritis, settled Marja down to find out what had brought this pretty stranger to his shop.

Responding to this kindness, she must have explained her difficult circumstance, sealing her fate. Because, not soon after, the fish man had called to his sister, Dolly. A porker of a woman with a sour snout of a face, Dolly made it quite clear that she would arrange a taxi back to the ship on one condition only, that Marja would accept an invitation to visit for supper with the family after Friday prayers at the mosque. Brooking no excuses from Marja — that the ship was due to leave that Saturday — Marja was deposited into a warm taxi and sent on her way.

†

Now, I am quite sure that you, the reader, would find it hard to believe that Marja would accept such an invitation to dinner after Friday's prayers. After all, the common saw is that "once bitten, you are twice shy". But Marja needed affection, and validation, and was in a foreign country quite on her own. And desperately lonely. She was just emerging from a bout of depression and self-doubt, the depth of such despair not easily fathomed by those of us who have been more fortunate in life. In addition, she was about to embark for Holland, uncertain of what was in store for her there and burdened with grave misgivings: could she, or did she even want to, face Willem after the defilement of her rape? At times she had wished she were dead, but here she had found salvation. The imam and these welcoming people were providing it. What harm could there be in accepting such a kind invitation? After all, the fishmonger and his sister had looked after her when she fainted and had put her back on the taxi to the ship. God gives us free will, and so we decide our fate.

†

Marja disembarked for Friday night's prayer. The muezzin's call dispelling any doubt of the rightness of her actions, she hailed a taxi on the wharf and was driven to the Aspeling Street Mosque, dressed brightly for the family dinner afterwards. All went according to plan and by all accounts the fish dinner was a delight, according to Marja telling of it to me much later. But there was something fishy about it, if you'll excuse the pun. Marja was a little surprised by the range of people encircling the huge table. It was not at all the sedate dinner she had anticipated. There was much raucous laughter, boisterous behaviour, and Dolly's family must have been considerably extended, for those seated were multihued and colourfully dressed, and unabashed in their friendliness, making Marja feel most welcome and comforted in their midst. Dolly, the most solicitous of them all, sat alongside Marja. Here she heard a new term that she was not familiar with. Strooi Meisie. Turning to Dolly to ask about it after a long draught of her cool drink to wash out the fishy taste from her mouth, Marja suddenly felt woozy. Whoops. The room clouded in on her; she felt hot and must have fainted, because she remembered nothing further of the evening. Indeed, nor of the next day. Her ship had sailed, so to speak. She woke up in the familiar alcove bed. Curtained as before, she opened one side and peered into the gloom. She was feeling faintly sick, as if poisoned or drugged. The fishmonger's crooked hand appeared again through the curtain.

"Marja, here, let me help you up. You will come to no harm if you work with us. Dolly put some sleeping tablets in your cold drink. You must be very sensitive because you have slept the long night and this whole day. You will be staying with us here in Cape Town."

Still feeling groggy at the time of this news, Marja told me that she just gave up there and then, ready to accept her fate. It must have been Allah's will. She didn't have the strength to resist or fight. She just wanted to be at peace from the turmoil and be calm in herself.

"Could I have some sweet tea and melktert? That should make me feel a little better. And I need to clean myself, please, I am feeling dirty all over," Marja asked the fishmonger, clutching her wrist between her finger and thumb.

Things unwound from there. Marja had been kidnapped into prostitution, like so many strooi meisies before her. She was a perfect mark for the Mongrels, one of District Six's notorious gangs, which ran illegal shebeens, gambling dens, speakeasies and suiker huisies, needing a steady supply of prostitutes, able to service the many sailors from all over the world that frequented the busy harbour.

For the first years Marja accepted her fate passively. After all, she had been trained as a geisha, knew her way around men in a professional sense, and really had no other option. Having been kidnapped, she was a slave. She had no identity documents, no money, no family, nothing that she could call her own; she was cut adrift, though imprisoned. The only home she had was a room in a boarding house set up by the Mongrels to accommodate their gaggle of strooi meisies. She became more depressed and emaciated and tried to commit suicide.

Dolly, who turned out to be the matriarch of the suiker huisie that Marja was forced to bring her clients to, despaired of the situation, and so the gang's profits, contrived to reawaken her charge's spirit by bedding her with a Japanese sailor. Knowing full well of Marja's past in the Japanese concentration camps, Dolly unleashed a Javanese tiger.

†

I have been told that Marja's response to the situation was not atypical for survivors of abuse and rape. Shamed by life's turn against them, victims like Marja attempt to find a new identity to endure and, yes, may eventually thrive. The fact that the Japanese sailor had a massive penis heavy with ballitos may have been the trigger for this metamorphosis, because Marja became indomitable. She turned from being a victim into a promiscuous predator, becoming hypersexual, probably to exact revenge against the men that had brought her into disgrace. Surprisingly, she found some healing and fulfilment in the sexual act. It set free her pent-up emotions and, although it did not bring the comfort or validation of love, it allowed her a measure of control over her life. Over the next years Marja made her way deep into the illegal world of District Six, plotting to get from under the men she detested and regain her liberty and feelings of self-worth.

†

CHAPTER 8

South Africa

Now that you know a lot more about Promise, Willem and Marja, let me fill you in on some political detail as we fast-forward to 1955, where I will pick up their stories.

By 1955 the Nationalist Party had been in power for a full seven years and their planned scheme of grand apartheid was gathering pace. You have already heard of the National Defiance Campaign of 1952, where Promise Madiba cut her resistance teeth within the African National Congress. Launched to counter repressive laws like the Population Registration Act and the Group Areas Act, engineered by the government to classify, separate and marginalise all non-whites in South Africa, the regulations made criminal the commonplace: customary relations between a black and a white, be they a man or a woman, were prohibited by legislation. The government stamped out any opposition with the draconian Suppression of Communism Act (1950) under which guise the Special Branch felt empowered to summarily imprison or ban a person from meeting with others. An Act that was rumoured to impel torture by the Special Branch to counter sedition.

The ANC had not sat on its hands in the matter. Quite the contrary, it had been growing in strength and militancy since 1952, when Nelson Mandela declared publicly that violence was the only strategy that could overthrow apartheid, non-violence as a stratagem having gained no traction over the previous forty years of the ANC's existence. The government countered by preventing Mandela from giving his inaugural address as president of the Transvaal ANC in 1953 through serving him, and twenty-nine fellow ANC members, with a banning order, restricting their movement and political activity for the next two years, forcing Andrew Kunene, instead, to give Mandela's inaugural address, entitled "No Easy Walk to Freedom", in his place.

Two important events would mark 1955 as a watershed, one each on both sides of the fight.

The Congress of the People, formed by the ANC, would agree to its Freedom Charter, which promoted equal rights for all South Africans irrespective of race.

At the same time the government-initiated Tomlinson Commission for the Socioeconomic Development of the Bantu Areas rejected the idea of integration between the races completely, and instead proposed separate development as the only way forward. In short, the Commission sketched out a blueprint for grand apartheid by proposing the formation of eight separate Bantustan homelands that each black tribe, like the Xhosas of the Transkei, would be declared citizens of — each black individual as a consequence losing their South African citizenship rights in the process, disenfranchising all but white South Africans from participating in a democratic society.

†

CHAPTER 9

Willem, Cape Town

Just a few days after my first tape-recorded interview of Willem in 1960 at Attorney Labuschagne's offices (just after he and Marja had been charged under the Immorality Act), I decided to follow up with another interview in more congenial surroundings. So, I invited the surgeon to join me for a fine fish lunch at my favourite restaurant on Cape Town's wharf.

It was a sparkling day at the Duncan Docks. Black seals wallowed in oil-glistened water. Circling seagulls plunged to their catch in the heaving sea lapping softly beneath the eatery's creosoted beams. The smell of salt, oil, and fish slick, I hoped to draw out his story — plying him with a sprightly Paarl white from my father's wine farm that I had brought with me to the restaurant.

Dr. Jansen looked anaemic and withdrawn, dressed all in black. His thin blond hair, parted in the middle, stretched behind his ears to his collar. The bruised eye visited on him by the police had shaded. His hooked nose matched the nasal tones that welled up from his darting Adam's apple. "Why have you brought me here?" He contorted his neck upwards to the right, while gazing downwards to the left. It took all of fifteen seconds before I felt it right to continue.

"Well," I said, "if I am to be of help when I report on your case for the *Cape Times Herald*, I need as full a picture of your lives as I can get. Promise told me that knowledge is power. I think she is correct. The more I know about you, the better I can help your situation. I have invited you to lunch because I want to hear more about how you got on in South Africa. Didn't you disembark just two hundred yards from here in 1955?"

Willem writhed again, his face guarded and inscrutable. I took this as a somewhat hopeful sign, pulled out my notebook and licked my pencil, and this is what he told me, jerkily at first, but then, upon further lubrication, more fluidly.

Willem had been roused belatedly by the brash horn announcing the ship's arrival at the Duncan Dock. He had overslept. He had wanted to be on the foredeck as they steamed into Table Bay, but the previous night's Bols Jenevers at the captain's dinner party had put that to rest. Hungover, Willem straightened out his crumpled summer suit, stooped out the narrow cabin door and headed up the gangway to the foredeck as the *Randfontein* steamed alongside the wharf. Just in time to see the coarse ropes cast to bring the ship in, he looked up at Table Mountain, a cloudy blanket already curled over its top — wisping down the slope like threads of dissipating smoke.

His nostrils up to appreciate the salted breeze, Willem turned to speak to a lean, dark-skinned man atop the deck. Dressed in a beige thobe, the Muslim was tamping down the cotton cloth against the gathering wind.

"Agh, but your land is beautiful. Can you point out Groote Schuur Hospital to me?" Willem twisted to examine the man's face.

"Ja, nee. Our land is beautiful. But troubled." The Muslim rolled his brown-veined eyes, "No, you can't see GSH from here. But you can see District Six rising up on the slopes of Devil's Peak over there." He pointed to the east. "And De Waal Drive curves around the mountain. There. Just below that is Groote Schuur — over the ridge. Can you see that white ambulance against the brown slope over there?" He aimed a knotty finger at the mountain. "You sound Dutch. Are you a doctor?"

"Ja. I am hoping to work at the hospital. What is the best way to get there?"

"Get a taxi. A *whites-only* taxi. Welcome to South Africa. You have a lot to learn about our country."

An hour or so later Willem followed his new deck acquaintance on to the wharf, the posted signage directing in two languages where disembarkers needed to go: *Doane — Customs. Net Blankes — Whites Only. Net-Nie Blankes — Non-Whites Only.* Struggling to keep up with the Muslim, Willem's two suitcases heavy, perspiration broke out under his panama hat, despite the earliness of the hour. Willem felt a rising tension, an enervating beating in his chest. Guilt-struck, he anticipated the probing questions from the customs officials and gripped his baggage tightly. The dread of authority fogged his brain. Willem progressed into the narrow customs hall and stopped in front of a counter behind which two blue-clad police officers stood.

"Goeie môre. Good morning," Willem stammered in both official languages to ingratiate himself. He had put down his luggage and reached for his travel documents, hoping for the hundredth time that all would be in order to secure this entrance to his new life.

"Good morning, sir." The stocky officer stroked his regulation moustache. "You are in the wrong room. This is for Non-Europeans. Non-Whites. Did you not read the sign? Please go to the other side."

Willem felt stupid. *How could he make this blunder? He always became agitated when he had to cross borders and confront the police: Japanese, Dutch, Indonesian.*

"I'm sorry, officer. Can I not just have my passport stamped here?" Willem had opened his passport to the picture page and handed his immigration papers across the counter.

"No, sir. That is not how we do things in South Africa. I see that you are a Dutch doctor." The policeman looked up at Willem. "Just like Jan van Riebeeck in 1652. Kaptein of the *Dromedaris*. He was Dutch, and a doctor. He started the first colony here. You can see it has grown a bit since then." The officer chuckled to himself as he pointed Willem back whence he came. "Good day. Next! Next!"

Willem needn't have worried so much. After hauling himself to the whites-only entrance, his polite passage into Cape Town was as smooth as the cut of a surgical knife. He didn't make the same mistake twice in selecting a taxi bound for Groote Schuur Hospital.

The next morning Willem arose early. It was not that the bed in the doctors' quarters was unsound. It was solid imboya wood. The past came crowding back, inescapable in his new surroundings, redolent of his Indonesian youth. The small sparse room. The dark heavy furniture. The dove cooing in the early-morning light, promising the warmth of a hot day. The fragrance of frangipani in the window box. Willem needed to see what his future would look like and be rid of the confining space.

Willem pulled on his plimsolls and escaped. Out round the back of the doctors' quarters, past the nursing home and up over De Waal Drive, rising along a footpath coursing up Devil's Peak, his heart apace with his step as he strained upwards brimming with energy. He would run till he was dead tired today. A smile broke on his strained face as he turned around some fifteen minutes later to look back down at the hospital and out over the Cape Flats. Built on the lower slopes of the great mountain he ascended, Groote Schuur's starkly white hospital wings spread out like two arms to receive the city's sick from below. Crowned by an ornate water tower rising dizzily at its centre, two tall turrets flanked its red-tiled roof, making the vast hospital look more like a place of worship than of healing.

Willem stretched his spindly arms. Both palms reaching out towards the magnificent building below that held his future. He whooped once and doubled his pace up the path to find a crumbled fort-like structure, settled high along the mountain's fynbos-covered ridge. He decided to rest and reconnoitre. Learning from a battered plaque that the edifice was known as the King's Blockhouse, he was thrilled by the view that the strategically placed lookout afforded. Groote Schuur now only a shoebox collection in the distance, Willem beheld the immensity of the African continent splayed before him: the Atlantic and Indian Oceans curving the narrowed waist of the Cape Flats below, the Hottentots' Holland Mountains deep in the distance. Willem had read that one half-million people called the great continent's tip home.

Turning to the sheer rock face that capped Devil's Peak some five hundred yards above the Blockhouse, Willem decided to leave that daunting climb for another day and cast his eye along the adjacent Table Mountain range. Only a bit higher, the enormity of the steep massif overwhelmed the senses as the solid bare mountain dropped past Lion's Head and Signal Hill into Table Bay's icy waters. So, instead, he descended the rock-strewn path he had come on, his mounting stress about the new job at hand softened somewhat by the energy expended and the raw beauty that surrounded him.

The next day Willem had an appointment with the hospital superintendent, Dr. Piet Visagie, who would decide his fate. Worried that his past had preceded him, the young doctor dressed fastidiously for the interview. He wore a dark suit, aligned his blue-grey Leiden tie, and spit-polished his black shoes to a fine sheen.

Arriving early, Willem was bid to sit down in the office waiting room. He could not help from asking the severe looking secretary a few questions, interrupting the noisy clack of her typewriter.

"Juffrouw, miss. Do you know if there are any other applicants for the job?"

"No, doctor. Rest assured; you are the only one. The superintendent spoke highly of you."

That matter assuaged, the superintendent duly welcomed Willem into his smoke-hazed office, invited him to take a seat in front of his paper-strewn desk, sat back, lit a cigarette and inhaled deeply with evident relish. Peering from below bushy eyebrows, his face cragged yellow, he exhaled and explained the new job's responsibilities.

"I see that you have had extensive training in surgery. But here in South Africa we take nothing for granted. You will have to show us what you are made of." Visagie leant forward. "You will first be an assistant surgeon to the head of the surgical firm, Dr. William Camden-Smith."

"Dr. Visagie, that sounds fine to me. When can I start?"

"Not too soon, I am afraid. You will first have to complete all the paperwork. That will take a little time. The Cape Provincial Administration is a stickler for that." He coughed once, then again, stubbed out his cigarette and reached for another. "And then you will need to get a car and get a place to stay; the doctors' quarters is only for temporary accommodation and overnight call. I would say in about two weeks; that will give you time to get yourself in order."

"Do you have any recommendations?" Willem asked.

"Yes, here, take this newspaper. I like the *Cape Times Herald* best. Look in the classified section for motor cars and flat rentals. I would recommend a Volkswagen. A good German car made right here in South Africa. And Rondebosch is a nice place to stay. A nice white suburb not far from here; you don't want any trouble in the mixed areas below the hospital, now, do you? You being Dutch, just like Verwoerd, minister for native affairs, was. That Nazi is no friend of the blacks. Although he pretends to be!"

†

Willem followed Dr. Visagie's advice and purchased a brand-new Beetle. One would have thought that given Willem's length he wouldn't have fitted into the cramped car, but he just pushed the seat all the way back and told me he was quite comfortable. He wanted a yellow car, it elevated his mood, but all they had was a black one, so he made do with that.

Finding accommodation went well too. Having read the classifieds, he drove around Rondebosch to scope it out before committing to anything. He knew he was considered a loner but wanted a fresh start — to be at the centre of things — so he could try to socialise. At least, that was his excuse for the slate-grey flat he settled for, a stone's throw away from the Pig and Whistle public house in Randall's Hotel. He found rooms on the first floor of the corner apartment overlooking the famous Rondebosch Fountain, an ornamental Victorian-era horse trough centred on Main Street, topped by a towering, hexagonal, multicoloured lantern. A further selling point for the gabled flat was that he could see the pub's front door from one of its windows, and St Paul's Church across Main Street should he need absolution after a drinking bout. Not quite as wonderful, though, was the fact of the Rondebosch Police Station, just a little further along Church Street, but hidden from view.

†

I acquired the date of Dr. Jansen's first day of work in Cape Town from an entry in his diary: December 5, 1955. Willem had just turned thirty-one when he started afresh as an assistant surgeon at Groote Schuur Hospital.

The day was bright, windless and filled with cheerful birdsong emanating from the park that angled Church and Main Street, so Willem felt almost good about himself when he unlocked his parked V.W., luxuriated in its new car smell, and drove the three miles along Main Street to bustling Observatory. I imagine Willem warily whistling to himself as he turned left past the ageing cemetery and sped up the steep roadway leading to the front of the hospital and the doctor's parking spot awaiting him. He was to meet Dr. Camden-Smith in his ward office on the second floor at eight o'clock.

The South African surgeon typical of the day, and in the British tradition, wore a dark waistcoat under his white jacket and sported a grand grey goatee to compensate for his failing hairline. "I dare say. You must be the new man, Dr. Willem Jansen. Dutch, born in Indonesia. I know those parts a little. Served in Singapore, before the fall. Glad to get out of there in time. Stopped off here and never looked back."

"Yes, I am grateful to be here. Ready to work." Willem kept his face straight and stopped his left hand from turning outwards.

"Alright, then, we'll start our ward rounds on the white side and then, after tea, repair to the black side; no surgeries planned for today unless we get an emergency, then we'll see what you can do, eh?" Camden-Smith turned to the nurse standing beside him. "Sister would you please get Dr. Jansen his white coat?"

Willem felt cramped in his new doctor's coat; his black suit sleeves stretched well beyond its limits. Fully aware that he must never again lose control of himself, no matter the provocation, he caught up with the Camden-Smith firm as they wheeled into the ward to see the first patient, an army of medical students from the University of Cape Town in tow. The bespectacled sister led the entourage. Dressed all in white, with a red-cross-emblazoned cap at the helm, she commandeered a trolley heaped with medical equipment and patient files. Willem braced at the smell of ether when a medical student took out a glass thermometer, cleaned it with cotton wool soaked in the pungent liquid, shook it out, and inserted the device under the waiting patient's tongue.

"Good morning, Mrs. Plumbottom. How are you today?" Dr. Camden-Smith addressed the recumbent patient, looking frail in her pink hospital gown, as he removed the thermometer and glanced at its rising column of silver mercury, before he continued, "I see from the chart that your blood pressure is fine, but your heart rate is up and your temperature rising. I would like my new assistant, Dr. Willem Jansen, to perform an examination of your tummy to determine the cause."

Willem bent to the purpose. Having noted that the patient's wide-eyed stare had deflected modestly at his approach, he pulled the thin curtains carefully closed around the patient's bed, and gently palpated her pale abdomen, finding it rigid to the touch. He released his hand's pressure rapidly and elicited rebound pain; the young woman gasped in distress, clinching the diagnosis. Colouring red at the pain he had caused, Willem stammered out a quiet apology, straightened up, opened the curtain, and announced in his usual nasal twang: "Dr. Camden-Smith, I believe the patient has peritonitis. She will need an exploratory laparotomy to establish the cause. The sooner we operate the better."

"Dr. Jansen, I think you are correct. Sister, prepare the patient for surgery. We will operate after lunch. Let us finish our ward rounds at the double."

†

Thus, on his first day on the new job, Willem performed his first surgery in the operating rooms on the second floor of the hospital. He gave me an account of how he felt.

"I was very nervous. I had rather hoped that I would not have to operate on that first day. I did not yet know where I could get some ether to calm my nerves. In Holland, I had some stashed away in the toilet cistern. If I was anxious, I could drink some before surgery. It helped to stop my hands from trembling so I could cut straight. But here I had to go in cold. Not only that. I was the one who had made the diagnosis of peritonitis. What if I was wrong? The patient would undergo unnecessary surgery and my reputation as a new surgeon would be shot. After all, I was under the gun. I was pretty sure Camden-Smith had contacted my former chief in Holland and knew about my problems there. I could not let anything show. I needed to calm myself.

"We gathered at the front entrance to the theatre suite. I was given my white scrubs to change into and told to select a set of rubber boots in the changing room. It reeked of toe-jam and urine, despite the red carbolic stains on the floor. I was then taken to Theatre One, *Saint's Theatre*. Mrs. Plumbottom had already been anaesthetised. I could smell the ether and heard her uneven pulse clicking a trace on the oscilloscope at the head of the operating table. She was lying quite bare under the intense overhead lights when I was introduced to the scrub sister, who was painting her abdomen with an orange antiseptic.

"'Dr. Jansen, this is Sister Promise Madiba,' Camden-Smith announced. 'She will be assisting you today. I will scrub in, but I want the two of you to perform the operation together. I want to see how you work. Also, by the way, this is a first for Sister Madiba too. She usually works in the trauma theatres downstairs, but we're short.'

"'Good afternoon, Docatela,' was all she said from behind her mask as our eyes met. She was magnetic: I was drawn in, her hazel irises reflected by light, an upward crinkle played at her darkened eyelashes. I felt something in myself release, a tenderness, like with Marja. The warm welcome had set a long-forgotten emotion anew.

"'Good afternoon, sister. Scalpel.'

"I put out my gloved hand — my trembling palm waiting over the patient's belly to receive the instrument.

"'Knife, Docatela.' She gently placed the razor-sharp implement, her fingers lingered lightly, steadying my hand, imperceptible to all but the two of us.

"I cut a slow but unwavering stripe bisecting the patient's abdomen, splitting the skin, red blood oozing out, dabbed away by Promise's deft fingers under the bright light.

"My surgical concentration kicked in. I became oblivious to all but the operation before me. It's like coming home. The patient's anatomy dictates the way, like an old friend met again in a familiar place. Well-known to the touch, I examined each internal organ in turn to detect the cause for the patient's disease — the appendicitis that would surely kill her if left undiscovered.

"I felt Promise's presence helping me through that first operation — as if we had met before and knew one another. She stilled my gloved hand with gentle pressures and calmed my nervous spasms when I sought relief in her lively eyes.

"The operation almost over, I straightened up to survey the theatre around me, taking in the green tiled wall, the anaesthetist, and the few onlookers that surrounded us, as if for the first time.

"Promise broke the hushed silence that had reigned in the theatre from the first incision. 'Well done, Docatela.' Lost in contemplation of the new operating room, I glanced down once more. Her averted eyes forsaking my thankful gaze, I readjusted to Camden-Smith's peering directly at me over the slight sister's shoulders.

"'Yes, Dr. Jansen, I think you'll do. Congratulations.'

"I tried not to show my relief and elation and replied rather nonchalantly for me — I was quite pleased with myself at having passed this first test: 'All in a day's work. I look forward to many more.' I then closed the abdomen with interrupted sutures, careful to leave a drain to the abscess cavity in her belly. And, at the end of that day, I drove home proudly in my black Beetle, rather hoping that I would be working with Promise soon again.

"However, that was not to be. The next day, she had been transferred back to the Casualty Unit. I felt a sense of loss, of what might have been. Not knowing then, what I know now: the great peril of love across the colour bar, a consideration completely alien to me."

†

Over the next year or so Dr. Jansen adjusted to his novel environment and progressed at Groote Schuur Hospital. Over weekends he explored the Cape Peninsula, almost always alone; he preferred it that way. He didn't have to trouble about other's feelings, and Marja was a distant memory. Her carved figurehead still held pride of place in his bedroom, though.

He usually ventured forth in his car early on a Saturday when he wasn't on call. He had found a nice parking space on Church Street. All he had to do was turn either left or right at its intersection on Main Street as he passed the Tudor-styled Randall's Hotel at the corner. The orange indicator bevelling out of the side of the black car pointing in the direction of travel — left past the hospital and on to Cape Town Central, or right to the Southern Suburbs. Claremont being the next. Here Willem liked to stock up with Douwe Egberts tobacco to replenish his Falcon pipe, a constant aromatic companion.

Another Dutch penchant that Willem indulged was a fondness for alcohol. A few stiff Bols Jenevers allowed him to console himself after a long day. But, failing that, the wines of the Cape were close at hand at Groot Constantia, about eight miles along Main Street, as it wound on to Muizenberg and the Indian Ocean, the site of his favourite beach for a body-surf in the breakers that curled on to the miles upon miles of yellow silty sand.

Driving to Muizenberg on one of his first forays, he parked his Beetle at the retaining fence that separated the car park from the wide beach, facing its blunted bonnet directly out to sea. He got out and surveyed the long coastline. He could see white signs with black lettering posted strategically along the shore. *Net vir Blankes — Whites Only*; Willem remembered clearly how put out he felt about all of this. What if he brought Marja, or Promise? The black nursing sister he had so recently met was now ever-present in his mind. Her gentle help had steadied his frayed nerves at his first operation in this new place. He wished he could see her again.

Willem would learn later, though, that both Marja and Promise would have been apprehended by a white police constable patrolling the beach. They were the wrong colour. For them there was a Coloured beach at Strandfontein — about ten miles up the coast from Muizenberg. And, if they could not show their dompass, they would be locked in the back of a caged police van and charged at the Muizenberg Police Station — ordered to present the passbook within twenty-four hours or be summarily convicted.

From this favoured beach, Willem often drove up the steep roadway of Muizenberg Mountain to its lookout. Here he liked to train his binoculars to look for passing whales. Starting at the roiling waves that foamed white on the yellow beach far below, he raised the glasses and watched the sea as it first turned sky blue, then cerulean, to navy, before darkening further to a deeper tone to engulf the hoped-for mammals in the far-off distance.

Alternatively, Willem drove southwards along the Cape Peninsula. He followed the curving coastline on a far to narrow road that inclined through Fish Hoek, passed the Naval Base at Simonstown, and travelled on to the distant Cape Point, where the two great oceans met.

"You would have thought that there would be a ridge in the sea line where the two oceans collided." Willem puffed on his pipe, the embers glowing in its briar bowl, emitting a sweet fragrance. "But there is nothing of the sort, just the massive ocean, the briny smell of rotting brown kelp, and the wind to tell you that you have arrived at the continent's tip, reaching out to the Antarctic. There is a timelessness in it. All on your own, you think that you are but a lonesome speck in the Universe. Will you ever make a difference to anyone or anything? And now look at the mess I am in." Willem bit hard on the stem of his Falcon, thinned his lips, sucked his teeth. "Just because I love someone. All I set out to do was become the best surgeon possible. Perhaps that is how I could make a small contribution to life. To heal people and so improve their lot. A little simplistic, don't you think, John? But I had seen so much death. So I felt hard inside but now Promise has softened me. Before her I didn't have feelings for much. For the sheer beauty around me? Yes. I was falling in love with the country. But not for people. No. Being with people didn't make me feel warm inside, like I remember with Marja, so I focused on my work. Surgery allowed me to concentrate on one thing at a time. But, John, I am only telling you these things because you have a gift for listening. I don't usually speak so much. But… in short, I wanted to make a difference, despite my shortcomings."

†

After this monologue, I stopped Willem. I saw he was tired and a little drunk and I wanted to coax more out of him. So I asked him whether we should go for a walk along the quay to still his evident agitation. He bared his teeth but agreed. He relit his pipe, puffed once or twice, unfolded from his seat like a giraffe after a drink of water, and we headed out along the docks, he rail-thin and swaying a bit, and me rather weightier and more steadfast beside him. Seagulls soared overhead, the sea slapped below and we were surrounded by the tumult and benzine fumes of a working harbour. It seemed to calm him, though, and we were fortunate to see a whale out at sea. Willem pointed it out to me, a rictus of pride shadowing his face. It started to rain so we went back to the restaurant, had another glass of wine, and he continued.

"As I said, I wanted to advance as a surgeon here in South Africa. And so had to learn techniques that I was not trained for in Holland. The surgical management of the stabbed heart is a good case in point. A tricky condition that Cape Town was notorious for, on account of the gang warfare that plagued District Six and the Cape Flats. Rival gangs would settle festering scores with their adversaries by sinking a dagger into their foe's chest. The blade often penetrated the heart and its surrounding sack and left only a small tell-tale sign on the man's chest, which was easily missed, while the heart exploded inside. The victim's blood leaked into the pericardial sack and compressed the collapsing heart with every pump, throttling the patient's blood flow like a cardiac lynching. The surgical approach to the problem had not yet been well established at the time, and the diagnosis was often difficult to make by an inexperienced surgeon like myself.

"I was called to the Casualty Unit on one of my first nights on call in the hospital. The black side. A coloured patient was deteriorating fast.

"'Doctor. The patient, he is dying.' A black nurse pointed to an unconscious patient, lying akimbo on a stretcher, blood pooling on the floor below.

"'What is the problem?' I asked, hurriedly taking in the scene unfolding around me.

"'Too many stab wounds, here, and here, all over the chest and abdomen. I think he has lost too-too much blood. I think we must take him to theatre.'

"I examined the patient, could not record a blood pressure, and decided that urgent surgery of the abdomen was required in the Casualty Unit's theatre adjacent to admissions. I was anxious. I could feel my neck and hand twitching. I yelled. 'Get this patient into theatre now! Now! He is going to die! If he is not dead already!' to get people's attention. They glowered at me in alarm. I could see them thinking: this Dutch doctor, he doesn't know what he is doing. Well, they were right. I didn't.

"We pushed the stretcher into the cramped operating room and the anaesthetist administered ether and told me to move fast; the patient was worsening. I scrubbed my hands quickly, donned sterile gloves, and was helped into a surgical gown by an assistant — all the time taking in the scene: the patient at the centre on the operating table attached to the anaesthesia machine, still bleeding from his lacerations. The disc-shaped light hanging from the ceiling above, bathing him in a wan glow. (The light didn't seem to be working properly.) I hesitated, gathered my thoughts, but went for the abdomen. Incising it quickly, in search of the source of the blood loss that was fast killing the stab victim. To no avail. The problem was in his chest. The patient's heart stopped, compressed to death by the unrelenting leakage into the pericardial sack. I should have opened the chest, through the ribs, to relieve the tamponaded blood — to save his life. But I didn't know that at the time. I had not been trained in the procedure back in Holland. There was rarely a need for it. I hung my head. My contortions were intolerable. I felt a failure. I had failed to rescue this man. I am rarely moved by death any longer but this was my fault. I shuffled out of the theatre to search for any members of his family that I could find. I wished to console them, but I was also seeking consolation for myself, forgiveness for this wanton death.

"The patient's post-mortem told me later where I had gone wrong, but Dr. Camden-Smith made doubly certain: he crucified me at the next surgery morbidity and mortality conference, held in the tiered hospital auditorium on Friday afternoons. Beckoning me to the front of the auditorium to face the gathered surgical department and present my case — the senior surgeon allowed forcefully from behind his lectern that I should have known better.

"'Firstly, Dr. Jansen' — Camden-Smith pointed at me — "you should have recognised the ballooning heart on the chest X-ray. That is pathognomonic of pericardial tamponade. That tell-tale sign is a give-away. You should have acted with speed and without hesitation."

"'And, secondly, Dr. Jansen' — he pointed again — "you should not have screamed in anxiety. A surgeon NEVER loses control. This is a time for calm, concerted action." Camden-Smith pressed both hands down on the lectern, then traced an arc with his right index finger across the room. 'A chest incision should have been made. The ballooning pericardium should have been opened to release the constraining blood, and the knife-hole in the heart should have been sutured closed with silk. That is how a patient stands a chance. Cutting into the abdomen instead was a gross mistake, an assured death sentence for the patient.'

"I didn't know where to look, so I just shut my eyes. And then, God help me, Camden-Smith gathered further steam. He held forth at pitch, his voice megaphoned up into the far reaches of the wood-lined auditorium, the whole surgical department a witness.

"Surgical research was currently being performed in the department on the best approach for managing the stabbed heart, given the high incidence of the problem in Cape Town. Experiments were being conducted on the condition in the J.S. Marais Animal Laboratory, down at the university's medical school, adjacent to the hospital graveyard. Perhaps, he said, again pointing at me, I should join them there to get some practice in this important surgical technique. Better still, I could study the matter further, write a few papers on the subject, and my work could become the basis for a Ph.D. thesis to secure a future professorship. I hadn't thought about it. But there it was. Another goal. I planned to become an expert on the subject. I didn't want to fail again."

†

"Speaking of Fridays, I did try to socialise. Usually after the morbidity and mortality meetings, the department repaired to the medical school. There was a bar set up behind the dean's office. Just a short walk across from the hospital, it was a great way to end the week, if you were not on call. A few drinks always made me feel better, so, when the bar closed at seven, I would regroup at the Pig and Whistle.

"I drove home and got ready. I like to dress well. Women like a sharply dressed man, and after a few drinks I become more interested in female company. I have my proclivities like any other, John. I gather that you would understand that.

"I put on my navy double-breasted jacket, over a tight silk shirt, open at the collar, and added a matching white pocket square. I tamped down fresh tobacco in my pipe, lit up for confidence, and walked down the stairs on to Main Street, and then over to Randall's Hotel across the road. I love the smell of beer, smoke and varnished wood as you walk into the hubbub of a busy pub. Suitably fortified with a pint in my hand, I turned from leaning against the bar and surveyed the clientele, seated on low bar stools around circular tables. I paused to see if there was anyone I knew.

If not, I casually took in the scene and bided my time. I cast my eye at the food menu scrawled on a blackboard or pretended to be enjoying the multicoloured herald shields that festooned the Pig's wooden beamed stucco walls, yellowing from the tobacco smoke that fogged the capacious tavern. Always, though, I kept my eye on the double doors left wide open to let patrons in, ready to make my next move. And sometimes I came away with success, but it never lasted.

"I have never been confident with girls. If I saw one coming in that was attractive, I feared rejection, but nevertheless I watched her carefully and then, if she went and sat by herself, approached, and tried my luck. But only in this setting, at the Pig, when I'd had a few drinks and wanted female company. Otherwise, I couldn't be bothered.

"Take, for example, Sally. I had been in the country about a year by now. It was in December of 1956. Nelson Mandela, the president of the African National Congress, had just been arrested for high treason, and I was becoming politically aware about South Africa's repressive laws. The University of Cape Town students had led a protest march through Rondebosch and afterwards many had stopped off in the Pig for a few celebratory drinks.

"Sally was on fire — long blonde hair, blue flashing eyes, stoked up with righteous anger. She was thrilled to hear that I was a Dutch doctor, and what did I think about this outrage? Well... of course, Mandela's arrest for high treason was an outrage, but that was not so much on my mind as I sought to win Sally over. She was. So I suggested that we go outside into the beer garden, order a few drinks, and she could tell me all about it.

"'Willem.'

"I leant closer to hear what Sally was saying in the din surrounding us. 'The apartheid government is corrupt.' Her eyes flashed. 'You know of course that over the last three years the state has made a case against the leadership of the ANC, after throwing a lot of them in jail or banning them.'

"'Yes, Sally. After the Resistance Campaign of 1952 against the pass laws. I have been reading all about it in *The Star*. One hundred and forty-four people arrested all over the country just a few days ago, mostly blacks.' I showed my concern by moving closer, her rosemary-perfumed hair touching my alcohol-pickled cheek, hypersensitised by increasing inebriation.

"'One hundred and forty-four! And Nelson Mandela imprisoned at Marshal Square in Johannesburg. Unbelievable,' she said and moved still closer. Not flinching, even a bit, when I put my hand high on her thigh under her dress, hidden from view by the beer-soaked table. 'All arrested on charges of high treason, and an alleged conspiracy to overthrow the state.'

"And so I absorbed a fiery lesson on the political situation to know Sally better, much later that night in my flat, conveniently close at hand. But the next day I felt very little for the girl. I could not enjoy the simple pleasures that other men might from a pretty girl like her. I could not talk to her intimately of my past. I became passive again, closed and irritable. After a few weeks she did not want to see me again.

"John, please do not misunderstand me. It is *not* that I was unconcerned about the deteriorating political situation in the country. In fact, the opposite. I was deeply troubled then and even more so now. What was happening to the blacks, the imprisonments and repression, reminded me of what the Japanese Secret Police, the Kempeitai, had done to us. Every time I came across a South African policeman in uniform, I mentally checked myself: was I doing anything wrong or illegal? And, if I heard a wailing police siren or a percussive helicopter overhead, the sound would trigger intense uncertainty and fear in me, an incessant free-floating anxiety, hyper-amplified by events. And those feelings are ever-present now.

"Any authority figure is an instant reminder, unlocking the terror of torture or some arbitrary justice. I wake up some nights sweating in bed. Sparked by who knows what, I arouse bewildered and fearful that I am back in a prison. Coming to, I am only able to calm myself once I have run through a mental checklist and realised that I have neither committed a crime nor a punishable offence, and am truly in my bed at home in Rondebosch, and not in Indonesia.

"Sometimes even that cannot calm me. And only a jog helps. Plimsolls on, I race up Stanley Road, over to Mostert's Mill at De Waal Drive, and up one of my favourite paths on Devil's Peak, till the panic leaves me and some semblance of serenity allows me to return. And now, since I have been charged and face possible imprisonment again, it is all coming back. That's why I'm in such a bad way."

†

CHAPTER 10

Promise, Cape Town

Getting Promise to speak to me again after the first tape-recorded interview was not as straightforward as it had been with Willem; it needed subtlety, nuance and strategy. Promise was a notorious black activist. An African National Congress Women's League organiser, trained to be suspicious. Especially of a white reporter asking questions. She treated me with outright disdain and would not take any of the telephone calls I placed to the Casualty Unit, where she had become the sister-in-chief. I had asked Willem during our conversation at the fish restaurant to convince Promise of my good intentions in seeking another interview with her. I wanted to create a fuller picture of the events that had led up to his arrest with Marja under the Immorality Act. He averred that Promise was of the "distrust but verify" persuasion. She first wanted to see evidence of my good offices: a favourable newspaper article penned by me as the court reporter covering their case for the Cape Times Herald, *my employer. Hence, I had written pointedly about* the immorality of the situation in the newspaper, witnessing the fact that both Marja and Willem were Indonesian-born and that he was a Dutch citizen. In this way I hoped to convince Promise that through my reportage we might be able to engage the Netherlands government to exert political pressure on the Nationalists, given that one of its country's citizens was being charged with an infraction of the apartheid law.

The very day the article appeared in the Cape Times Herald, *the Caledon Square Police Station chief loudly — very loudly — noted his displeasure by telephone — only relenting somewhat when I told him that I had to write the article in this fashion to get Promise to speak to me again.*

At a loss for what else to do, I decided to visit Promise in person. To catch her when she was coming off duty, at the entrance of the Groote Schuur Hospital. This was of course highly irregular, but I think I set it up quite well. I parked my red Porsche, top down, on the curved driveway that abutted the hospital's garden terrace. I had chosen a warm, windless summer evening for the intercession. I had put on my best brown jacket, matched it with a fawn cravat, Brylcreemed my hair back into place, and positioned myself on a bench nicely shaded by a palm tree in full view of the hospital's doorway. Just in case Promise needed further persuading, I had the newspaper article in question readied under my arm. I lit my Marlboro, leant back and waited. I hoped to bring just the right touch to the essential encounter.

Promise didn't fail me. She appeared prettily at the front door in her white nursing uniform just after five o'clock, but seemed a bit taken aback. She told me that she didn't want to be seen with a white man outside the hospital like this. I must say, I lost my cool a bit. The interview was critical to piece together the whole story. So I remonstrated, I pleaded and then I opened the newspaper to point out my good offices. Seeing the article with her own eyes finally convinced her of my bona fides, for she relented and let me drive her — top up so she couldn't be seen — to Signal Hill. There we sat alone overlooking the bay, the sunset soothing her into telling me far more than was good for her. She was nevertheless guarded, and so I have needed to back-fill to provide the complete story for you from other sundry material I could lay my hands on during my intensive investigations, and from the diaries that Willem left me — what follows is the best summary of events that I can muster.

†

Promise was pleased with the small cottage she had moved to in District Six necessitated by the bulldozing of her uncle's house and her start as a nurse trainee at the nearby Groote Schuur Hospital in 1951. Debbie, her Namaquan friend, liked its cosy nature — sisal mats, beadwork, wooden carvings, soft rugs — and the location was just right for their purposes, situated as it was at the upper reaches of District Six, a neighbourhood designated a mixed area by the Cape Administration. Promise could reach the hospital by taking a short cut (criss-crossing De Waal Drive) on one of the footpaths that coursed the lower reaches of Devil's Peak, while Debbie could walk the length of Queen's Park Road and take a bus on Main Street to Dr. Ebrahim's offices in Woodstock. Lying halfway up a steep, cobbled side road leading up to De Waal Drive, the steel roofed cottage was outfitted with two tiny bedrooms. One too many as far as Debbie and Promise were concerned; they loved to lie together on rainy nights and listen to the riffs that pattered the corrugated iron that protected their entangled heads, Promise goading Debbie to open the window, wide, after they had had sex, so they could view the mountain up in the distance and feel the mist-cooled air tempering their sweating, sensual bodies. They were content together and not in need of a man to feel complete, but had to navigate a man's world nonetheless. The white man's world, just outside. The reality of a non-white woman's existence was inescapable. Promise was explicit in her condemnation of the inequity to me.

"Fuck it, Mr. Terreblanche. You can write about that in your fucking newspaper. I was determined to get out from under white men. Do you have a cigarette? My hands are shaking."

She inhaled deeply, savouring the rich Marlboro I had passed her, and exhaled through her upturned nose, gazing out to sea, "I don't think you men know what it's like to be a small black woman. The overbearing stupid masculinity. All those male hormones swilling uselessly around. Like my father, who used to shout down my mother. Like the policeman that locked me up in jail when I forgot my passbook in high school. Like those brutes that bulldozed my uncle's house, there in District Six!" She stood up from the bench, sucked in her cheeks to a pucker and pointed in the general direction with a well-scrubbed finger, shaking with passion.

"I was determined to take it on. I wanted to prove myself as a woman and a black. From that first day at GSH as a nursing student, I was determined to succeed. And be better than the other white nurses. I was an exception, I know, the only black nurse in training at the time. Yes, there were coloureds, but not blacks. It was only because of Dr. Ebrahim that I got in, and the hospital was short, so they let me stay. But they tried to hide me away as best they could. On the black side of the hospital and in the operating theatre, where no one cared whether a black nurse was looking after them. We are just as good as anyone else, no matter what the government officials will have you believe. Hau, hau, hau, it is just too-too frustrating."

Promise had very quickly ingratiated herself at the hospital; she was kind and caring with patients, quick to learn, and unequivocally facile with the procedures nurses were taught to perform. She rapidly mastered the humdrum of bed rolling, temperature taking, heart rate recording, and the organising of the wards, and studied the science of nursing diligently at the Carinus College behind the hospital. Two years of training soon behind her, Promise was identified as ideal to be taught the fine art of becoming a scrub sister: the nursing sister that assisted the surgeon in the operating theatre. Here she learnt about each necessary step and every instrument required for the different types of surgery performed at Groote Schuur. As if this was not difficult enough, she also had to learn to abide with the irascible surgeons and their favourite peccadilloes in performing these operations, often differently. The surgeons, almost singularly white men, obliged Promise to constrain her political passion; to succeed, she hid her fury with a mask of innocence.

One Saturday, it must have been in 1955, Debbie and Promise went shopping. Arms entwined, a bag apiece balancing their gait, the lovers made their way down their steep road to Hanover Street. Impassioned by the rhythmic beat of the African music that played on Radio Bantu, their expedition had at its heart a visit to Decca Records in the Western Building on Tennant Street to buy one of Miriam Makeba's latest recordings. Situated at the district's retail epicentre, catty-corner to the Hanover Building, the couple had a long trip ahead. First, they had to run a gauntlet of low wolf whistles as they breasted the fishmongers opposite the Aspeling Street Mosque, so they crossed the road to avoid the frank fish-stench and continued on the pavement, all the while looking for a gap in the perpetual Saturday morning traffic jam to slip back over Hanover Street to visit the Seven Steps. Here they stopped to listen to a trio of buskers — clarinet, saxophone, ukulele — the ragged music echoing off the stepped alleyway fading as they progressed from shop to shop dodging the grocer and fruit carts stationed on the broken sidewalk. The cacophony of the cluttered street vying with the snuff of petrol fumes, as they visited Van der Shyff's Material Shop, Strand's Shoe Shop, Mark's Furniture House, and Dulah Khan's Store and walked on into the Westminster Cafe for a cup of rooibos tea and a koek-sister, their bags now bulging with collected shopping. Then, suitably refreshed and hoping to catch a practice stage performance, they made for the Blue Lagoon, the infamous night club situated on the second floor of the Hanover Building. A grand sight all by itself.

Cornered on Hanover and Tenant Streets, the three-storeyed structure had a flat bevelled facade topped by a red brick turret — its two set-off flanks, trimmed by a continuous encircling balcony and protected by an iron railing, stretched the full length of the construction on both sides.

A little wary of being caught entering the dark building without permission, Promise tested the two front doors gingerly, hopeful that either the blue or the red one had been left unlocked by the tradesmen who frequented the Blue Lagoon to restore its supplies. Finding that the red door opened after a second hard pull, the girls entered the gloom inside and snuck up the stairwell to the second floor to gain entrance to the cavernous crimson-curtained room. They were in luck: a group of performers were practising a routine on the half-circle stage under a low-slung light, so Promise and Debbie made their way to one of the outermost cocktail tables readied for the evening's entertainments and sat down to watch the free show from the shadows of the curtains that surrounded the club. And, as no one seemed to mind their presence, they rolled a Navy Cut cigarette and enjoyed the smoke while holding hands under the table.

Looking down underneath the table to gather her belongings, Promise thought she spied a ball of white paper, just beyond her reach, lit up by a sliver of light that fell underneath the shifting curtain.

"Hau, Debbie. I see some paper over there. Pull up the curtain so I can see better." Promise bent underneath the table to grab it, but it rolled away in the draft from the lifted curtain.

"It looks like a scrunched-up evening programme, Debbie, should I just leave it?"

"No, get it. Perhaps it's Miriam Makeba performing here." Debbie laughed.

Promise crouched under the table, retrieved the crumpled paper and then smoothed it out on the table for both to read.

"Hau, it's a letter. Confirming a speaking engagement. Signed: Nelson Rohihla Mandela. That's impossible. He is banned by the government and cannot leave Johannesburg. Shoo, shoo, this is too big." Promise sucked in her cheeks. "Who should we give this to?"

Debbie took the paper and scanned it carefully. "September 27. That's next week. I think we should burn it. And you should go and see what Mr. Mandela has to say. Perhaps you can convince him that you want to join the ANC Women's League. You're cut out for the job. You are a good organiser and can convince anybody of anything. Now, let's go to Decca Records before they close." Debbie pocketed the paper, gathered their bags, put her arm through Promise's and they descended the stairway together, exited through the red door, out onto Hanover Street — the bright sunlight outside beating back any doubts as to their course of action.

†

Just a quick aside here: I was raised a strict Calvinist in the Dutch Reformed tradition but am not confessional by nature; nevertheless, I must briefly pause this exciting narrative to admit that I was deeply taken with Promise.

Although the feeling clearly wasn't mutual; the dismissive shrug of her slender shoulders that followed most of my questions told me that. Promise was ravishing. That was patently obvious once she had settled herself down on one of the rough-hewn benches encircling Signal Hill and taken off her nursing cap and untangled her hair. Tawny ringlets bobbed around her doe-like face, sharp hazel eyes dilated with passion as she spoke, and she had nice breasts too: a black beauty if ever I saw one. I was convinced that Debbie was right in her assessment of the situation. Mr. Mandela would be entranced by Promise and easily persuaded to take her on if she could engineer an encounter when he appeared at the Blue Lagoon. I offered Promise another cigarette. She declined but continued the story.

†

"Hau, Mr. Terreblanche. My problem was getting into the club and then in front of Mr. Mandela. I suspected that this would be a secret meeting later in the night, after the main performance of the evening was over, and the regular patrons had left the Blue Lagoon. So I contacted my uncle, Mr. Dlamini, for help. I had to call him at the house he was forced to move to in Langa Township. At first, he was pleased to hear my voice, then hesitant when I told him of my finding the letter, and then warmed to a plan. Turns out that he had joined the ANC after his house was bulldozed flat and now, quite active as an officer, had been invited to host the clandestine meeting — a rare opportunity for Cape Town's ANC leaders to meet with the organisation's former Transvaal president. Mr. Dlamini told me to dress sharp — Mr. Mandela liked to dress well himself — and walk into the Hanover Building through the blue door at 11 p.m., exactly. My uncle would be inside to take me up to the Blue Lagoon himself, and we could figure it out from there.

"I arrived fifteen minutes early. I know what men like, but I wanted to dress just right for the occasion: official, but with a touch of class. I wore a tight black low-cut dress, did up my hair in a fashionable pile, but left a bunch of ringlets gracing my shoulders, and applied just a hint of mascara on the eyes and black edging around my lips; a slender gold necklace completed my ensemble. I had to cover it all with a dark green coat against the cool night. I paced outside and smoked a cigarette. Took a last draw, crunched the stub under my stiletto heel, and marched in. My uncle looked suave in his dark dinner jacket and green bow tie. He escorted me up the stairs, seated me at a dinner table, introduced me to a few people, and bade me sit back, relax, and watch the proceedings unfold.

"Hau! I couldn't sit still. I was filled with excitement. The place was transformed at night. The encircling crimson curtains, dead before, pulsed with life: spot-lit by semilunar ceiling lights, they riffled in the breeze from the surrounding outside windows, left open to dispel the smoky miasma within. The strong smell of bourbon and cigars suffused the place, while the slapping of shoulders, and the handshakes of greeting and departing guests signalled a changing of the guard: the cabaret-going patrons left, and a new exhilarated crowd arrived, all sporting the black, green and gold colours of the ANC faithful — each new patron's bona fides carefully checked before they gained entrance to the secret meeting.

"My uncle returned to my side, sat down at the table in front of the stage and told me to look snappy. 'Promise,' he said, smacking his fat lips after he had taken a great gulp of bourbon, 'you are about to see a great man. I will bring him here to the table. I will introduce you after his first speech. You know he comes from Qunu, in Thembuland? He'll be pleased you are from Pondoland.' Then he rose to announce the renowned speaker, his sweating face interrupting the beam of white light trained expectantly on the podium.

"The hum of excitement smouldered, as my uncle grunted his introduction, kindling to a fire when the audience learnt who the evening's speaker was: Mr. Nelson Mandela. The ANC leader strode magnificently onto the stage to loud applause. Mr. Mandela wore a wide-lapelled double-breasted suit, a white handkerchief aflame in its top pocket. His broad forehead, covered by a mat of thick black hair, furrowed by a carefully sheared side parting, coursed atop a generous nose and abundant lips that curled apart into a gleaming white smile of greeting. He paused, breathed in deeply, his bright eyes scouring the room before uttering a single word. 'AMANDLAAAAA!' Mr. Mandela raised his right arm in a fisted salute. The gathered crowd responded in unison: 'NGEWETHUUUUU! NGEWETHUUUUU!' And then we clapped and clapped and clapped, till he raised his hand again and addressed us in more measured tones, his voice burning with the sing-song spirit of the veldt.

"'COMRADES. FREEDOM IN OUR LIFETIME, LONG LIVE THE STRUGGLE.' He settled, and his broad shoulders narrowed as he continued. 'I am here with you today to talk of two things, the Freedom Charter and the Bantu Education Act. Mr. Dlamini tells me that I must give you all a break in between, so let me start with how I see the situation as a lawyer practising in Jo-burg.'

"'Our people are desperate for legal help. In our country, it is a crime for an African to drink the water from a *Whites Only* drinking fountain, ride a *Whites Only* bus, walk through a *Whites Only* door, or swim at a *Whites Only* beach. It is a crime to be unemployed and a crime to be employed in the wrong place, a crime to live in certain places and a crime to have no place to live at all.'

"'A crime, a crime, a crime,' chorused back a few audience members. Mandela took out his handkerchief and continued. 'Every week I see old women who have brewed African beer to supplement their income, or people who have lived in the same family house for decades evicted without compensation because the town was declared white under the Group Areas Act.' Mandela wiped his cheeks.

"'Every day I see the thousands of humiliations that ordinary African's must confront. This must end.' Mandela pointed up, the handkerchief clutched in his hand. Sounds of unhappiness charged the room.

"'The ANC has brought together the Congress of the People, at Kliptown in June of this year. There, in a small village situated on a scrap of veldt just a few miles outside Jo-burg, three thousand people came together. They travelled to Kliptown by bus, by car, by truck and on foot, with at least three hundred Indians, two hundred Coloureds and one hundred whites attending. We talked, we sang, the platform of delegates was a rainbow of colours. The Freedom Charter was read out in English, Sesotho and Xhosa and approved with singing, and shouts of *Afrika!*'

"'Ewe, ewe, ewe, yes, yes, YES,' the room responded.

"After waiting for calm and looking down at me once, catching my eye to my surprise, Mandela continued, 'Policeman and Special Branch members tried to intimidate us, taking notes and photographs with large cameras, but we persevered that first day and into the next.' Mandela paused to look around. We were rivetted to our seats, waiting to hear what happened next.

"'Each section of the Charter was read out and adopted with loud acclaim. We needed only the final vote of approval from the Congress when a brigade of police and Special Branch detectives swarmed the platform brandishing Sten guns.' Mandela dabbed at the sweat on his forehead, glowing in the bright spotlight and then continued.

"'An Afrikaner policeman commandeered the microphone: *By order of the South African Police force, this meeting is prohibited,* he said, *it must stop. It is an act of treason.* The clipped voice continued: *No one may leave until we have your particulars and your pass books have been checked.*

"'Then a cordon of police constables, armed with rifles, surrounded the crowd. Our people were hemmed in but having none of it. They started singing "Nkosi Sikelel" in full voice and mighty unison.' Mandela paused when he heard a few of us starting to sing, but we stopped when he raised his hand-kerchief again.

"And then Mr. Mandela continued. This is what I remember of what he said — so impressive.

"'Fortunately, I had kept to the periphery of the gathering because I was still under a banning order. So I made my way back to Johannesburg deeply troubled. This unwarranted police raid signalled a harsh turn on the part of the government but cannot stop the will of our people.' Mandela pointed up again. 'Although the Congress had been broken up, the Freedom Charter prevails.' He then closed by reading a few important sentences from the Charter, which I can't remember now, and then looked up from his reading, tucked the handkerchief back into his jacket pocket, waited for the applause to die down, smiled invincibly, and walked off the stage to come and stand right next to me at my table. I got up quickly. I was flustered.

"'Promise Madiba?' he asked. 'I have heard about you from your uncle. May I sit down?' He patted his jacket, took out a packet of cigarettes, offered me one, and then lit both before stretching out and continuing, 'We were born neighbours. I'm a Thembu and you're a Pondo. We are one family.'

"'Yes,' was all I could offer.

"'I see you are wearing our ANC colours. You look very nice in them. Have you been active for the people's cause?' Mandela smiled warmly at me.

"'Hau, yes. I have marched during the Defiance Campaign but would gladly be more actively involved in the Woman's League.' I made myself even smaller to demonstrate my humility and sincerity.

"'I will see that it is arranged.' Mandela exhaled a last puff, stubbed out his cigarette, took a long swig from the whisky that Mr. Dlamini had poured into a glass next to him, bowed rather formally to both of us, and made his way back up on to the stage.

"'Now to the Bantu Education Act, Minister H.F. Verwoerd's attempt to limit the education of all Africans, condemning our children to be fit only for the tasks of menial labour.' Mr. Mandela looked up from the text, flicked a white speck from his dark jacket, and continued. 'The ANC fears that this act will permanently set back the freedom struggle of the African people. We must resist.' Mr. Mandela raised his fist, and the lights went out.

"A police whistle shrilled. Dogs barked in the stairwell. A faint light billowed through the Blue Lagoon, released by the now-darkened curtains moving in the breeze, wafting in streetlight from the outside. I could just see Mr. Mandela's silhouette disappearing through a side door before an electronic voice magnified through a loudhailer heralded the Special Branch's arrival. 'This is a police raid. You are all under arrest. This is an illegal gathering. We believe a banned person is speaking. Where is he?'

"The lights came on. But of course Mr. Mandela was gone. They never found him. I am told that the next day he left for Kimberley up north at his usual time of travel, three in the morning. As you know, Mr. Terreblanche, he became known as the Black Pimpernel, moving from safe house to safe house — but Mr. Mandela was as good as his word. I moved up in the ranks of the ANC. I organised the ANC cells that he told me of. I became responsible for recruiting as well as coordinating boycotts, conducting education programmes, running safe houses, and the like across a designated area of District Six. Thrilled by the opportunity to be of larger service to the black cause, I remained largely in the shadows so as not to jeopardise my position at the hospital. As you no doubt know, the Afrikaner government has its fingers on everything — measuring the pulse of resistance through informers that are everywhere, often paid by the police, out of Caledon Square Police Station. I had to be very careful that I was not detected and reported. I was unwilling to give up my freedom for the cause. Freedom, it is said, is having nothing left to lose. Hau, I had lots to lose. I was determined to be the very best nurse I could be. To care for those in need of my services, and to advocate for our people.

"Mr. Terreblanche, the sun has set. I see that you have got quite tense. You are shivering. Are you cold? Or is it something I said?"

You can imagine that that question, coming directly at me from an impassioned Promise, was quite a shock. I had to win her trust, to get her side of the story. I had to think fast. I got up from the bench we had been sitting on and adjusted my gaze. Taking in the beauty around me, I turned to the beauty in front of me. "No of course not." I wanted to change the subject quickly. "Can you tell me how you first met Willem?"

Promise shrugged and just sat, as if in a trance. She gazed out at the darkening sea, the white coastline curving sand far away into the dusk-fading distance. Focusing her flashing eyes on the rugged Robben Island centring Table Bay seemed to jerk Promise back into the present. She said something both puzzling and, in hindsight, possibly prescient. "Mr. Terreblanche, as a black in this white jail of a country, I feel like one of the lepers that was banished to that island in the past. I just hope I will never be imprisoned there in the future like many of my Xhosa forbears." Then she quietly rolled tobacco into a Rizla paper held on her lap, Promise's white dress trestled by shapely black legs crossed at her ankles beneath the slatted bench. The cigarette rolling soothing her, Promise looked up and asked for a match light; the flame flickered appealingly off her white-clad bosom, creating an intimacy between us in the gathering gloom that darkened the lonely spot on Signal Hill.

"You ask when I first met Dr. Jansen? Hau. All the scrub-sisters had been talking about him, even before he arrived. We had heard that he was from Holland and a fine surgeon, but that he was deeply troubled. One of the sisters had seen him enter the hospital. She said he was tall, but wiry and bent and seemed to have an uncontrollable contortion of the neck muscles, which caused his gaze and head to freeze in opposite directions. His head up to the right, his eyes down to the left. Hau. Hau. Hau. I could not see how this man could be a good surgeon with such a problem.

"And, then, there he was. I had been transferred from the Casualty Unit that day to work in the Saint Theatre on the first floor. The regular scrub sister was sick. I was told to get ready for a laparotomy. Dr. Camden-Smith would be operating on Mrs. Plumbottom, or so it said on that day's theatre list posted in the passageway behind the changing rooms. The patient had been anaesthetised and I had just finished painting her abdomen with an orange antiseptic when the two surgeons walked in together.

"'Dr. Jansen, this is Promise Madiba,' Camden-Smith announced. 'She will be assisting you today. I will scrub in, but I want the two of you to perform the operation together. I want to see how you work. Also, by the way, this is a first for Sister Madiba too. She usually works in the trauma theatres downstairs, but we're short.'

"Dr. Jansen was nervous. His eyes shot downwards, his head upwards, and his face became a sneer. His gloved hands trembled and he barely spoke. He just nodded in my direction and then stared deeply into my eyes, looking for confidence, I suppose. I am sure my pupils must have dilated. I was nervous too. So, I greeted him as I would any other surgeon: 'Good afternoon, Docatela.' But something dormant was awakened. I wanted to help this foreign surgeon. I needed to soothe his fearfulness by calming myself. I took a deep slow breath. I listened to the clicking oscilloscope unevenly beating Mrs. Plumbottom's heart rate. I took another deep breath, readying for his response:

"'Good afternoon, sister. Scalpel.'

"He put out his gloved hand, his trembling palm waiting over the patient's belly to receive the instrument, translucent in the glaring overhead light.

"'Knife, Docatela.' I gently gave him the razor-sharp implement, letting my fingers lightly linger to steady his quavering hand, imperceptible to all but the two of us.

"He cut the patient's belly open — straight and true. Blood leaked from the seeping wound. I dabbed it away with gauze feathered in my nimble fingers. I assisted Willem through each step of that first operation. I like to think that my goodwill helped carry him through. I encouraged him with a soft, even tone when he stopped and looked around to take in his unfamiliar surroundings, before finally completing the operation: 'Well done,

Docatela.'

"Averting my gaze when he looked down at me — it would have been too forward to do otherwise — I was pleased to hear Dr. Camden-Smith's compliment as I turned to pack away the remaining surgical instruments into the waiting surgical tray. 'Yes, Dr. Jansen, I think you'll do. Congratulations.'

"And, upon hearing the final golden words, 'Sister Madiba, thank you very much for a good day,' I taught Willem what we do at Groote Schuur to celebrate a successful operation: the surgeon reaches out to clasp the sister's hand, held high over the patient — an inverted V for victory, lit up sharply by the overhanging surgical light. I then tidied away the instruments, while Dr. Jansen made his deliberate way out of the theatre into the corridor. I was well pleased with the new surgeon; a glow of satisfaction spread all over me.

"I remember that day for two reasons. I was thrilled to be the one to work with the foreign surgeon on his first day. He was as good as we had heard. Maybe even better. But there was something very wrong within him. I had sensed his trouble, and I thought I had helped.

"That first day was strangely windless. A rarity in December. When I left the hospital at five o'clock, there was no howling southeaster outside to meet me. Usually, you must put your shoulder against the wooden entrance door to stop it from blowing closed in your face. But that day it swung open freely and I was in for an easy walk home, up over De Waal Drive to meet Debbie. Because there would be light for at least another three hours or so, I ran barefoot from my house up Devil's Peak to the King's Blockhouse, my favourite spot for a view over the Cape Flats, as the sun sets.

"Hau! Mr. Terreblanche, that is quite enough for today. Please take me back to my house in District Six. Marja will be waiting, and it is my turn to make supper. I have told you more than enough. You must write another op-ed that will help exonerate Willem from this charge under the Immorality Act. And keep my name out of it, completely. DO YOU UNDERSTAND?"

I nodded in agreement but involuntarily lowered my eyes.

"Now, put away your pencil and your notebook, and please take me home."

†

CHAPTER 11

Marja, Cape Town

"Nooit, Mr. Terreblanche, No! I don't want to sit in the tea garden any longer." Marja locked her right hand over her left wrist, stood from the heavy wooden bench, tightened her short bright sarong across the brown birthmark livid on her chest, and shook her head for further emphasis. "I have had enough tea and melktert for a week. If you want to talk more, we must walk."

I had invited Marja to join me at the Rhodes Memorial Tea Garden, nestled on the lower slope of Devil's Peak above the imposing granite monument dedicated to Cecil John Rhodes, the British imperialist. As she had continued her story, the low stone-walled terrace we sat on afforded a magnificent view of the wind-blown terrain below.

"Mr. Terreblanche, I had to make the best of a bad situation. I had been kidnapped to become a strooi meisie. To serve men and their pleasures. I did not like men. In fact, I hated them. But that was not my choice. The rape in Indonesia had put me in a state of terrible shame.

Verschrikkelijk. Like fear, shame weighs you down. I couldn't get over shame; I couldn't get under shame; I felt so alone that I felt like dying. But Desi, my girlfriend, saved me: she took me to Somerset Hospital and they pumped out the pills I had taken. I took this as a sign. I would set aside shame and do what I must to survive. I felt worthless and had lost my identity. I did not know who I was in this strange country. I was no longer an Indo, but was I a Coloured now? I was working in the underworld. The Mongrels owned me and kept me as a slave in a tenement boarding house over there in Canterbury Street in District Six. I became a cunning fox; a vixen, you might say, determined to get out of the prostitution business and create my own life.

"During the day we were left to our own devices. We painted our nails, coiffed our hair, sewed or knitted or went shopping if we could afford it. Nice clothes were expensive and the only money we had to spend was what we cadged in extra tips from our customers. There was a going rate in pounds, shillings and pence for what we did. A hand job. A blow job. Or the full Monty. We had to hand over what we earned to Dolly. The fat sow. She was in charge of us. She would always be bothering us. Nothing was ever enough. 'Why did you not let him in the back door?' she'd shout.

"In the early evening, Dolly packed five or six of us, all dolled up, into a battered red combi and drove down to a bar at the waterfront. There we plied our trade. You got quite good at picking out marks: ones who paid the most and you could bear to deal with. The Japanese seamen were the alpha clients. They paid well and were the most loyal. The Filipinos were the great romancers. The Koreans fought too much, and the Indonesians were on the lookout for Muslim women. I had long ago lost religion, my hijab, and wanted nothing to do with them. They looked down on me. Most were playboys, pretty boys that didn't like to pay or leave tips. So good riddance. The Portuguese, Germans and Brits were fine, but the Russians were trouble. Fortunately, they mostly went to Alf Wylie's Bar, which we only frequented when our regular place was quiet. It was on the corner, across from the Cape Castle wall, quite close to the strooi huisie we called the Riad, up Primrose Street, where we took most of our clients for rest and relaxation.

"The Riad was nice. Fronted by a high wall, no one could see the coming and goings inside once you had knocked and slipped in through the heavy oak door. It was an oasis: a garden and a central water fountain, ringed by bedrooms, their French louvre doors painted a deep red. Here we entertained our patrons, extorting as much as possible by our careful ministrations.

"The Sea Tavern, our go-to bar on the docks, was a little less tasteful. It stank of booze and sweat and kerosene and smoke, like a noisy oil rig. The Tavern drilled you into submission. The unwashed seamen cursed in languages foreign to my ears. The place was backed by a forbidding wooden bar, illuminated by a display of colourful glassware: a kaleidoscope of alcohol promising consolation to the hard-bitten seafarers visiting the port. To the side was a small stage for karaoke and pole dancing and surrounding the centre, where the melee of sailors mixed and matched with the girls, was a ring of tables at which free fish and chips were provided.

"The girls had different approaches to securing a man for the night. Of course, we were not alone. Many other gangs placed their prostitutes at the Sea Tavern, so competition was fierce. Some girls would sidle up to a mark and ask for a light — 'Light my fire' — and take it from there. Others displayed their wares by energetic pole dancing, coming off the stage with sweat-strained bodies irresistible to the hungry men. Others still sang karaoke, inviting sailors on to the stage to compete with them at the microphone. Some simply sat down at tables and introduced themselves.

"I was not so brazen. I wanted to be alluring. So I dressed with a geisha's care. Exotic. A tight-fitting bright-yellow sarong, my breasts protruding *just* above the nipple, two long slits revealing my golden-brown legs, a soft promise of endless wonder on offer. I sat demurely, but conspicuously, at the bar. I rode my stool solo. I lit my own cigarettes and positioned myself as a prize. Like a light attracting inevitable moths. I intrigued men by looking exclusive and acting hard to get. I was discerning. I took only officers to the Riad. And, there, I showed them a good time. Mmmmn, a very good time.

"Saturday was our busiest day, but of course Sunday night we had off. Then, if it was a nice evening, I liked to take a wooden bankie and place it on the balcony so that my roommate, Desi, and I could sit and look up at Table Mountain; the setting sun reflected a warm glow on our faces. She too was an orphan. Even shorter than me, she was quite pretty and had a sultry look. Her mother was a prostitute and had died at her birth. Desi had grown up in the boarding house secure in the knowledge of her chosen profession: she knew the ins and outs of the business. Please excuse the pun.

"To get away from it all, we rolled zolls filled with dagga — Durban Poison was best — inhaled and succumbed. Dit was nou lekker. Then we curled up together, getting closer and closer, our senses sharpened by the marijuana, and watched the shadows descend from the mountain as the streetlamps flickered alight, casting a pool of life on the dark cobbled street below. A hush settled over the district in the gloom, our quiet voices echoing softly within the high balcony, Desi spelt out my escape. There were three routes. Make money and become independent. Become famous. Or marry the boss, Mr. Henry Plaatjies.

"'Marja, first you must negotiate with Dolly. Tell her that you will bring in the Japanese. You're good at that. You speak their language a bit and you can provide special service.' I think I knew what that meant, but I wasn't going to let Desi dwell on it, so I egged her on with my eyes, a beseeching look worthy of any trained geisha.

"'You must become more than a prostitute. You must negotiate to become a hostess for the high-paying customers. Fat Dolly can make the arrangements. You could take them to the Blue Lagoon for dinner and cabaret. And then to the Riad for the rest of the night's entertainment.'

"You will recall, Mr. Terreblanche, that it was Dolly who drugged and kidnapped me in the first place, that fateful Friday night after my visit to the Aspeling Street Mosque, the day before my ship to Holland sailed.

"I approached Dolly in the kitchen, where she was happiest sitting wide-legged on a short stool, doing absolutely nothing of importance. Stocky, with a puffy piggish face, Dolly was usually sullen as a sow, but brightened up considerably when I made the proposition. She had seen my potential and this new plan to become a hostess would pay dividends on her investment. There was a catch, though. I told her that I wasn't going to do it unless she paid me a percentage in cash so I could become independent. Twenty per cent, I said. She said fifteen, but I was very well pleased when I received my first payment. It was more than enough for the final two instalments on the tip-top Gallo radio I had on lay-bye at the O.K. Bazaar on Adderley Street.

"Being a hostess was far more lekker all around. Dolly booked the clients. They were no longer just Japanese sailing captains (my forte) or, for that matter, marine officers, per se, but often wealthy private citizens or business associates that the Mongrels' boss, Mr. Henry Plaatjies, wanted to have serviced and entertained.

"The client was told to meet me at the Seven Steps at 7 p.m. For identification purposes, white was the colour. My mark wore a white pocket square and I held two white carnations, borrowed from one of the flower sellers' buckets that lined the alleyway's grey walls.

"Once our eyes met, I had been told to introduce myself as Buttercup, and say quite simply: 'Please follow me.' Usually a little flustered, they did so haltingly. We walked side by side down Hanover, turned left across from Decca Records and entered the bright blue door of the Hanover Building, went up the stairs into the Blue Lagoon and on to my favourite table, just to the left side, where it was a little more discreet and quieter, but with a clear view of the stage set out for the cabaret. Then, like a perfect hostess, I awakened their ardour with a fine champagne, fanned the flame with small talk in any direction the client wished to take it, never forgetting to add that an extra tip on the side would be highly appreciated.

"The meal served, the cabaret complete, the evening was pleasurably consummated with the lekker sex I was notorious for, most assuredly besting their wildest sexual fantasies, for my little piggy bank needed to become bigger. I began thinking of a place to stay of my own.

"I approached Dolly again in the kitchen sitting on her stool.

"'I want to move out of this stinking harem to my own place. I know I have made you a heap of money, and now it is time for you to give me my independence,' I said.

"Dolly reared up and pointed her snout in my direction. 'You are a whore; there is no escape from working for us. You are an illegal, with no identity. Mr. Plaatjies protects you from prosecution by the police.'

"I nodded my understanding and she continued.

"'But there is one job you can do that will secure your independence. A sting operation for the Secret Police. Your next client will be a white one. An ANC sympathiser who they want to put away using the Immorality Act. If you agree, the police will catch you in the carnal act, red-handed with a white man.' Dolly chuckled, a smirk of disgust on her bitter face. 'They will book you both at the Caledon Square Police Station, but you will not be formally charged. Mr. ANC sympathiser will be, though.' Dolly sneered. 'Do this and we will let you get your own place. Otherwise not. Your choice. Suit yourself.'"

†

"Well, Mr. Terreblanche, I kind of didn't have a choice, did I? I wanted to be a free agent, to come and go from my own place, and take control of my life. If I didn't do it, someone else would. So I suffered the indignity of the police raid, the barking dogs, the horrible policemen and the terrible scene that unfolded in the Riad. I will never forget the look of dismay in my mark's eyes as he realised what I had conspired to do. To this day, I feel a great guilt for my treachery, my role in the man's imprisonment. Especially now that it has happened to Willem."

Marja stood up and walked off at a great speed, up the track behind the tea garden terrace we had been sitting on. I quickly gathered my belongings, paid the waiter and followed suit. I caught a flash of her yellow sarong as she turned a craggy corner way up ahead. The blazing sun above, hidden cicadas whirred in the midday heat. Marja disappeared up behind a big grey boulder surrounded by brown brush. Climbing steadily higher, she reappeared along the ridge, a silhouette making her determined way upwards on Devil's Peak. She had four hundred yards on me but I had the sturdier legs, so I caught up with her, narrowing the distance slowly, only finally reaching her as the path levelled off on to a wide, yellow-grassed plateau, before curving up to the King's Blockhouse looming above — the observation post's crumbled walls protruding squarely in front of the grey-capped mountain, the bright blue sky beyond tinged by a gathering cloud that threw a long shadow over us.

"Wait, Marja. Wait!" I yelped, trying to catch my fast-coming breath. I'm about fifty pounds overweight and

141

not very fit. I puffed onto the plateau where Marja was pacing about. She circled round and round, short steps alternating with long strides.

I offered a drink from my hip flask. She first said no. Then yes. Then shook her head from side to side.

"Shush, Marja. Shush, Marja. It's not your fault," I said. This seemed to quieten the wild look in her eyes and stilled her agitated gait. She slowly regained her composure. We sat down on a grassy knoll and Marja continued the story while we gazed over the Cape Flats.

"Ja. Nee. I had had it being a nobody. A tart, a whore — a prozy in Afrikaans. Especially after this degrading affair. The police sting where I was used as a bait. I had become a lady of the night but I had set my sights much, much higher. I wanted to become a lady of influence, like Cissie Gool, the Cape Town city councillor. I wanted to become famous — not notorious — to alter my identity to become someone to be proud of; I schemed some more.

"One night at the Blue Lagoon my mark had become quite undone from the flow of sweet champagne. He snored it off, a mound of flesh heaving on the table between the silver cutlery. The cabaret was in full swing. Under dimmed lights, a minstrel played a lament on a sad trumpet, brassy in sound and colour. A silvery waif shimmied close, swaying to the sad melody, both caught in the spotlight that stalked them across the stage. The audience, all a-hush at the spellbinding act, broke to loud applause as the duo took their bow, the last trumpeted notes echoing in the smoke-filled chamber.

"I continued clapping and glided over to the stage manager. He stood smiling on the side-lines. I told him

I could do even better: a sensual geisha act. I could dress up sexily, sing and play the shamisen, perform kabuki and create an oriental cabaret, a sensation that would become the talk of Cape Town. Would he give me a chance? I had done it all before in the Japanese camp in Indonesia.

"'Okay,' he said. 'Come in on Saturday morning. You will do an audition. I need a new enticement to bring in the crowds. And what is your name?'

"'Buttercup, sir.'

"*Buttercup, the Geisha Girl* is what the stage manager called my show. At first, the audience was titillated by my low-cut lamé kimono, then fascinated by my Japanese-styled hair, fashioned into a split black peach upon my head, before becoming shocked when I turned around, showing off the red rose that nestled in its apex. It looked to the discerning eye for all the world like a vulva. The men followed my mincing steps hungrily as I performed the kabuki, a come-hither sashay in my step, fine-tuned to entice any red-blooded male in the audience. My bookings rose rapidly like their hidden erections, and I became the talk of the town. Well, not quite, but at least of District Six."

Marja turned to me, her brown eyes quizzical, her smile a query on her silky face. I gulped twice before responding, "Yes, yes, that is quite a story." And, quite inexplicably and ill-advisedly, I blurted out my newspaper's involvement in Marja's experience with the Immorality Act.

The Cape Times Herald is a tabloid paper, like the British *Sun*, and has fashioned itself as a mouthpiece for the people — a community ambassador with the slogan "The Paper that Cares". Apart from political and social commentary, the editors liked us to cover, salaciously, detailed reports of gang fights, rapes and murders, as well as transgressions of the Immorality and other Acts that the National Party was legislating. (I had cast myself as a Liberal reporter, but my police paymasters knew well where my true sympathies lay.)

I explained to Marja that I was ideally positioned to advocate for Willem with respect to the Immorality Act, because I had experience in the area. I admitted that I had reported on Marja's involvement in the police sting operation of the ANC sympathiser. I thought I'd better come clean, to regain her trust. So I explained my role in detail.

Marja listened carefully, twisted her fist around her wrist, turned and walked slowly upwards towards the Blockhouse's wall, and sat down on a gritty verge to rest in its coolness. I wasn't quite sure what to do but we had come this far, so I followed her, sat down next to her and she softly continued her story.

"Mr. Terreblanche, I am sure you know of the Kaap Klopse, the Coon Karnival Parade that is held every January 2 to celebrate the slaves' freedom. Well, that's how I got to meet Mr. Henry Plaatjies, the boss of the Mongrels, at the front of the procession.

"Business and my reputation as a performer had been picking up at the Blue Lagoon. Dolly, the sullen pig, had been well pleased because she took a cut from the pay for my performances and I was much loved as a hostess. Advance bookings were through the roof, my sense of worthlessness decreased, and I started enjoying myself. I found that I liked to act but could do without the male sex. *That* was becoming tedious. Just a means to an end.

"One day, while waiting for my mark at the Seven

Steps, my eye fell on a pink poster plastered against the alley's cement wall.

> *Miss District Six Competition.*
> *Isaac Osberg Hall*
> *Pretty Girls Only.*
> *Acting Ability a Plus.*

"My heart quickened. I read the small print. A first for 1956: the winner would win a big prize and be the first ever Coonette to lead the District Six Star Spangles Troupe for the Coon Karnival Parade through Cape Town. I saw myself already in a tall white top hat, sexy short skirt, and high boots, twirling a silver baton — photographers flashing their electrifying bulbs in my face to capture the historic event for the newspapers.

"My reverie was rudely interrupted by my mark. He had spied the two carnations held behind my back as I peered at the poster.

"'My name is Buttercup. Please follow me.'

"I was in luck, or maybe out of it. This man was one of the Mongrels' lieutenants. His reward for a job well done — a night with me. He was full of information. Did I know that Mr. Plaatjies owned this club, and that the Mongrels controlled pretty well all the prostitution, the shebeening, the gambling, and the racketeering in this area of the district? I didn't. But I listened even more carefully, pumping my mark with ever more champagne and questions.

"It turned out that I was out of my league. This was a dangerous man. He looked the part. An ex-prisoner from

Pollsmoor Prison, his hooded eyes peered out along a nose crooked by the many fist fights he had endured. Violent, he oversaw protection. He explained what that meant. If someone wouldn't pay, or encroached on the Mongrels' territory, he killed or maimed them. Retribution was the name of the game. There was a constant war among the gangs. Usually with the knife. Sometimes the gun. Each gang member was identified by their signature tattoo. The Mongrels by a triple star, the Sea Boys two anchors. They infested District Six with their carnage. I shivered and tried to turn the subject to happier matters. The Coon Carnival next year, and the Miss District Six Competition.

"Turns out he knew a lot about that too and was thrilled to talk about it, because, being one of the Mongrels, he marched in their troupe — a minstrel known for his banjo work.

"'Ja. Nee. Ek. Sê,' he lisped, his tongue lapping his gums through the gap left by his missing upper two front teeth. 'I am a very good musician. Each October, we start practising. Plaatjies puts the troupe together and we form a band, organise the marchers, and identify a "voorlopertjie" — the one who walks in front.' He trailed off and took a sip of his drink, then continued.

"'This year Plaatjies wants to change it up a bit. Good for business. Ek. Sê! He wants a pretty girl in front as the voorlopertjie. What do you think? I saw you looking at the poster at Seven Steps.'

"I hesitated. I could have sworn that I saw him lick his lips. He looked like Dracula, his remaining fangs imprinting his lower lip. I was scared he was going to bite. So I nodded and said, 'What are my chances?'

146

"'Good. I've seen you do your geisha girl act. That's why I am here tonight. And, if you win, you get to meet Mr. Plaatjies.'

"So you see, Mr. Tereblanche, all my scheming to get from under these men was slowly falling into place. I just had to win the competition, practise with the Star Spangles and then I would get to dance in front of Henry Plaatjies all the way from Hanover Street to Green Point. I asked Dracula to describe his boss to me given that he could be my ticket out of prostitution.

"'Ja. Nee. Hy is 'n baie groot man, big and fat and round, with slit eyes like a Jap. They say his father was a Japanese sailor, his mother a whore like you. He must have taken his mother's Afrikaans name, because Plaatjies doesn't sound Japanese to me! I think he looks a bit yellow like your dress. You'd fit well together. I hear his wife is ailing: TB.' He shuddered. 'Not long for this world. Finish!' He clapped his open palms together above the table, wiping them over each other four or five times to make his point. Got up slowly and said loudly: 'Nou gaan ons naai,' in Afrikaans. Now we will fuck. Not very nice, but that was what he was being rewarded with. An approaching waiter skittered off in another direction. He must have heard my mark's final comment and opted for discretion instead of valour."

†

"Mr. Terreblanche, I think you can guess I won the Miss District Six Competition at the Isaac Osberg Hall. Fame at last. I was crowned queen and received the first prize — a boat trip for two on the *Union Castle* ship to Durban — and was photographed for the social pages of *The Argus*, the two princess runners-up smiling sweetly each side of me. I was looking forward to taking Desi on the boat trip if Dolly, the fat swine, gave us a release to go. Even more motivation to get involved with Plaatjies, the boss.

"Now, Mr. Terreblanche, let's walk down back to the tea garden at Rhodes Mem. You can buy me another cup of tea and a koek-sister before it closes."

Marja got up, stretched her arms skywards and made off down the path we had come up on. I followed in the wake of her yellow sarong, rippling before me, eyeing her bare legs, careful not to slip on the rocks that rolled underfoot. We sat down on the terrace and ordered tea and she continued her story.

"Mr. Henry Plaatjies was a queer fish. He smelt and looked like one. All the time. He had big bulging eyes and the thick downturned mouth of a grouper. He favoured grey and his silky clothes clung to him like fish skin. He ate raw fish, which was a typically Japanese thing to do and was patently evident on his rank breath. And, I learnt later, Henry was in and out of the Fish Market, checking over the girls and trading in abalone, which was illegal. Not that anything being illegal was of great concern to Mr. Plaatjies. He was above and beyond the law: he paid off police officers right and left and seemed to have a free pass in and, more importantly, *out* of the Caledon Square Police Station.

"Mr. Plaatjies's great passion was the Klopse Karnival, the highlight of us Coloureds' calendar. He wanted the Star Spangles to win, just once, the Best Troupe Trophy at the Grand March Past held at the Green Point Stadium, the focal point of the Parade. Conducted on tweede jaars dag, the procession amassed troupes from different sections of the district and passed along Hanover, up Adderley, left on Strand, and then onto Waterkant and via Somerset Street to Green Point: a splash of green fields curbed by the dark-blue ocean just beyond Cape Town's harbour.

"Henry was the captain of the Star Spangles. Like many other gang bosses, his troupe was his pride and joy. He had the resources needed to field a winning team: the tailors to sew the uniforms, the venue for the rehearsals, the musical coach to teach the troupe songs and train the accompanying band, and the power to enforce practice and discipline.

"He had arranged that the winner of the Miss District Six Competition (little old me) would be the first ever Coonette to perform as a voorlopertjie for the Star Spangles and so was quietly confident — and ferociously adamant — that we win the trophy this time. He spared no expense, and we practised our routines endlessly, but he was never at the practices until the grand day dawned: January 2, 1957.

"That day I woke to a brighter future. The sun slowly rising over the Indian Ocean to the east tinted the receding darkness with a soft warmth, promising a scorching day. Sparrows flitted under the awning of my balcony, tweeting a good morning's welcome. I heard the bustle of gathering voices and the soft playing of a banjo, down on Clifton Street. Table Mountain dwarfed the scene with its dark presence, illuminating District Six in reflected light as the sun rose. I smelt smoky fires frying sizzling breakfasts. Lower Clifton Street had been chosen as the collection point for the Star Spangles. I got myself into tip-top shape before joining the fray. I oiled my skin to a sheen, feathered my eyelashes ultra-black and puckered my lips with scarlet red. This was my chance to snag the boss.

"There were two opportunities as I saw it. One, I could seduce Mr. Plaatjies as I pranced sexily in front of him as the voorlopertjie and, two, I could titillate the crowds and enthral the judges to help win the Best Troupe Trophy at the Grand March Past at Green Point. In fact, I could get two for the price of one. I put on my best smile, piled my hair extra high under my tall white top hat emblazoned with a tinsel-sparkled fire-red star, shortened my white miniskirt beyond the limits of decency, and twirled my baton. I was going to use all my assets to our advantage.

"The Star Spangles marched out of Clifton and onto Hanover Street in full regalia. Our singers warmed up with *Januarie, Februarie, Maart... April. May. June. July...* singing the well-known moppie accompanied by our sprightly band's brass, wind, guitar and drum sections — the music echoing along the built-up street. Purple-attired marshals directed us to join the swelling procession, contriving to separate the swaggering troupes sufficiently so that their music did not clash into cacophony. I streaked ahead proudly at the front, Mr. Plaatjies, in his grand captain's outfit, just behind me. Profoundly rotund, he wore a dark-blue waistcoat and a tall white top hat. His plump boot-blackened face pushing down a bright red bow tie. But for his Falstaffian figure and absent moustache, he could have passed for America's Uncle Sam, who he was trying mightily to impersonate.

"Plaatjies pointed at the throngs crowding the pavement, stopped, crouched and hollered: 'Vote for us. Vote for the Star Spangles.' He repeated the refrain, goading the bystanders to our cause, as we proceeded on the long march to Green Point. A hot cauldron of bubbling festivity, bystanders hooted and whistled their approval, the unrelenting midday sun enlivening the sweating procession undulating through the streets.

"About three hours later, we made our swinging way on to the green fields that surrounded the oval stadium and came to an excited halt. We stopped and awaited our turn to enter the stadium and make our way past the judges' stand. Mr. Plaatjies exhorted us to greater heights. He cavorted, spun about and cajoled us. He raised the stakes. If we won, there was money in it, for all eighty of us. Then he passed around five bottles of golden-brown Klipdrift brandy, told everyone to take a few doppies for strength, and started practising his own routine: 'Vote for the Star Spangles.'

"The sweating marshals directed us to follow the Dusky Dinah Coons while the American Yanks fell in behind us, somewhat stealing our thunder. We circled the ochre track to loud applause from the overloaded stands, redoubling our efforts as we passed the band stand, where the judges had taken their elevated seats to adjudicate the spectacle. The judges were comprised of the chairman; secretary; two organisers of the Coon Carnival; and a fifth judge, the only female, Cissie Gool, my hero. They held up paddles emblazoned with the passing troupe's final score: 10/10 the highest one could fetch. So the best score possible was fifty. I shimmied about to be especially alluring and launched my baton on high, catching it smartly, my final curtsy releasing a roar of approval from all but the female judge. She gave 7, the others 10. We were unlikely to win the competition.

"Nevertheless, on exiting the stadium and coming to a final rest, Plaatjies came over to me. He was so pleased; he took slender little me into his bountiful arms. He clasped me to his hot chest and I favoured him with a lingering hug. My mind was not quite up to seeing the affair through just yet. Nonetheless, although we hadn't won the competition, I would eventually win the prize.

"Two days later, a smart rat-tat-tat was banged on my front door. Mr. Plaatjies was outside, dressed in his usual grey outfit and smelling of fish. He scowled like a grouper and asked to be let in. Fortunately, I was in one of my most stunning yellow sarongs at the time.

"I bade him sit in the only chair in my lounge that was strong enough to support his weight, and offered him a cup of coffee, which he waved away. I sat opposite him on a low pouffe and cradled my chin on my balled fists. My elbows rested angled on the coffee table. I focused my brown eyes on his bulging ones. My head felt like a camera on a tripod, ready to shoot a picture.

"'Marja de Koning... Buttercup... I would like to get to know you, if you will allow me. I am strongly attracted to you, and I would like to keep you to myself.' He scowled a little less but perspired a lot more. Drops trickled from his black angled sideburns down his yellow face. The weak fan that churned over our heads had little cooling effect on the situation. I bowed my head but favoured him with a slight smile to show him he was on the right track.

"'If you are willing, I will ask you out on a date. If things work out, you will no longer have to work as a hostess, nor prostitute. Do we have a date?' Plaatjies attempted a smile, his deflected lips turning marginally upwards, to my surprise.

"'What, today?'

"'Yes, today. I know you are performing at the Blue Lagoon tonight, and I would like to accompany you to the show. It's geisha, isn't it? That runs in my body — I have Japanese blood from my father — so I appreciate that sort of thing.'

"'But what of your wife? I hear she's ailing.'

"'Yes. Yes, she has died of TB.' Mr. Plaatjies looked crestfallen; his scowl returned. 'I am very sad, but I need a new companion. My late wife gave me two beautiful girls. But I still want a boy. Have you any children, Marja?'

"'No, Mr. Plaatjies. Despite many men, I am not good in that department.' But I added quickly, 'I hope that will not make a difference to your proposition.'

"'We'll see,' he said. 'But will you be my dinner guest at the Blue Lagoon tonight after the show?'

"'Yes,' I said, fully convinced I should take advantage of the situation. After all, this had been my strategy all along. The one Desi had advised me of when we got stoned on Durban Poison on the balcony of the tenement building. I remembered clearly what she said. There were three routes: *Make money and become independent. Become famous. Or marry the boss, Mr. Henry Plaatjies.* I had managed two, and now three was on offer. I just had to play my part.

"I swallowed my revulsion at Henry's fishiness and thought through some of the advantages. I would only have to deal with one man and never have to prostitute myself again. I could live under his protection. Perhaps I could live a respectable life. Time would tell.

"We were married at the Blue Lagoon a few months later and I was his from then on. No longer a prostitute, I now had marital obligations, which I strived honourably to fulfil with limited success.

"Tidak apa-apa."

Marja shook her head from side to side and looked inquiringly at me again. "Do you know what that means, Mr. Terreblanche?"

I screwed my eyes and gave a shake of the head and she continued.

"It is Malay for 'it is okay'. Well, it really wasn't. I had always wanted children myself but I never got pregnant. At first, I thought this was because of the rubbers that I made the patrons wear when I was still a prostitute. But with Plaatjies I really tried. I wanted to please him as part of the marriage deal. He wanted a boy to take over from him when he retired from being a gangster. That business was already taking its toll. I learnt that Henry was under constant stress and threat of usurpation. As a mafia boss, he was like a big spider with a web of connections across the district. But there was always the threat of a takeover. He was often in debt from the gambling he enjoyed, and so had to extort money from others. He ran a shopkeepers' protection racket. Henry double-crossed the owners. His boys first robbed a shop, after which Plaatjies offered protection at £25 a month. So Henry had many enemies.

"And then there was the prostitution, the blackmail, the dagga trafficking, the smuggling and the shebeening, as well as the political retributions that the Mongrels were involved in. Henry had to pay off policemen to look the other way and, in turn, did work for them, performing hits for the government.

"To stay up to date with political developments, Henry listened avidly to my Gallo radio tuned permanently to Springbok Radio. My radio played constantly and had pride of place in the well-outfitted kitchen of the fine house on Caledon Street that I had moved into after our wedding.

"So, Mr. Terreblanche, my life was not altogether bad. In fact, it had much improved. I took the *Union Castle* boat trip with Desi to Durban and said a sad goodbye to that part of my life. Henry didn't mind because he thought she was just a friend who was owed a payback.

"I settled into a fine life as a kept woman. We went to the cinema often. To the Star Bioscope on Saturday afternoons to see the next episode of *Zorro Rides Again* in black and white, or to the National Bioscope at night to see Movie Tone news and watch Technicolor films made in Hollywood. We wondered out loud how great it would be to live in America and sing like Gene Autry or talk like Charles Starrett.

"On Friday evenings, I went to Millard's Fish and Chips to pick up supper and walked back home quickly to keep the parcels hot. I window-shopped a lot, bought the occasional gramophone record at Decca Records, and visited Moodley's, the local Indians' shop, to get most of our food supplies. You could say that I became a respectable citizen of District Six. When I eventually got a passbook, I was classified as Coloured. So I had the new identity I had mislaid. I rested with my lot in life, and only very rarely thought of Willem. What was past was past. I thought he must still be in Holland, practising as a doctor. I was now a Cape Coloured, and this was my adopted country. I wanted to make something more of myself, though. I aspired to become someone like Cissie Gool. She was a voice for the Coloureds and considered the jewel of District Six. She had trained as a lawyer and served on the Cape Town City Council. I had high aspirations, even though my husband was a gangster. I left my past as a prostitute behind me and over the next years I became civically active with a determination that would define my future."

†

"Of course, I remember that fateful afternoon well. Almost like it was yesterday. Henry and I had been listening to Springbok Radio. There were reports of a massacre at Sharpeville in Vereeniging. A great clamour arose up and down Caledon Street. Shouts of BETOOG, BETOOG, PROTEST, PROTEST, there is going to be a protest march in Langa Township! Join us! Join us! Uproar in the streets reigned, police sirens howled as army helicopters growled overhead. Henry and I got into our car and picked our painful way, sluggishly, through the heavy traffic — a slow seven miles to our journey's end."

†

ACT II

CHAPTER 12

The Cape Times Herald
The Paper that Cares.
April 17, 1958

National Party Wins: Coloureds Upset
John Terreblanche

The first all-white general election is over. The Afrikaner Broeders have won again. The National Party beat the United Party into the dust of the veldt. For the first time in South Africa's long history, the Coloureds, disenfranchised by the Nats, did not vote. Instead, the government created four stooges: four white Members of Parliament to represent the Coloured voters of the Cape Province. This was after a long battle of the Franchise Action Committee, which was formed in opposition to the Separate Representation of Voters Act of 1951. I sought out Mrs. Cissie Gool, who had served on the FRAC, for her opinion on the matter. The vocal Cape Town city councillor — who is of course Coloured — did not disappoint. Known to many as the "jewel of District

Six", she is rumoured to be a member of the South African Communist Party, and is no shrinking violet. "It's a crying shame," she said. "We can't just watch the experiment. We must join the struggle; it's yours, it's mine; it's ours. We shall resist." She wanted to shrug me off, but I persisted, knowing full well her background (her father was Dr. Abdullah Abdurahman, the first African elected to the Cape Town City Council in 1904, and her mother Helen Potter James). "Do you approve of mixing the races, then?" I asked. "Of course I do. I am a result of such a mixing. If my father had not had the opportunities of meeting my mother, I would not be here." She pointed the way forward: "We must walk the talk. We must march on Parliament again to voice our resistance."

†

CHAPTER 13

Willem and Promise

Sheets of rain came off Table Mountain in vertical waves. Willem loped out of the bus that had delivered him on to the drenched pavement, tenting a newspaper above his gaunt head. The downpour gathering thunderous force, he made his laborious way up the glistening street to Groote Schuur's front entrance. He had taken the bus because his car had failed to start and was now late for his first case of the day. He trudged past the graveyard that fronted the hospital, not for the first time thinking sombre thoughts. He had just read my opinion piece, now dissolving over his head; he despaired of a way forward. But his immediate problem was his greatest concern: the patient, first surgical case of the day. Willem had been named the head of the Casualty Unit. Each morning he had one or two elective surgeries, non-emergent operations that could be exceedingly complex to perform. He had lain awake most of the night, tossing and turning and planning the operation over and over in his head. His brain buzzed, he couldn't think straight, and now he was late on top of it.

Usually, he started his day with a run to calm his nerves, but the bad weather had precluded that. He prized open the hospital's great oak door into the entrance hall, thankful to be out of the deluge. He dumped the sopping newspaper into a wire basket. His wet footsteps imprinted the red sheen of the terracotta floor dulling the fine polish. He felt guilty for spoiling the work of others. His eyes shot down; his neck curled right. Usually, if he focused intently, Willem could attenuate the torsions, but not today. He made his way to the doctors' lounge on the ground floor and spoke to the anaesthetist having a cup of tea. "I am sorry I'm late. Car didn't start. Probably the spark plugs. I'll get changed and see you in theatre. You can start."

Willem told me that he liked the changing rooms, even though they smelt of dirty socks; he found relief there. Fronted by a square serving hatch, Willem stuck his head in and called out to the attendant.

"Tall, please."

"I know, Dr. Jansen. Here they are. Good luck today." The smiling girl placed the freshly cleansed items on the worn counter and shoved them in the surgeon's direction.

Willem picked up his white scrubs and bleached boots, a fading imprint of his misspelt name on each spine, and elbowed his way through the male entrance door. He sat on the wooden bench opposite his aluminium locker to gather himself for the operation at hand. His distorted image reflecting back at him, Willem listened carefully for approaching footsteps in the adjacent corridors after he had changed into his scrubs. Hearing none, he opened his locker to retrieve a plastic mug and then quickly walked over to the urinal and pretended to pee. Willem clamped the mug between his teeth to free both hands, pushed up the cover of the overhanging cistern with his left, and with his right found the brown bottle of ether he had secreted there. He poured himself a measure, savouring its pungent smell, returned the bottle to the cistern quickly, pulled the toilet chain, added water from the washbasin tap into the cup, and downed the acrid concoction in one gulp. The urinal gushed its whistle of water and the cistern refilled and clanked overhead. Willem coloured and sweated a little, his nerviness stilled, his hands trembled less, and, feeling a whole lot calmer, he made his way to the operating room in the Casualty Unit. Willem was ashamed of this need but it was essential to success, despite the risk. He had to quieten himself to do the difficult operation justice.

Willem hoped that Sister Madiba would be the scrub sister for the operation. He had come to depend on her serene composure during a surgical crisis. She steadied his trembling when he most needed it, applying firm pressure as she placed surgical instruments into his waiting hand. Few words were necessary, and not many had passed between them, save for this silent connection. He, distant, taciturn, and traumatised; she, submissive, remote and proud: they were of different countries — their languages a world apart, except when they united in front of a patient in the Casualty Unit. Then they were one.

Willem never failed to look at the patient's chest X-ray before starting an operation, so he stopped at the light box before going into the theatre, where the patient had already been anaesthetised. To his relief, Promise stood ready to assist. He grunted and walked over to the scrub sink, washed his hands, donned a white gown and sterile gloves, and approached the operating table before stopping to look around.

The theatre was too cramped. Too much equipment and too little space.

Against the back wall was a row of glass cabinets stocked with equipment and supplies for emergency use. At the patient's head, the anaesthesia machine with its colourful shiny vaporisers delivered ether or chloroform or halothane to keep the patient unconscious and free from pain. The patient had been intubated; Willem could hear the swish of the ventilator inflating the man's chest hiss loudly in the quiet operating room. The click of the patient's heartbeat lit up the round green oscilloscope with a reassuring bright luminescent trace. Overhead, the bright surgical light focused everyone's attention on the problem at hand.

"Knife, Sister Madiba. Ready, Dr. Ozinsky?" Willem turned to the anaesthetist.

"Yes, Dr. Jansen. Let the surgery begin."

Willem contorted once, then once more — his scalpel poised.

"Cut, Docatela. Cut," Promise said softly. Willem leant over the patient's chest towards Promise, placed the sharp knife against the skin covering the man's rib cage, and sliced between the bony ribs, drawing the scalpel back to end at the breastbone.

"Stop ventilation, please, Dr. Ozinsky," Willem muttered as he carefully pared the intercostal muscles, inserted a retractor between the ribs and splayed the chest cavity wide open. He continued the meticulous operation on the patient's punctured lung, Promise attending to each request with perfect timing. Promise and Willem were synchronised like trapeze artists angled over the patient. Willem placed a life-saving patch to plug the rent that had caused the lung's collapse. Salvaged, it heaved pinkly in its shell, ballooning up and down, when the anaesthetist restarted the arrested ventilation at Dr. Jansen's request.

Willem completed the thoracic surgery masterfully — Promise's unruffled presence stilling his anxiety. His nervousness at bay, Willem was able to concentrate on the operation without the fear of failure sapping his confidence. They straightened from bending over the steel table together, their close heads separating. Willem looked deep into Promise's eyes with gratefulness. They held each other's gaze just for a moment longer when Willem raised his gloved right hand above the operating table and Promise her left to meet in Groote Schuur's V for victory. He said thank you and added something that he had never offered before: "If you need my help, Sister Madiba, please don't hesitate to ask." Then he turned on his heel and marched out through the theatre door.

†

Later that dreary day, an urgent metallic voice peeled from the hospital's public address system: "Dr. Jansen. Dr. Jansen. Please come to Trauma Bay One. Trauma Bay One. Dr. Jansen!"

Willem ambled over. Not often in a hurry about anything, he came across Promise standing beside a stretcher encircled by listless flannel curtains bearing a dead patient. She was a picture of woe: her head was bowed, the curve of her nape prominent under tied-up hair; her doe-like features sagged; the flare of her nostrils sought self-control. In slow motion, Willem witnessed Promise's eyelids pressed tightly closed, releasing tears that dribbled two darkening lines down her hollow cheeks. They dripped on to her trembling breasts held up by her starched white dress. Her face distraught as she sobbed.

Promise looked up at Willem. "My Debbie. My Debbie. Car crash. Car crash. Hau. Hau. Hau. Au. Au."

He felt her loss deeply, her whimpering unbearable; he didn't know what to say. Willem reached across the stretcher and placed his right hand on her heaving shoulder and held it there until Promise's shuddering stopped — a full ten minutes passed, the pale curtains enclosing this intimacy, hiding it from view.

Then Willem asked, "Who is Debbie?"

Promise pushed aside the curtain a little to assure herself that no one else was in earshot. She blew her nose on the handkerchief Willem had given her before whispering an answer. "Debbie is my umthandi."

"Your what? You can tell me, Promise. Everything is safe with me." Willem leant closer to better understand.

Promise's sobs quickened again. "Debbie is my partner, my lover, my friend. She lives with me. She must have taken the car in the rain. She was not ready yet to drive alone. But I was here on duty. Now she is gone. Taken from me. Au, Au, Au, my heart, it is broken."

Willem put his arm around Promise's quivering shoulder and guided her towards the nurses' station at the side of the Casualty Unit. He addressed the sturdy matron overseeing the unit.

"Matron Jantjies, Sister Madiba has suffered a great loss. A friend has been killed in a motorcar accident. The patient is lying in Trauma Bay One. Can you help Promise manage the situation? And can we release her from work for the evening? I will make do with the other staff nurses for the rest of this shift."

The matron turned to Promise and put her arm around her. "Come, my dear, we will help; aitsa this is terrible." The matron shook her big head, her mouth an open O. "That will be difficult for you, Dr. Jansen, and for us. But Promise has a great loss to carry. We will take care of her."

†

According to his diary, the next day Willem had off. He had been up all night in the Casualty Unit looking after case after bedraggled case swept in by the raging rainstorm's motor vehicle carnage. The place had seen bedlam. Here a patient with a leg fracture screaming in pain sitting on a chair, and there a collision victim spurting blood from a head wound lying on a stretcher in the corridor, because the seven trauma bays had already been taken. The dead had been dispensed to the mortuary and the disabled restored. He had been exhausted and dispirited, even more so when he remembered that he had to take the bus home. Willem had alighted at the Fountain bus stop in Rondebosch, took one look at his lifeless car parked across the road, and struggled up the stairwell to his first-floor flat. All he had thought of was his bed, sleep, and then a run to enliven him later in the afternoon.

Willem awoke. Sunlight slanted across his face, making him sweat. A bit dazed, he turned to look at his travel clock, ticking loudly. Three o'clock. Good. Then he regarded Marja's carving standing alongside it. The bright light burnished the brown wood. Whatever had become of her? He felt miserable — how Promise must feel. He had wanted to console her last night but was constrained. He had felt the banging in his chest subside as her crying stilled. He had offered help but there was none to give. Debbie was dead. Like Marja. He shook his head, brushed his teeth, put on his white plimsolls and black running gear, shuffled down the stairs and ran across Main Street and over to the Pig and Whistle. He took the hilly road upwards along Stanley Road, his pale downy legs attuning to the gradient, his stride strengthening as he made his way over to De Waal Drive at Mostert's Mill. Willem loved that Mill. It reminded him of Holland when he was young. He took the rock-strewn path upward on Devil's Peak. He gazed up the windy track as he bounced along, the cicadas buzzing in the bushes that flanked the mud-caked path, drying puddles evaporating in the sweltering heat. A fresh breeze feathered the fynbos, releasing their honey-peppered scent. In the distance, Willem saw a black figure in a white outfit running barefoot. Her tan soles rose as she ran. She was fast. But he was faster. He closed the distance and then came to an abrupt halt on Mowbray Ridge. It was Promise, sweating in the hot sun. He smelt her amber fragrance and recognised her fluid gait. Compelled, and yet restrained, he restarted, hesitantly, in pursuit. His doubt receded as he drew abreast when the pathway widened. His feelings aroused by her womanly shape, he quickened his pace, and ran rapidly past her. His shoulder brushed hers in passing; he stopped to apologise. She looked up. They both panted heavily.

"Promise. Going to the King's Blockhouse?"

"Hau. Yes!"

"I will see you there then," Willem exhaled, exhilarated, despite his trepidation.

Promise stopped running and walked the final incline that led to the Blockhouse. Every time she visited; she was impressed by its grandeur. Built from brown rock hewn from the mountain, and seamed into place with white plaster, it stood four storeys high and a cricket pitch wide. A series of vertical lookout slits made the square building look more like a fort than an observation post. But for its stark symmetry, the structure looked like a natural extrusion of the mountain's face, camouflaged further by the surrounding khaki brush that wagged and waved in the interminable wind.

Willem had climbed on to the grassy terrace that flanked the side of the building and sat waiting, his long legs hanging down its lichen-covered wall. Promise approached, her eyes downcast. She had bundled her mass of tawny hair into a blood-red, cotton doek. Severely tied back, it strained her hollowed-out cheeks. Willem invited her to the terrace, the white of the girl's hazel eyes flashing bright in her sweat-darkened face. She shook her head from side to side. "Aikona!" she hissed. "We must not be seen together. There are too many people about. Follow me to Woodstock Cave."

She was right. Their innocent meeting out in the open would look like a tryst — the deep rocky crevice, an open gash in the mountainside further up, was a far better meeting place. Promise wound her way up the contour path to get there and leant against a boulder to wait.

Willem entered Table Mountain's vast cave, stooping despite its great height. He nodded to Promise, checked that no one else was around and then sat on a wide sunburnt ledge, the bronzed boulder warming his thighs. He invited her to sit. He patted the warm stone beside him. He was reluctant to get involved but felt helpless in the face of the grief he had seen the previous evening. Promise had given him so much strength, and now it was his turn to give back.

Promise sat across from him, curled her naked legs into a ball in front of her with a protective arm, and pointed beyond the green slopes below with the other. "Hau. Docatela. The people down there look too-too small. Too small. That is where I lost Debbie. On Hospital Bend."

Willem reached out and gently squeezed Promise's shoulder, his long hand cradling the thin flesh. His face tightened; his lips narrowed. "Please call me Willem."

"Hau, Docatela?"

"Yes, Promise. You have given me much comfort. When I am scared in theatre, you help calm me. With you by my side, I can manage any operation, no matter how difficult. You give me confidence."

"No, no, but you are too-too good." Promise relaxed her shoulder into Willem's hand and raised her eyes to meet his.

"Now I must help you. Please tell me again about Debbie. And please call me Willem when we are alone."

"Debbie was my love, my umthandi," Promise sniffed. "She made me whole. Softer. I am like a prickly pear. Sharp outside but soft inside. Debbie was my softness. She was from Namaqualand. A land of bright flowers and cruel cactus. She lived with me." Promise whimpered, her generous lips swelling.

Something expanded in Willem's chest. He could not call it love. It was caring. Something that had been lost in the past reawakened within him. He felt her sadness, her punishing loss. He wanted to take Promise into his arms to console her, to still her shuddering shoulder within him. A spirit of goodwill stretched out to this girl that he barely knew. He felt the need to care for her like a wounded patient. Willem softened his grip on Promise's shoulder, and then firmed it with a new resolve, willing Promise to relate the story she needed to tell.

"It's my fault. I was teaching Debbie to drive, and she only had her learner's licence. She should not have been in the car on her own but I was at the hospital. She must have been late for her afternoon shift at Dr. Ebrahim's and taken the car to be out of the rain." Promise wept as Willem tried to console her.

"Tidak apa-apa. Tidak apa-apa. Tidak apa-apa." Willem surprised himself with the comforting words from his youth. They came out as they had in his past, but in a different country and with a different girl. He could not understand why he spoke Malay to an African woman.

The words soothed Promise. She got up, pulled her white T-shirt up to her nose, blew snottily into it, exited the cave and disappeared down the contour path. Willem sat back and left it at that. He peered into the distance and last saw Promise looking back up at him as she stopped to round a boulder-strung corner. She turned towards him and held up her slender arm. Her pink palm, turned in his direction, was at first wide open — in greeting or thank you — but then clenched into a firm fist. A Black Power salute. She swivelled round and headed down to the fort-like Blockhouse beyond. Willem had felt the soft; he now witnessed the sharp that Promise had spoken of. She stirred an old fire within him, long lost in the concentration camps of Indonesia. He experienced an unlocking, a release, a fresh beginning. It was another world displayed before him that he knew little about but would become a cautious participant in. Promise was both the key and shackle. He got up and ran slowly home as dusk came down from the steep mountain, a faint mist descending gradually behind him.

†

The next time they met, ten days thence, was with grave purpose. Dr. Ismael Ebrahim, a man of considerable means and Debbie's boss, had arranged that she be buried at the Groote Schuur Hospital Cemetery, situated at the corner of Anzio and Main Streets. The majestic burial ground had witnessed many internments over the years and was resplendent with row upon row of man-height white-washed headstones, interspersed by the occasional red brick mausoleum and many simple crosses. Elegant angelic sculptures pointed heavenward, all separated neatly by well-tended grassy lanes, while dark green fronded palms provided merciful shade for the afterlife, creating a tranquil haven from the traffic-clogged streets siding the enclave.

Willem had not been specifically invited but felt compelled to go. After his chance meeting with Promise on the mountain, she had not been back at work, but Willem had seen an announcement of the church service and time of burial in the *Cape Argus*. Held up by emergent surgery, Willem was too late for church but entered the graveyard just in time for the reverend's Bible reading. He made his way towards the crowd standing around the freshly dug grave. Cut from the dark red ground, a pile of stones and earth lay to one side on the grass, like a wound to be stopped. Alongside the burial site, a mausoleum, crested by a life-sized marble angel, towered over the host gathered tightly beneath the edifice. The angel's finger pointed to Promise, dressed all in black. Her head was bowed, her hair tied up with a black doek. A large rotund man stood next to Promise, providing comfort. A few other black-clothed people were sprinkled around the grave. Muffled sniffs could be heard carried on the wind. Willem took position underneath a pine tree, a few paces distant from the proceedings.

"Ashes to ashes, and dust to dust." The preacher's last words reached for a higher place as he made the sign of the cross over the waiting grave. He turned to Promise and handed her the shovel for the first load of dirt to be cast upon the casket lying deep within the ground.

She couldn't. "Au. Au. Au. Au," Promise wailed as she crumpled, knelt on the grass beside the grave, teetered

173

over its edge, and shed tears on the coffin below. "Au. Au. Au. Au. My Debbie, my Debbie." The big black man next to her bent forward and patted her on the back gently. He couldn't control his own sobbing. His broad shoulders heaved as he mourned for the girl beside him.

Dr. Ebrahim couldn't contain his grief either. The only one present dressed in a white safari suit, his brown face creased as he snuffled and stepped back from beside the grave to regain his composure. Promise's left flank thus deserted, Willem stepped forward uncertainly to fill the gap beside her, and tenderly put his hand on to her neck, stroking gently. Restored somewhat, Promise spaded the first clods of red earth into the gaping ground, then turned away, leaving others to complete the closing. She left the grave, not once looking back on her way out of the cemetery and onto the busy road outside.

The solemn job was completed with care, the thud of the remaining clods changing pitch as the grave was filled, the rude violence of a passing ambulance's siren coinciding with the final shovelful.

Mr. Dlamini turned to Willem; he had taken the space left by Promise. "You must be the Dutch doctor Promise spoke of? Call me Goodwill. I'm her uncle." He offered his meaty, sweat-stained hand, then didn't let go.

"Hau. You must learn to shake in the African way. Let me teach you. First you do a traditional handshake like this. Then a mutual thumb clasp, like so, and then back to the traditional handshake. Yes, now let's try it again but in slow motion so you get it just right." Promise's uncle gripped Willem's hand again, his broad grin widening. Willem responded in kind, his thin lips stiff with concentration.

The black hand engulfing his white one, their pink palms blanched from the pressure they both applied. As their grip loosened, their hands pivoted in tandem to ring each other's extended thumbs, forming balled fists. Willem recognised the significance immediately. A Black Power salute in a handshake. Willem could see Goodwill's beady eyes registering his recognition, Promise's uncle's toothy grin expanding even further; the men undid their mutual thumb clasp and reverted to the closing handshake. And then didn't let go again. They squeezed and squeezed, looked deeply into each other's eyes, and then relented.

"Aikona. You are too-too strong. Surgeon's hands?"

"Yes, they are. And yours?"

"Black hands. Hau, hau, too funny!" He stepped back and bent over, both hands at his knees, before looking up, "now that the funeral is over, let's go and celebrate Debbie's life. Promise is a queer one — always different; she is holding a wake *after* the funeral at her house." Goodwill stood up. "I am inviting you. Do you have a car? I can show you the way."

Willem wasn't sure about going to the wake, or about visiting Promise's house, and said so.

"No, Dr. Jansen. I won't take no for an answer. I know Promise would be pleased. She doesn't go for men, especially not white ones. But she told me you were different. Must be because you are a foreigner: colour-blind. She tells me you treat all your patients the same. Now, where is your car. Let's go."

Having bade their farewells to the few people still around the grave, Willem and Goodwill walked together out of the graveyard to where the doctor had hastily parked his car. It stood askew in the parking space. Willem was much relieved when the car started at the first key crank and he could ease the Volkswagen up Anzio Road and over on to De Waal Drive and follow Goodwill's directions to Promise's place.

He manoeuvred the black Beetle in behind a badly damaged white one parked in front of a cottage, painted pastel green. Willem pulled the handbrake hard against the steep road, before getting out, carefully testing whether the car would roll forward. Goodwill joined him on the covered front porch, took a playful swipe at the leafy bougainvillea flowering the side wall, and rapped hard on the dull-red front door, not stopping before going in. Willem followed uncertainly behind him, not sure of the reception he would get. Miriam Makeba's mesmerising click song played softly on a gramophone as he stepped over the threshold. The place was packed; a low hum of subdued conversation filled the room. Willem was the only white in a tumult of black. All eyes fell upon him as he entered. Some nodded; others mouthed "Sawubona — I see you" in his direction and then continued their conversations in clicked Xhosa or flowing Zulu. Willem felt an outsider; he did not understand the languages that surrounded him. He fastened his eyes on the wall-hangings so that he didn't have to engage in conversation. He was drawn to the expressive mask carvings that crammed the small cottage's walls. Embossed with teeth, feathers or animal hide, and caked in mud, they gave off a rank, swampy odour, an African smell he had not experienced before. Through Promise, Willem had stepped into the unknown. He was thrilled and daunted all at once. He feared entanglement but was captivated by the woman. He made his way slowly through the throng to seek her out.

He found her at the centre of the square kitchen. The floor had black and white right-angled tiles. The walls were painted green. She had a glass of white wine in her hand, held up to her mouth to take a sip, when he walked in. She was still dressed in black but her tawny hair had escaped from the constrictive doek she had worn to the funeral. She stopped the glass at her black tinted lips and turned her shiny eyes in his direction. She held his gaze and slowly arched her neck back to swallow a taste. She drank down. Promise lowered her glass and her gaze.

"Good evening, Dr. Jansen." She took two steps towards him and shook his hand gently. "Thank you for coming to Debbie's funeral. May I introduce you to some of my friends?"

"Yes, please do."

Promise guided him around the cottage, proud of his presence. He glanced down at her full mouth each time she made an introduction. His name on her lips, she always introduced him in English to make him feel welcome. Willem practised his newly learnt handshake at each encounter, many warming to the foreign doctor in their midst.

†

Over the winter months, Dr. Jansen and Sister Madiba worked side by side in the Casualty Unit — none of the other staff any the wiser that the pair's relationship was developing. Communicating only by light touch and gaze while in the operating theatre, Willem and Promise feared discovery and separation by Groote Schuur's hospital authorities. Promise had told Willem that there were informers everywhere. The most seemingly innocent personnel could be police spies, paid to report on suspicious activity, no matter how trivial, that might compromise the security of the state: resistance was building among the black and coloured people against the apartheid government, which needed to be stopped in its tracks.

Yet anyone who observed closely might have seen a change in the surgeon and his scrub sister over the ensuing months. He appeared less irritable, his contortions less common. He had turned from taciturn to more talkative, and likeable, while she got over the loss of her friend's death and returned to her buoyant, prickly self much quicker than anyone would have expected.

†

Initially — in the way such things go — they were unsure of themselves and each other. They knew one another's work schedules, however: the sisters' and doctors' rotas were pinned on the notice board in the Casualty Unit, and so they contrived to time their runs up Devil's Peak, ever hopeful that they might intersect along the way, often starting out their runs expectantly but invariably disappointed. On other days, bad winter weather made running in the mountain unpleasant.

One unusually fine winter's morning, after Dr. Jansen and Sister Madiba had just completed an operation to repair a patient's fractured skull, known as a Le Forte operation, Willem communicated his intentions for the afternoon. He raised his hand above the patient to meet Promise's in the V for victory and said two words, "Le Forte", before "Thank you". Then he turned away from the operating table and loped off.

This time, when Promise arrived at Woodstock Cave, she did not need to be asked to sit on the hard-stoned ledge, quite close to where Willem had been sitting, waiting for her. Sweating profusely, she offered a gleaming smile, fine droplets pearling her doe-ish face. "Well done, Docatela. Now we can speak in code in theatre."

"Agh, yes. You make me smile and happy about myself. I haven't felt this way for a very long time. How do you do it?"

"Hau, it's easy. You need some joy in your boring life. And I am the one to give it to you. We have been invited to a party at my uncle's house in Langa Township. He told me to tell you that you need some education about the African way of life. He wants you to take me to his birthday celebration next Sunday. Will you take me?"

"Agh yes. I would love to." Willem's taut face became almost attractive when he smiled.

"I must warn you, though," Promise said, "it is not allowed. No white man is allowed into a black township without permission from the authorities." She shook her head from right to left three times. "So, it is a risk. Are you willing to take that, to have fun with me?"

Willem's face pulled again into a knot. He thought of Marja and his visits into the kampong to watch the bloody cockfighting. He had to wear a cap to disguise his blond hair from the Indonesian villagers. He remembered how fearless he felt, and how delighted he was with the adventure. Some of his spirit was returning. "Promise, I don't think there is any going back anymore. I will take you." He inhaled. "Now let's run back together, until we must separate. I like being with you."

†

An overnight gale-force northeaster had cleared Cape Town's city smog, leaving a cold bright sky, as grey winter clouds scudded out of sight over the Atlantic's horizon. Willem appreciated the view as he parked his black car behind the damaged white one outside Promise's cottage. One of its front wheels had been removed, and its shattered windshield lay scattered over the rust-scarred bonnet. There was no way someone could have survived such a crush. Willem sucked his teeth, lips apart, and wrapped on the front door three times, his left fist curling further outward with each knock. He had dressed in the colours of the Dutch flag for the party. Red tie, white shirt and a navy suit; he hid one feathery protea in the small of his back.

Promise flung open the door and stood back for effect. She was transformed. Like the flower of a prickly pear, Willem thought. Erect on high black stilettos, her halo of tawny-brown ringlets crested at the level of his beaked nose. He involuntarily glanced down to take in the whole of her. The overall impression was one of sheer loveliness. A short black dress, cleaved into a deep V to set off the curve of her breasts, wrapped her elastic skin. A white pearl necklace complemented Promise's sparkling smile.

Willem twitched. Promise laughed. "Docatela. You haven't seen a black girl before? You don't know what you've missed. So, what are you hiding behind your back? Out with it."

They drove on to De Waal Drive and out past Hospital Bend. Willem at the wheel looked over at Promise to gauge her reaction, now that four months had passed since the fatal accident. She had been telling him about her youth and had become suddenly quiet. She pointed to the little white crosses at the verge of the road but said nothing further till they were well on to to Settlers Way and could see the Athlone Power Station cooling towers rising in the distance. Grey and massive in size, they looked like two conical toilet rolls, tapered to funnel out white steam, which rose like a cloud into the blue sky over Langa Township.

"Willem, now signal to turn left over there on to Bhunga Avenue." Promise pointed, adjusted Willem's panama hat above his dark sunglasses and draped her black scarf around his pale neck: camouflage to disguise his entrance into the *Blacks Only* area. The change in scenery was abrupt as they turned left through a wide-open gate and onto the tree-lined central road.

Although the main roads of the township were paved, most of the side roads were muddy, potholed and dishevelled. Mangy dogs, chickens, an assortment of horse- and donkey-drawn carts and a few broken-down cars were arrayed between the dilapidated cast-iron roofed houses, glinting in the bright sunlight.

Willem turned into Washington Street. Towering overhead were floodlights on poles twice the height of the double-decker bus parked at the bus stop on the corner. Far in the distance, Table Mountain's great flank fell, then rose to become Lion's Head and Signal Hill, backlit by a blinding bright azure sky.

Willem winced, despite his dark glasses, and pulled the sunshade down so that he could spot Promise's directions to her uncle's place on Harlem Street. He was thankful when they finally parked. Willem sweated, despite the cold outside.

Promise touched him lightly on the leg. "What's wrong?"

"Nothing, Promise."

"Hau. That's not nothing. You're shaking like a rattlesnake."

"This place reminds me of the camps. The floodlights overhead. The barbed wire fence outside."

"What camps?"

"Agh, Promise. This is not the time for that. Let me light my pipe."

"You smoke? Me too. I roll my own."

Willem primed his Falcon. Promise rolled her tobacco, took out her Lion matchbox, pulled out a red-tipped stick and struck the box's side sharply. The flame fizzed to life; sulphurous smoke whelmed in the small car. Promise lit her cigarette and then passed the flame over Willem's pipe. The molten tobacco glowed with each grateful tug. They settled down to smoke together and rolled down a window to let in fresh air. Music from the party blew in.

"Let's go, Willem," Promise coaxed. They opened the front door to Mr. Dlamini's house and were welcomed with great heart. A cheer arose as they stepped in. The swing music was deafening. The smoke-filled air in the dark threadbare room stung their eyes. A crush of smartly dressed people danced, while others whooped with delight. Cigarettes were inhaled and drinks downed to loud approval from the swaying crowd.

Promise pushed Willem through the upheaval and out the back door. The backyard was fresh with air and the tang of sizzling meat on the braai. The assortments of meats had been carefully roasted on an oily iron grate, fired from below in a half kettle drum. The cook bent to his task. Birthday celebrants gathered round for heat and to savour the smell of burning rose wood and charcoaled flesh.

"Welcome to Langa. Welcome to our humble abode." Goodwill grinned, his broad neck jiggling above his yellow-bordered dashiki shirt. He put out his hand to Willem for a ferocious handshake and gladly accepted the Johnnie Walker whisky Willem and Promise had brought.

"Now, Willem, for your education. We must teach you African ways if you are to be with Promise. Here she is at home, amongst our people. Just look at her."

Promise had walked over to the group gathered around the barbecue, moving fluidly among them. Joy shone on her face. Willem felt happy for her. She was a fuller person, completed by the Africans clamouring around her.

Goodwill offered Willem a brandy and asked, "Do you know where Langa Township gets its name? Aikona — I didn't think so. From Chief Langalibalele, king of the AmaHlubi. He was from up north. The British tried him for treason in the last century. He was taken from the Drakensberg and imprisoned on Robben Island over there." Goodwill pointed in the general direction, swaying with emotion, alcohol dense on his breath. "A year later, the king was set free and was moved here." He stamped his foot, dust dulling his well-polished shoe. "At the turn of the century, the British wanted to move the blacks out of Cape Town. So they created this location in 1923. I had to move here some years ago, when the government bulldozed my house down in District Six. That was heavy." He shook his head from side to side like a great wide animal, snorting its disgust.

Willem hunched closer, his face colouring under the panama hat. He felt embarrassed to be a white man and wanted to show respect for Mr. Dlamini's pain.

Goodwill lightened the spoilt mood upon Promise's return. "Langa is Xhosa for 'sun'. We have lots of that. And it's free!" He raised his glass, "Ah, here is my lovely niece. Take Willem for a dance inside. I've been making him feel guilty. And that is no way to treat a foreigner."

Promise, glad to see the warmth building between her uncle and Willem, wrapped her arm around the doctor to steer him into the throbbing room, hot with perspiring dancers toy-toying to the wild beat of township music blaring from a loudspeaker hung from the ceiling.

"I can't dance," Willem grumbled.

"No matter. I can. Join me." Promise guided Willem through the steps, clasping his stiff frame close, her languorous dance relaxing his rigidity. They melded together as they shuffled closer. Willem put his arms tentatively around her slight shoulders. He felt her yield, her rounded form filling his taut one.

†

184

Neither Promise nor Willem wanted their time together to end. But the party was over and the night yet young. They drove past District Six, skirted Table Mountain along De Waal Drive, and climbed the dark winding road up Signal Hill to get a view of the city. Willem parked his car at the lookout point, glad to see that no one else was about. The isolated spot, fringed by fynbos, was darker than dark. Only the soft moonlight and the lights from the city hovered. The stillness was penetrated by the rumble of traffic, which came in little surges. They were both nervous, like children. They sensed the danger.

Aroused and excited, Promise took the lead. "Come and open my door, Willem, and put the lights off." Her face was the colour of her people. Willem got out, walked round the car and opened its door from the left side. He stood with one hand on the car door and the other on the roof, waiting. Promise stepped out and up within the confines of the angled door. She brushed his neck with her moist lips. Willem, at first, strained away and then towards Promise. His chin caressed her shaggy hair. They closed their eyes and took deep slow inhalations, expelling the air as they tightly embraced. They stood quite still for a while in the dark and the quiet and the comfort. Their chests together, they felt each other's heart thump. The knock to be let in. Neither yet ready for that immutable step; closure took a back seat and was parked for a future date.

Willem sighed. "Promise, Promise, Promise… I must take you home."

†

CHAPTER 14

The Cape Times Herald
The Paper that Cares.
August 11, 1958

Treason Trial in Pretoria: Who is in the dock? The South African government or the defendants?

John Terreblanche

Almost two years ago, on December 5, 1956, the South African Police rounded up 140 people from across our beloved country and charged them with high treason under the Suppression of Communism Act. Preliminary hearings held at Johannesburg's Drill Hall provoked a riot. The state alleged that the defendants were subversive because they had attempted to undermine the government by seeking help from abroad, purchased firearms to arrange an insurrection, or had attended the recent Congress of the People at Kliptown, where the ANC's Freedom Charter had been created.

A few thousand black South Africans voiced their

186

discontent outside. Like a Zulu Impi going into dusty battle, they sang Nkosi Sikeleli i'Afrika, waved sticks, toy-toyed and threw stones, injuring a policeman. The S.A.P. retaliated in typical fashion. They fired into the heaving crowd, hemmed in by the surrounding shops and cars, injuring fourteen people. The preliminary proceedings were halted and the international press went berserk. They accused the South African government of being a police state; the apartheid regime victimised and imprisoned those opposed to its ministrations. The government was not for turning, however, and pushed on regardless of the bad press. Trial hearings to determine whether the state had a justifiable case against the accused continued doggedly in Johannesburg over the next year. Oftentimes interrupted by boisterous crowds and the occasional rioting, the state nevertheless gathered more than six thousand pages of testimony and ten thousand exhibits. More than sufficient evidence for the magistrate, the Honourable F.C. Wessels, to instruct that the remaining ninety-one defendants be tried for high treason.

The Treason Trial began in Pretoria on August 1, this year. Fifty-seven blacks, sixteen whites, sixteen Indians, two coloureds and, most importantly, in my opinion, the government, were in the dock. The prosecution alleged that between 1952 and 1956 the defendants had sought to overthrow the government and replace it with a communist state. The chief defence lawyer countered pointedly. According to him, the mass of documentary evidence — impossible to read in less than two years — was an abuse of court proceedings, and the prosecution had not brought a legitimate case. In fact, the indictment should be thrown out with contempt. The government's ineptitude in bringing

187

the case against the accused was plain for the whole world
to see. The trial was adjourned and will resume on the 12th.

†

S.A. Nursing Council: African Nurses Must Complete Forms for Population Registration Act
John Terreblanche

Not satisfied with leaving well alone, the South African Nursing Council has rubbed salt into their charges' open wounds. The Council has sent out registration forms to all nurses that need to be completed by filling out their official identity numbers, and population group, under the Population Registration Act. This forces African nurses to register for a reference book to obtain the all-important identity number. There has been uproar around the country. Demonstrations have occurred at Baragwanath Hospital, Johannesburg, and King Edward Hospital in Durban. The Cape Peninsula may be next. Here, in the past, under the Natives Consolidation Act of 1952, certain categories of women have qualified to stay in urban areas without a permit and I.D. number. They have been exempted by their workplace from doing so. Nurses working at the Somerset, Peninsula Maternity, Mowbray or Groote Schuur Hospitals fall within that category. But now, in Cape Town, "exempted" African women have been informed they must obtain documents proving their right to be in the urban area. I expect that the African nurses' wounds will need more than salt to heal from this new mandate.

†

CHAPTER 15

Promise and Willem

Unseasonably, the southeaster churned a full-throated windstorm. The Cape Doctor blew all before it. Trees bent, litter flew, and dirt pelted Promise's exposed calves as she made her hurried way to the entrance of the Casualty Unit. She stopped to catch a stray newspaper that flipped and flopped into view. She felt duty-bound to clasp it in her right hand as she pulled hard on the front door of the hospital with the other to open it against the gale. But couldn't. She stuck the paper under her armpit and pulled the door open with two hands, then slipped in quickly as the door slammed behind her. A loud thunk reverberated in the porticoed entrance way. Promise unfurled the crumpled page and was about to dump it in the litter basket when my headline caught her eye. Something about the S. A. Nursing Council, all-important to her, given her livelihood.

She backed into a corner to read it. Intermittent blasts of wind from the opening and closing hospital door cooled her rising temper only slightly. Promise had not received any notification from the Nursing Council at all. My article said that she needed to get an I.D. number to fill out the nurse registration form. She would have to get a new reference book. A new passbook. A dompass! She still had her old passbook from the Transkei, but she had not needed to get a new one here in Cape Town as a nursing student. But now she did. And she would have to register as a "native" because she was black, my article said. She backed further into the corner and looked up in aggravation as the next person, Willem, blew in through the front door.

"What's wrong, Sister Madiba?" Willem kept it formal. "You look like you have lost something."

"Hau, Docatela. This is too much."

"What is?" He stooped closer.

"This bloody nursing form," Promise blasted.

"Come with me, into the Casualty Unit. We can go to my office and you can tell me about it." Willem put his hand on Promise's exposed collarbone, guiding her out of the entrance way, and into his private room. He locked the door and they sat down across from each other, faced off, like a doctor and his patient, separated by a wide wooden desk. Promise clasped her two hands as if in prayer and tucked them between her white-clad thighs; her dress lifted, showing elegant legs and dark knees. She took the opportunity to look around while Willem lit his pipe.

A roof fan turned above their heads; its centred bulb-light illuminated the windowless office. The wall behind Willem was a massive bookcase filled with textbooks and medical paraphernalia. Promise spied a microscope, bent into a question mark, a telescopic light left on to focus on a glass slide cradled below. Next to that, a grey portable blood pressure manometer, its heavy box folded open — a mercury-filled glass tube glinted vertical in the overhead light. A curious-looking clock ticked the time softly. The size of an Encyclopaedia Britannica, the clock's face was a wave of black metal, bounded by two erect brass cannon shells. Promise thought the clock might have come from an armament factory. The soft tick-tock calmed her. She swayed forwards and backwards in her chair, as the pipe smoke thinned above Willem's head.

"Willem, I don't think you have any idea what it's like to be foreign on one's own soil, to be black in this land run by whites."

"I don't... but... maybe I do: I am a foreigner here too." He wiped the crumbs of tobacco still flecking his white safari suit on to the terracotta floor. He stooped under the desk, picked up one side of the striped zebra skin, shoved the brown leaves under the hide with a white-shod foot, and then leant closer to Promise across the desk.

"Here, I want you to read this." She plunked the crumpled page of newspaper on the shiny surface; a thin dust settled as the printed page came to rest in front of Willem. "Do you read Mr. Terreblanche's op-ed pieces? He seems to be on the black side, despite being Afrikaans. Are you on our side, Docatela?" She narrowed her eyes to slits.

"I am here to support you, if that is what you are asking, Promise. But, to be honest, I am afraid to take sides. I am a guest in this country. I must behave accordingly and don't want any trouble with the police. I've had enough of that sort of thing in my past." Willem's neck muscles bulged as he arrested their pull; he used his left hand to steady his pipe, exhaling smoke into the close room.

Promise softened slightly. She swayed back in her chair, crossed her legs, watching Willem's eyes carefully for a hint of downward deflection, and put her hands, palm upwards, on the desk in front of him, the fawn of her upper arms exposed beyond the sleeves of her white nurse's uniform.

"You must tell me about Indonesia later. There are more pressing matters now to deal with. I have to get a new passbook I.D. to continue nursing. The Nursing Council says so there on the page. I must register at a police station to get it. Hau. I don't like visiting the police. I was locked up once overnight in the Transkei. I had forgotten my passbook when I went shopping in Fort Beaufort. I felt like a black animal imprisoned in a cage."

Willem couldn't arrest the neck twist this time, so he tried to hide it by waving the smoke away with his right hand, "Agh, I cannot ever be imprisoned again. I hate police stations too. Anything to do with authority, really. I become anxious just at the thought of it. But I'm here to help you, Promise, in the best way I can."

Willem leant back, put his hands behind his head, and sucked slowly on his Falcon, the coal glowing in its walnut bowl. Overhead, the fan spread the sweet-scented smoke around them.

Promise tented her hands and leant in closer, "Alright, Willem, so far you have only seen a part of me, not the whole of me. Which do you want to help?"

"The whole."

"Well, then, you must learn about us. Me. The blacks of South Africa. How we live, how we work, how we love and how we struggle."

A high feeling swept between them, like the wind outside. It felt like a barrier had been blown down. They took turns to tell their life's story.

Promise spoke of her growing up in a mud hut, herding cattle, and her joy of the veldt and of the red earth of Pondoland. She spoke of her father's death and her long walk from Mtshiso to enter the household of her new benefactor, Chief Ziyabonga Dlamini, and of how inspired she was by the chief's indabas, held in the courtyard.

She spoke of her education, first at the Clarkebury Boarding Institute in Engcobo, where she encountered foreign teachers from England and Ireland and developed her love for running. And then her move to Healdtown School, where she was awakened to the great struggle for Africa sparked by an African historian's enactment at the school's annual Dingaan's Day commemoration.

She told him her real name. Tembisa. Tem-bis-a.

"That is beautiful, Promise. What does it mean?"

"It is Xhosa for Promise; my English name was given to me by my first teacher," Promise stood up from her seat, lifted her opened hands above her head and stretched, her fingertips just short of the revolving fan, touching the down draft of air, the curve of her breasts a shadow in her tight dress as she arched backwards.

There was a knock on the door. "Dr. Jansen, can I bring in some tea and cookies for you?"

"Just wait a minute. I'll unlock the door." Willem beckoned to Promise to hide in the corner, then turned the key to open the door and thanked the pink-dressed tea lady as she passed the tea tray into him.

"Doctor, I heard voices, so I have given you two cups."

Willem placed the tray on his desk and poured the tea. "Promise. Sugar? Milk?"

"No, thanks. I like it black."

"So, what brought you to Cape Town?" Willem poured the second cup.

"My uncle, Goodwill Dlamini. The chief's brother. Goodwill has many connections, as you most likely figured out. I started work at Dr. Ebrahim's general practice in Main Street. He got me into nursing school here. It is him I have the most to thank for." Promise felt heartsick as she remembered that bright day at the practice when she had met Debbie for the first time. How she was attracted to her instantly. The sensation of her slow smile of welcome, the reassurance she gave, the warmth she exuded. Willem and Debbie were polar opposites — but both magnetic.

Willem observed Promise's face change.

"Now, Willem, tell me about Indonesia?"

Willem spoke of his youth, but not of Marja. His birth in Bandung and the Japanese invasion of Java. He told of his imprisonment in Japanese concentration camps, the solitary confinement, the beatings and the torture. He felt a great release, a feeling of kinship with Promise. He had never spoken of his trauma at such depth before.

"Shoo, shoo, shoo, Willem." Promise dropped her head, the whites of her eyes setting in her darkening face. "This is unimaginable. Although I have heard it happens here too. Our people are tortured in prison by the police. When the cops don't get the answers they want, they shock with electricity or douse with water, till the prisoners confess."

"Agh. Agh." Willem's severe face hardened further, his lips pared tightly over his two crooked front teeth. "That is exactly why I don't want to get involved."

Promise reached over the desk and placed her soft palm over Willem's clenched fingers. They sat for a while in silence, the fan faintly turning above. Then Willem compressed his lips and continued.

He told of his move to Holland to study medicine, and his deep disgrace: his addiction to ether, to steady his nerves. He lamented his blunted feelings, his intense fear of authority, and spelt out his desire to do right by others but never to contravene the law. He could not face imprisonment again. He related his love for running and the great need to climb mountains, for elevation, and the feeling of freedom it brought. Climbing reminded him of the trips he had taken with his late father in the mountains surrounding Bandung.

When it looked like Willem had finished his confession, Promise sat for a while just looking at him, then smiled encouragement, and countered with the same question she had been asked. "So, what brought you to Cape Town?"

Willem locked eyes with Promise. "I was disbarred from medical practice in Holland for hitting a man in a fit of anger. I came to Groote Schuur to find work in another country. I cannot go back to Indonesia."

With his secret laid bare before her, Promise felt she could trust Willem with her whole. Not just her professional self as a nurse but the fact that she was undercover in the ANC resistance. She reached over the desk again and placed her right hand over his left and gave a little squeeze.

"Willem, I know you are scared of involvement, but it's the only way forward for us. If you wish to help me, you must learn more about the ANC. I am chair of the Women's League for District Six."

"What?" Willem's hand shifted from under Promise's. "What, the ANC?"

"Yes. The ANC, and we could use some more white members like you. The ANC stands for multi-racialism. Especially now with the ongoing Treason Trial, we need all the support we can get."

Willem felt a heat flush his neck, a crawling feeling his hair and a contraction cut into his throat. He shook his head and glanced down at his hands, now splayed wide on the desk between them. "Promise, I can't." Willem raised his wild eyes to meet Promise's.

She fastened his gaze and continued, "Next Friday, meet me at my place at seven in the evening. We will walk to the safe house together."

"Promise, no, never, I can't." Willem got up gradually from his chair. "Sister Madiba, please see yourself out; there is work to be done."

†

That evening, Willem woke in his flat in Rondebosch, all in a sweat. His bed sheets were drenched. As sleep's smog cleared and his focus sharpened, he interrogated his conscience. He mentally clicked off a register of potential wrong doings that might get him in trouble with the authorities.

*No, not that one. No not that one either. No, no, no, no, definitely not; that wasn't something he could get into trouble with the law for either — he needn't worry about those. But then he thought of Promise's invitation; now **that** was a real problem. A risk of ending up on the wrong side of the law.*

She did make him feel good about himself, though. Just being with her gave him confidence again. She was changing him for the better. He was happier in her presence. Just thinking of her made him feel more alive. She was like a shot of ether, elating and calming at the same time. Promise was addictive.

He went back to sleep and awakened the next morning in two minds. *Should he? Should he not? He had not done anything against the law yet; should he chance it to be with Promise? He would decide Friday.*

†

Willem was late. He parked his Beetle behind Promise's car wreck and saw her disappear around the corner, beneath a bowed streetlamp, in a dark green coat. He hooted, just once. She spun round and raised her finger to her lips, then urgently beckoned that he must join her. Willem remained in the darkened car. Promise walked back up the steep street. She got into the car, sat beside him. Willem went into a fifteen-second contraction. His head stretched upwards; his eyes glazed downwards;

his hand clutched the car's gear lever. "I can't, Promise. Promise, I can't."

"Yes, you can." Promise covered Willem's hand with her own, soothing his grip. They sat quietly in the confined car. The dashboard clock ticked for a while. Promise palmed Willem's hand again, twice, got out of the car, gathered her coat around her and started walking in the direction of the dim lamp post. Willem arose, as if from the dead, and slowly followed Promise through the darkened streets to the safe house.

A double knock on the door, followed by another two, allowed them entry to the meeting house. Promise and Willem were shushed down a short corridor by a tall black man wearing a brown hat and bade into a large humid room hazed by smoke. Dark curtains drawn against the night; the strong millet smell of Bantu beer permeated the secret get-together.

A wafer-thin man stood at the room's centre on a pile of books fashioned into a make-do podium. Droplets of sweat glistened on his brown careworn forehead, bathed bright by an overhanging light. His staccato voice rattled like a machine gun; he was holding forth about the Treason Trial. The ANC finally had a megaphone, he said. The score of sympathisers gathered around him agreed. They clapped their hands or stamped their feet. Half leant against the walls; the others had a seat; all had two things in common. They were black and they had committed to the struggle for freedom. They wore the black, green and gold of the ANC. A black suit here, a green dress there, a golden sash or arm band tied proudly in place.

When Willem and Promise entered the room, the speaker stopped. The clapping did too. Willem wore a black suit with a matching polo neck noosed high up his thin neck to just below his stand-out ears. He had slicked his thin blond hair back off his bony forehead. His large beaked nose protruded beyond the depths of his narrow-set eyes. He hunched forward and twirled his black hat between long bony fingers and averted his gaze from all that sought to pierce it. His neck pulsed pale against the black cloth. Promise engaged Willem's stiff arm within her supple elbow and stood erect beside him in her long green coat.

"Comrades, this is Dr. Willem Jansen. He is from Groote Schuur. You can trust him. I do," she said, and clutched his arm tighter against her flank, bracing them both for the group's response.

"Aikona, Promise, Aikona. He is a white man. Aikona." The wafer-thin man stretched for height upon the book-stacked platform. He raised a gangly hand in the air and continued. "I know we have white brothers in arms like Joe Slovo, who is this very day at the Treason Trial in Pretoria with Nelson Mandela, but I don't trust these Afrikaner Broeders. And you bring this man into our midst?"

Promise fired back. "He is not an Afrikaner. He is not a Broeder. Hau. He is from Holland, born in Indonesia."

The wafer-thin man shook his head; the crowd muttered; a few took loud slurps from their foaming beer, while others shifted in their seats or pressed their backs more firmly against the wall. A buffalo-sized man dressed all in green, who had wedged himself comfortably in a barely lit corner, picked his unsteady way across the room towards the couple. His black hat slouched low, Goodwill slurred apologies as he pressed on to where Willem and Promise still stood arm in arm. The assembled hushed as they gathered Mr. Dlamini's intent. He placed a manly hand on Willem's scrawny shoulder, pumped an African handshake with the other, and then clasped the white man's thin frame with both, lifting Willem off his feet. Setting him down with a flourish, Promise's uncle turned towards the centre of the room to break the impasse.

"Willem is my white brother. You can trust him… with your life. He is a doctor, after all." He chuckled.

A few laughed; others stirred: "Hau." "Agh, nee." "Ewe." "Can we believe you?" The proceedings continued where they had left off.

Promise, in turn, was asked to mount the collection of books, to give her address as chair of the Women's League for District Six.

"Sisters, comrades, today we must rise again against the pass laws. The state is resolved to impose passbooks on all women, so that we can be controlled like our men. As you know, passbooks are now called reference books by the Nationalists. We are not fooled — they are no different. Not at all. There are protests around the country. In Port Elizabeth, Frances Baard and Florence Matomela organised women to refuse passes by protesting on Main Street outside the pass office next to the police station. When women rise to meet the struggle against apartheid, no power on earth can stop us from achieving freedom," Promise raised her fist.

Willem, his black hat returned to his head, interlocked his hands at the waist.

A woman stood up. "Sister, how will we do this? The police will lock us up if we stop women from entering the pass office. That is what the police did in Johannesburg. They arrested hundreds of women and put them in prison, till they got bailed out. Most will lose their work permits and we cannot risk that." The woman sat down and looked around in a huff.

"Hau. Hau. Aikona. Aikona," arose from the room.

"Yes. That is a problem," Promise countered. "As a nurse, I have to get a new reference book. Otherwise I cannot work. But, for those who do not have government employment, perhaps there is a way. We can organise and go from door to door in District Six. A whispering campaign against the pass laws for those who can manage it. I will organise the campaign, if you agree."

Wild clapping ensued — the answer Promise had hoped for affirmed, she stepped down from the bank of books and returned to Willem's side while the wafer-thin man got up again to close the proceedings.

He addressed the audience. "Comrades and Dr. Jansen, I now close tonight's formalities with an invitation. There is still plenty of drink and I have brought some dried biltong for your pleasure. Abide in fellowship with us. Amandla. Good night."

Goodwill lost no time in introducing Willem to the gathered ANC stalwarts. One by one. He started with the wafer-thin man.

"You must be thirsty after all that speechifying. I have a drink ready for you. Dr. Jansen, please meet our local director."

Willem inclined his head, stuck out his right hand

and performed the African handshake ritual in the way Goodwill had taught him to. A slow smile of pleasure creased his pinched features as he felt the firm handclasp returned and watched the director beam — both harried faces transformed by the goodwill each had extended.

Promise brought up the rear as Goodwill worked the crowd with Willem. He cajoled and glad-handed the couple around the room and brought drinks, biltong and good cheer to win Willem over to the cause. Goodwill must have succeeded because the couple were one of the last to leave the safehouse. Late, but elated, they departed quietly into the dark night.

†

The reader will no doubt notice that I have let the telling of the story roll on a bit without too much interjection. I want you to get the "feel" of it without interruption on my part. Nonetheless, I want to assure you of the story's veracity. I have meticulously tapped the considerable resources at my disposal as a police reporter and journalist, conducted innumerable interviews, performed extensive archival research and accessed all manner of (shall I call them) 'retrieved' reports, documents and tape recordings for my reportage.

Bear with me, please; we will get to the prosecution of the Immorality Act in due course.

†

Promise needed to apply for the all-important passbook to continue as a nurse. She was disinclined to do so, hoping that the storm of protest against the S.A. Nursing Council might force them to lift their mandate, but Willem had convinced her otherwise. He wanted everything to be legal and in order.

He had promised to take her to the police station in Rondebosch, up on Church Street, across the way from his apartment on Main Street. He was familiar with the station, which lay across the street from St John's Church, because he had had to pick up his own South African I.D. document there. The black plastic-covered booklet contained an unflattering passport-sized photograph and had Willem's unique identification number imprinted on the first page. Coded to note Dr. Jansen's date of birth, gender, population group (white) and the fact that he was a non-S.A. citizen, he knew the I.D. number off by heart: 251030 5069 10 7 — nothing official could be achieved without filling out one's I.D. number on the government document in question.

The police officers had been most cordial with him when he had first picked up his I.D. document and, later again, when he had to have his driver's licence appended in the booklet's enclosed pages. Willem realised that Promise could not go in the *Whites Only* side of the police station as he had, and would have to use the *Non-Whites Only* entrance, but had planned to park his car along the road outside and observe matters from across the street. After all, the two sides of the police station were probably served by the same policemen because it was a small secondary office, unlike the central Caledon Square Police Station, which bordered District Six, and served greater Cape Town and its docks.

The Rondebosch Police Station was not much more than a bisected cottage. Two white gables separated a green corrugated roof common to both office entrances, each fed by a short-paved walkway abutting the street. On the left for coloureds and blacks; on the right for whites. Willem imagined that the police offices inside would be mirror images. He had found the half-door entrance and the red-tiled floor leading to the counter not unpleasant to navigate. It was true, however, that once inside you had to wait on a wooden bench, until you were beckoned to the front, but all had been done in an orderly and respectful fashion. The blue-jacketed police constables, seemingly restrained by their tight brown belts, their epaulette-squared shoulders and their close-fitting caps, were polite and pleasant in the conduct of their duties.

Willem sat back in the car and watched Promise, white in her uniform, walk up to the black entrance, her hair tucked neatly under a nursing cap, her blue cape nestling over her slim shoulders. Willem had reminded her not to display any attitude, before giving her a gentle shove out the car door.

He wound down the window. Birds chirruped, a plane circled in the clear sky above, revving its engine, and the rumble of cars in Main Street provided a backdrop. He looked at his watch: 12.15. Promise needed to be back at the hospital at one. Petrol fumes and the sweet smell of recently mowed grass from the church yard mingled. Then he thought he heard something else. Something he had been afraid of. The hateful raising of voices. Yes. It came from behind the *Non-Whites Only* door. Its upper half had been closed when Promise had stepped in. Willem sprinted out of the car and into the police station, not stopping to knock. Two white policeman, one short, the other tall, both red in the face, screamed at Promise from behind the polished oak counter, in broken English and clipped Afrikaans.

"Jou Hotnot. You must get your bloody pass at your police station in District Six. Not here in Rondebosch. We have called the Caledon Square Police Station and that is where your file is. Not here. Don't you know any bloody better?"

Promise stooped her head. She stood quiet and defenceless, helpless in the face of brutality.

"What gives you the right to treat someone like dirt underfoot? Your white skin?" Willem glared at each police officer in turn.

The short one yelled: "Sir, get out now, and take this girl with you or we will have you both arrested. You are on the wrong side of the police station. Can you not read the sign outside? And she is in the wrong police station altogether."

Then the tall one barked at the short one. "Get the police dog from the kennels if they don't want to move. I'm going on lunch break. I've had enough of this nurse and the doctor. He turned, looked directly into Willem's eyes and snarled: "I can remember you from when you came in for your I.D. document. You're from Holland, aren't you? A Kaaskop! A foreigner." Then he walked out the back to the jail cells, to have his much-needed lunch.

"Come, Sister Madiba." Willem made to drape his shaking arm across Promise's shoulder but thought better of it. He paused and clenched his fists instead. They turned and walked out of the police station together. Willem pushed Promise in front of him as they exited on to Church Street. He had just enough time to make up his mind as to his next steps.

"Promise, will you follow me?"

"Hau. Yes. Two steps behind." She exhaled, a catch in her breath.

They walked in tandem, quick-stepping across the recently mowed garden that fronted the church, down the hilly mound upon which it had rested since the last century, and on to Main Street. They crossed the busy road. Promise took in the bright-coloured lantern atop the horse-trough-shaped fountain in a blur, but had no idea where Willem was going until he beckoned her to follow him up a set of concrete steps. They stopped on a first-floor landing, and he unlocked a varnished wooden door.

"Hau, Willem. This is your place?"

Willem pulled Promise into the flat shaking; he held her upper arm tight. "I am so sorry I brought you here; you must feel terrible. Those bloody policeman."

"Yes, it makes my blood boil. I get upset and get a stomach ache. I hate argument. They treat us like kak!" Promise stepped into the lounge, and after calming herself continued, "Shoo, shoo, shoo, this is a beautiful place." She sat down on a chair and continued, "But you know it is not a good idea to have me here in a white area like Rondebosch. I can't pass for the servant girl. Especially not in my uniform."

"I don't give a damn. These fucking police…" Willem raged. "I will call the hospital for you, and tell them that there has been a complication, and Sister Madiba cannot make the afternoon shift today. Please look around and make yourself at home while I call them. Then I will try and make up for this mess. I will make you us a pot of coffee and a proper Dutch lunch to make amends. It is about time I tell you a bit more about Holland."

Promise took off her cap, unbuttoned her cape, kicked off her shoes and shook her tawny hair loose, letting it rest lightly upon her shoulders as she padded around the apartment, hoping to put together the puzzle of Willem's past from the artefacts he had surrounded himself with.

She started in the lounge that windowed over Main Street and the Rondebosch Fountain. Sunlight blazed past the drawn-back curtains onto a set of four dark stinkwood chairs, their seats strung with cow gut like large square tennis rackets. They squared off a low gleaming yellowwood table covered by small Hessian mats to protect the finely seamed surface from the inevitable stains of life. The parquet floor was covered with a rich array of animal skins, soft under her bare feet. Promise identified zebra, lion, tiger and — would you believe it — giraffe, as she stepped into Willem's bedroom. The walls hosted fine oil paintings, in grey, blue and light-green tones, displaying Javanese fishermen, boats and rice paddies, from the country of his birth. There was a loud ticking travel clock by the side of the bed. A slope of sunlight illuminated the brown carving of an Indonesian woman's face. Promise moved in closer and took in the fine detail of the girl's carved features: the slightly upturned nose, the slant of her eyelids, the curve of her mouth and the puff of her cheek. The carving reminded her of Debbie. She felt sad all over again. But she had another feeling. She thought that she had seen this face before. But where? Perhaps in a dream of Debbie?

"Promise. Promise. Where are you? Come to the dining room. I have prepared lunch for us."

Promise made her way into the dining room and sat down on the leather-cushioned chair that Willem had pulled out for her. He had filled the round yellowwood table with all manner of Dutch delights that he proceeded to describe. "Over here is roggebrood. First you smear it with butter from this botervloot." He pulled a white oblong ceramic dish in front of Promise and showed her how to scrape just enough from the yellowing block of butter settled there, and then shaved some pieces of cheese with a kaasschaaf from the rounded triangle of mature mustard-coloured Gouda, to put on the thick bread slice.

"Next we add two rollmops." Willem pulled the rolled-up pickled herring fillets from a glass jar filled with a vinegary brine and plunked them on Promise's plate. "Then some black coffee." Its rich smell replaced the vinegary one as Willem poured the thick dark liquid into small white stoneware cups placed at the side of their plates. "A meal fit for a king... and queen. Beware, though, Promise, the rollmops can take some getting used to. Just eat it with your fingers from the plate."

"Hau, Willem. I know what to do with my fingers. I eat with them all the time, instead of with a knife and fork." Promise glanced at Willem, holding his stare, as she popped a rollmop into her wide-open mouth, grimaced, chewed slowly and swallowed down the sour fish. "Talking about knives, you are a great surgeon. I know one when I see one. Did you carve that beautiful woman's face that I saw on your bedside table?"

"Agh. Promise, that is the only one I have ever done."

"Who is it?"

"Promise" — Willem leant back his hands folded behind his head — "that is Marja." He nodded. "We were born on the same day and grew up together in Indonesia. Although we were like a brother and sister, Marja… was my first love… only love, I should say." Willem cast his eyes away from Promise and looked at his bony hands, now draped on the yellow table in front of him. Traffic sounds came through the opened window. A curtain riffled in the gentle breeze.

Promise took a deep breath, waiting for him to continue.

"Promise… Marja and I were separated during the Japanese invasion of Bandung, where we were born, and I have never seen her again. Never." Willem shook his head three times.

"Hau, Willem, I am sure that I have seen that face somewhere before. I never forget a face. And certainly not one as pretty as that."

"Promise, I am afraid that is impossible. Marja was lost at sea. Woman overboard," Willem's eyes slowly deflected. "But let us talk about more pleasant things. We have had more than enough trauma for one day, and we are not even in the Casualty Unit." Willem looked at Promise, swallowed. "I would like to invite you to the late afternoon film show at the Rondebosch Cinerama. *Gone with the Wind* is showing. I can drive you home afterwards."

"Willem, that is too-too kind of you. But impossible; I have just read in the newspaper that blacks have been banned from bioscopes in white areas."

"What? That cannot be true. What is the sense of that?"

"It's nonsense. Seemingly the government is doing it to get rid of the bad elements, or so it says. Am I a bad element?"

"No, no, of course not, Promise, but there is nothing I can do about it. I am so sorry for my mistake today. We shouldn't have come to this police station. I just cannot accept the system here." Willem suddenly pushed back his chair, leaving a deep scratch in the parquet floor, picked up a coffee cup, held it above the kitchen basin for a moment and then dropped it. He stood looking at the smashed stoneware, trembling. "Promise, I am so, so sorry; please let me take you home."

†

The chilly Cape winter had changed to sweltering summer. Promise ran fast, turned up the contour path on Devil's Peak, and left the King's Blockhouse behind her. "Race me, Willem."

He preferred to follow in her slipstream but caught up as they entered the mouth of Woodstock Cave arresting her motion on the familiar copper-toned boulder. His left arm clamped her perspiring midriff from behind. His right hand opened to catch her pink palm hanging down slack by her side, their fingers enfolded. They panted, exhausted and exhilarated, dripping with mingling sweat, and clung together facing into the deep dark cave. Willem tightened his hold as their breathing slowed and rotated them both 180 degrees outwards to look over the Cape Flats, the sun still fierce on the horizon, three hours above dusk. Promise's head was capped by Willem's for a moment in time, a single dwarfed silhouette in a vast crevasse of the mountain's ragged face, far too distant for the naked eye to see from below. But, aided by binoculars, an interested person could have seen Promise disengage and turn inwards towards the cave's darkness and reach up to put her slender arms around Willem's neck. She took a long look at him.

Focusing the binoculars to catch a fuller picture, the beholder could have seen the two take off their dripping running clothes, the contrast of their nakedness where they stood. They lay down together, disappearing from view, and merged upon the warm rough rock that Promise and Willem had come to regard as their own.

†

CHAPTER 16

John Terreblanche, Paarl

While Promise and Willem are making love in Woodstock
Cave, let me tell you about my own political awakening
and a little of South Africa's fraught history.

You may recall that I am an Afrikaner by birth. Our
family goes back to the French Huguenots, who settled
in the Cape Peninsula during the seventeenth century,
fast on the heels of the Dutch colony created by Jan van
Riebeeck at the foot of Table Mountain in 1652. Hence,
Terreblanche (white-earth) is a common surname in
South Africa, especially in the Cape.

The French refugees were granted freehold parcels
of land by the Cape's governor of the time to settle at
Stellenbosch, Franschhoek and Paarl. The Dutch East
India Company wanted to extend its reach across the Cape
Flats to the Hottentots' Holland and Klein Drakenstein
Mountains. They envisioned fertile valleys of farms gracing
the lee of the great massif's hills to provision the ships
docked at Table Bay, newly protected by the Fort de Goede

Hoop (today's Cape Town Castle). Over the years the three farming regions became famous for their wines: the French settlers brought their knowledge of wine-craft; the sandy terroir proved perfect to the task. I grew up on our family's wine farm in Paarl, steeped in Afrikaner tradition.

Nonetheless, my father named me "John" rather than Johannes, a very *English* name. As the younger son, I was not going to inherit the farm, so my father wanted me to become anglicised, for purposes that I would only appreciate much later.

By 1930, I was in the final year of school at Paarl Boys' High. Five years after Afrikaans, the potpourri of Dutch, French, Xhosa, Malay and German, had replaced Dutch as the second official language of the Union of South Africa. (English was the first.)

Afrikaans and Afrikanerdom had a long journey in the making.

Not soon after the Cape Colony had been established, Afrikaner trek-Boers had tired of the Dutch administration's restrictions and so had migrated into the hinterland in ever widening arcs. They packed their belongings in oxen-drawn huifkars and travelled first east to the Great Fish River, where they clashed with the Xhosa, and then north in the Great Trek, where they fought with the Zulu and seized and plundered African tribal lands.

You have already heard from Promise about Dingaan's Day, commemorating the Battle of Blood River, now celebrated each year as the Day of the Covenant, and a prominent feature in my high school history book, but it requires further telling to understand the Afrikaner politics of today.

On December 16, 1838, Dingaan, who had murdered both Shaka (to become chief of the Zulus) and Piet Retief, the Voortrekker leader, sent an Impi of ten thousand Zulu warriors to attack the advancing Boer commando of five hundred Voortrekkers. Forewarned of the advancing Impi by Boer outriders, their new leader, Andries Pretorius, circled the seventy wagons into a laager in the veldt. Backed on one side by a steep Donga-ravine, a second flank of the laager was protected by the Ncome River. Three field cannons had been placed between the huifkars to cover the remaining unprotected flank, pointing out across a flat treeless plain. Pretorius mounted one of the gun carriages and asked his men to enter a vow with God. Should they survive victorious, he pledged a covenant: the day of victory would be celebrated in honour of the Almighty.

That day, wave upon wave of Zulus attacked. But were repulsed again and again, their assegais and hide-shields no match for the musket balls and lead shot that the farmers blasted at them. The Impi attack faltered. Pretorius ordered the Voortrekkers out of the laager to give chase on horseback and the rout turned into a massacre. The Ncome River ran red with native blood and was renamed Blood River by the victorious commandos. Three thousand Zulus lay dead, with only three Voortrekker casualties. The Boers had exacted a horrible revenge for the assassination of their leader, Piet Retief.

In similar fashion the Voortrekker commandos conquered the land and founded the Independent Boer Republics of the Transvaal, Orange Free State and Natalia. Independent, that is, from Great Britain, which by 1805 had taken over the Cape and its hinterlands from the Dutch, for the second time but now for good.

The independence of the Boer Republic of Natalia would, however, be short-lived. In December of 1838, the British governor, Sir George Napier, sent British redcoats to occupy Port Natal, effectively cutting off the Voortrekkers from use of the harbour, weakening their hold on the territory. And, when the Boer Natal Volksraad resolved to drive all Africans not in the employ of whites southwards into the Transkei in July of 1841, a British military intervention followed, crushing the Boers' stoic resistance.

Thus, battle lines were drawn and redrawn between the Afrikaner Boer and the British Imperial colonialist; the next decades would become a raging tug of war for land rights that would culminate in the South African War, the Anglo-Boer War of 1899–1902.

By then the British Imperial Exchequer was out of pocket because its colonies around the world were expensive to keep. But diamonds had been dug in Kimberley, and great seams of gold unearthed in the reefs surrounding Johannesburg, motivating the British to annex the two remaining Boer republics, the Orange Free State and the Transvaal, despite the fierce resistance from the Boers. The Afrikaners battled for their right to exist; their Bibles told them they were the chosen volk, and their Promised Land had been stolen by Britain's Imperial might.

Atrocities abounded during the Anglo-Boer war, chiefly on the side of the British soldiers, who outnumbered the farmers tenfold (500,000 to 50,000). The redcoats imprisoned the Afrikaner women and children in concentration camps, where half died of starvation. They exercised a scorched earth policy on the land and destroyed the Boers' farms, burnt their livestock, and broke their hearts. The British devastated the Boers' livelihood, leading to their vast impoverishment and dereliction.

By the conclusion of the war, the rupture between Afrikaner and Englishmen had turned to hatred stoking the Boers determination to exist as a people, as Afrikaners in the land that God had granted them. Accordingly, although the Boers had lost the war, they sought to win the peace. They strove to maintain their hard-won identity as a volk no matter the cost. And so the terms of the peace treaty signed at Pretoria in 1902 was a harbinger of the apartheid policies that would follow. Although the Boers had given up independence of the three republics and recognised King Edward VII of England in the peace treaty, they sought constraints on the voting rights for Africans, who, as far as they were concerned, were getting "out of hand". And, thus, the final surrender document included a key condition that the plebiscite would *not* be given to blacks in the ex-republics *until* full restoration of self-government had been ensured.

It was thus unsurprising that, when elections were finally held in the four territories — six years later in 1908 — the Afrikaner vote predominated in the Transvaal and Orange Free State by sheer preponderance of the Boer farmers who had migrated northwards to secure it. And, when colonial representatives from the four parliaments met to discuss the unification of South Africa two years later, the two Boer republics allied with Natal to ban blacks from the common voter's role. The Cape Colony was the only holdout of the four; the Cape maintained their colour-blind franchise and further entrenched that Coloureds could vote in their newly drafted constitution.

The Act of Union of South Africa of 1910 thus united the four colonies together under one flag but disunited the country. It excluded the natives of the land, the Hottentots of the Cape Peninsula, the Xhosas of the South, and the Zulus in the north.

The British were far from innocent in the matter of black subjugation; they had waged relentless colonial war against the Africans. Over the intervening years the Cape-Xhosa and Anglo-Zulu Wars raged up and down the vast country, killing tens of thousands of Africans as the redcoats sought to plunder and control South Africa, a key strategic crossroad.

In response, the long-suffering Africans, robbed of their country, organised politically. They created the South African Native National Congress in 1912, the forerunner of today's African National Congress, the ANC.

†

Now, all of this occurred before my birth in 1913, but it helps you to understand the Afrikaner nationalism I was brought up with, and — dare I say it? — coloured my point of view, so to speak.

As I learnt to read, I remember looking forward to *Die Brandwag*, a family-style magazine created by the assistant editor of *Die Volkstem* specifically to appeal to simple folk. The well-known journalist had embarked on a campaign to reframe our Afrikaans history. The simple stories, colourfully enhanced by obvious stereotypes with accompanying cartoonish pictures, painted the Afrikaner as the hero, the British as wicked and devious, and the Africans as barbarians.

And then there was the influence of religion on my upbringing. Of course we belonged to the Dutch Reformed Church in Paarl. My father was an alderman. And very proud of it. He was imposing and the spitting image of what I look like today.

A man of outsized proportions, thickened by life's excesses, his rotund face was kind but stern and split by fat purple lips. Sunbeaten, when he took off his hat his scalp revealed a ring of pale skin set off by scant black hair brilliantined back on its way to baldness. His eyes, flecked blue and half-hidden by sagging eyelids, were enjoined by a ruddy nose that flared to the rhythm of his substantial torso. His ears, fleshy question marks, dotted heavy lobes. Two extra neck-folds creased his crisp white alderman's collar. His three-piece suit, dark, crimped his widening girth and pushed out a broad farmer's chest. His hands were large and hairy, like warm shovels.

Each Sunday my older brother, Theo, and I had to dress up for church. As early as I remember, we had to wear a jacket and tie. Sunday school was first, followed by an 11 o'clock church service that droned on and on in a mixture of kitchen Dutch and High Hollands. Eventually of course this volkstaal would become die Taal — the Afrikaans we hold dear today.

After the service, the dominee shook everyone's hand as we filed out of church, before the whole family —

children, uncles and aunts, ailing grandmother, and stoere Opa — returned to our house for the Sunday lunch.

This was a grand affair centred around a massive stinkhout table in the formal dining room of the Cape-style farmhouse that my forbears had built against the lower reaches of Paarlberg. Named Buitenkyk, it stood elevated at the end of a long gravel driveway fed by ripples of neatly rowed vines stretching into the distance. Like a white cross at the end of the road, Buitenkyk dominated the landscape. Darkly thatched, and whitely gabled, front, back and on both sides, it was a splendid example of the Cape Dutch building style. Scant windows and thick walls ensured cool, despite the fierce summer heat, richly burnished terracotta tiles echoed underfoot.

The Sunday meal had been prepared by the coloured cook and black servants in the kombuis adjacent to the dining room while we attended church. Candles had been lit in silver candelabras, and the family cutlery gleamed on the starched tablecloth readied for our arrival, frumpy, and hot in our Sunday best, sweaty from the bright day.

My father sat at the one head of the table and opened the proceedings. He reached out to my mother and Opa sitting next to him and grasped their hands in his, then bowed his head. The host of twenty or so sitting around the table, in descending order of age, followed suit.

"Here zeegen dezen spijzen. Amen," my father said.

"Amen," we replied in unison. And then "Smakelijk eten," was repeated to each other, as the small talk began, and the food was served and the rich wine poured by the servants.

Usually, we were served a roast of sheep, or cow, or pork, with baked potatoes. Fresh vegetables, peas, or carrots, or cauliflower lay steaming on our porcelain plates embossed with the family coat of arms.

I wasn't a big talker. I wasn't confident enough. Instead, I listened and observed. I was a careful witness to the conversations around the tables of my youth. I kept a diary and wanted to be a writer.

One conversation that year would change my life's course. I couldn't observe on that occasion because I was hidden in a cupboard, in that same dining room. But I listened carefully and wrote it all down, like the good journalist I would become.

†

My father was a very important man in Paarl. I didn't quite know why. I assumed that it had something to do with the church or farm, never politics. That is not to say that I hadn't heard a great deal about politics from my father: about the Afrikaners' rights to exist in this country that was rightfully ours. We were the true white Africans, not the English, who had stolen the country from the Dutch and settled here so much later, starting in 1820, in Port Elizabeth. This was our country and our people, and we must ensure the purity of our white Afrikaner race. We must have large families (it was a pity he could only have two sons) and weave our volk into the fabric of South Africa. We needed to organise, to redeem the dishonour of the capitulation of the Anglo-Boer war. We should be able to hold our head high in our own country. The country of our birth.

Every month, Tuesdays, late into the night, my father hosted a dinner meeting solely for male guests. Theo and I were never introduced to the visitors and commanded not to talk about the events to others outside the family. Motor cars crunched up our gravel driveway and parked in straight stripes in front of the elevated flagstone terrace that led onto our arched, double front door, varnished black. Two flaming torches flanked the entranceway, their fire turning to black smoke faint with paraffin.

The dining room was prepared as for a Sunday meal, and because the leather-bound family Bible lay at my father's place I thought these were prayer meetings. By now, in the final year of high school, I had learnt the forbidden pleasure of a good glass of wine. On the fateful evening, I had snuck into the fine room and sampled one of the dark reds warming on the sideboard in anticipation of the guests.

I was almost discovered. Voices grew louder from the front door hallway that led into the dining room. I could not escape through the adjacent kitchen, still busy with servants. Instead, I found a narrow space in the new jonkman's kas that my father had recently built. I hunched over, my head on my knees, thighs tight against my chest, and closed the two tall doors from the inside. The rank smell of linseed oil suffused the dark space, my breathing fast and shallow.

There came the murmur of voices, the clink of glass and the occasional sound of a backslap of greeting or heavy tread on the terracotta floor. I pictured what I could only hear. The large, curtain-draped, high-eved, candlelit room. An imboya glass-paned display cabinet next to the open door through which the men entered. The long stinkhout sideboard, conveniently next to the closed kitchen door, upon which the food would be placed, and the wines were displayed, the red still warm in my stomach. The freshly oiled yellowwood jonkman's kas framed the back wall behind my father's seat at the head of the table.

Murmurs turned to indistinct conversation and the scratch of wooden chairs on hard stone, until my father pushed back his chair, stood up (I saw his back through the jonkman's kas keyhole) and started the meeting.

"Broeders, you come in God. May God be with you." He opened the Bible and read a short passage, then set up the order of proceedings:

"First, a roll call. Mr. Marius Swanepoel will take the minutes. Then, we eat and drink. I will have my wife, Marie, bring in the food so that the servants cannot identify you. As you know, Marie is sworn to secrecy and, to be double sure, I have given the servants the rest of the night off."

I settled in for a cramped evening, too scared to reveal myself, especially after the names of my school headmaster, the police chief, our dominee, our doctor, the mayor of Paarl, and what sounded like a high official from the Cape Administration had been recorded, and the woody smell of cigar smoke permeated my confinement.

"Broeders, we are gathered in secret, not for fun but for purpose: we have important work to do for our Broederbond. In this year of the Great Depression, our volk suffer mightily. One-fifth of all Afrikaners are paupers. Poor whites! Three hundred thousand of us!" Through the keyhole, I saw my father point three thick fingers skywards.

"It has been twelve long years that we have organised to insert our Broeders into the economic engine and political machine of our country to lift our people from destitution. We must uphold our Afrikaners' rights against the British, who took them away. Ever since van Riebeeck arrived and the Voortrekkers settled this great land, we have been suppressed by the English. God dank that in the year of our Lord of 1929, Hertzog's National Party won the majority in the election. It is high time that we win back the country stolen from us. Not through the barrel of a gun" — he patted his Bible — "but through influence. Through cultural, economic and political influence. We must place Afrikaners, tied together in secret Broederskap, in the higher echelons of power in the country – right up to the president."

"Ja." "Ja." "I can toast to that." "Ek, ook." I heard a shifting of chairs and imagined glasses filled with brandy raised and downed, before my father continued.

"We have come a long way. We have established FAK, the Federation of Afrikaanse Kultuurverenegings, our most important public front. We have charged the Federation with spreading our Afrikaner culture, country-wide. We have promoted Afrikaans in single-medium schools, created Helpmekaar to help buy land and finance businesses for our brethren, and need to create a bank, a volkskas, to support our members with money matters. With geld." I saw my father's fat thumb and two fingers rubbing together.

"A trade union is possible too. We must fight the English capitalism. There must be no class division amongst us Afrikaners."

"I agree, Mr. Terreblanche, but we must please get on with the business at hand, the business on the agenda." I recognised the secretary by the reedy voice that piped up to arrest my father's monologue.

"Ja, ja, ja, it is your turn now. I know the ANC is agitating again. Over to you, Mr. Swanepoel."

I am sure you can appreciate that I was now in a very problematic position in the jonkman's kas. I had just heard that my father was a most important man in a clandestine organisation set up to advance Afrikanerdom. I was shocked. I had heard whisperings about this organisation. I was cramped tight in the kas. My body ached; sweat warmed my face and ran down my chest. If I were discovered, my father would likely be expelled from the Broederbond. I could not have that happen. I respected my father. He was a lion in my estimation. I could not see him shot down.

Mr. Swanepoel continued shrilly. "Broeders, the blacks are restless."

"Agh." "Ja, nee." "When was it ever not so?" someone said to loud harrumphing. "Never." "Never." "Never."

"They are on again about the passbooks," Swanepoel continued. "The Communist Party and the African National Congress and other black organisations want to stage a new pass-burning campaign and nation-wide strike starting on Dingaan's Dag this 16th December. In this year of our Lord, 1930."

"Right," said my father, rising from his seat. "Do we know who the ringleaders are?"

"Yes. Johannes Nkosi in Natal, but we are not yet sure who is in charge in the Western Cape," my headmaster responded.

"Well, we know what we have to do," my father said. "Let's arrange it. And now I must close this evening's proceedings. The hour is late, and you must be tired and need to get home to your wives and children. In closing, we must remember what each of us committed to at our initiation ceremony into the Broederbond. Lest we forget, let us say it together in unison:

"*He who betrays the bond will be destroyed by the bond. The bond never forgets. Its vengeance is swift and sure.*"

I thought I recognised each distinctive voice banding together, despite my discomfort.

Then my father finished. "Good evening and good night," and I heard with relief the pushing back of chairs, conversation receding, car motors coming to life, and the scrunch of gravel as the Broeders departed into the black night.

†

Just when I thought it was safe to get out of the cramped kas, I heard my father's heavy step on the terracotta tiling. He yanked open the cupboard and hauled me out by the scruff of my wrinkled overalls. He stood back, breathing heavily, "What the hell are you doing in the kas, John? You bloody idiot! I thought I heard something moving behind me; thank God the others didn't find out. There will be hell to pay."

"I'm sorry, Pa."

"You better be. Why were you there, anyway? Another school writing project? Well, you cannot write anything about any of this. Do you understand?"

"Yes, Pa." I bowed my head and writhed my cupped hands over and over each other repetitively.

My father slaked a deep sigh. I could smell the brandy on his breath. "My son, my son, we are in deep, deep trouble if anybody finds out. Did you hear what we said about Nkosi in Natal?"

"Yes, Pa."

"Then I am duty-bound to have you swear secrecy to the cause. Here, now, on the family Bible."

We moved to stand over the weighty book, its silver clasped corners glinting in the candlelight.

"Place your right hand flat on the Bible," my father said and then placed his over mine. I could feel his strength and his warmth feed into me. "Now say after me: I promise to keep secret all I have heard today in service of the Broederbond."

"I promise to keep secret all I have heard today in service of the Broederbond," I repeated as requested, and, like Saul on his way to Damascus, was converted to the cause.

†

CHAPTER 17

Willem and Promise

The next morning Willem woke up in a sweat. The taste of Promise still on his lips, he sat bolt upright in bed, his boxer shorts drenched with despair. *Mijn God, what have I done? What if someone was spying on us? What if I get Promise pregnant?* He reached a trembling hand to grasp the glass of water on his bedside table but knocked it into the woodcarving of Marja's head — both falling to the parquet floor with a thud and crash.

"Godverdomme. Godverdomme." He clasped his hands to his narrow face, shaking it from side to side. He remained sitting on the dishevelled bed sheet, still wet with the night's perspiration, trying to calm himself. Willem took a few deep breaths and watched the sunlight play through the open window, sheening the pool of water surrounding Marja's sculpture. The brown wood darkened moist in the puddle. The church bells outside struck eleven times for the Sunday Service. Willem bowed his head. The sound reminded him of Leiden, of medical school in Holland.

I've got to get control of myself, he thought, his heart beating at his throat. *Tidak apa-apa. Tidak apa-apa*, Marja would have said back in Indonesia to soothe him. It will be alright. *Tidak apa-apa.* Willem got up, washed his face in ice cold water, mopped his clammy chest and bared his teeth in the bathroom mirror, forcing his downward-curled mouth upwards to adjust his mood. He remained standing for a time looking at his sallow face. Then he splashed some more water, patted his cheeks with a towel and then, after carefully drying his hands, went into the kitchen. He made a strong cup of black coffee and sat down to read the recently delivered newspaper.

†

The Cape Times Herald
The Paper that Cares.
December 20, 1959

ANC and PAC Launch Another Campaign Against the Hated Pass Laws
John Terreblanche

You might have thought by now we could get past the pass laws. Think again. They are the crux of our existence in South Africa. The means by which the government controls the non-whites, their place of residence and labour. The country has paid a high price in blood and treasure for the diktat that harks back to the Hottentot Proclamation of 1809. The Khoisan of the Cape were compelled to have a "registered place of abode" and to carry a "certificate" should

---

they chose to travel beyond their district, forcing them to live and work on white farms.

Over the intervening years countless protest marches, strikes and pass burnings have deteriorated into rioting, bloodshed and death. I recall hearing of a pass-burning campaign when I was seventeen years old in Paarl. And then reading about the four deaths at Cartwright Flats in Natal; the shocking allegations that the ringleader, Johannes Nkosi, had been murdered while in police custody.

It is true that there have been thrusts and parries in the Pass Law's application. In 1906, 3000 Asians protested (2000 were jailed or deported); in 1930 the above events transpired, and in 1942 Prime Minister Jan Smuts spoke of scrapping the pass laws altogether, to galvanise the whole nation against a Japanese invasion. But, since the National Party came to power in 1948, the pass laws have become ever more oppressive.

In 1952 the 'Abolition of Passes Act' made matters worse. Created to make policing of Bantu influx control easier, the bizarre sleight of hand embittered Africans and brought great trauma. The pass was abolished in favour of a 96-page reference book. Rendered in standard green or brown issue, the 'dompass' contained the owner's thumb prints, photo, permits and work history, and had to be carried on one's person on pain of punishment. Failure to produce a valid reference pass at the request of a policemen could incur a fine of £10.00–£50.00 or imprisonment for one to six months, or both. In 1958 alone, 396,836 Africans were convicted for offences contravening the governmental laws created to control Bantu migration.

It is thus no wonder that at this month's national conventions both the African National Congress and the

229

newly created Pan African Congress have planned Anti-Pass Campaigns for early next year, the ANC an Anti-Pass Day on 31 March and the PAC "decisive and final positive action against the pass laws" under the slogan: "no bail, no defence, no fine" on March 21.

Don't hold your breath waiting for what the government's response will be.

†

Willem put down the Sunday newspaper containing my article, looked out the window at the Rondebosch Fountain, and closed his eyes. He made up his mind on the matter, bypassing his heart. Promise would need to be locked out to protect himself. He got up from the dining room table and walked into the bedroom, gathered the shrapnel of broken glass lying on the water-stained parquet into a tin dust-tray, and picked up Marja's carving. He looked her in the eyes and gently cradled the cool wood against his pulsating neck, as he had done so often before. It calmed him but it also made him feel guilty. He had been unable to keep the family promise. Willem thought back to the festive rijs-tafel dinner their two families had enjoyed at the Dago Falls Club to celebrate his father's promotion to major. Held a week before the Japanese invasion of Java, they had enjoined hands around the table. Willem remembered how thrilling it was to feel the tightening of Marja's unsure grasp to match his own. Both fathers, smart in their military uniforms, had stood up to propose a toast and a pledge: that, no matter what the future might bring, each one would promise to look after one and the other.

"A promise till death do us part," they had said in unison. Willem had sought Marja's golden-brown eyes and held her glance until she looked away. That was the last time he had seen her. The war had separated them and killed their parents. He was quite alone. The church clock struck twelve, breaking Willem's reverie.

†

Promise found herself strangely energised. The wetness left by Willem felt like a warm glow rising within as she ran down the mountain path at increasing speed. Her gait more sure-footed than on the way up, a broad smile of bright teeth marked her pleasure. *Hau! Promise you've done it. You, a girl born in a mud pondok, you've got yourself a doctor! He's not at all like the other whites. So impressive; such a gentleman. He doesn't look down on us. Treats me like a lady.* Promise swerved to miss a boulder protruding onto the crooked pathway, a tussock of sage smelling fynbos hiding it from view in the lengthening shadows. *Hau, he really likes me. And I him.* She slowed her pace. *I have pulled Willem on to our side and put him in danger.* Then brightened again. *I can have a baby boy. Maybe I'm pregnant already. I must look out, for all our sakes.* Her footing faltered through a sandy donga. *The child will be a mixture for all to see. Shoo, shoo, shoo.* Promise slowed to a walk, crossed De Waal Drive at Mostert's Mill, looking right and left and right again, and picked up the pace to get home before sunset.

Two days later, on duty at Groote Schuur Hospital, Promise was in high spirits. She wanted to see whether

Willem had altered, transformed somehow, by their intimacy in the cave. Whether he would give off a sign — that only she would recognise — when he walked into the theatre to operate on the first patient of the day.

Promise staged the morning after meeting to her best advantage. She had wrapped her white surgical gown with special care, gathered her tawny hair in a white doek to highlight her fawn-like face, and applied black lipstick to outline her perfect teeth in a welcoming smile.

Willem, gowned in white, shuffled into the operating theatre, masked face down. He produced one long contraction: his head writhing upwards right, his gaze fixed left-down, before he slurred: "Goeie môre, get ready for surgery… sister." And then swayed to the surgical table, waited for Promise to ready herself, demanded the knife, and cut. Promise was sure that she smelt ether on Willem's breath when she leant in close to dab blood from the chest incision the surgeon had opened.

She couldn't whisper a warning to him — it was morbidly quiet in theatre save for the beep of the EKG, the gurgle of blood being drained from the patient's cavity, and the swish of the ventilator — for fear of being overheard. Not that it would have made much difference. Willem seemed oblivious to all but the surgical task at hand, which he completed perfectly nonetheless. Promise straightened up and raised her hand above the patient, readying for the V for victory clasp. But Willem just stood back from the table, thanked the anaesthetist, turned around and walked out of theatre, leaving Promise standing with her left hand in the air.

"Promise, that is *very* strange," remarked the

anaesthetist, Dr. Ozinsky. "I wouldn't worry about it. Dr. Jansen is just an oddball."

But Promise did. She thought she knew what was going on. She dropped her arm and busied herself packing away the instruments as Dr. Ozinsky woke the anaesthetised patient. She couldn't see the instruments very well until she had screwed her eyelids tightly together, tiny droplets bathing the inside of her mask.

The next days, at Groote Schuur, the weather worsened. The hot summer southeaster turned to a barrage of rain. The parched Cape Peninsula, aflood with water — the slopes of Devil's Peak offered no protection from the onslaught; the hospital's storm drains and gutters overflowed; the Casualty Unit was awash with puddles. The building's red-tiled roof had suffered leaks that buckets failed to contain.

†

From what I learnt later, Willem was not having a good time of it either. He hated what he was forcing himself to do — close himself off from Promise for his own safety. He felt like a coward. He had given to Promise and then withdrawn out of fear. Fear of being caught in the act of love that was prohibited between black and white. On pains of imprisonment. Willem had read all about the Immorality Act in one of my newspaper articles. He became anxious again. Running long distances up the mountain didn't help either, as it used to. The anxiety welled up out of nowhere, like an electrical short-circuit in his brain, he couldn't reason himself out of it, however hard he tried. It wasn't just a mental thing. It was physical. A hot shiver in the nape, a thudding heartbeat in the throat, and sweat in the palm. He couldn't get any relief. He just couldn't get any relief. The only relief was with Promise, and that was forbidden.

Willem endured Christmas Eve at home on his own and was thankful that Promise was not on duty the following day when he started his round-the-clock shift in the Casualty Unit. He would not have to pretend that he did not care for her. He did. His attraction to her must be plainly visible. Willem had to mask his emotions in Promise's presence. And surgery required all his concentration — working with another nursing sister in theatre those twenty-four hours proved a strange reprieve.

†

On the evening of December 26, Promise was utterly miserable. A week had passed since the couple's life-changing act when they had agreed to meet at the annual Boxing Day celebration held atop Signal Hill. Cape Town celebrated the holiday with a fireworks display over the city, after which floodlights were ignited to illuminate Table Mountain for the summer season. There would be a large crowd and Promise and Willem could easily enjoy each other's company undetected in the thickets of squat trees that flanked the fields surrounding the Noon Gun emplacement. But Willem was nowhere to be found; Promise accosted her uncle, yelling to overcome the jazz band playing nearby.

"Goodwill, did you see Docatela anywhere? He said he would meet me at the Noon Gun. I have been watching for him for two hours now."

"Aikona, Promise. No. Let me finish braaiing this sausage and then come and have some with me. He's not coming." Dlamini's beaming face sweated in the firelight, the smoke of charcoaled meat rising above the clutch of barbecues semi-circled on the sandy field fronting the cannon emplacement: the wide-open space a rainbow of celebrants mixing in bonhomie. Partygoers enjoying Boxing Day to the full, the guttering barbecue fires lit up green beer bottles arched aloft to quench the ever-present thirst that such events occasion.

†

Willem had seriously considered going to Signal Hill. After all, *a promise you make is a promise you keep*, he thought wryly. But he couldn't, shouldn't, and so went to the Pig and Whistle, across the road from his flat, and got drunk instead. Perhaps he could make amends for not going by meeting Promise at the Klopse Karnival Parade a week from now. They could meet in the crowd that watched the New Year's procession from the Company Gardens at the top of Adderley Street. That would be completely innocent, could be passed off as a chance meeting, and might allow them to figure things out. Willem got another beer and a scrap of paper from the barman and penned an apologetic letter to Promise with the proposal. (She had told him never to call her at home because her telephone might be tapped.) He walked home, put the message in an envelope, and posted it at the street corner letterbox. He felt much better about himself. A little less drunk and more hopeful. He would continue to mask his emotions for Promise at work in the intervening days, then on the New Year's day they could work things out seated on a nice bench in the gardens. He wondered whether she had already given up on him, in disappointment. He wondered whether this was the right course of action. He fell asleep wondering — Marja's carved face, the last thing he remembered seeing, beside his hard bed.

†

The colourful voorlopertjie raised her baton high and mince-stepped forward to navigate the corner of Adderley Street, waving to the jubilant crowd waiting in the gardens to view the Klopse Karnival Parade march past. A cacophony of string, brass and wind instruments became ever louder as the minstrels strutted up Cape Town's main thoroughfare to celebrate the arrival of the 1960s. The garden's crowd met the first wave of Coons fronted by the Star Spangles troupe, with whoops, clapping and loud heckling:

"Jy lyk mooi. Jy lyk mooi. Beautiful!"

"Show me some leg."

"Wys die bene. Wys. Wys."

Two people who might have recognised Marja as she tightened her hold on the baton and wheeled around the corner were absent from the festive crowd. Promise had never received Willem's letter and Willem had, again, had second thoughts; he preferred to spend the day alone, climbing. Promise had wanted to get away. Away from District Six and the madness of the Coon Karnival.

†

Willem edged his Beetle behind another car, parked next to Signal Hill Road, across from the eroded footpath that led up Lion's Head. He switched off the engine and sat quite still. The view of Kloof Nek and the city below was glorious in the midday sunshine. The percussive sounds of the Klopse Karnival came in cool waves on the faint breeze that stirred the smell of the fynbos encroaching the roadside. He stretched, pleased that there was only one other car and so he would likely have the mountain to himself. Willem tightened his boots, pocketed his pipe in his shorts, and made sure to attach his water bottle to his belt. He loosened the two top buttons of his khaki shirt, crossed Signal Hill Road, and started the long trudge upwards to encircle Lion's Head, twice, before reaching the final climb to the summit. Table Mountain's neighbouring massif gigantically presented itself along the way up to the first switchback, when the Twelve Apostles range, arduously, came into view — their vertiginous slopes a deep purple splendour that ebbed and flowed into the southern distance to meet the curve of the Atlantic Ocean frothing on to the rocky coastline below. As Willem rose around the mountainside, rusty stones replaced fynbos shifting in the wind, the beat of his heart and the crumble of pebbles underfoot outdid the cicadas' incessant buzzing, and the air surrounding him felt purer; the smog and the complications of life below slowly fell away. He made the turn upwards around the lone fir tree that had carved its life into the mountainside and headed for the final steep climb onto the flat-topped summit he had been looking forward to reaching. Willem clamped his right hand around a rock, positioned his left foot against another and crested the rock face, anticipating the vista he knew so well. There it was in all its glory, but he was not alone. In the distance, standing at the black and white striped mountain beacon, was Promise.

Willem froze in mid-climb, his eyes level with the mountain's edge. His heart notched a rate higher; he could feel the thumping in his ears. Promise looked around, in search of something. She was wearing her sheer white running outfit, her tawny hair wild in the stiffening wind. Sunglasses glinted in Willem's direction; a lovely smile arched across her face. She was barefoot. "Willem. I can see you. I have been thinking about you all day. Now you are here. On Lion's Head. You can run but you cannot hide. Come up here. Please."

Willem completed the climb, and walked over to stand next to the beacon, the black and white sign separating them just for that moment in time, for he stepped around it and pulled Promise towards him. And there they made each other's acquaintance for a second time, the compelling act of love far stronger than the rule of law. And then, high above Cape Town, they planned for a life together.

†

Let me tell you, that wasn't simple. Nothing ever is in South Africa between black and white. Promise was not allowed to be in Rondebosch after nightfall unless her reference book showed that she had business there, and the police station was a stone's throw from Willem's flat. So they couldn't risk that. The only option was Promise's house in District Six, which was still classified a mixed area by government planners, but not beyond the reach of the Immorality Act, the Mixed Marriages Act and, soon, the newly repurposed Natives Resettlement Act. The latter Act had just recently been used to evict all Africans from Johannesburg's Sophia Town, and had now been extended the length of the country to forcibly evict non-whites from newly declared whites-only areas to grubby blacks-only townships, with predictable consequences: riots had flared across the country that couldn't be quelled by the undermanned police force and so army units had been brought in to implement the Native Resettlement Board's mandates. The upshot: there was fierce resistance and resentment against the white government's rules, which raged relentlessly, finding no outlet.

Fortunately, for Promise and Willem in Cape Town, the situation was not quite as bad as in the north: although two new blacks-only townships had been proclaimed for resettlement purposes at Duinefontein on the Cape Flats, the central city area had not yet been declared white, and so expulsion was not imminent. Consequently, although protests, strikes and demonstrations were common around the city, riots were read about only in the newspapers: in Paarl and Somerset West, and in Worcester beyond the Drakenstein Mountains. Sometimes, though, when they ran up a footpath on Table Mountain, Promise and Willem could see the smoke trails from protest fires burning across *the Cape Flats and watch the helicopters traverse the Peninsular neck to throttle the distant disturbance.*

†

Willem stretched back on Promise's prickly couch. He didn't like the stiff zebra-hide covering, nor the black and white bristles that poked through his anaemic safari suite. He took a deep drag of his Falcon pipe, inhaled some more, and watched the smoke turn blue as he breathed into the sweltering sun light passing through the opened window. Children played outside; he could hear them running their toy cars noisily on the pavement.

"Vroom. Vroom. Vroom. My car is faster than yours."

He thought about how he used to play with Matchbox cars back in Indonesia. Now he had his own. He had parked his Beetle a good walk away from Promise's house. He chose a different site each time he came. He had let his car become dirty, so it mixed with the neighbourhood. Most cars were barely working jalopies that had seen better days or had been abandoned in the dilapidated districts' streets altogether — the depth of their rust and flatness of their tyres a witness to the length of idleness.

Willem didn't want to rouse suspicion, so he usually visited at night; the dimness of the streetlamps matched the quarter in poverty. It looked like the government was trying to evict the coloured folk by other means. Subsidies were strained; the place was a slum. Only a few inhabitants could afford their own house. Most doubled or trebled or quadrupled up, not having enough money to pay for their own like Promise. It was her birthday today and Willem wanted to surprise her by cooking an Indonesian meal, a rijs-tafel, nasi rames. A little of a lot. Fried rice, pork saté, egg omelette, and sambal and kroepoek and atjar and seroendeng. He would explain it all with great delight when she arrived. They also had to talk. After a month together, he felt they needed to look at their options considering the deteriorating state of the country and its prospects.

Promise sniffed twice as she entered. "Hau, what is this? Is it the Indonesian that has come to visit? Is that why you weren't at work?"

She wrapped her arms around Willem as he rose from the couch to meet her. "You naughty boy." She kissed him once on each cheek, grabbed his hand and led him into the bedroom. "I know you have a birthday present for me; I can feel it between us."

The handshake of love duly spent, Willem and Promise rose again for a chilled glass of pale wine around the kitchen table. Promise had lit two white candles, which guttered greenish shadows on the darkened walls, providing the only light for the savoury meal that Willem had prepared. The molten aroma of candle wax sharpened by chilli pepper.

Promise put a saté stick into her mouth and bit into the pork cube at its tip. "Delicious! Just like you." She pulled out the stick and swallowed the spiced meat after a short chew, pressing her lips firmly together.

"Promise, we have to talk."

"What about, Willem?" Promise pulled another cube from the saté stick.

"Our situation. You know that if you — me — we are caught like this we're in big shit with the police."

"Not if we're not doing anything, we aren't. They must catch us in the act. We can stay together, live together, just not have sex, nor children together."

"But I thought you wanted a boy. You've been telling me that ever since we met, or almost," Willem said.

Promise smiled. "Yes, that is a problem."

"And with this situation, there is no future here. The United Nations is sanctioning the country; many countries are boycotting us." Willem shuddered. "I don't want to get caught here. We could go to America. We can both easily find work there; I see advertisements for doctors and nurses all the time, and we can have the child you want and not live in fear of the police."

"Never." Promise stood up and spat out the last cube onto her plate. "I belong here. This is my country. The ANC will prevail." She sat down and shook her head. "Aikona, Willem, I'm sorry, I should not have overreacted like that." She took a sip of wine and continued. "But you must understand. This is me. I am an African, I belong in Africa."

"For me it is different, Promise. I don't know where I belong. Am I Dutch? Am I an Indonesian? All I know is that I am a foreigner, and I would like to find a place to belong." Willem sniffed. "This is what I admire and love in you. You are an African, and… brave… and beautiful."

He lowered his head. Promise reached out her hands to Willem's, their arms rectangled across the table. The candles guttered lightly, to and fro, with their breath.

†

The Cape Times Herald

The Paper that Cares.

February 4, 1960

British Prime Minister: 'Wind of Change' Speech: Can it blow any harder in the Cape?

John Terreblanche

The British Prime Minister, Harold Macmillan, blasted Dr. Hendrik Verwoerd at a meeting of both Houses of Parliament yesterday. In front of a full court press, Macmillan provided a frontal assault on apartheid and its architect.

The British Prime Minister was nervous. He fiddled with his papers, read in a reaching voice, and added emphasis by slapping the microphoned podium.

He stressed the importance of the Union of South Africa, now 50 years old. He stressed the beauty of the country and all its people. He thanked our Prime Minister for the invitation, and then turned to the key impetus for his visit: to state that his Conservative government had no intention of blocking the road for its African colonies to seek independence from Britain. In fact, the opposite, he said:

"The wind of change is blowing through this continent. Whether we like it or not, this growth of consciousness is a political fact. Our national policies must take account of it."

And then he made his telling points:

A government's aim should be to "create a society which respects the rights of individuals — a society in which individual merit alone is the criterion for a man's advancement, whether political or economic.

"We, that is the British, reject the idea of any inherent superiority of one race over another. Our policy, therefore, is non-racial. It offers a future in which Africans, Europeans, Asians... will all play their full part as citizens in the country where they live and in which the feeling of race will be submerged in the loyalty to new nations."

Macmillan ended in a conciliatory tone:

"Let us therefore resolve to build, not to destroy. And let us remember always that weakness comes from division, strength from unity."

What happened next will surely go down in the history of our time. Prime Minister Verwoerd was visibly shaken by the speech; he got up immediately but spoke calmly at the microphone:

"To do justice in Africa means not only being just to the Black Man of Africa, but also to the White Man of Africa."

†

"Hau Willem! Come and read this newspaper article." Promise had spread the paper on the kitchen table, cleared of the last evening's emotion.

"This means the British Prime Minister is on our side. It will be a windfall for the Anti-Pass Campaign, excuse the pun."

"And a black eye to Verwoerd. Promise, you know that he was born Dutch, don't you? He's an embarrassment. The puppet master, pulling all the strings. He makes me angry, a bit ashamed. It is just not right, what they're doing to your people. At least it looks like Macmillan put Verwoerd in his place. I'll bet the National Party will want

S.A. to become a republic now, independent of Britain. Just like the Republic of Indonesia became independent from the Dutch after the war. I didn't understand the hatred for colonialists, until I met the Pemipin at Kebon Jati Camp, when I was a P.O.W. Have I told you that story?"

"Yes. Once or twice at least." Promise continued. "On Konininginne Dag they lined you up, to salute the Japanese flag. Someone had displayed a Dutch flag in a window to protest and the camp commander went berserk. He beat a man who had placed a red disc on his backside half to death."

"Yes, and I did nothing, just stood there spineless and watched the beating."

†

March 21, 1960, broke like any other Monday at Groote Schuur Hospital, the date indelibly etched on the back of the photograph I found in Willem's album. I suspect that the shot was taken for the hospital's yearbook. Promise and Willem are standing on either side of the grand entrance. All on their own. That's strange. A white doctor and a black sister. It looks like an official photograph to document that Dr. Jansen and Sister Madiba were now in charge of the Casualty Unit behind them. What's even more strange is that they are smiling. And, although they are standing at least three feet apart, they look closer. As if some intimacy has passed between them, just before the photograph was taken, that was not meant to show, nor be recorded.

The rest is history. Reports started coming in over the

radio that afternoon. The PAC Anti-Pass Campaign had started. People had gathered in their thousands at police stations around the country without their reference books to be arrested. So far in the Cape Peninsula there had been no bloodshed, although there had been many arrests at Wynberg, Philippi and Nyanga police stations. Agitators were fanning violence in other parts of the country. In Sharpeville Location, outside Vereeniging, it was bedlam. Thousands upon thousands had beset the small police station and then the shooting started. Reinforcements had to be brought in. Forty-five were dead, many more injured. In Langa Township outside Cape Town, trouble was brewing. Multitudes had gathered, reinforcements were being brought in, and police helicopters were monitoring the tense situation.

†

CHAPTER 18

Marja, Langa

Piet, the helicopter pilot, adjusted his visor against the flash of dying sunlight cast up from the ocean. He pushed the joystick forward to descend, anticipating the lurch down, the thudding rotors' shudder turned to a howl in the updraft. A smell of burnt kerosene lay across the globed cockpit as his rapt eyes 360'd the angled view of Langa Township below.

"Daar is kak in die land." Piet's jarring voice crackled in the co-pilot's headphones next to him.

"You're right Piet, big shit. There must be ten thousand," Johan replied, craning forward to see past the instrument panel, his bulk shifting as the aircraft scrawled downwards. The view gained more definition with each falling foot.

Piet and Johan looked at the altimeter — 400 feet — and took a glance at the clock: 5.30 p.m. They could see a crowd of people on the dusty field in front of the Langa Police Station and a volley on their way there. A line of cars stretched to Cape Town; wire-screened police vans flashed their blue lights, ambulances their red, and wide-bodied Saracen armoured trucks lumbered towards the disturbance.

"Piet, hover over the field at 200 feet, and I will report what we see." Johan clicked the microphone with two cocked fingers to connect with Caledon Square Police Station. "This is alpha-tango-bravo-one. Do you read me? Over."

There was a sound of static on their headphones. Piet and Johan witnessed the massive crowd below, dirt kicking up from the helicopter rotors. They saw a makeshift podium with a man standing on it. He was trying to read from a book the size of a Bible. A lot of people seemed to be just sitting on the ground listening.

Both pilots focused their hearing, while Piet steadied the aircraft.

More static wheezing, then, "This is Caledon Square. Give your report. Over."

"Caledon Square. This is Johan, it doesn't look good. I estimate about ten thousand people here at the clearing outside Langa Police Station. And many more on their way. We can see them coming from the barracks and from New Flats... in fact from all over the township. Many are carrying sticks. We don't see guns. Over."

"We have reinforced that police station with sixty extra policemen armed with Sten guns. How many Saracens can you see? Over."

"Caledon Square, we see three. One has a Browning machine gun. We also saw two on Settlers Way. Over."

"How many police vans? Over."

"Ten, sir, round the south side of the field. Two are moving into the crowd. We can see the people getting restless. They are throwing stones at the police. I can see a black man with a gun on the top of a flat. Over."

"We cannot lose a police helicopter. Johan and Piet, get the hell out of there and report back. Over and out."

†

Marja De Koning had watched the helicopter hover above the field. The sound of aircraft overhead often made her think of Indonesia and the Japanese invasion of Bandung, which started with bombing from the air. Her husband, Henry Plaatjies, wanted to join the protest organised at Langa Township. They had travelled from their home on Caledon Street in District Six, parked their car along Washington Avenue and walked the rest of the way to Langa Police Station. They had dressed for the event, Marja in one of her tight, bright-yellow sarongs with her long black hair bunched high and Henry in his usual outfit: a silvery grey suit crowded his ample figure, and his grouper-like face was set off by a stark-white open-necked shirt, unbuttoned to three. They were both not much given to protests. As the gangster boss of the Mongrels, Henry kept a low public profile, while Marja had become civically active and long outgrown her reputation as a prostitute. But the terrible news about Sharpeville was all over the radio, and they were both outraged by the government's violent response to the Anti-Pass Campaign. Henry grabbed Marja's hand and pulled her through the teeming crowd, nearer to the podium. He cupped his hand to her ear and yelled to overpower the percussive thud of the overhanging helicopter.

"Marja, I want to hear what they are going to say. This helicopter will go away. It will be better closer to the podium."

Marja nodded and followed Plaatjies, her brown eyes alert to the surrounding danger. She could see a chain of heavily armed, blue-uniformed, police officers at the field's edge some hundred yards away. Two tractor-wheeled army trucks crouched high between them, flanked by innumerable wire-screened grey S.A.P. vans, their blue lights flashing, and tall radio aerials waving as they took their positions. She could hear the sharp snarl of caged dogs barking within. Surrounding the field, but at a distance, were row upon row of three-storey flats, their sides long ago faded by the Cape sun.

Marja and Henry had not yet reached the podium when the helicopter started climbing above them. A police van, its headlights on, bumped forwards, its windshield reflected the setting sun, blinding Marja for just a moment — she felt dazed and panicked, and cried out to Henry. He tightened his grip and bundled her out of the way into the jostling throng, who were not taking the car invasion lightly. Shouting started and fighting sticks were banged together.

"AIKONA, AIKONA, AMANDLA, AMANDLA." The protesters changed from a smouldering mass to an Impi on war footing, stamping their feet in the dust. They surged towards the oncoming police van. They beat at its sides and cracked the windscreen, occasioning a hasty retreat. But not before a metallic megaphone command spread:

"Disperse or we will arrest you. Disperse in three minutes or we will arrest you."

And then the command "CHARGE. CHARGE" took the wind.

"Caledon Square, Caledon Square, this is Johan, it doesn't look good. Another Sharpeville. Over."

†

Now, I suspect, you may be wondering why I, J.T., am bringing in this device of a recorded cockpit helicopter conversation to give credence to parts of the story. You're probably thinking, where is he going with this? It's breaking up the narrative. Well, I am rather proud of it. And purloining the material was hair-raising.

*One day (once I had finally decided to write this novel and before I fell out of favour with the police), I saw my chance. I had realised I needed to get as much authentic historical material as possible to paint the full political picture to tell this history well and grabbed the opportunity on one of my regular rounds at Caledon Square Police Station. I was being accompanied by an officer down to the prison cells, when we heard a disturbance, on the floor above us at the station's "front desk". The officer pushed me into a side room, said "Wait here," and retrieved his steps upstairs. Noting that its door had a brass plate marked **Private** — **Keep Out**, I closed it gently and looked around. There was no one about (it was a Saturday); but for two shuttered windows, the room was wall-to-wall filing cabinets marked with jurisdictional labels: **District Six**, **Woodstock**, **Langa Township** etc. along one wall and **Case Reports A–Z** along* *another, a broad oak table and scattered chairs at its centre. But one black cabinet caught my attention: **Flight Records**, four drawers tall standing right next to the doorway adjacent to an almost new Xerox machine. And, wonderfully, it had a bunch of keys dangling from its top corner lock, begging me to investigate. I have always been intrigued by helicopters ever since I went up in one and they are a ubiquitous "eye in the sky" for the police here in Cape Town. Well, to cut a long story short, the officer never came back; he must have gone off duty and forgotten about me, and I managed to get a wealth of information (including on Promise, Willem and Marja) out of Caledon Square, in my satchel, that you are now the beneficiaries of in this fine book.*

†

CHAPTER 19

Groote Schuur Hospital

Groote Schuur Casualty Unit overflowed with victims from the Langa riot. Deposited at the front door by a chicane of red-lit ambulances wailing the nation's distress, many had to be turned away to less busy centres like Woodstock, Peninsula or Somerset Hospital.

Although staff had been relocated from other parts of the vast hospital, mayhem reigned. Gunshot, batons and riot sticks had wreaked havoc on human flesh. Trails of blood showed the way from the front door towards the seven trauma bays the victims had been triaged through. There the normally well-polished terracotta floor was awash in pools of blood, vomit and discarded medical detritus: bandages, splints, empty fluid bottles — there wasn't time to tidy up before the next wave of patients.

Dr. Willem Jansen was in his element. This is what he had become very good at. He was an outstanding trauma surgeon and head of a unit that was used to such onslaughts. He managed the stress of life-and-death decisions by remaining dispassionate. He didn't bring emotion to the cold act of surgery. Instead, Willem went into overdrive and dispelled all thought of the human consequence of his actions. Otherwise, he couldn't concentrate on the surgical task at hand. He had taught himself to do so and thus far it had served his patients well.

Sister Promise Madiba loved the work but hated what had been done to her people. She cried inside but composed her exterior. She fought to save the lives of her patients. During a crisis like this, Promise was stationed in one of the two Casualty Units' theatres while Dr. Jansen alternated between them. Willem operated on one casualty with a different sister, while another patient was being prepared next door by Promise, to speed the surgical turnover. Sometimes Willem saw the patient in the trauma bay before going into surgery, other times not. Another doctor had. Instead, he quickly reviewed the case history and X-rays outside on the lightbox, and then stepped into the adjacent theatre, where the patient had been already anaesthetised, prepared and draped so all he had to do was start surgery — the identity of the patient hidden, their face out of view behind the ether screen: a sterile barrier erected by the anaesthetist separating the patient's face from the surgical site, all the better to administer the anaesthetic.

Promise observed the next patient wheeled in through the double doors of the theatre with growing curiosity. She had prepared her theatre rapidly with special care. This was a "stabbed heart", a patient near death. Willem and Promise had operated on many such patients in the past and it was always touch and go. The anaesthetic alone could kill them. The hole in the patient's heart had leaked into its surrounding sack, throttling the heart with its own blood, beat by beat.

Promise had quickly put out two surgical trays draped in sterile white cloth and arranged the sharp surgical instruments in perfect order upon them. The implements reflected silver against the glass-paned cabinets, painted a sickly green, that made up the back wall of the close theatre. Fully dressed in her white sterile outfit, Promise ordered her things precisely with her long rubber-gloved fingers and watched the anaesthetist, Dr. Ozinsky, on her right preparing the anaesthetic machine, his greying hair covered by the multicoloured surgical cap he liked to wear; the weathered anaesthetist was always ready with a quip. He drew up drugs into glass syringes, put them on a purpose-built tray, and checked the anaesthesia machine, backed against the side wall of the room, for good function.

Then he busied himself with the patient, who had been placed on the operating table by the surgical orderlies. He spreadeagled her mottled brown arms on two boards attached for the purpose and hung two bottles of blood high above to drip dark red through twin intravenous catheters, one in each hand, the bright overhead disc-shaped light reflecting its warm glow against the life-giving bottles. He attached an inflatable blood pressure cuff on the right arm, felt the radial pulse beating fast, faintly, and compressed the measuring device's orange rubber bulb, again and again, to extinguish the pulsation at the patient's wrist, its connecting tubing quivering with each pump. Then he released the bulb's valve with a slow hiss and peered intently at the attached foot-sized dial, positioned above the anaesthetic machine to record the blood pressure. The dial's clock hand flicked at 70 mmHg. Much too low. Ozinsky attached three EKG electrode straps and switched on the green-paned oscilloscope: a bright trace marched across its round screen matching the patient's heart rate with a loud tock. One hundred and thirty. Much too high.

He turned to the patient and muttered some encouragement. She was pale and struggling to breathe despite the plastic oxygen mask attached at full flow. Her long black hair matted with sweat was caked with blood. He looked at her heaving chest: a gash over the heart bubbled blood with each rapid breath.

"Promise," he said, "we're in shit. Yell out the door for Dr. Jansen and get him in here fast."

Ozinsky anaesthetised the patient, with thiopentone, placed a breathing tube and connected her to the green ventilator attached to the anaesthesia machine. He put up the ether screen and draped it with the white sterile cloth Promise had passed off to him. Except for her exposed chest, the patient was now hidden under the drapes, her blood pressure unrecordable.

Willem had heard Sister Madiba's plaintive yell and the banging of the double door of the operating theatre as it closed behind her. He was standing at the X-ray box, looking at the black chest film, illuminated from behind. Unmistakable. Cardiac tamponade. The balloon shaped heart before him was the tell-tale sign. He pictured the foot-long incision he would make between the fourth and fifth ribs to get at the heart behind. The release of contained blood as he cut into the pericardial sac, which usually stopped the heart altogether. He would have to squeeze it again to get it going. If it did, he would need to find the hole in the heart, but first lift it out of the chest and look around to find the laceration. Then Promise would have to plug the gash with her finger and he would need to suture it closed. Ozinsky would give blood to keep the patient alive.

Willem walked through the double doors into the hot theatre, scrubbed up, gowned in white, and ready. The smell of ether on the air and the tock of the heartbeat on the EKG machine signalled that it was going far too fast.

"Dr. Ozinsky, what's the blood pressure?" Willem looked down at the patient's chest, moving gently to the swish of the ventilator, the prominent birthmark accentuated further by the glistening iodine wash that had been used to sterilise her chest.

"There is none, Willem. There is no blood pressure."

Willem faltered. The brown birthmark broke his concentration; it could not be possible. The birthmark was like none other; he could recognise it anywhere. But Marja was dead, lost at sea. It was unmistakable, unmistakable.

"Did you see the patient's face, Sister Madiba?"

"Yes, Willem. Yes, Willem, it is like the carving," Promise hissed.

Willem glanced down again, dazed.

"Mijn Godt, het is Marja. Mijn Godt, het is Marja." Willem went into a prolonged spasm. His head arched painfully up, his gaze down, as perspiration beaded his white cap and ran down his tightened face behind his mask, sheening in the overhead arch of light. His hand held hovering above the patient as the paralysis slowly dissipated.

"Dr. Ozinsky, please dab some cold water on Dr. Jansen's brow. The patient is a relative. Willem must concentrate." She turned to Willem, willing him in, even closer to the patient, beckoning him with bright hazel eyes.

"Cut, Dr. Jansen, cut. For God's sake, cut." Promise pressed the scalpel into his shaking hand.

"I can't, Promise. I can't. What if I kill her?"

"She's dead already. Cut. For God's sake, cut."

"I can't," Willem croaked, his knifed hand quaking.

"You must. You must. Cut."

"Okay… stop ventilation, Dr. Ozinsky," Willem cut a wide swathe through Marja's chest, punctured the ballooning heart sac, and released the tamponaded blood, Marja's collapsed heart shrunken in its cavity.

"Give blood, Dr. Ozinsky. More blood. We need to fill the heart." Willem pulled the slippery organ out of Marja's chest and massaged it gently with his cupped hand. He let it go when he felt the first pulse course through its soft muscle, hardened by its life flushing back, and watched it gather strength within her chest. The EKG registered the heart rate: 80. He found the hole that had caused the problem in the atrial appendage, sutured it closed, and stood back, sweating. His hands, which had become faithful, now started shaking again. He looked at Promise, holding her returned gaze steady, until they both looked down at the heart strengthening between them.

Dr. Ozinsky called out the blood pressure: "Ninety. It looks like it's going to work."

"Yes." Willem repeated the phrase in Afrikaans softly: "Dit lyk of dit gaan werk." He raised his right hand above the girl he had promised to protect and clasped the left of the one he now loved — a V for victory. He didn't let go but hung his head and whimpered instead. Erect but prostrate.

Until Dr. Ozinsky lightened the mood. "Dr. Jansen, if you don't let go of Sister Madiba, people will start talking about the two of you."

"Ja, ja, you are correct. Forgive me, Promise." He dropped his right hand and thanked her again with his eyes. Then he sutured closed Marja's gaping wound, taking extraordinary care to perfectly align the cut edges of the brown birthmark exactly. Back to its former lovely shape. He had teased Marja about the mark, that first time under the Dago Waterfalls, in Bandung.

†

From Willem's sixth diary I established that, the very next day, Dr. Willem Jansen and Sister Promise Madiba visited the Intensive Care Unit in their official capacity, burdened by bad news.

Marja Plaatjies née de Koning was clothed in a light blue hospital gown and propped up in bed, still foggy from the powerful sedatives that had been administered post-operatively, and oblivious to last night's events. Her long black hair spread on the white pillow; a thick white plaster covered the sutured gash in her chest. Blood had returned colour to her round face. Her long eyelashes perked up with surprise when Willem came into view and put his bony hand over hers, resting helpless on the white sheet beside her.

"Marja, Marja, Marja. I thought you were dead." He

sat down on the wooden bedside chair and softly caressed her hand.

"Willem. What happened? I thought you were in Holland."

"Agh, Marja, it is a long story. For some other time. But first we must look after you. I am your doctor. And this is Sister Promise Madiba." He beckoned her to come closer. "She saved your life last night."

"My life?" Marja asked. "All I remember is blood exploding from Henry's face and a policeman spearing my chest and then a long ride in the ambulance in pain, and the operating theatre, and the anaesthetist and then nothing till now."

"Au, Au, it must hurt." Promise stepped into Marja's view on the other side of the bed and pressed her hand softly to Marja's exposed shoulder.

"Please, just call me Promise. We have something to tell you about Mr. Henry Plaatjies. Is that your husband's name?"

"Ja, I mean yes. It is. Is he ooraait?"

"I am afraid not," Willem said, holding his hand still on Marja's.

"Hij is dood." Willem moulded her hand gently. "I had to certify him last night."

Promise and Willem watched Marja deflate. Her eyelashes dropped, her shoulders sank, she shrunk smaller into the ample pillows that supported her.

"Then I'm all alone. Unprotected and all alone." She looked down. "I might as well be dead."

"Why, Marja?" Promise asked, the palm of her hand a gentle stroke.

"Henry has many enemies. He was head of the Mongrels. I cannot go back home." A wisp of black hair fell over her crimped face.

"They will take over my house and make me disappear. I know what they are like."

"Okay. Marja. We will make a plan. But first we must get you better. You had a stabbed heart, as we call it here. The policeman's bayonet went through your chest into your atrium. I sutured the hole in your heart, and it takes a while to heal before we can get you home." Willem became the good doctor he had trained so hard to be. "Are you in pain? Let me take your blood pressure."

†

CHAPTER 20

Promise and Marja, District Six

"Marja, are you comfortable? Is there anything I can do for you before I go?" Promise asked, looking into the narrow bedroom warming in the March sunlight, the rumble of distant traffic a hint through the open window.

"My chest hurts when I try to get up and my throat is sore." Marja pressed two anaemic fingers against her neck. "Not tip-top, but on the way. Don't worry yourself." Looking frail in Willem's far-too-large white pyjamas, Marja shifted to get up out of the rattan chair. It creaked as she relented.

"Well, that's my job."

"Not when you are at home, it isn't. Your house is very nice. Thanks for putting me up. Baie dankie." Marja stretched out both hands, her fingertips barely reaching beyond Willem's rolled-back sleeves, to straighten the pins coiffing her bun of dark hair but winced with pain. "Agh, nooit, this won't do. Promise, on second thoughts, can you put a chair out on the stoep? It's such a nice day. I will sit out there later. I like to look up at the mountain."

Promise framed the open doorway in an unbecoming outfit. A white cloth hat held down raging hair; grey shapeless trousers covered agile legs; an ashen shawl shrouded her shoulders.

"You look more like a man than a woman. Where are you going?"

"I'm going on a march." Promise leant into the room, her hands stenting the doorway. "There will be mostly men and so I don't want to stand out."

"Not stand out? That will be difficult in your case, Promise."

Promise sucked in her cheeks, pursed her lips, leant in further and spoke softly. "While you were in hospital much has happened. There have been protests and riots all over the country. A national day of mourning was called by the ANC, and just two days ago a crowd of five thousand of our people gathered in Langa for a funeral to honour your husband and the two others that were killed."

Marja tented her hands tightly over her eyes. Promise stepped into the room, pushed back her floppy hat opening her face and continued, "Shoo, shoo, shoo, it is just too-too bad. All the Africans in Cape Town are out on strike in sympathy. Nothing is working. Nothing. No buses. No trains. They say that even shipping has been delayed in the harbour."

"Well, I'm very, very sad. It is all just terrible. Terrible. Tidak apa-apa." Marja shook her head from side to side until Promise gently stopped her — palming Marja's face.

"But you went to work, didn't you, Promise? Despite the strike," Marja asked in her low voice.

"Yes, I got into Groote Schuur, round the back way, over De Waal Drive. No one could stop me. I'm of more help at the hospital than sitting here with you." Promise stood back and observed Marja, using both hands to gather the shawl that had loosened about her neck.

"I agree," Marja said as she wiped the wetness from her face with Willem's pyjama sleave and slumped back in the snug chair.

"But, Marja, there is something big that I must tell you since you will be staying here with me in this kaia. It might put you at risk." Promise bent forward and gripped the bamboo armrests on Marja's chair, and carefully leant closer.

"What is it?"

"I work for the ANC Women's League. Nelson Mandela asked me to join, so I did. I met him one evening at the Blue Lagoon; my uncle introduced me."

"The Blue Lagoon?" Marja whispered, hoarser than usual.

"Yes."

"I used to work — I mean... perform there." Marja flinched. "As Buttercup the Geisha Girl."

"Hau. That must have been quite something. Perhaps when you are better you will show Willem and I. I'm looking forward to it already. But now I must go to the march."

Then Promise surprised both of them. She bent even closer and kissed Marja lightly on her forehead. Then she stood up, turned briskly and strode out the front door.

†

"Caledon Square. Caledon Square. This is alpha-tango-bravo-one. Do you read me? Over." The army helicopter whirred above Settlers Way en route to the squiggle of De Waal Drive, etched grey against the olive-brown slopes of Devil's Peak. The red-tiled roof of Groote Schuur Hospital pitched into view as Piet, the pilot, banked the aircraft, setting course for the city — the triple-storeyed water tower that centred the striking white building making it look more like a monastery than a hospital.

"This is Caledon Square. Give your report. Over."

"Not good news, I'm afraid," Piet said into the microphone, throttling back to level the aircraft. "Johan will take it from here."

"Caledon Square. This is Johan." The co-pilot yelled to overcome the howl of the turbines thundering overhead. "We saw a pack of people leaving Langa — maybe forty-five minutes ago — stretched from the Athlone Power Station cooling towers all the way along Settlers Way, I would say about a mile long, and now moving along De Waal Drive below. Over."

Static crackled as the helicopter swung.

"This is Caledon Square. How many? Do you see weapons? Where are they heading?" A guttural voice staccatoed the questions.

"Thousands. Ten thousands! I've never seen so many people on the march. De Waal Drive is wall-to-wall people. They are peaceable. No weapons in sight. They are letting cars drive past. I see no disturbance. In fact, they are letting three Saracens through. Over."

"Do you see a ringleader? Someone in front. Describe him to us. Over."

Piet pushed the joystick forward, opened the throttle and descended above the crowd, banking right to give Johan a better view through his binoculars.

"Yes, I see him. Black man. Round face, big smile; he has a brown jacket on, white shirt, grey pullover and blue shorts. No hat. He's got his arms out wide, like many in the front row behind him. He's holding the crowd back from running. Just walking. Over."

"That's probably Philip Kgosana," crackled the guttural voice. "Anyone else suspicious? Over."

"Yes, there is a woman in the front row. I can't see her properly — she has a white hat on and brown hair. Sunglasses. Over."

"Ooraait, take position above the crowd and let us know what direction they take in Cape Town. We have Parliament cordoned off with army tanks — go and check that out so we are sure they are in place. Over and out."

†

Promise arrived right on time to join the mass of people advancing along De Waal Drive. Marching twenty abreast, the crowd was in a celebratory mood, but walked silently, straddling both sides of the highway. Every now and then, marchers moved aside to let traffic past. Many had taken off their coats and pullovers and wound them around their bodies; it had been a long, sweaty journey from Langa and Nyanga Township two hours away. But still they had come, people had joined from the surrounding neighbourhoods

— the swelling throng first climbed the road against the mountain and then descended to the city bowl. A helicopter throbbed overhead, blanking out the hot noon sun as the aircraft's shadow slowly passed over the front of the crowd. Promise could smell a blend of perspiration overpowered by the downdraft of heated oil from the engine floating above. She looked up through dark sunglasses and down again at Philip Kgosana marching to her left on the side. She saw a man shoot out of the crowd and start running ahead as the helicopter ascended away. He was shouting: "Burn down Parliament. Burn down Parliament. Amandla."

Kgosana sprinted after him. Promise could see that his brown jacket was frayed and his blue running shorts had seen better days, but his legs were true. He apprehended the man. Kgosana stopped and talked quietly to him, both their heads bowed. Then, when the column caught up with them, they blended back into the crowd, which descended en masse down Roeland Street, gaining momentum with each new participant, till they came to the crossroads — go to Parliament on the left, or to Caledon Square Police Station on the right.

The multitude chose right, into Buitenkant Street. An extraordinary mass of thousands upon thousands compacted between the tall buildings and funnelled like an advancing wave into the tight street space that fronted the police headquarters for Cape Town. They surged around the grey police van that had been parked on the concrete driveway in front of Caledon Square's arched entranceway, and then extended three swimming pool lengths further along Buitenkant Street — excited protesters pouring down from the mountain to fill the space.

The nervous mass came to an expectant halt at the focal point of the march: the magnificent concrete arched entranceway that centred the forbidding red-bricked police station. Arched high and broad, a polished black police car had been parked beneath it, behind the grey van, creating ten feet of open driveway space between the two stationary vehicles where two blue-jacketed police lieutenants stood guard. An army helicopter rumbled overhead.

Philip Kgosana picked his way to the hub of the crowd, Promise following closely at his side. He stopped in front of the parked police car, eyed the two officers standing to either side, and then asked for an audience with the highest-ranking officer in charge.

Kgosana waited patiently, the crowd hemmed in place restless behind him. Others to each side — some had climbed onto concrete parapets lining the police building; others hung from its barred window coverings to get a better view of the proceedings.

Ten unarmed policemen marched out and positioned themselves along the driveway to stand still at attention. After two or three minutes, Colonel Ignatius Terblanche followed. Cleanshaven, and in full uniform, he had been delayed by a telephone call from the Minister of Justice. The two police lieutenants stood to attention at his side.

(Please note that Colonel Terblanche is not a relative of mine. I was sent out by the Cape Times Herald *to report on this demonstration. It was terrifying to be at its epicentre.)*

"Good afternoon. I am Colonel Terry Terblanche." He fiddled with the leather swagger stick clapped under his left arm and looked into his opponent's dark eyes.

"Gentleman to gentleman, what are your demands, Mr. Kgosana?"

"Colonel Terblanche, we have marched to seek the release of all the prisoners that have been arrested this past week in contravention of the pass laws." Kgosana spoke forcefully but smiled, his cheekbones prominent over his short goatee.

"We seek an urgent audience with the Minister of Justice, Mr. F.C. Erasmus."

"Mr. Kgosana, he cannot be disturbed. He is at lunch."

The crowd, quietened to a shiver to hear the crucial conversation taking place in front of them, released a collective groan at this riposte.

"However, Mr. Kgosana" — Colonel Terblanche sharpened his voice, squared his back and tautened his sweating face — "I give you my word that if you turn back the crowd and march back peacefully the way you came, I will arrange an interview for you with the minister this afternoon at five o'clock. You can return then. I will promise you that." Colonel Terblanche continued, noting the broad smile of satisfaction that played on Philip Kgosana's face. "We will provide you with a police megaphone so that you can speak to the crowd, if you agree."

"Yes, I agree, I will take you at your word, Colonel."

"You have my word." The black and white hands shook, formally.

A photographer took photos, catching Promise in the image with Kgosana.

A cheer of jubilation arose from the assembled mass at this great victory and Philip Kgosana was hoisted onto a marcher's shoulders in celebration. He was handed a wired microphone connected to a gleaming loudspeaker that was held aloft by a plain-clothed policeman who jogged beside him. A great beaming smile across his young face, Kgosana megaphoned the march's success from his elevated position — his metallic voice enhanced by the public address system provided by the South African Police. He enjoined the swarming crowd like a goatherd his flock. They made a collective turnabout and jostled and jived, back through Buitenkant, up Roeland, and onto De Waal Drive, cheering, sweating but peaceable — a victory march back to the townships where they had come from.

†

CHAPTER 21

Marja and Promise, District Six

Marja wept. Tears trickled down the faded surface of her face. Her long black hair — now suddenly streaked white — funnelled her despair like a flue. Late April's sunlight cast bright reflections against the gleaming green-walled room; a leaking tap dropped in loud sympathy within a rusted enamel sink. Marja clutched her left lapped wrist with anaemic fingers and rocked back and forth in her seat in front of the kitchen table.

Promise attempted consolation. She draped her arm around Marja's shrunken shoulder and drew her kitchen stool closer. They sat looking out the open window, the white flecked sky and Devil's Peak a magnificent presence beyond.

"I'm sure it will get better with time, Marja, shush, shush." Promise milked Marja's shoulder, kneading rhythmically.

"No, it won't. No, it won't, I have been here before. I don't want to die. I don't want to be afraid of death all the time." She shook her head, her gruff voice coming in short gasps. She tightened the grip on her wrist. "Always looking over my shoulder for someone to get me. I feel so vulnerable, and I am so ashamed."

"Shoo, Marja, shoo," Promise sounded softly. "Ashamed of what? Whatever can that be?"

"Ashamed now that Willem has found me. I would rather die than tell him the truth."

"I am sure Willem will accept everything. He suffered greatly from the camps. He is quite broken but I think he still loves you. He told me that you had been lost at sea on the way to Amsterdam, too-too many years ago. He has a wooden carving of your pretty face. He made it himself in Indonesia. He has carried it around with him ever since. That's how I recognised you during the operation. I had seen it standing on his bedside table at his flat in Rondebosch."

"It is just unbelievable, unbelievable, that we have lived in this city unknowing, unknowing of each other's presence. Do you know, when Willem came to Cape Town, I thought he was still in Holland?"

"Oh yes, about five years ago, I remember it clearly. Willem was quite a sensation when he arrived at Groote Schuur Hospital. I was the scrub sister for his first operation. He was terrified, shaking. I could see he was deeply troubled. But he was a very good surgeon. Straight and true. And you know of course that he was the one who saved your life, not me. He fixed the hole in your heart. I assisted him. How could he ever not accept your past?"

"Ja. Nee. But still," Marja whispered, "the shame is terrible."

"You can tell me." Promise lowered her eyes and gave Marja another caress.

"Agh." She started sobbing, and then silenced. A hadada cawed overhead loudly, breaking the trance. "Perhaps I should start at the beginning?" Marja took the offered handkerchief, blew her nose wetly, knitted her brow and, with strength gathering in her raw voice, started slowly. She told of Willem and her birth on the same day and of their growing up together like twins, the only children of two neighbour military families in Bandung. The schooling, the cycling, the kite-flying and the million pleasures gathered. She told of their budding love for each other, and Willem's silly remark about the brown birthmark on her chest that so embarrassed her and he found cute. She spoke of the impending threat of the Japanese invasion, the celebration at the Dago Falls Club, the solemn family promise made, and their separation upon the fall of Java. She told of the bravery of Willem's mother in the camps, in trying to protect her from the Japanese soldiers and of her own decision to become a comfort woman. Anything was better than starving to death. And then of her (little Marja) — she shuddered — becoming a much-favoured geisha for the Japanese officers.

She had learnt how to manipulate men to her own advantage. She told of the Japanese capitulation, the setting free from the camps, and the marauding Indonesian resistance fighters that were massacring the whites and the Indos like her. (She omitted the rape; she had packed that away in her subconscious.) She did tell Promise that she was attacked beside a kali in Bandung and left for dead; she washed up on its shore surrounded by floating corpses. That's when Marja de Koning missed the first boat to Amsterdam. The next she could travel on stopped in Cape Town, on its way to Holland.

Marja sniffed, blew her nose again, looked Promise in the eyes. She noted her unruly thatch of copper hair, lit up by sunlight, the window's reflection in her hazel eyes, the sharp features of her angled face, widened by a spreading smile. Promise's full lips flattened as her mouth opened pink on perfect sparkling white, the small pores of her radiant face.

"How old are you?" Marja asked. "You look so beautiful."

"Thirty-one and you?"

"Thirty-three, same as Willem, but I feel old and frail. My chest still aches, beneath the scar. It feels like my heart is still open to the air, under my sarong. The pain is always there, reminding me. I could have been dead. Still… talking to you helps. Thanks. Terima kasih banyak. Do you know what that means?"

Promise shook her head; her hair swayed gently.

"Baie dankie. Thank you. See, I have learnt Afrikaans like the locals. I have had to, to get by."

"So, what happened next, Marja? Why are you in Cape Town? Or don't you want to speak about it?"

"Well, agh, I might as well tell you. Maybe you can tell Willem for me. Will you do that?"

"Ewe, yes," Promise said.

Marja continued, her head down.

She told of her suicidal depressions: on the ship from Batavia, and after her capture by the Mongrels in Cape Town. She told of the forced prostitution, and the fact that she grew to accept it, to survive. Sex gave her power but she came to hate men. Marja became good at prostitution, could manipulate men, and so fight back against the shame. She told of becoming Buttercup the Geisha Girl at the Blue Lagoon, and setting her sights on the Mongrels' boss, Henry Plaatjies, to become his wife, get from under prostitution, and lead a more respectable life. (She thought it better to leave mention of Desi, her girlfriend from District Six, for another time.)

Marja closed with what brought her to Promise. The day of the riots at Langa. Henry's face exploding blood on to her hair and the jagged pain of the bayonet plunged into her chest. She cried a little more, sniffed and stopped.

"You know, the strangest thing is, I don't even miss him. Henry is just gone but I am so lonely; I feel so, so alone."

"Shush, shush, shush." Promise gave Marja's arm another squeeze and held her hand in place firmly until the shaking stopped. Then she stood up to make a cup of tea for them. She bent over the green enamel stove, positioned at the window, struck a Lion match to life — the puff of smoke rich with the bracing smell of sulphur — opened the gas flow to the burner, secured the blue guttering flame and put the battered aluminium kettle to boil. Then she went into the adjacent room to find some cookies and compose herself.

Promise picked up an old newspaper and turned to the op-ed page.

†

The Cape Times Herald

The Paper that Cares.

April 11, 1960

Verwoerd Assassination Attempt – Philip Kgosana Arrest Unleashes Backlash.

John Terreblanche

The assassination attempt on Prime Minister Verwoerd at the Rand Easter Show two days ago should have surprised no one. David Pratt, the perpetrator, wanted to shoot the "epitome of apartheid". There had been no alternative for redress against the Nats as far as he was concerned.

After the deadly riots of Sharpeville and Langa just three weeks ago, the country has descended into mistrust and chaos. Protest marches, arson and strikes are violently suppressed by bannings, arrest and arbitrary justice. On March 30 the National government irretrievably fractured the people's trust. I was there to witness it, in the front row.

Colonel I.P. Terblanche offered Mr. Philip Kgosana a guarantee. Should he lead the 30,000 people that had marched to the Caledon Square Police Station in protest back peaceably whence they came, Terblanche would arrange an audience with the Minister of Justice that afternoon. Kgosana honoured the agreement, thereby averting certain bloodshed, but the government didn't, breaking all trust. Mr. Philip Kgosana and a few others were arrested that same afternoon when they returned, and a country-wide state of emergency was declared the same day.

†

"Marja, hau, Marja, I'm in the newspaper." Promise folded the broadsheet open on the kitchen table and pointed at the photograph of the jubilant crowd wedged in front of the Caledon Square Police Station.

Marja stood up to see better, leaning over the paper to do so. Her long hair fell across Promise's shoulder. "Yes, definitely, you should have kept your white hat on so the police couldn't recognise you. Now they know that you were there." She turned her head sideways to look in Promise's eyes. Something unformed passed between them.

"Yes, I'm too-too vain. I wanted to look nice, and that hat was bothering me." Promise smiled. "But it may well have been a stupid move. Only time will tell. I wasn't doing anything wrong so there is no basis for an arrest."

"Well, you look on fire, smouldering; let's hope the police don't set a trap for you. You must be extra careful now... Isn't Willem coming over next Saturday?"

"Yes, it's high time that we have a celebratory dinner together now that you are well recovered from your surgery."

"Would it be ooraait if I make nasi goreng rames? That was Willem's favourite dish." Marja asked.

"Alright? That would be great. We can go out shopping together, Marja, when you feel ready. I'm sure you know where the best spices can be bought. I have Debbie's — ah, ah, I mean... an extra shopping bag for you."

"Yes, and I need some new clothes. May be a bright sarong will help cheer me up. And some hair colour. Do you know The Little Wonder Store on Hanover Street? They import batik from Indonesia."

†

CHAPTER 22

Willem and Promise and Marja

Willem ran. Arms knifing the air, he jogged up past Mostert's Mill over De Waal Drive and onto the mountain along a dust track that felt gratefully familiar to each footfall upwards. He was confused, sad, panicked and burdened by guilt.

Panting with the effort, hot sweat running the length of his body, Willem watched the surroundings change as he set his mind to work through his problems. The fine-smelling fynbos turned to craggy rock, the sparse resinous fir trees left below, as he sprinted up to the King's Blockhouse. His emotions sharpened with the elevation.

He could not fully believe it was Marja, till the next day after the operation, when he went to visit her with Promise. She had been dead to him, but he had brought her back. But was he not responsible for her fate in the first place? Had he not abandoned Marja when he couldn't find her in Bandung, and left for Amsterdam on the M.S. *Johan van Oldenbarnevelt* to start medical school? (Promise had told him about Marja's horrid story in the camps.) He felt responsible for Marja's state. But Marja had changed irreparably. Although she still looked like her carving, her spirit had turned. From something gay and free and bird-like to reptilian. Tarnished and spent. Her smile a hesitant smear. Did he still love her? No, only time could tell, but he thought that was gone. He detected only traces of past feelings as he watched her, but they had little resonance within. He wondered if she felt the same.

Willem was grateful to Promise for giving him the strength to save Marja but was anguished by the fact of the police attack that almost killed her. The random unpredictable violence of their past in Indonesia had returned in South Africa. Nowhere was safe. He could not protect Marja from the authorities. And worst of all he had a sense of wrongdoing; he had failed Marja. Willem stopped running, his arms at his side. He was hyperventilating, his head arched up and his gaze locked down on the footpath, his white plimsolls covered in fine dust. He doubled over and retched in a bush; the vomit stunk on his breath. He stood panting and keened softly to himself, shook his perspiring head free and started up the steep footpath again, stones crunching underfoot as he climbed unsteadily.

There was only one way; they had to get out of the country. But Promise wouldn't leave; she had told him so before. And he couldn't leave without her. Willem's feelings towards Promise had heightened as he watched her kindnesses with Marja and Promise's willingness to take Marja into her home in District Six and look after her. She offered the protection from the Mongrels he could not give. (The District Six mafia was all too aware that Promise Madiba was underground in the ANC and should be left alone.)

In fact, if he thought it through, Willem was in thrall to Promise. He needed to be with her, to make love to her. Then he felt complete, calm and brave again. He could picture Promise running in front of him up the hill. The flash of her fluid brown legs, the crux of her skintight shorts at their silken apex, her graceful hourglass figure crowned by ringlets of tawny hair bobbing as she accelerated away ahead of him. He couldn't get enough of her. Strange that!

†

Promise was scared. She walked at a fast clip. Her white nurse's cap alert on her shag of hair, her red and blue cape trailed in the funnel of wind that her quick steps fetched. Out the front door to Groote Schuur Hospital and back round alongside the nursing school and then, past that, up the little pathway that led to De Waal Drive. She paused at the roadside and looked left towards Hospital Bend, where Debbie had died in the motor crash. That always gave her pause; it didn't feel like just two years ago. Almost to the day. That terrible rainy day when Willem had first showed his kindness, comforting her in the trauma bay where Debbie lay. Promise shook her head, looked right and left and then right again, and sprinted across the road and then walked up the mountain path beyond. (She took off her white nurse's shoes and walked barefoot to keep them dust-free.)

Promise feared losing Willem to Marja. She had come to love the strange and damaged man. His drawn skull-like face, pale wiry frame and elegant fingers. His shy hidden strength, sparsely clothed by quiet kindness, courage and fairness. His occasional bright smile when she amused him. Promise could not fathom Willem's reaction to Marja. Had he idolised her in death and was now uncertain of the reality of eighteen years gone by? Promise liked Marja. She felt sorry for her and wanted to help her get better; help bring a smile back to her faded face, to wipe away the tears and start afresh. Free to choose her own path, really, for the first time. (Her nurse's training had taught her how survivors of near-death experiences often reset their lives upon recovery.) But she didn't want to lose Willem to Marja. Why should it be one or the other? Perhaps there was room for both?

†

Marja tilted in the rocking chair. She liked the smell of the blooming red bougainvillea that decorated Promise's porch but feared the buzzing bees that gathered pollen from the potted plant at the side of the opened front door. She rocked back taking in the bouncing view of Table Mountain in front of her as she moved up and down, her brown feet flexing on the smartly painted balustrade that enclosed the oblong stoep. She was proud of her newly bought bright-yellow sarong, tightly bound across her chest, her surgical scar an enflamed stripe through the brown birthmark at her breast line. The wound felt contained and protected by the new batik cloth. The fabric's faint smell of candlewax reminded her of Indonesia. Iron tablets and vitamins had restored colour and texture to her cheeks, Clairol jet-black lustre to her hair. Marja was, yet again, beginning to accept her fate. *Inshallah*, she thought. What worried her most was what Willem would think of her damaged past now that he knew. Would he be understanding and loving like before or disgusted and repelled? And what was the situation between Willem and Promise? Clearly it must be more than professional, but how much more? *Oh well, time would tell*, she thought. *The Saturday dinner would be a litmus test.*

†

So, as I pictured it later, all three must have been suitably nervous about the Saturday dinner. And all three prepared in their own way.

Promise freshened the small cottage. She opened all the doors and windows to air out the rooms; she let a vigorous northeaster funnelling up the steep cobbled street outside blow through. Then she dusted and polished each space in turn. Starting with the terracotta stoep that spanned the front, she progressed through to the parquet-floored lounge that matched the length of the compact house — four oak doors opened on the adjacent rooms. First, the square black and white tiled kitchen painted light green, which doubled as a dining room, then a sliver of a pink-tiled toilet-cum-bathroom, to be followed by the two bedrooms: the "master", a tad bigger than the "guest" but both with glorious views of the slopes of Devil's Peak off in the near distance. Promise loved those views. She rearranged the soft animal hides that covered the lounge and bedroom floors, made sure that the many

African masks hung straight on the walls, the zebra-skin-bedecked furniture was angled just right, and the imboya coffee table placed just so. She looked on with satisfaction; she wanted to create the atmosphere of an African Boma, a dwelling of safety.

Marja prepared the planned Indonesian meal. She could have spent all day on that. Rasping and frying the coconut with spices to make seroendeng; creating searing sambals; boiling the oil, to transform tapioca shrimp wafers to kroepoek; frying plantains to a crisp; sauteing spiced rice and firing pork saté slices gathered on sharp bamboo sticks to a succulent crisp. Making nasi goreng rames was something she had learnt from her mother and so it soothed her; the pungent smells brought her back to Bandung. She thought of happier times with Willem as a boy — little did they know what was ahead of them; how could they? And how could they now? All she could be was herself, with Willem. Emotion rose like the pressure in the cooker on the gas stove in front of her, finding release in a watery stream.

Willem got drunk. He first got dressed for the evening and packed his well-worn leather valise for an overnight stay. A good suit always gave him confidence. It being autumn with a nip on the evening air, Dr. Willem Jansen donned a grey pinstriped worsted, matched a white pocket square with a crisp open-neck shirt, polished his black boots, put on his matching hat and drove his Beetle to an unobtrusive parking spot within a half-mile walking distance of Promise's house. Then he took out his bottle of Bols Jenever from the car's glove compartment and settled down to enjoy the street scene playing out before him: the hustle and bustle of a side street in District Six on an early Saturday evening. He didn't feel like he was drinking alone because he was parked outside a shebeen. The shabby place was fronted by a dinged-up door in constant motion, the clientele noisy and of unsteady gait. Two tapped on his window and asked for a dop. Willem shooed them away and then, feeling a little less apprehensive about the dinner, returned the half-emptied earthenware flagon to its hiding place, locked the car and made his unstable way to Promise's dimly lit street corner.

Turning the corner clutching his valise, Willem appeared quite surprised to come upon my Porsche convertible parked across the street; such fancy cars were rare in this area of the district. He must have been only vaguely aware of my hulking figure hunched over the steering wheel because he crossed the road in front of me without another glance in my direction, looked up to the mountain, adjusted his bag's strap over his shoulder and continued the hundred or so cobblestone yards up to Promise's stoep. I could see him knock on the door and disappear inside via my right wing mirror.

Promise and Marja had prepared well for the dinner celebration. Indonesian dishes simmered deliciously over blue flames on the three hobs of the gas stove. Two long white candles, atop amber wine bottles, guttered on the centred kitchen table reflecting green light from the gloss of the painted room; bright moonlight shone down through the windows from high above Devil's Peak silhouetted in the distant evening glow. Soft gamelan music played in the background from the record player in the lounge. An occasional car could be heard shifting in the street. Voices of passers-by fluctuated through the opened windows.

The women had dressed for the occasion, Promise in a sheer white lace dress that revealed more than it hid and Marja in her signature low-cut yellow sarong — both with their long hair down, falling tawny-brown and black to their bare brown shoulders.

Neither seemed to impress Willem, who was even more taciturn than usual when they welcomed him at the door. He took off his hat, dropped his bag in a corner and meandered through to the rectangular kitchen table to sit down at its short side, where a place had been set for him. He tapped the wine glass standing at the ready with his index finger and asked for the red. Promise poured some while Marja dished up the plates, upon which they proceeded to eat. Promise next to Willem and Marja next to her along the long flank of the table, both facing towards the windows, they watched the full moon slowly rising while they ate in silence, outside noises the only disturbance — the record had stopped — until Willem broke the strain.

"What of the promish? What of the promish?" He took yet another sip of wine and glared first at Marja, and then at Promise and then at Marja again, fixing her eyes.

"Well, what of it?" Marja cast her eyes down to the table.

"I didn't keep it, Marja. I abandoned you to your lot in Indonesia. All alone. I knew your mother was dead but not the fate of my mother nor of our fathers in Burma. It was only when I got to Holland that I found out we were orphans. I prepared for you to come and join me in

Leiden; you sent me a letter but you weren't on the ship. I never heard from you again, not another letter, telegram, nothing! Nada! Why not? Whyever not?" Willem's eyes were wild and wounded, Marja's dull in her pained face.

"I was ashamed. So ashamed." Marja started crying; Promise patted her hand, stretched on the table before them.

Willem looked down at the spent Indonesian food. "Yes," he said, "Promise told me all about it. But that should surely be in the past. I hear that you are trying to lead a respectable life now. Ssurely, ssurely, that is all anyone can asshk for."

Promise interjected for them both. "Yes, that is in the past. Let us now look to the future." She softened her lips, looking them both in the eye in turn.

"That's what I'm worried about too. Our future," Willem said. "We have to get out of this bloody country to stay alive."

"But, Willem, you are the only one who can do that," Marja said. "Promise and I have discussed it. We would both need exit visas, and the government will *never* grant special exceptions for the likes of us. Never in a hundred years. And this is my home; this is me now. I am a Capey now, and this is where I want to be."

"Me too," Promise said fiercely. "I'm not going nowhere but here. Now let's lighten up a little, Willem. You can go but I don't want you to. I want you in my bed tonight, nowhere else." Promise pressed the palm of her left hand to Willem's cheek and stroked his face.

Marja stiffened, turned a quick glance at Willem — who looked down — and then sideways at Promise, who met her gaze. Marja moved her hands below the table and wrung her left wrist with her right repetitively, until Promise reached down to stop the motion. Connecting the two with her caresses, Promise continued, "Let's have no further talk of leaving the country, please." She looked from one to the other and, relinquishing her touch, picked up the bottle of wine left on the table with two hands and divided its remains equally into the three glasses glinting in the sputtering candlelight in front of them. "Let me propose a toast to the three of us. To our good health and a long life in freedom. Drink up and let's go to bed." She blew out the guttering candles. "Tomorrow is another day."

†

CHAPTER 23

Groote Schuur Hospital

As autumn turned to rainy, cold winter and gradually to sun-blessed spring, rumours at the Casualty Unit intensified. They had started when the hospital authorities realised that Marja Plaatjies was being discharged into the care of Sister Promise Madiba, and were fanned volubly by an orderly, Japie van Wyk, who had witnessed the drama unfold in the operating theatre that fateful day. Van Wyk had overheard Promise tell Dr. Ozinsky that the stabbed heart patient in extremis was a *relative* of Dr. Jansen's. The hospital orderly, a sinuous curved creature who seemed to live on cigarette smoke, had gadded about his theory that what had unfolded in the operating theatre that day was a ménage à trois, a drietal. He was not shy to provide updates to anyone who would listen on his take as to the temperature of the surgeon's and the scrub sister's relationship (warming) and was a stalwart National Party sympathiser who spoke only Afrikaans, insisting that this was the only true Boere language: "None of this English kak!"

Van Wyk was nicknamed *smokie* because he had a perpetually burning cigarette stuck at his lip when he wasn't carting around patients and prided himself on being a font of information to the police reporters that frequented the hospital. A little money on the side loosened his tongue further, and copies of medical records, later entered into court proceedings, were not unknown to have been lifted, although their source was never verified.

†

ACT III

CHAPTER 24

Police Raid, District Six

The police helicopter, rotors thundering, scribbled down towards the small cottage embedded among the row of houses sloped up the dark road. The faint gloss of its corrugated iron roof glinting in the midnight moon.

The pilot spoke into his helmet microphone: "This is alpha-tango-bravo-one. Caledon Square, do you read me? Over."

"We read you. Do you have the target house in your sights? Over," crackled in the two pilots' headphones.

"Yes, we do. We have levelled off at 700 feet. Piet here; Johan has the searchlight at the ready to light the way… over."

"Hold steady and tell us when you spot the police van, over."

The pilot chuckled. And added, "By the way, who is the raid on? Over."

"Well, the word from the Groote Schuur is that a head of the ANC's Woman's League has taken a Dutch doctor as a lover. We want to catch them in the act, over."

"O.K., I see the police van coming along Hanover Street. Tell us when you want Johan to switch on the searchlight and cone down. Over."

"Alpha-tango-bravo-one, hold your position, till we tell you. We are communicating with the police van. Over and out."

The helicopter hovered high in the dark sky, a speck of turbulent noise reverberating off the great shadowed mountain; a cloud had shifted across the quarter moon.

Then.

"This is Caledon Square. Do you have the house in your sights? Over."

"Yes, it has a steel roof. Over."

"O.K., Piet. Searchlight on when the police van is at the bottom of the cross street. Keep us informed. Over."

The buzz and wheezing crackle in their headphones electrified the two hyped-up pilots floating above the target.

"Caledon Square, Caledon Square, police van at corner. Johan, light on, were going down, 350 feet, 300 feet, 250 feet; Caledon, we can see the police van outside the house next to a black Beetle; 200 feet, three officers are getting out, one dog. Levelling at 200 feet. Aitsa! Caledon Square! Caledon Square! I see a naked black girl. She's jumped out the window. Fok! She's running up the street. Over."

"God dammit. Follow her. Over."

Piet angled the helicopter in pursuit, its rotored tail lifting so the two pilots momentarily lost sight of their target, the searchlight beam useless.

"Johan, where is she? Can you spot her?"

"Nope, I think she's already in the mountain, under the trees. I couldn't get a photo."

"Caledon Square, Caledon Square, we have lost her. Over."

No response, just wheezing and crackling through the headphones. Piet pulled back the joystick and the helicopter circled back for another look, in search of their prey.

"Alpha-tango-bravo-one, this is Caledon Square. Do you read us? Over."

"Yes, loud and clear. We have lost her. Over."

"Ooraait, ooraait, moenie worry nie, the police officers will sort it out on the ground. But have one more look, boys. After that you two are released from duty; fly back safely. Bravo Zulu. And don't forget, gentlemen, tomorrow you must vote in the referendum. Over."

"Yes, Kaptein," came two shrill pilot voices. "For the Republiek. Baie dankie. Over and out."

†

"Hau! We're in kak," Promise shouted as the thundering throb of a descending police helicopter enveloped the bedroom, its blistering light penetrating the dark cottage in a white blaze. Rousing from under Willem, Promise catapulted out of the back window and shot out onto the cobbled street, the dead streetlamps silhouetted by the police searchlight hunting for its quarry. Promise could almost feel its warmth and smell the kerosene that powered the hovering aircraft, her nakedness making her feel even more vulnerable as she ran up towards De Waal Drive. She knew that if she could get into the fir trees that populated the lower reaches of Devil's Peak before the police could take a night-photograph there could be no evidence against her. Willem and Promise had talked often of a possible police raid but never envisaged that they would use a helicopter. Promise started panting with the effort; she could hear the helicopter circling. It was pitch dark as she crossed the road. No cars at this time of night. Now she had to scramble up a steep section of the path, another 400 yards to the trees. Run. Run. She could sense the helicopter closing in from the distance. Panting, she made it into the trees, the overhead searchlight useless as she recovered her breath sweating under the canopy hidden from sight. She slumped onto her haunches, bowed her head, and covered her nakedness with her arms into a ball, her calloused soles equal to the harsh mountain. *What now?* she thought. She was starting to shiver; it was a cold night. *The police can only find our soiled sheets and Willem will say that I am working at GSH, so there is no evidence of a crime. And Marja didn't have sex with Willem, that's for sure. But you can never trust these bastards. They'll do anything to make an arrest.*

After an hour or so, an uncontrollable shake racked Promise back into motion to warm up. Knowing well the peril of hypothermia, she slowly jogged back the way she came and stopped at the higher reaches of Upper Melbourne Street. A dog barked and then settled; the streetlights were still out, the moon low behind a cloud, so there was very little light to see by as she crept to the cottage stark naked. Feeling like a furtive animal returning to her lair, Promise slunk onto the stoep across a slice of dim light. The front door ajar, she slipped in and closed it softly.

"Willem, Marja, anyone here?" Finding no one, she went to the bathroom, filled the tub with warm water and lay down for a while. Then she sat up, pulled her arms around her knees and bowed her head. Her wet hair drooped over her shoulders; drops of water plonked loudly in the stillness. She shook her head. "Aikona. Aikona." A shower of droplets battled the quiet.

†

During the police raid, Officer Piet Marais had ordered Willem and Marja to sit on the lounge couch together while the three policemen looked for evidence. Marja had been asleep in white pyjamas, while Willem had quickly dressed before the uniformed policemen had burst into the front door, a barking dog and the sound of a receding helicopter filling the tiny cottage. Having been served with a warrant for the search, both Marja and Willem sat quietly awaiting developments when the raid came to a climax.

"Kaptein, come and look here, Kaptein."

"Viljoen, what is it?" Marais had exited the kitchen, looked at Marja and Willem to reassure himself they were still sitting on the couch, and then walked into the bedroom.

"The bed sheet is sticky with spunk. And black curly hairs. Doctor Jansen is blond."

"Very well." Marais walked over to stand in front of the pair, the pitch of his voice sharp with tension, "Dr. Jansen and Miss? Miss…? What is your name again?"

"Marja de Koning."

"Whatever it is. You are both under arrest for contravention of the Immorality Act."

Willem exploded. Incensed, he got up from where he sat and took a swipe at the officer, narrowly missing his moustached face. Unpractised in the art of fist fighting, he proved no match for the trained policeman, who responded with a vicious upper cut that landed on Willem's eye, launching him back onto the couch.

"That will teach you to mess with the police, Dr. Jansen. In South Africa you *do not* mess with the police." Officer Marais bristled, patting his fist with his left hand to soothe the impact of Willem's face.

"Yes, officer," Willem replied, cupping his hand over his eye, while Marja, rubbed his leg.

"Right! Now! We will have no further nonsense from the two of you. We are taking you to the police station to be charged. Get dressed and bring your I.D. documents at the double."

Willem and Marja sat across from each other in the back of the caged police van. Allowed to change before being taken away, Marja had put on a black sarong and a canvas jacket while Willem had added a blazer to his outfit. A large Alsatian sat slobbering next to them. The animal had been put into the van after Marja and Willem had been ordered to sit on its steel benches and was attached to a handle at the back door by means of a steel-ring choker that throttled the dog if he got too close to the two prisoners. Hence docile, the animal sat panting, drooling and licking his lips, and gave off a rank smell that filled the enclosed car space completely sealed off from the front driving section, where the three police officers commandeered the car at speed on its way to the Caledon Square Police Station.

Willem had to sit hunched over because of his length so their foreheads bumped lightly when the police van hit a pothole.

"Aitsa, Willem, not to worry, we will get out of this mess. I've been in this situation before. It's a case of mistaken identity and they can't have anything on Promise, so we should be fine once we get to the police station; they can clear it up there."

"Agh, Marja, I don't think so. I think they'll put us in jail tonight. I shouldn't have got so angry."

The van hit another pothole, so they both clasped their seats to steady themselves and watched the Alsatian's choker tighten around his neck.

"Marja, I always thought it would come to this with Promise. I was so scared of getting involved with the police, especially with that Immorality Act hanging over our heads. And now, no matter what, I think they are going to put us in jail for the night. That's what I am most scared of."

"Toe maar, Willem." Marja bent to rub both his legs wedged to the side of hers, her silken hair bouncing on her shoulder. "We should be out in a day."

"Ja, I prepared for that eventuality. I have a lawyer's card in my wallet. To post bail if we need it. But I don't want even one night. I have had too much of that. Too much." He clasped the seat tightly with both hands and bared his teeth. "Too much."

"When, Willem?"

"In the camps. In solitary. And torture."

"Torture?"

"Ja, like this dog with a choker around his neck, they tried to throttle me with water — to get me to confess."

"Agh, Willem, dit is verskrikkelijk, verskrikkelijk."

The van lurched to a halt, the back door was wedged open and, after the dog had been relieved of its choker and jumped out, Officer Marais marched the two into the front office to be charged, and, despite Dr. Jansen's many protestations, remanded them into custody overnight.

†

Two days later, having been released on bail after an overnight stay in prison by Mr. Lamprecht Labuschagne B.A. L.L.B., Marja and Willem sat waiting in the vestibule of the lawyer's plush office on Buitenkant Street. The barrister was late for the appointment, detained in court. He rushed in all a-fluster, nodded to me sitting quietly in the corner smoking my Peterson, and then led the couple into his mahogany office, sat them down across from his smart desk, and flopped into his leathered chair. A large befreckled man with a mop of ginger hair, he sported a stout moustache and an affable smile.

"Well, Dr. Jansen and Miss Marja de Koning, it seems we have got into a bit of a pickle, haven't we?" Noting that only Marja nodded, he nevertheless continued. "Doctor, it seems you have also got into a spot of bother with your eye there. What happened?"

Willem told him, holding his hand to shade the injured eye as he spoke.

"Except that it hurts, I am not sure that it will injure your case much as it is about as bad as it can get," the lawyer said.

"Surely that cannot be the case, Mr. Labuschagne." Marja twirled her loose hair around her index finger. "It is simply a situation of mistaken identity with only circumstantial evidence."

"Yes, I aim to prove that, but it may be complicated by your past record, Miss de Koning." Labuschagne turned to Willem to gauge his response to this point.

Willem just sucked his teeth and ran his hand once back through his hair.

"I am afraid that after reading the police's charge sheet — which I have made a copy of for you to take home — they have thrown the book at you. You see, because you are a Dutch citizen, the government may wish to make an example of you, to show their independence of foreign influence." Labuschagne looked at Willem, who stared in front of him, his face unmoving. "A political statement of rectitude with regards to the Immorality Act. You know, of course, Dr. Jansen, that the Treason Trial is not going at all well for the government and that they are nevertheless forging ahead to become a republic, with only half the *white* population in favour of it. In the face of this the government may want to demonstrate their piety and resolve by prosecuting a foreigner like you transgressing the Immorality Act with a Coloured girl. After all, the Immorality Act and the Mixed Marriages Act are the bedrock of apartheid. As far as the Nats are concerned, there must be no interbreeding allowed to sully the purity of the white race. So I expect that the court — that is, the *government* through the attorney general — will likely prosecute your case strenuously and ask for the maximum penalty — seven years of imprisonment, if not the two whiplashes mandated by the law of old."

Marja turned to look at Willem for his reaction; having placed her hand on his leg, she could feel he had tensed under the black trousers of his suit.

Willem looked directly at Labuschagne and said, "I cannot go to jail ever again. Never. What can you do about it?"

"I think we can win the case. First, we will have to go in front of a magistrate. If that works, fine, but, if not, I will attempt to get you immediate bail and we will petition the Supreme Court. Trust me, I'm good. I will get you both free." He stood up behind the desk and leant over to shake Willem's hand. Then he moved around the desk towards the two and shepherded them into the vestibule. He concluded with a request. "I would be very pleased if you would meet with my friend, Mr. John Terreblanche; he is a police reporter. Good day to you both."

†

CHAPTER 25

Willem, Promise, Marja and John Terreblanche

"Willem, I don't think we should have spoken with that Terreblanche slug," Marja said, rolling down the side window of his Beetle parked along Promise's street to let in the October air. "I don't trust that fat bastard."

"Agh, ja." Willem winced; the bruises around his eyes stretched as he frowned. "Nor the police." He fingered his tender brow above his blackened eye and rolled down his car window to better gaze across a stretch of barren veldt — nestled between two dilapidated houses — and up the mountain now turning to fresh green: early spring rising up its slopes. They were both startled by a piet-my-vrou chirping its piercing refrain from a scraggly tree beneath which a fire still smouldered wood smoke from a kettle drum, left abandoned in the veldt now that the sun had risen high and dispelled the morning's mist.

Marja and Willem had just returned from their meeting with Barrister Lamprecht Labuschagne, who had arranged their bail, after which they had met with me. I had been sitting in the lawyer's grand Buitenkant Street office when they arrived, but Marja and Willem had probably not noticed me as they entered the office's vestibule because they were far too troubled about what Labuschagne would have to say about their impending court case.

With a little help from Labuschagne, I had managed to convince Willem and Marja to sit for tape-recorded interviews. I had taken great pains to explain to them that, if I knew their life stories in depth, I could provide a more favourable account when I reported on their case for my newspaper, *The Cape Times Herald*, and so they had reluctantly agreed.

"Ja, but, Labuschagne seems alright, don't you think?" Willem looked fixedly through the window but activated the windscreen wiper by mistake.

"Agh, Willem, I've lost trust in men." Marja clasped her left wrist in her right hand, her arm wound tightly across her lap. "They've done me no good. And I don't trust Terreblanche's tape recorder. It might suit him to have us tell our story on tape, but God knows where it could show up as evidence. I'm not going to speak into his microphone ever again." She giggled a little, her pressed lips upturning and her cheeks rising in little balls. "Oops, that sounds naughty, I didn't mean it that way."

Willem stretched his thin arm across Marja, gently unclamped her right hand from her wrist and brought it to cradle between his, linking across the close gap of the adjoining car seats. He held her hand for a time, gazing up at the mountain and listening to the piet-my-vrou and the screeching seagulls circling overhead. Her hand was warm in his. He took comfort from the familiar gesture of the past. Marja broke his reverie.

"Willem, I don't think we should be seen together like this. Let's go inside. We need lunch and a cup of tea. Promise will know what to do when she comes back from work."

†

I, on the other hand, was quite pleased with myself. When I played back the tape recordings from the interviews with Marja and Willem, I realised that I had got a lot more than I bargained for. I leant back in my Cape Times Herald *office chair and puffed on my Peterson pipe with satisfaction.*

Previously, on October 5, on my daily rounds at the Caledon Square Police Station, I had ascertained that overnight Dr. Willem Jansen and Miss Marja de Koning had been charged under the Immorality Act. This puzzled me. I had been informed that there was something afoot at the Groote Schuur Hospital between a Dutch doctor and a Xhosa nurse from my contact there, the porter Japie van Wyk, so I was quite surprised when I was handed the charge sheet to find that a Coloured *female, and not an* African *one, had been arraigned. I asked the duty officer if I might interview the prisoners immediately to provide an accurate police Report for the* Cape Times Herald.

"Mr. Terreblanche, I am sorry, not today. No one is to visit with prisoners today. It is strictly not possible. Today is the referendum. We want no political agitation." The policeman pursed his inadequate moustache, wrote something on a piece of paper, folded it into a pre-addressed

envelope readied on his desk, winked, licked its flap closed and handed it over the counter. "Good day, Mr. Terreblanche; please come again tomorrow."

Disappointed at the refusal, I visited the men's room, crammed myself into an uncomfortably tiny stall and sat down on the toilet seat with a thud to prise open the envelope with my fountain pen. I had been well rewarded: there was twice the amount of cash agreed to, and on the scrap of paper was written a telephone number and Lamprecht Labuschagne B.A., L.L.B., as well as the address on Buitenkant Street, where I had just been, to get said tape recordings.

I repositioned my legs on the ironwood desk in front of me — my back was aching — refilled my Peterson and contemplated the opportunities that had unfolded from the telling of Marja and Willem's strange story. If I could get Sister Madiba to co-operate, I might be able to write a world-class story that I could sell to the Daily Mail in London. Now, that would be some real pound sterling, I thought. My debts had been mounting to grotesque proportions: the downpayment on the Porsche, my fancy flat in Sea Point, and the nice meals with high-priced girls — a divorcé's life on a reporter's salary was a precarious endeavour.

Although the police work made some money — and tax free! — it was a risky business. In public I masqueraded as a liberal English reporter; in private, well, that was my own business, but if I was outed by the Secret Police my career as a journalist would be shot. Over! Caput! And so too my legitimate livelihood. I walked a tightrope every day. Beholden to opposing masters, I wanted out. Out of my debt and out of the country. If I could dig to the root of this strange story, maybe I could write a novel about it, *I mused.* And with some luck, I might create a bestseller. But I would need to publish in England, where the book wouldn't be banned, and where I could escape too. Back to Cambridge University, my alma mater. *I shifted my legs on the desk to ease my back pain.* Away from the Secret Police and out of reach of the ANC — neither would take kindly to an exposé. Whatever I did, the next step was to find that Promise Madiba sister, the one that should have been caught in the raid in the first place. I needed to get her story on tape too.

†

Not much more than six weeks after the above planning session, Promise had gone into her house livid. Tricked twice, she unlocked the door quickly and never looked back at me sitting happily in my beautiful Porsche parked along the kerb.

"Marja, I am back to make supper as promised," Promise called as she pulled off her sister's cape, walked into the kitchen and set the kettle. "Come in here and speak to me."

"How did it go today? Why are you so late?" Marja asked, sitting down at the table.

"It's that bloody Terreblanche reporter fellow. That fatso, after the tape recording, he tricked me into speaking to him again. When I came out of the front door of Groote Schuur at five, today, he was there in that fancy car of his, waiting." Promise started slicing a bread loaf for their tea.

"Ja, I never trust that man. Watch that you don't cut yourself, Promise."

"I won't. I'd like to slice him, though. I wasn't going to go with him but he showed me one of his newspaper articles and convinced me that talking to him might help Willem's situation and so I agreed."

"So where did you go? He took me to Rhodes Mem for tea but that's closed after five."

"Signal Hill. I told him to put the car's top up so nobody could see us together. And that's why I am so late. He is a real journalist. He's got that knack of getting you to talk too-too much. And now I am pissed off. Let's talk about something else, please."

The kettle whistled its readiness, tea was poured, and Marja and Promise settled around the familiar table to a troubled supper.

†

Dr. Willem Jansen was in a torrid state. Ever since his night in jail, his nightmares had returned with a vengeance. He thought himself back to the suppressed horror of the Japanese concentration camps. He woke up in a sweat: heart pounding, a crawling, squeezing of the spine, warming his neck. He felt horrid and guilty. He had done wrong and had to pay. He had broken the country's laws. But he couldn't help himself; he needed Promise's love. And when they had put him into the cell at Caledon Square Police Station he had feared being punched again so he had gone in quietly, his head burning and sweating and trembling with the terror of the cold stone-walled cell, the clanging of the steel door, the closing of the peephole with an iron clash. The square empty space with the bunk and grey blanket ready for a disturbed night. Dreadful memories recalled. He couldn't do it again — go to prison. He would rather die.

Not knowing where to turn after Barrister Labuschagne had explained their predicament, Willem grasped for a lifebuoy. Me, John Terreblanche, sitting waiting outside in the Buitenkant Street office. Willem put his trust in me, coming back again and again, finding solace in sharing his story — I, apparently, was such a good listener. I had promised to help him out and Willem believed me. And… if I am to be perfectly honest, I rather liked him. May be a bit too much for my own good. He was a Dr. Jekyll to my Mr. Hyde — a good, admirable man, while I was a skullldugger. I had to watch myself. I must not get emotionally involved with my subjects.

†

Promise and Marja, with Willem at the rear a steady hundred yards behind, had trudged up the concrete jeep track that wound its steep way up the southern flank of Table Mountain. They had parked their black and white Beetles, separately, under a clump of oak trees at Constantia Nek, and had then picked their way past tiers of sage-peppered fynbos to the planned rendezvous site: a rocky outcrop hidden out of sight of the crumbling pathway by a thicket of swaying Port Jackson willows fed by an updraft of warm air from the Cape Flats below. The rocky outcrop protruding from the side of the mountain created a perfect hiding place for Willem and Promise to rejoin, while Marja sat guard outside the sheltered copse. A trill whistle, like a passing bird, the sign to cease the tryst.

After the police raid, the threesome had decided that it would be better for Willem to visit the District Six house only in preparation for the court trial at hand, and certainly not for the business now being conducted hidden from view. That would just be too risky; Promise was sure that her telephone had been tapped — she had heard two extra tell-tale clicks and a gap in time when she had picked up the handset, before the dial tone snapped on — and was convinced the house was now under police surveillance; spending the night was out of the question, so other means of congress needed to be arranged. Marja preferred to walk, not run, like the other two, so she suggested the Constantia Neck walk up to the top of Table Mountain as a way they could be together.

"We can take a picnic and swim in De Villier's dam at the top."

"I can't swim; can you, Willem?" Promise had responded with a broad smile, turning her glad eyes on him as he sat at the kitchen table.

"Agh, ja, of course. Marja and I learnt at the Dago Falls Club. We'll show you."

And so it was settled.

Marja rose from where she sat on the rock looking downward at the rising path — having noticed some climbers in the long distance — uncreased her yellow sari, turned her head as far left as she could in the direction of the Cape Flats, curled her tongue upwards to her teeth, stretched her lips tight and pressed out a shrill trill. Then she slung her kit bag across her shoulder and launched up the jeep track, her mountain boots grinding the crumbling concrete despite slender legs.

Next, Promise emerged from between the Port Jackson trees. Dressed in her white running outfit, she wore a clay jacket against the morning cold and sprinted to catch up with her companion.

Later, but well before the climbers were close enough to identify him, Willem shot out of the copse, jogging at pace, a Japanese army cap slung low over his head, the neck flaps trailing behind, a canvas backpack tugging at the straps around his midriff as he accelerated. Willem ran like the wind. His bony legs, equal to the precipitous incline of the jeep track, cut up the side of the mountain. He crouched a little to lower his centre of gravity as he ran, giving him more power and purchase. He flew past Marja and Promise, as if they didn't exist, and reached the summit and its glorious view, panting only slightly despite the exertion. He felt elated but knew not to stop suddenly at the top: he would become dizzy and collapse — his blood pressure low from the strenuous exercise. So, instead, he continued jogging slowly over to the De Villiers Dam wall, traversed its walkway and descended on a path to its white pebbled beach. Finding a private spot where a jut of rock and a clump of high fynbos provided shade, Willem settled down to wait for the women.

"Shoo, you are too-too fast, Willem." Promise sank down to sit next to him on the grey blanket he had placed to cover the sandy stones. "Marja, come and sit here." She patted the prickly wool blanket next to her. "Are you going to teach me to swim? That water looks seriously cold."

Marja took off her boots and, barefoot, squatted next to Promise. Eyeing the brown water gently slapping the curve of beach they were sitting on, she leant over and touched its surface with a flat hand. "Perfect," she said. "The water is tip-top. But I forgot my swimming costume."

"Me too." Promise laughed. "I guess there is no alternative."

"Ooraait then." Marja stood up and stripped off her colourful sari, naked in the brilliant sunlight. "It's not deep here at the edge; follow me, Promise, I'll make sure you don't drown. Willem, are you going to sit there and mope, or are you coming in with us?"

"No, I'll leave you two to it and go for a quick jog around the dam. I'll join you later for lunch; best not that we are seen in the water together. Here no one can see us. But out there in the middle, it's anyone's guess. Let's not chance it."

Promise thrilled to the sight of Marja in the nude. The dark birthmark across her bared chest, bisected by the still darker scar. She stood up, shed her clothes and stepped gingerly into the murky water. Her unsure feet gripped the slippery stones as she went deeper in pursuit of Marja, who had turned back to egg her on, water lapping at her exposed hips.

"Come in further. Come on. Don't be scared. It's only water."

Promise wasn't so sure but stepped cautiously on, feeling unsteady in the deepening water; the grey stoned dam wall came into view as she waded in further. "Stop, Marja. Wait for me."

Marja, her long black hair slick from a quick refreshing dunk, turned to face Promise and waited, the water not much deeper than before. Promise came nearer. Marja could see the perspiration on her face, her tawny hair still dry in the mid-summer heat.

Coming closer, Promise seemed to slip, pitching forward into Marja, who stood her ground. Their arms clasped around each other's backs, their breasts pressed together lightly, hot breath on their lips; they both held on for a moment longer. And then giggled. Marja unclasped and said, "Oops, Promise. Not so fast. Now let's try some swimming. You lie over my arms, and I will show you how to move your legs. I promise I won't let you down."

They continued the swimming practice, spending more time laughing than swimming, until they heard Willem give them a shout from the beach. Lunch was ready. Promise grabbed Marja's steadying hand underwater, held it, and let go, and they splashed their way to shore.

Willem had readied a Dutch picnic on the blanket. Roggebrood, cheese, and rollmops herring from a glass jar. Hot black coffee in three plastic cups from the thermos flask. Three shining green apples ready for dessert. They sat down in the accustomed semi-circle to eat after Marja and Promise had redonned their clothes, but Willem, sitting between them, stared fixedly out at the dam water.

"Cheer up, Willem. We're at the top of the world," Promise said, throwing back her head to gulp back a pickled herring.

"Agh, you know. It's the trial. The thought of it never leaves me and they haven't set the date yet." Willem sucked his teeth. "It's just all so degrading... so humiliating. For this... this man-made law. Is it a crime to love you, Promise?" Willem threw a pebble into the water.

"Hau, hau, of course not. Of course not." Promise clenched Willem's arm.

"That bloody policeman during the raid. I just exploded when I got up to hit him. And then, when he punched me, it struck me like a beating in the camps. The endless pain and the hurting from the past. That's going to come back if I go to prison. I felt the horror of it all over again when they shoved me into that cell at Caledon Square. All over again." Willem pulled up his legs, cradled his arms across his knees and bowed his head between them. Promise stroked his neck.

"And going to court. The shame. The shame. Me. A doctor. I have only tried to do good in this world." Willem let his head hang deeper. "I just can't face it all. I just can't."

"Tidak apa-apa, Willem, tidak apa-apa; isn't that what you always say?" Marja reached over to place her hand on his shoulder. "We will work it out somehow. We have a good lawyer; he will know what to do. He told us he will get us out."

"Agh, yes, but there is no way forward in this country. I want to be with you, Promise... all the time." Willem turned to Promise, searched her eyes.

"Shoo, I agree," Promise said, returning his gaze with equal ardour. "I agree... this bloody country and its laws." She stood up to contain her anger and sat down on her haunches. "And it's getting worse, you know. Just wait till South Africa becomes a republic next year. Then we will become even more of a police state. Wait for it! There will be nothing holding the government back. Not Great Britain, nor the Commonwealth. We will be a pariah. Willem, won't you pass my tobacco tin? I need a cigarette."

†

A rare summer rainstorm lashed Cape Town, breaking cool in the sweltering night. Sheets of water clattered on the corrugated roof, waking Promise from a fitful sleep. She lay naked under the white crumpled sheet in the centre of the double bed, listening to the rain fall. The moist smell of humid air came off the street through the open window. She tore off the sheet and lay quite still, under the slowly revolving fan, hoping for coolness. The storm suddenly ceased. The silence deafening. Until she heard a soft cry, and another, coming through the open bedroom door.

Promise got up and padded the five steps to stand in Marja's doorway. Just a wan light from the streetlamp fell on the bed through the narrow window, making it hard to see. Marja lay on her side, curved into a foetal position beneath her sheet. Her bare shoulders shuddered and her legs jerked a little — jet-black hair lay disarrayed across her pillow, Marja's face in her bosom.

"Marja, can I come in?"

"Yes."

Promise slipped into the bed behind her, cupping Marja's naked body with her own. She nuzzled Marja's neck and sensed her warmth and her smell and then reached down to help her insert the condom-covered candle between her legs. They held it still there for a while, both trembling. Then they moved the candle rhythmically together; starting slowly, they sped up until Marja gave another cry. A cry barely audible in the deafening downpour that again gathered force from above.

†

CHAPTER 26

The Cape Times Herald
The Paper that Cares.
January 5, 1961

Trial Date for Prosecution under the Immorality Act Set for Dutch Doctor: Can love across the colour bar only be immoral in South Africa?
John Terreblanche

Following a police raid, Dr. Willem Jansen, a Dutch citizen, and Marja de Koning, wife of the recently deceased Henry Plaatjies of District Six, will be prosecuted for contravention of the Immorality Act. The couple were charged on October 5, now better known as Referendum Day. It has taken the Crown a good while to set the trial date for January 10. I wonder why. Could it be that the trial will draw unfavourable international attention, given that a Dutch citizen is being prosecuted at a time that many countries (including Holland) are already boycotting South Africa for such apartheid laws. Or is it political calculation: the

---

government wants the trial out of the way, dead and buried, before celebrating Independence Day on May 31, when South Africa will divorce from Great Britain and become a republic. The government has a tough road to hoe: just 52% of the only-white electorate voted for independence…

†

CHAPTER 27

Immorality Act

Cape Town Magistrates' Court, Room A, was all a hubbub.

"All rise. All rise," rang out a reedy voice. The wrinkled usher, dressed in a dark suit, pushing back his chair, stood up to set the day's proceedings in motion. The Honourable B.J. van Niekerk swept in from a side door at the front of the wood-panelled chamber, gathered his black gown about him, stood still in front of his high-backed chair, took a deep breath and settled down to the business at hand — comfortably ensconced on an elevated wooden dais recently polished to a deep glow.

Before proceeding, the wigged magistrate took in the scene in front of him. He narrowed his close-set eyes and pointed his ferret-face up at the gallery.

Bisected by ermine-carpeted steps leading up to a double mahogany swing door at its back, the terraced gallery sported inquisitive black and white spectators. Separated, but equal in their bustling curiosity, they hung over the brass guardrail straddling its length, a scatter of anticipation gradually stilled into submission by the magistrate's scrutiny: "Shush, shush, shush, SHUSH," echoed back from the high plastered dome of the august chamber.

Satisfied that he had controlled at least that part of the room, Van Niekerk concentrated next on the white press corps on his left, restrained within our mahogany enclosure, and, after acknowledging my presence with a curt nod, levelled his glare at the non-European press in their box across the way. He then proceeded to scan the room again, front to back. The empty witness box to his right and the clerk of the court behind the desk five feet in front of him. The three transcript writers that sat silent behind their red-baized table in the pit before him. The bench of solicitors, advocates and barristers of the court facing him. He acknowledged the skeletal attorney general, A.P. Treurnicht, prosecution for the Crown, and the jowly ex-Springbok rugby player Lamprecht Labuschagne, for the defence. He raised his eyes to a row of three police officers, in blue-grey uniforms, girded by leather shoulder straps and tightly brass-buckled belts, who sat proudly on the side among an assortment of other witnesses.

Then, finally, he looked up at the two defendants sitting far apart in the dock, behind which were rowed yet another mass of rowdy spectators.

A gaunt white man with thinning blond hair who had dressed in a dark-blue suit, white shirt and red bowtie. It looked like he had cut himself shaving this morning, because he had a bloodied piece of tissue paper fluttering on his chin. He held his face almost still despite the obvious straining of his neck muscles and looked malevolently in front of him.

And a pretty coloured girl, dressed in a yellow sarong, her long black hair bundled atop a bedak-whitened face cut by cherry rouged lips. Van Niekerk tried to catch her eye but she glanced downwards, immediately.

The magistrate raised his gavel and rapped the table three times, his neck pale above the black mantle.

"On this day of our Lord, January 10, 1961, I am calling the court to order," he said in a high-pitched voice. "Dr. Willem Jansen, please rise."

The defendant rose, looked down to button up his jacket and then fixed his gaze on the magistrate.

"You are charged with the Immorality Act 23 of 1957, Section 16 (2) (a), specifically subsection (ii) and (iii), and here I read: *Where any white male person who commits or attempts to commit with a coloured female person any immoral or indecent act; or entices, solicits, or importunes any coloured female person to have unlawful carnal intercourse with him*, shall be deemed a crime and a sexual offence. How do you plead?"

"Not bloody guilty," Willem beat back, straightening from a stoop to his full height, a lick of his parted hair falling over his forehead.

"I beg your pardon. It is guilty or *not* guilty, no *bloodies* allowed. Otherwise you will be sentenced immediately: seven years maximum." The magistrate rapped his gavel twice in irritation. "Now, for the second time, Dr. Jansen, how do you plead?"

"Not… guilty." Willem sat promptly, quelling his neck's torsion, the tissue paper still stuck to his chin.

The magistrate noted that the second defendant had already risen in the dock.

"Miss Marja de Koning. You are charged with the Immorality Act 23 of 1957, Section 16…" the magistrate inverted the gender classifications but droned on, intermittently peeking at Marja between clauses, before finishing. "How do you plead?"

"Guilty… a… a… I mean *not* guilty, I… I… am nervous… sir."

"Very well. I see that Advocate A.P. Treurnicht is present for the Crown's prosecution of the defendants. Am I correct?"

A wigged, bespectacled, fragile man, with a thin grey beard and threadbare cloak, stood to be recognised. "Yes, Your Honour."

"Please speak up. Please speak up and slowly. Our stenographers must get everything down for the record." The magistrate turned his weasel-face ten degrees left. "And, for the defence, I see my venerable colleague, Barrister Lamprecht Labuschagne."

The barrister heaved his square, cloaked frame to stand over the papers strewn about on the table in front of him, wrinkled his puffy face, grinned, and said, "At your service, Your Honour." He then sat heavily, but not before turning to look behind him and smile encouragement at Willem and Marja. He looked up at the gallery to nod to Promise, sitting in the front row.

"Very well, proceed. Will the attorney general please have your first witness take the stand."

Erect and sure, the police officer took the stand and doffed his cap, revealing shining combed-back hair. He had a black pencil moustache and a chiselled face, his thin lips primed, ready to tell the truth.

"I am Warrant Officer Piet Marais of the Caledon Square Police Station. On the night of October 4, 1960, I was ordered to investigate at Number 83 Upper Melbourne Street, District Six, because of a report. We could not find the place. The streets signs were missing and the lighting was poor. We radioed Caledon Square Police Station, and they called in a police helicopter to light the way. The owner of the house, Sister Promise Madiba, was under police surveillance. I took an Alsatian from the back of the police van and knocked on the front door. No one answered, so I knocked again and again. I blew my police whistle. Still no answer. So we forced open the door. Dr. Willem Jansen — I mean, Defendant Number 1 — was standing in the lounge when we entered. He had on a light blue shirt and khaki trousers but was barefoot. He seemed upset. I introduced Sergeant Viljoen and Constable Botha and told Defendant Number 1 that we had a warrant to search the place. He said that we had no right to do so. He swore at us and told us that Sister Madiba was at work at Groote Schuur Hospital. This was a lie. We later heard that the police helicopter had seen an unidentified naked black girl running towards Devil's Peak. That was probably Sister Madiba." The warrant officer raised his curt head and sneered in the direction of the balcony. "There she is, all tarted up in her nurse's uniform."

All who could looked up to see Promise Madiba. Impassive, but for a demure smile, her white sister's cap contained her unruly hair — her sparkling teeth bright from a sunbeam trespassing the skylight.

"Objection, Your Honour." Barrister Labuschagne rose heavily behind his table. "This is not a fact but conjecture on the part of the officer. And… furthermore, Sister Madiba is not in the dock."

The gavel hit the table. "Please sit, Lamprecht. You will get your turn. Let the witness finish first without interruption. Continue, Warrant Officer!"

"Agh, waar was ek? Oh yes, the bedroom door was closed. I commanded Sergeant Viljoen to search the two bedrooms and Constable Botha the rest of the place. Then Defendant Number 2 suddenly appeared. She was dressed in white pyjamas. Men's pyjamas, far too big for her. She came out of the main bedroom and lay down on the couch in the lounge. She was barefoot too and had red lipstick. She looked like she didn't have panties on. She is very familiar to me and to this court."

"Stop." Labuschagne rose, agitated. He glanced at Marja, who had covered her lips with four red-tipped fingers.

"What happened next?" countered the frail attorney general.

"Viljoen yelled that I should come and look in the bedroom. He had found a crumpled sheet, which was still warm to the touch. There were gooey stains on the sheet that looked like spunk. There was black pubic hair on the sheet. I noted that Dr. Jansen was blond."

"Sies." "Sies!" "Hau." "Hau!" And other exclamations of "Aitsa!" "Up and at 'em" dropped down from the gallery upon the proceedings, while the newspaper men, present company excluded, had their heads down, penning the headlines that this revelation would surely bring.

Marja sat slumped, her face hidden by the palms of her hands.

Willem stared straight ahead, his inscrutable face stretched thin, the cut on his chin faintly bleeding — the tissue paper gone.

"Silence in my court," commanded the magistrate, then banged the gavel twice.

The warrant officer pointed at the evidence table, where the sheet and pyjamas now lay folded, then continued, "The window out to the street was wide open. I remember thinking that someone could easily escape through it. Then Constable Botha came rushing back into the lounge. He held up a used condom that he had found in the rubbish bin. I thought we had enough evidence for an immediate arrest. So we took the two defendants in the police van back to Caledon Square Police Station and booked them in for the night."

Marja stayed still, impassive; Willem started rocking in place.

"Right. Now, it's finally your turn, Barrister Labuschagne, to ask questions," the magistrate continued. "I need silence in the court. Or I will have the ushers throw you out!"

Labuschagne rose and addressed the warrant officer, who now stood, arched forward, hands knotted from clutching the banister of the witness box.

"Warrant Officer, is it not so that the apartment was dimly lit?"

"Yes."

"Well, how can you say that Defendant Number 2 had no panties on?"

"We found this out from the medical examiner's report. Miss de Koning was examined by a district surgeon that night in the prison."

"And the condom," Labuschagne continued, "what

evidence is that? Didn't Constable Botha find the contraceptive in the dustbin outside? Couldn't anyone have left a condom in there?"

"Yes, but we found an open wrapper in the second bedroom, and five unused condoms in the night drawer next to the bed." W.O. Piet Marais pointed again at the evidence table.

Labuschagne sat, looked back at Marja, noticed her distress, stood up again and redoubled his efforts.

"Is it not so, Warrant Officer, that the dustbin is not outside the bedroom in question?"

"Yes." The W.O. tweaked his moustache and patted his oiled hair. "Constable Botha wrote in his report that it was outside the *second* bedroom, readily accessible from its opened window."

"No further questions, Your Honour."

"Now it is the Crown's turn." The magistrate craned in the direction of Attorney General A.P. Treurnicht.

"Warrant Officer Marais, could you enlighten us as to the summary findings of the District Surgeon's report?" Removing his spectacles and polishing them with his thin cloak, Treurnicht elaborated. "Why, for instance, was the examination performed at all?"

"To establish penetration."

"Well, was there evidence of immorality, of… of… penetration?"

"Yes."

There was a collective intake of breath in the court room.

Marja sat small in the dock; her hands had moved to cover her bowed head.

Willem started to rise in protest but was stayed by a whack from the magistrate's gavel.

Promise remained unmoved, aloof in the gallery.

Marais continued, "Yes, there was evidence of recent penetration with an *object*, but no evidence of spermatozoa."

"With an object? What do you mean, man, an object?"

"I'm making that assumption. May I read the report, sir?"

"Yes."

"There is evidence of penetration. The vaginal introitus is erythematous and demonstrates recent cracking of the skin with mild bleeding and abrasions."

There were two loud gavel bangs to arrest the flying commentary from the gallery; the witness from further testimony; and Defendant 2 from further embarrassment. "The court will adjourn for twenty minutes," said the magistrate. "The two defendants must remain in the dock. Treurnicht and Labuschagne, join me in my chambers."

†

Promise Madiba remained in the gallery, her hands blanched almost white around the balcony's brass handrail.

I hot-footed out of the court into the terracotta-tiled hallway to find the nearest telephone to submit my report and returned as soon as possible.

Marja stayed on her side of the dock, shrunken.

Willem shifted stiffly to sit close beside her. He put his hand on her thigh, gently stroked her leg, and whispered,

"Tidak apa-apa, tidak apa-apa," through clenched teeth, his neck a knot of muscle.

†

"All rise. All rise."

The magistrate marched in, sat down, glanced at the clock, 11 a.m., and marshalled his court room. "The court has decided that we do not need further testimony presented by the two other policemen present at the arrest, Sergeant Viljoen and Constable Botha, because the prosecution and defence believe that the previous testimony by Warrant Officer Piet Marais has done this sufficient justice. However, the Crown wishes to bring further lines of evidence to bear in this case. The attorney general will now address the court."

The A.G. rose, adjusted his spectacles and discharged his throat before addressing the court. "The Crown has long been suspicious of Defendant 1, Dr. Willem Jansen, a Dutch citizen, and a certain Promise Madiba, who serves as a sister at Groote Schuur Hospital, where they both work in the Casualty Unit. But I must stress in the most strenuous fashion that the activities that Sister Madiba is currently under police surveillance for are NOT relevant to these proceedings, as she has NOT been charged by the Crown under the Immorality Act, except in so far that the crime, if this becomes proven fact, occurred in her home at Number 83 Upper Melbourne Street. What is of relevance therefore in the Crown's present two cases, *Regina vs. W. Jansen,* and *Regina vs. M. de Koning,* is where the surveillance by the police of Dr. Jansen, and, separately,

328

Sister Madiba's home, draws into question Dr. Jansen's proclivities, his character, or bears on his relationship with Miss Marja de Koning.

"The prosecution thus submits into evidence an undated letter that came into the possession of the police at Caledon Square Headquarters, written to Miss Marja de Koning but posted to Promise Madiba, resident at Number 83 Upper Melbourne Street.

"It reads as follows:

"Dear Marja,

"I'm sitting in the Pig and Whistle feeling sorry for myself and you. I promise that I will not stand you up again. I should have met you on Signal Hill, but I just couldn't.

"Promise will you meet me at the Gardens January 2nd, during Klopse Carnival?

"I have the day off and I know you do too. There is always a big crowd of onlookers, and we can find each other there. I will be there from 11 o'clock. Please come. Willem."

Having finished the reading, A.G. Treurnicht handed the letter to the usher, who walked it over to the clerk of the court to admit the document into evidence, while a hum of conversation arose from the spectators.

Taken aback and having glanced at Willem quickly to gauge his reaction, Barrister Labuschagne intervened: "Point of order. Point of order, this letter is inadmissible. I must confer with my client."

"I give you leave to confer with Dr. Jansen. Five minutes. The court will stay in place." A loud bang resonated from the magistrate's much-abused table.

Labuschagne joined Willem in the dock and they bent their heads together.

"Willem, what the hell is that?"

"Agh, agh." Willem grimaced. "I... I... sent the letter from Rondebosch when I was drunk. It was meant for Promise but I mistakenly wrote it to Marja instead of Promise. The letter was never delivered. I am certain of it. I mailed it that same evening after drinking at the Pig. The police must be sifting Promise's mail. Her telephone is also being tapped." Willem covered his face with spread fingers and spoke into his wrist. "So as not to implicate Promise in any way, you should say that I must have made a mistake in the writing. I wrote *Promise will you*. It should be corrected to *Promise you will*. Otherwise, the authorities are sure to put two and two together, if they haven't already."

"It's a mess. Why didn't you tell me about this? It's a written admission of a relationship with at least one, if not two, non-European women. The papers will have a field day. Just look at the press corps over there licking their pencils," Labuschagne said. "And look at the girls."

They both turned up to the balcony, where Promise glared fixedly into the middle distance and then looked across at Marja. She had dissolved, whimpering quietly behind her hands, her scarlet lipstick haemorrhaging.

Two table bangs brought the court to order. "Barrister Labuschagne, please bring your objection," the magistrate said.

"Your Honour." Labuschagne faced the magistrate. "I fear that this letter was seized by the Secret Police illegally, and thus cannot be admitted in evidence. Furthermore, my client would like to point out a mistake in the writing of the letter — if it is not to be wholly withdrawn from evidence."

"Overruled. The evidence stays. You can correct the letter with the A.G. later. Bring the next witness to the stand!" the magistrate yelled.

An unkempt-looking fellow mounted the two steps into the witness box, removed his workman's cap and was sworn in, with an Afrikaans Bible. "I am Japie van Wyk, residing in Woodstock. Can I light my cigarette?" he asked in Afrikaans.

"No, there is no smoking in my court room! Continue your testimony."

"I am an orderly at Groote Schuur Hospital. I ferry the patients on stretchers from here to there and everywhere, but chiefly in the casualty theatres. In point of fact, I brought Defendant 2 — he pointed at Miss Marja de Koning — into the theatre after she was stabbed during the Langa Riots. And he operated on her." The witness pointed at Dr. Jansen with a tobacco-stained finger, then faltered as the chatter in the court room amped up.

"Go on, Mr. van Wyk. What else did you wish to tell us?" the prosecutor enquired.

"Only that I heard a nurse, Promise Madiba, tell another doctor in the theatre that Defendant Number 2 was a *relative* of Defendant Number 1."

"Aitsa." "Hau." "Hau." "Aitsa, how can this be? A relative?" exploded from the gallery, requiring repetitive bangs with the gavel.

"That's enough; no further testimony. Mr. van Wyk, you are released. Go and smoke your cigarette, OUTSIDE."

The prosecution and the defence got up simultaneously and called out in unison, "Your Honour, I must protest."

"Alright, the defence goes first. What do you have to say, Barrister Labuschagne?"

"Merely that we need to assure that Mr. van Wyk's testimony is based in fact, rather than hearsay."

"You have made your point, thank you." The magistrate pivoted his attention towards the A.G. "What did you want to add?"

"I wanted to bring another police witness."

"No, there is not time. Please summarise what he will demonstrate for the court."

"Very well. He will testify that Dr. Jansen and Sister Promise Madiba have been subjected to police surveillance for some time now." The prosecutor hesitated before continuing, "And allege that via binoculars, from below, the policeman was able to see Dr. Jansen undress in front of a brown girl in the mouth of Woodstock Cave on Table Mountain."

Pandemonium broke out: catcalls, wolf whistles, clapping, drumming of feet and hoots of laughter echoed around the resonant court chamber.

Promise, high in the balcony, shook her head from side to side. "Aikona, Aikona, that is a lie. It is a lie, Aikona."

Willem made to get up, thought better of it and instead clenched the bench with both hands at his sides, his face a blank mask.

Marja, who had recovered her composure somewhat, smirked redly.

The cacophony was stilled only by the incessant banging of the gavel on the worn table. The magistrate had lost it.

When order was finally restored ten minutes later, the

magistrate shouted, "The court will recess and reconvene for sentencing after an examination is performed *in loco* at Number 83 Upper Melbourne Street, District Six. The defendants are remanded on bail of £50 each but are free to go if Barrister Labuschagne has the cash. Does he?"

"Yes, Your Honour."

"Court adjourned." Bang, bang.

†

If Willem and Marja were not immediately convicted and jailed, the three had planned to meet on the Grand Parade, just down Parade Street from the magistrates' court. Promise was the first out of the forbidding building and made her way quickly along the street bustling with secretaries, legal clerks and robed barristers going about their daily business upholding the law. It being lunch time, many were stopping in eateries or cafes to prepare for the afternoon's court sessions. The Parade was packed, a market day. The height of summer, the sun was at its zenith, with just a hint of wind starting to curl a wisp of cloud over Table Mountain — Promise needed to find somewhere sheltered along the castle wall side. She spied a concrete bench under a eucalyptus tree, commandeered the space and sat down to wait for the others.

Marja and Willem looked diminished, despite their smart dress, the contrast between them stark. Tall, Willem stooped and shuffled, and looked like he was in a trance. Marja, about two-thirds his size, held her arm around his waist but seemed to have recovered her composure somewhat.

Promise was unsure how to greet them so she stood up, and hugged both, summoning them to her bosom by putting her hands at their shoulders and pulling in. They stood there for a while, heads down, just breathing. The chime from the Grand Parade's clock tower, mixed with the noon-day gun salute from Signal Hill, broke their commune. Promise bade Willem and Marja to sit down beside her on the bench and put her hands on each of their adjacent legs. She patted each softly and said, "Hau, what is this matter of *examination in loco*? I thought we would be finished and klaar and free by now. The case is such a nonsense. Willem, who would have thought the police would be chasing us up Table Mountain to photograph us in Woodstock Cave?"

"Ja," Willem said, putting his hand over Promise's, "and that problem of the letter I posted to you and you never received. The bloody police stole it. And what about the Japie van Wyk fellow, the informer? That's such bullshit that you said Marja was a relative. Agh, they'll throw anything at us to make it stick."

"But, Marja," Promise said, "I didn't know that they gave you a medical examination. You poor thing, that must have been awful."

"Yes, and totally unnecessary; het was verschrikkelijk — terrible," Marja replied, waving her hand in front of her face.

"And, Marja," Willem looked across at her, "what's this business of the condoms?"

"Shoo, shoo, Willem, I think we should leave that." Promise turned her shoulders towards him to protect Marja from further inquiry.

"Maar, maar."

"Aikona, Willem, Marja has suffered enough embarrassment for one day."

"We all have. This is the last thing we need," Willem said as he got up to leave. "I hope that Labuschagne knows his oats. I'm not having a good feeling about this at all. I think we're fucked."

†

Two weeks later, the Taj Mahal restaurant in District Six was jam-packed with dinner guests. Situated not far from the Seven Steps on Hanover Street, the eatery was wildly popular, drawing not only locals but clientele from far and wide for its signature biryanis and tika masalas. The décor, although a bit seedy, was colourful and exotic, and gave off a sense of being in India. The aroma of rich spices circulated from the kitchen hidden behind a purple curtain, which was kept in perpetual motion by red-turbaned waiters, gloved and dressed in white, who tended to the diners and relit the dripping candles that were the only source of light in the smoke-filled room.

Willem, Promise and Marja had been invited to dinner by Lamprecht Labuschagne. He had coordinated the court-mandated examination *in loco* at Promise's house in their absence. The barrister wanted to report back on next steps and felt the trio were short on reassurance, and encouragement, and could do with a night out to relieve some of the tension.

"Let's raise a toast to our success," Labuschagne said as he angled the foaming beer towards his freckled face and took a satisfied slurp, coating his ginger moustache. "Willem and Marja, you can be sure that we will submit a notice of appeal, immediately, if Magistrate van Niekerk sentences you to prison. We will have the papers ready at the hearing to assure immediate bail."

They sat round a circular table tucked into the furthest corner from the entrance onto Hanover Street.

"But what guarantee do you have that we won't spend another night in prison? Do you have a date yet?" Willem asked. He had downed his beer in two long draughts and raised his hand for another.

The girls leant in to hear the response.

"No absolute guarantee that they will accept immediate bail if they think you are a flight risk. Have they asked you to submit your passport to the police?"

"Yes, I had to hand it in at the Rondebosch Police Station last week."

"Well, that will help secure immediate bail, and the court date is — let me look up here in my diary — yes, it is February fourteenth." Packing away his diary in his coat jacket, Labuschagne appeared surprised. "Aah, aaaah, but look who's here. If it isn't John Terreblanche." He swivelled his chair backwards and stood up to shake my proffered hand. "I believe you know each other." Labuschagne glanced at Marja, Willem and Promise, in turn, and continued, "Would you care to join us? I can get an extra seat. Perhaps you can play some light on matters from a police reporter's point of view."

"I don't mind if I do," I replied, sensing an opportunity, "as long as it is okay with you all — I don't want to impose on your conversation."

"This *is* a surprise!" Willem stood up to shake my hand warmly over the table and then clasped its white-clothed edge tightly. He rotated the unsteady table with both hands to put it back in balance before sitting down to his Castle lager.

Promise remained seated, narrowed her gaze, sucked in her cheeks and snarled, "You, you always show up like a bad penny." She swept her braided hair behind her ears and retied her red doek.

"Ja, nee, spent and unwanted." Marja had stood up; she unwrinkled her lamé sarong, patting it down, but then sat down again and repositioned the pins stacking her hairdo.

A turbaned waiter had placed an extra chair, so I unbuttoned my tweed jacket — it was feeling rather tight — and sat down with a grunt. "Lamprecht, Marja, Willem, Promise" — I looked from right to left, pausing to look deeply into Willem's narrow-set eyes — "this is a well-met opportunity indeed. Cheers!" I raised the cold Castle that had been placed in front of me and took a grateful sip. "Why don't you just all call me J.T.? This is a beautiful occasion to get to know all of you, off the record, so to speak. I must insist, though, you will do me a great honour… if I may treat you to dinner at this fine establishment."

"Ooraait," said Marja.

"Alright," said Promise, "but in turn we must get better help from you to get these two out and free. You have written only a few lousy police reports in the *Cape Times Herald*. We need better help from you, from your newspaper; your opinion pieces need to be stronger. STRONGER."

I nodded, edged the beer between my parched lips

again, sipped and said, "Yes, Sister Madiba, I am trying, I really am."

"I think he is too." Willem admirably came to my rescue. "But I cannot see how we can win our case; the magistrate is a fool. An idiot, an idiot." Willem looked at me and then fiddled with the table, unsettling it again.

"The trick is," said Labuschagne, "that we combat the magistrate's false reasoning by bringing the case to the Supreme Court if he decides against us. For the next court session Van Niekerk is basically just reading his summation and reasons for judgement. He has probably already made up his mind."

"That ferret-face" — Promise sipped her wine — "should be sacked. Willem, did you see how he looked at Marja, trying to give her the glad eye?"

"Nee, I was just staring him down, trying to psyche him out. But I can well believe it. The problem is the abject fools one must contend with when you're on the wrong side of the law." Willem sucked his bared teeth.

Labuschagne continued where he left off. "I get the summation a few days before Van Niekerk reads it out in court and so will lodge an appeal by letter to the Supreme Court beforehand. I will request that the appeal has immediate effect so that we can post bail for you both, and you will not need to go to prison. Then we will fight it in the Supreme Court."

"I understand, but how much is the bail going to be?" Willem had downed his third drink.

"I expect the same as the current bail, but we will bring sufficient cash to be sure," Labuschagne replied.

"And what are we to do if we do have to go to prison

immediately? Do we have to pack a bag and bring it to court?" Marja asked.

"Yes, that is a good idea to be safe. And you can leave it with me beforehand. I will keep the bags in my chambers should you need them," Labuschagne replied.

Promise then put her elbows on the table, a bowl of steaming rice between us, levelled her eyes at me, her doek a red warning, and said, "That's all very well, but why are *you* so interested in us? Tell me that. It seems to me your interest is not just a matter of police reports and politics."

The room was uncomfortably hot — I unbuttoned my waistcoat and tipped back my chair to ease the ache in my neck and put some distance between us. "Ah, well, as a journalist I am always interested in the story behind the story, and yours is worth telling." I raised my glass of beer. "Indeed, it *must* be told." I smiled and eased back further. I tried to transform my dour expression into something almost sunny to turn the conversation to where I wanted it to go.

"Well, I'm not sure I believe you; you're too-too slippery."

"Promise, these two are the only hope we've got." Willem fastened his eyes first on Labuschagne and then seemed to linger on mine. "We better trust them." He raised his Castle, said "L'Chaim" and turned the conversation to other things.

And then, gradually, as we spoke deep into that night, and as I watched the three's interactions, an excitement occurred within me. I was awakened to the easy intimacy between them: the caring hand placed to reassure; the soft shoulder touch; the nod of agreement and the knowing smile. Quiet, tender moments between the threesome that I had not seen when interviewing them individually and, to be frank, I was envious of the obvious love between them.

And so I began to understand things I could not from my own upbringing in black and white. The irrepressible love of one human for another, no matter the consequence. A loving display of that inextricable bond playing out right in front of me that very evening in the Taj Mahal. And then, gradually, my understanding deepened to the true heart of the matter — that love is unpredictable, and ungovernable, and colour-blind.

†

Much thus rode on Magistrate B.J. van Niekerk's final summation on February 14, 1961.

"All rise. All rise," rung out a reedy voice in Cape Town Magistrates' Court, Room A.

In the dock, Marja, in yellow and lipsticked red, sat separated from Willem, who was dressed again in his dark-blue suit with a white shirt knotted by a red bowtie. Both were demonstrably tense. Marja clinched her left wrist, while Willem restrained his neck and clasped the hard bench with his left hand.

Promise had retaken her seat in the gallery, dressed in her nurse's uniform.

I sat in my usual seat in the press box and fiddled with my fountain pen. I tried to appear non-committal but I was rooting for the two of them, especially Willem; he deserved better.

Magistrate van Niekerk, white-wigged and black mantled, took his high-backed seat on the elevated dais to provide his findings and closing arguments.

After banging his gavel, twice, to quieten the court room, he first glared at Marja until she looked down and then swivelled to Willem, who locked the magistrate's gaze like he must have done when he faced the firing squad in Indonesia. Van Niekerk broke it off, coughed, looked heavenwards, and then down to read from the notes placed in front of him — softly at first and then more strongly.

"This is Case Number. B. 616 B/1960: REGINA versus WILLEM JANSEN and MARJA DE KONING."

Van Niekerk stopped to see if he had had the desired effect. The court had hushed to hear the magistrate's prepared statement:

"Accused Number 1, who is a European male, and Accused Number 2, who is a Coloured female, were convicted under the Immorality Act, 1957, as read with Section 195(4) of Act 56/1955), of conspiring and/or having carnal intercourse with each other."

Sharpening his tone to underline the key sections of the conviction, Van Niekerk continued reading:

"The Facts Found to Be Provided. That on the night of October 4/5, 1960, based on a report provided to the Caledon Square Police Station, Warrant Officer Piet Marais, with Sergeant Viljoen and Constable Botha, gained forcible entry at Number 83, Upper Melbourne Street, District Six, the home of one Promise Madiba." The magistrate paused, took a ferret-like look at Willem and then continued. "Accused Number 1 was confronted by W.O. Piet Marais as he left the main bedroom. Accused

Number 1 was barefoot and dressed only in khaki shorts and a blue shirt.

"Accused Number 2" — he glanced at Marja — "dressed only in white pyjamas without panties, was also seen to leave the same bedroom after the warrant officer asked as to her whereabouts. As further evidence of carnal intercourse, Accused Number 2 was examined by the district surgeon at the Caledon Police Station and found to have evidence of vaginal penetration. In addition, on searching the premises, the policemen found disturbed bed sheets in the main bedroom soiled with semen and black curly hairs, probably of pubic origin. A used condom was found in the rubbish bin."

Marja gripped her wrist tighter, her whitened face fixed — Buttercup the Geisha Girl.

Willem turned to Marja and mouthed words inaudible in the erupted hullabaloo.

"Aitsa!" escaped from the gallery, followed by a peppering of "ooraaits" and "ek sês" and a few hand claps.

Promise, blank-featured, focused her concentration on Marja and Willem below.

Two sharp gavel raps brought the court back to order.

Magistrate van Niekerk took a deep breath, let it go, and continued:

"Reasons for Judgement." He looked up and returned to reading. "In my judgement as to the fact that the two accused had conspired to conduct an immoral act, I took fully into account the evidence brought by the prosecution of an ongoing relationship between Accused Number 1 and Number 2." Van Niekerk stopped, looked left and right, seemed to weigh his words and then continued.

"Under cross-examination, a porter at the Groote Schuur Hospital, Mr. Japie van Wyk of Woodstock, testified under oath that he had overheard that Accused Number 2 was a *relative* of Accused Number 1. In addition to this fact, evidence was provided of an undated letter addressed by Accused Number 1 to Accused Number 2 asking to meet at the Company Gardens during the Klopse Karnival on January 2."

An audible groan came from Willem, who sat looking at his shoes.

"In addition… In addition, police evidence was brought that Accused Number 1 was seen via binoculars disrobing in front of a brown girl at the mouth of Woodstock Cave on Table Mountain."

The magistrate looked up at Promise; she had bent forward and grabbed the balcony's handrail with both hands. A hurt expression played on her face.

"Further, it is to be noted. I say again to be doubly clear," Van Niekerk almost shouted, "further, it is to be noted that neither of the accused elected to testify on their own behalf to explain under oath why they were found in such unlawful circumstances in the house of Sister Promise Madiba. Hence, the only reasonable inference I can draw from the facts is that, at some stage during the evening of October 4, Accused Number 1 and Accused Number 2 had carnal intercourse." He paused for the final.

"I convict them both of conspiring to, and the conducting of, carnal intercourse." He gavelled the table for good measure.

Willem stood up shaking and had to be restrained

from leaving the box by a police officer. Marja bowed her head.

The crowd vented their opprobrium:

"Hau." "Aitsa." "Donner bliksem." "Hau…" resounded in the sweltering court room.

Van Niekerk stopped, gazed again at the two accused in turn, and then read again, at a register still higher than before.

"The Sentences… The legislature has seen fit to take a very serious view of contraventions under the Immorality Act by providing for a maximum penalty of seven years, with hard labour. My sentence for both accused, for contravention of this act is two — I repeat, two — years of imprisonment. Because the maximum penalty is seven years, I cannot therefore see any grounds for complaint against the sentences passed by me." Bang, bang.

Magistrate van Niekerk rose on the stroke of the second gavel and ordered Marja to stand up in the dock. She did, after which the magistrate read out her past convictions from a sheet of paper.

Past Convictions
Marja de Koning

Court & location of trial	Date of Conviction	Sentence	Crime
Cape Town	16.8.54	*£12. or 2 months*	Solicitation/ Prostitution
Cape Town	12.9.55	*£15. or 3 months*	Solicitation/ Prostitution

Van Niekerk looked Marja in the eyes. "Accused Number 2, do you acknowledge this past record?"

"I do, Your Honour." Marja stood up, grabbed her wrist across her yellow sarong, bowed briefly and then looked straight ahead. Two tear lines divided her white make-up.

"Accused Number 1 has no past record in this magistrates' court. Barrister Lamprecht Labuschagne will now address the court on behalf of the co-accused."

Labuschagne hove into upright position, mopped his freckled brow beneath his horse-hair wig with a tartan handkerchief, then leant on the paper-strewn table in front of him, both arms outstretched.

"Your Honour, Magistrate van Niekerk, and respected colleague Attorney General Treurnicht, ladies and gentlemen, you have just witnessed a gross infraction, a travesty of justice. Herewith, and with immediate effect, I lodge an appeal to the Supreme Court of South Africa. I have made the following key points in my letter to the honourable clerk of the Supreme Court here in Cape Town."

Labuschagne mopped his brow again with the moist handkerchief while he waited for the commotion from the gallery to die down and then continued, reading from the document laid out in front of him, in a booming voice.

"Point number 1. The conviction was bad in law and against the weight of the evidence.

"Point number 2. The magistrate erred in finding that the Crown had established beyond a reasonable doubt that Accused Number 1 and Accused Number 2 had committed an offence under the Immorality Act.

"Point number 3. The court erred in accepting the evidence of the Crown witness, Japie van Wyk.

"Point number 4. The sentence was excessive in the circumstances."

Labuschagne then stood back from the table, mustered his substantial girth and boomed out, "Given all of this, we ask — no, demand" — he raised the appeal foolscap clutched in his hand — "that the magistrate agrees to the immediate release of both accused upon provision of bail." Labuschagne waved the appeal for emphasis. "It is only right and proper that it should be so!"

"Hear, hear, hear, hear," echoed down from the gallery, followed by a smattering of clapping as the spectators awaited the magistrate's ruling.

Van Niekerk slammed down the gavel three times, rose, let his eyes sweep the court room, coughed, brought his hand up to his pointed face, scratched his scrawny neck and declared, "Very well, it pleases the Crown to set bail at £100 for Dr. Jansen and £115 for Miss Marja de Koning. Barrister Labuschagne, do you have sufficient bail money for an immediate release?"

"I do, Your Honour." Labuschagne lumbered back onto his feet.

The magistrate had the final word:

"Court dismissed. Court dismissed."

†

CHAPTER 28

The Cape Times Herald
The Paper that Cares.
February 15, 1961

Sensational Sentencing of Dutch Doctor and Coloured Girl Convicted under the Immorality Act: International furore ahead?

John Terreblanche

Two sensational court proceedings, on January 10 and again February 14, were conducted by the Right Honourable B.J. van Niekerk at the magistrates' court on Caledon Square, Cape Town. Dr. Willem Jansen, a Dutch citizen, and Miss Marja de Koning — wife of Mr. Henry Plaatjies, who was killed at the Langa Riots by the South African Police — have each been sentenced to two years of imprisonment for contravention of the Immorality Act.

Following a tip-off, the police raided the premises at 83 Upper Melbourne Street in District Six on the night of October 4/5 and allegedly caught the co-accused contravening the Immorality Act. The evidence presented in the court hearings was graphic, controversial and highly circumstantial in nature. This correspondent, for one, does not believe that the case will stand on appeal in the Supreme Court.

However, the government may wish to persevere in this case to claim the moral high ground; these are difficult times in South Africa for the Nationalists, faced with the prospect that the three-year-old Treason Trial — brought against the African National Congress alleging that they are a communist organisation — is likely to be thrown out of Pretoria's Supreme Court by Justice Rumpff as bogus. That and the fact that the country is under internal revolt and external siege.

The ANC is planning a national strike to coincide with the Declaration of the Republic on May 31, arguing for a National Convention to implement a democratic constitution based on "one man, one vote," given that the independence referendum was a whites-only suffrage.

And the United Nations — following a Security Council resolution after Sharpeville — has mandated that the government must "initiate measures aimed at bringing about racial harmony based on equality", and has endorsed an international boycott and economics sanctions campaign, which is hurting the Union and causing massive disinvestment in our economy.

The government needs all the moral suasion it can muster to navigate the international furore ahead.

†

CHAPTER 29

Cape Town

Promise was having none of it. "Aikona, Willem, Aikona, we must cheer you up. I know this is a serious situation but I am confident the Supreme Court will throw it out. Come now, come now with me." She looked back at Willem, who had stopped running, so she turned round, continued running backwards, C'd her arms repetitively to beckon him up and, when she saw him restart running, turned back around and ran off, up-up the familiar path, well above the tree line on Devil's Peak, her bare feet fleet in the soft dust. "Catch me and I'm yours."

Willem hesitantly gave chase. Swifter, he caught up and gently wrestled Promise onto the dusty ground under a canopy of khakibos frayed by the southeaster's gathering force. She turned on her back in its shelter sweating profusely, pulled her white shorts down to her ankles, slackened her legs and invited Willem in. He entered with a moan. They moved to a gentle, accustomed rhythm and then Promise arched up, her legs clinging around Willem's torso, they peaked together. Strained, and then relaxed.

"La petite mort." Willem buried his head between her breasts.

"What?"

"La petite mort, the little death. That's what the French call orgasm. Giving yourself over to someone else. It *is* a little death. Perhaps a big one, in my case."

"Aikona. Always so, so serious and so tense. We must hope that we will win with this appeal. That is the only way forward. Labuschagne was confident so let us be too. Now get out of me. You are going to get me pregnant. Or is that what you want? A little Willem?"

Willem rolled off Promise on to his back, his hand lingering, tracing her navel. They gazed up, the bright sky filtered by the waving khakibos. Willem shivered despite the heat.

†

Marja welcomed Promise home with open arms after her run. "You smell of Willem. It's that Old Spice aftershave. Am I right?" She tugged at her yellow sarong to pull it up beyond the still-aching scar on her chest. She liked to hide the disfigurement as best as possible, although she was secretly proud of the wound. It was almost a year ago that she had been stabbed at Langa Township; the scar reminded her how precious life was. She was going to live it to the full. "So, is he still depressed about the trial?"

"Yes, he tells me he has nightmares again. He wakes

up shivering. It brings back memories of being tortured in jail. And he can't escape."

"Yes, he told me about that awfulness when we were in the back of the police bakkie after the raid. With that horrid dog slobbering all over us." Marja dropped onto the zebra-skin couch and shifted to get comfortable among the bristles.

"That's why he's all screwed up. Have you seen how he flinches, and his neck starts twisting when he's confronted in the dock?"

"Yes."

"He tells me again, again and again how terrified he is of people in uniform — what they will do to him if he has to go to prison."

"Agh, ja. The protest marches and riots all over the place are not going to help *that* situation; there are so many people dressed in uniform, it looks like a military occupation," Marja said. "I walked down to Salt River to see some of my friends and Main Street was cordoned off again."

"Again? Shoo, shoo."

"By the police with two Saracen tanks. People were in uproar. There was shouting, toy-toying, and a tall Xhosa woman in a black doek started wailing one of those chorale laments. They were waving placards against the Riotous Assemblies Act. Apparently, now, it is an offence to even *talk* about a prohibited meeting to your friends or anyone else. Can you imagine that? Now you can be imprisoned for a year for *talking*." Marja tugged at her sarong to relieve the pressure on her chest and sagged deeper into the bristly couch.

†

Seated in a less-than-comfortable chair, Dr. Willem Jansen looked around the superintendent's untidy room. He had been summoned to Dr. Visagie's office for the first time since his arrival at Groote Schuur Hospital some six years before. Not much had changed. The superintendent still looked the worse for wear. His craggy features consumed in a haze of cigarette smoke, Dr. Visagie coughed twice and raised his bushy eyebrows before speaking from behind his desk.

"Good morning, Dr. Jansen. Comfortable? Let's begin." He leant back, the squeak of his chair competing with the woosh of the ceiling fan. "It has come to my attention that you are a regular feature in the *Cape Times Herald*." He rapped the newspaper, lying open on the desk in front of him. "We don't like that. Bad publicity for Groote Schuur. I think you know that I know that you had a less than honourable past in Holland." Dr. Visagie took another draw from his cigarette and leant forward across the desk.

"Yes, Dr. Visagie, I half expected that you had been informed from Holland," Willem replied stiffly.

"Well, what are we going to do about it? If I have the story straight, you are involved with not one but two non-white women." Visagie held up two yellowed fingers. "And this… and this," he stammered, "after I told you at your interview in this very office to stay clear of such situations, by moving to Rondebosch. A nice white suburb, and not to get involved in the mixed areas. These black sirens will get the better of a man." The doctor blew out a gush of smoke with a hiss.

"Agh ja. Agh, ja." Willem sucked his teeth, his eyes low. "It's complicated, very complicated."

"That might be... that might be, but we expect our doctors to be above such matters. We can have no impropriety on the premises. You can take it that your position here is now under review. You are being put on notice. I have launched an internal investigation and, if it pans out, *you* will be out on your ear. Understood? Verstaan jy?"

"Agh, ja. I do." Willem got up unsteadily and exited the office.

†

Marja felt compelled to go to the first anniversary of the Langa Riot but was scared to go alone. Although Promise was helping to mend the break left by her husband's loss, Marja had not been able to attend Plaatjies's funeral a year before as she had been recovering from her stabbed heart at Groote Schuur Hospital, and so had not found much closure. She had not made amends for using Henry, nor was his death *real* in her mind; it felt like he had just gone away.

Marja had heard announcements about the memorial service on her Gallo radio, now balanced on the windowsill of Promise's kitchen. Springbok Radio reported on the country-wide preparations for the first anniversary of the Sharpeville and Langa massacres to be held on March 21, 1961. There was a steady drumbeat of gathering tension around the country as police activity intensified to prepare for the inevitable unrest.

Townships were being cordoned off by tanks, meetings prohibited, and people banned or subjected to twelve-day imprisonment without charge. The government had banned the ANC and PAC for another year, again branding them illegal organisations, but had relented to enormous pressure from abroad and granted a passport to Ex-Chief A.J. Luthuli, former president of the ANC, so he could travel to Oslo, to receive the Nobel Peace Prize. Protest go-slows and work stoppage became the order of the day round the country.

"Will you take me, Promise?" Marja asked over a pot of tea brewing between them.

They took De Waal Drive round Hospital Bend, down onto Settlers Way, and drove past the high cooling towers before turning at the checkpoint into Langa Township, to park a short distance from the field where events had brought them together a year earlier.

They held hands as they edged their way through the crowd to stand in front of the makeshift podium erected at the centre of the field.

A bugler sounded the Last Post next to the lectern before a lean preacher gathered himself. His black cassock fluttered in the breeze.

He raised his voice to the crowd. "We are congregated to commemorate our fallen brothers on this sad, sad day." He raised his right hand to the Lord, his left planted firmly on the Bible weighing on the unsteady stand. "Let us pray for those who have trespassed against us. Let us pray for Mr. Henry Plaatjies. Let us pray for —" Their two names were lost, engulfed by the rising tide of "Amandla... Amandla..." which caused police hands to tighten around their Sten guns — a tight cordon of menace ringing the rocky field.

A loudhailer barked: "Please stay calm. Please stay calm. We respect the dead. We respect the dead. We will allow you to pray. We will allow you to pray. In peace."

Promise enfolded Marja in her arms to stem the grief.

†

In the lavish offices of Lamprecht Labuschagne B.A. L.L.B, on Buitenkant Street, Marja and Willem sat waiting in mahogany chairs across from the barrister's large desk. They had been asked to take their seats while the secretary got them a cup of coffee. Typically dressed in yellow and black, respectively, Marja fidgeted with her hairdo while Willem pressed his hands together at his face as if in prayer and looked straight forward; his jaw muscles bulged as he ground his teeth.

They were startled by Labuschagne's sudden appearance. Dressed in a flamboyant suit, he mopped his brow with a tartan handkerchief, settled himself in his leather chair and opened the conversation.

"So, how are you both? I thought it high time for an update and to consider strategy."

Willem barely suppressed a neck torsion; Marja tightened her clasped wrist.

"I know your bail was steep, and that is certainly concerning, but I believe I can make a superior case to the Supreme Court that will destroy Magistrate van Niekerk's case. Destroy it, I say again, forcing the court to set aside your case."

"Agh, ja, but I don't buy it," Willem said. "Once the state has made up its mind to put us away in prison, I am certain they will persevere. And I can't go to prison, I just can't." He crunched his teeth.

The secretary brought in three cups of coffee, and all three took sips and waited for her to exit before proceeding.

"Your case has been much in the news, and that can play to our advantage." Labuschagne took another gulp of coffee. "At least if we manage it properly. Last week I was invited to the Dutch embassy, to meet with the ambassador."

"The Dutch ambassador?" Willem bared his teeth.

"Yes. Obviously, they have taken an interest in your case."

"Hoe zo?" Marja asked.

"They wanted to know how likely you are to be acquitted. And what might be done to assure this. They certainly don't want a Dutch citizen imprisoned under the Immorality Act."

"And... and... what did you say?" Marja continued.

"I said it may depend on whom is assigned to be the appellate justice and gave them a name."

Willem, shook his bowed head, looked up and asked, "Lamprecht, do you really think that will do it?"

"That, and my superior argument. I am confident."

"Agh, agh, I hope so," Willem said and then turned to Marja. "Why don't you ask your question?"

A wailing police siren gathered and then receded before she continued.

"Yes, ja, I have been wondering how it happened that Mr. Terreblanche joined us for dinner, that night at the

Taj Mahal restaurant. Had you invited him?" She looked pointedly at the barrister.

"No, no." He lowered his eyelids and his face coloured redder than its usual pink hue. "I don't know how J.T. knew that I had invited you three to the Taj. All I can think of is that he must have got it off my daily calendar on my secretary's desk. J.T. has been in and out of here ever since he called me up to ask for an interview with you on that first day we met. How long ago was that?"

"Well, October 5, Referendum Day, till today, May 5, 1961," Marja read off the calendar resting on the desk between them. "That's exactly six, no… seven months."

"Marja, that is enough about that. I want to know about the court case. When are we going to have this bloody court case? I am sick and tired of waiting and wondering about my future." Willem lunged forward to glare into Labuschagne's now-wide-open eyes.

"I bet the government is calculating the date," Labuschagne motioned his arms expansively, "so that newspaper reports about your case will have the minimum political impact. I expect the 29th or 30th of this month. Certainly, before the 31st, when the newspapers will be full of the Republic Day celebration. I will call you as soon as I know."

†

CHAPTER 30

The Cape Times Herald
The Paper that Cares.
May 24, 1961

South Africa on War Footing for Republic Day Celebrations
John Terreblanche

Against the background of increasing sanctions, boycotts of South African goods, and condemnations by the international community of apartheid policies, the country will finally divorce from Great Britain and declare itself a republic next Wednesday, May 31. On this day in 1902, the Anglo-Boer War, fought against the British forces, ended with the signing of the Treaty of Vereeniging. Eight years later, the Cape of Good Hope, Natal, the Orange Free State and the Transvaal united to form the Union of South Africa. That union will finally declare its independence from Great Britain. Accordingly, a public holiday and celebrations are planned throughout the country.

But so too are protests. The ANC has organised a stay-away for the 29th, 30th and 31st to protest. Mr. Mandela, the ANC's spokesman, announced in a recent statement to the press that the demonstrations are not meant to be anti-white and are planned to be peaceful and disciplined. He has called upon the coloured people and Indians as well as "democratic" whites to stage demonstrations too.

Thousands of leaflets have been distributed around the country calling on "all freedom-loving South Africans of all races" to make the next six weeks "a time of active protest, demonstration and organisation" against the Verwoerd Republic.

Dr. Verwoerd has responded in kind in Parliament: "I am prepared to say that we regard the present position as very serious and that we shall be equipped to meet it... The government... has instructed the organisation at its disposal to prepare the most detailed plans."

Concomitantly, the Defence Amendment Act has empowered the Government to quell "internal disorder" using the means of war, giving the military the authority to commandeer vehicles, equipment, foodstuffs and other matériel that in the past could only be exercised in wartime.

And the Police Amendment Act has provided for a reserve police force, a citizen unit, to help to conduct routine tasks when policemen are needed for more urgent responsibilities.

Over the last two weeks thousands of police raids have been conducted and we have seen the greatest mobilisation of the military, commando and citizen force units ever seen in peace time in our country

†

When riots or protests occur, townships have been surrounded by the military to contain them and all gatherings of any kind have been banned from May 19 to June 26.

†

360

CHAPTER 31

Devil's Peak

As the telephone rang, the black handpiece bounced in its cradle on a side table at Promise's house.

"Yes, this is Marja de Koning, kan ek help?"

"Good morning, this is Mr. Labuschagne's office. Please hold and I will put you through to him."

"Miss de Koning, dit is Mr. Labuschagne. I have been trying to get hold of Dr. Jansen but he has not been answering his telephone at home. Your case will be heard in the Cape Supreme Court on the 30th."

"Hai, that's four days away. Anything we must do?"

"Yes, just tell Willem, and you should both probably pack a small suitcase just in case, but I am hopeful, and show up please, on time, nine o'clock sharp."

"Okay, we will do that. You make me worried."

"And remember, it's in the Cape *Supreme* Court on Keerom Street, not the magistrates' court on Parade Street."

"Okay, I'll tell him. How do you think it'll go?"

The barrister had hung up.

Willem floored the accelerator of his Beetle to run the red stop light. All the robots on Main Street seemed to be stacked against him. He wanted to get home to his flat and hide the amber bottle of ether he had repurposed from the operating theatre now lying beside him on the black seat, barely hidden under a yellow strip of chamois. He felt mortified and ashamed. What would his parents think if they were still alive? How had it come to this? He had broken the law and all he wanted was Promise's love. He wanted to belong somewhere and that was impossible.

Willem was convinced that the court case would go against him and there was no way forward. He passed the Rondebosch Fountain and parked his car one tyre sloping on the pavement; thankfully there was an open space right in front of his flat. He switched off the engine, opened the car door, and exited onto the roadway, all the while cradling the chamois-wrapped anaesthetic in his left arm to hide it from view. A fast-moving car honked and swept narrowly past as Willem barrelled upstairs and into the flat.

He placed the bottle of anaesthetic on the kitchen table and went looking for his pipe. Godverdomme! He was out of tobacco. He took a swig of ether instead. Goddamn, it burnt. He opened the fridge, yanked out a bottle of milk and downed half a pint, his Adam's apple jiggling with each gulp. Then Willem stretched out on a lounge chair and stared out of the windows, letting the afternoon's softening light and street sounds wash over him as he decided what to do.

He must have taken too much ether because he dreamt of being with his father. Willem climbed up the high mountains in Bandung with him. The captain looked back at his son, beckoning upwards. The beauty of the grand mountains surrounded them as they ascended the hilly track together.

Willem awakened and shook his head to stop his eyes from their twist; he controlled his left arm to stand up and noted from the clock that hours had passed.

He took the bottle of milk to his desk in the bedroom and sat down to his diary. He leant back in his chair, thought of his dead father's beckoning and made a final note, signing it for good measure. Then he collected all seven diaries from his desk and placed them in a cardboard shoebox from his cupboard. He took out his photo album and, after carefully looking through it from beginning to end, placed it below the shoebox back in the cupboard.

Willem sat thinking for a while and then got up to arrange his clothes, folding them into their correct shapes and place. He tidied the bedroom, straightening each Javanese landscape in turn and then, after pausing at some far-off place, hung next day's suit on his valet stand.

He put on his white pyjamas and got underneath the sheets — the last thing he saw was Marja's carved figurine, a flicker on the bedstand.

†

Monday the 29th, the first day of the stay-at-home, out on police patrol, Piet angled the helicopter at altitude over the Cape Flats. He loved the shudder of the powerful engine, the smell of gasoline, and the vortex as the machine descended over Settlers Way so that Johan, the co-pilot, could give a better report.

"Caledon Square, Caledon Square, this is alpha-tango-bravo-one. Do you read me? Over."

"Loud and clear. Loud and clear. How are you two fine fellows today? It's Johan and Piet, isn't it? Over."

"Ja." "Ja." they both responded into the helmet microphones brushing their lips.

"It's a beautiful day up here," Johan added. "Over."

"Well. Out with it, what do you see? Over."

"We've flown over to Somerset West, then out to the Strand and then back along the coast to Muizenberg and we're now back over Langa Township. There're fires all over the Cape Flats. I count ten out to Somerset West. And Nyanga and Langa Township have cordons around them, with Saracen tanks and army trucks surrounding the areas. When we were over Strand Township, we saw a clump of people gathering on the soccer field, so we hovered over them until they dispersed. That usually does it. Over." Johan said.

"Okay. Any sign of a riot anywhere? Over."

"No; except for the burning tyres, it's pretty quiet. All the police raids you guys have been conducting must have got rid of the Tsotsis causing the problems. Over."

Johan chuckled and looked over at Piet, who was manoeuvring the helicopter high above the slope of Devil's Peak. They looked down at two small figures running below.

Willem and Promise ran up the wide path abreast, the thud of a helicopter dissipating above, sunlight lowering on the Atlantic. Willem had invited Promise for one last run before his court case the next day. He had extended the invitation across the operating table without a word. A meeting and deflection of their eyes, upwards in the direction of the great mountain. Now they were beyond the tree line and halfway up to the King's Blockhouse, nestled below the ragged mountain's stony tip, a sheer climb that Willem had always wanted to attempt but turned away from as impossible. Now, he wanted to summit the peak, to stand at its top, just once.

Promise, running steadily beside him, faltered, and then bent double.

"What's wrong, Promise?"

"I'm nauseous, my stomach is a knot; please go on without me."

"I can't."

"You must. I am feeling weak, and it will get too-too dark for you on the way back. I will slow you down."

Willem spread his arms around Promise's shoulders from behind, marked her neck with three soft kisses, said goodbye, and trundled up the stony trail, not looking back.

He thought of what had brought him to this time, this place, as the rhythm of his running set in, the surrounding fynbos peppery in the rising breeze.

His playful youth with Marja, growing up in Indonesia.

His climbs with his father in the mountains above Bandung.

His first kiss under the Dago waterfall, Marja's breasts against his chest.

He side-stepped a rock that had blocked the stony pathway.

His first corpse, killed by Japanese bombing.

His gunrunning and capture by the Kempeitai.

His imprisonment and confinement, and the torture that hurt and hurt and sent his head spinning and the piped water that choked and choked him until he wanted to die.

His footfall now unsteady, Willem twisted into a curve steepening the path, took a deeper breath, and strained upwards.

The firing squad that didn't kill him but made him shit in his pants.

Then his cowardice in the Japanese concentration camps — his need to survive the only imperative.

His volunteering as a nursing aid and wish to become a surgeon.

His abandonment of Marja in Indonesia after being freed.

His travel to Holland to study medicine at Leiden.

Willem deepened his breath further, shivered, and laboured onto the contour path that led to the Kings Blockhouse. He stopped when he got there to look out over the dusking view. He peered up at Devil's Peak and started the slow climb up its steep face, clawing his way upwards along its bare stone wall.

His trouble with anxiety and paranoia and the recurring nightmares of imprisonment and authority figures.

His ether abuse to still his anxiousness.

His pervasive anger and banishment from Holland for hitting a colleague. The shame.

Then Groote Schuur.

And then Promise.

Willem panted, the rocks cool under his clasping hands. His plimsolls planted in crevice after crevice as he rose the sheer face; his grasp had the desperation of Russian roulette.

And then Marja.

And the police raid and apartheid and separation by race.

And the court case.

And prison.

Almost spent, Willem clawed to the top of Devil's Peak. He lay panting and broken — the life-threatening climb at bay.

And for what? Willem was beyond despair.

Promise could take care of Marja.

And, presently, Willem stood up and turned to gaze out at the Cape Flats — the sun lost beneath the horizon. And then, much later, Willem must have looked down, back at the dark tortuous path he had come.

And… fell.

CHAPTER 32

Court Record

IN THE SUPREME COURT OF SOUTH AFRICA

(CAPE OF GOOD HOPE PROVINCIAL DIVISION)

In the matter of

WILLEM JANSEN. Appellant: NOT PRESENT

And

MARJA DE KONING. Appellant: PRESENT

And.

REGINA

Lamprecht Labuschagne B.A. L.L.B

Respondent

JUDGMENT delivered 30th May 1961

Botha. J.A.

First Appellant, a European man, and Second Appellant, a non-European female, were charged together with contravention of Section 16(2)(a), subsections (ii) & (iii) of Act 23 of 1957 and Section 16(1)(b) subsections (ii) & (iii) respectively. Both pleaded not guilty but were found guilty by the magistrate of conspiring together to have unlawful intercourse (by virtue of the provisions of Section 54 of Act 68 of 1957) and sentenced to two years of imprisonment, stayed upon appeal, and without compulsory labour. The main point taken on appeal is that the conviction is against the weight of the evidence and, more particularly, that the Crown had not established beyond reasonable doubt that the accused had committed or conspired to commit an offence under the Immorality Act.

Three police constables, following up on a report, went on the night in question to No. 83 Upper Melbourne Street, District Six, the house owned by Sister Promise Madiba, who works at the Groote Schuur Hospital. They knocked on the door several times but failed to gain admission, so they forced their way in. All three constables entered the main room and first found Appellant No. 1, dressed in khaki shorts, with an untucked blue shirt. He was barefoot and aggressive towards the policemen. Then Appellant No. 2, a coloured female, appeared out of the main bedroom, dressed in a white pyjama. According to the arresting warrant officer, she was not wearing panties. The constables inspected the house and found,

in /....

in the main bedroom, that the bed sheets were crumpled, still warm, had black curly hairs in evidence, and were stained with a gluey substance. Upon forensic analysis, this substance was shown to contain spermatozoa. They also found a used condom (without spermatozoa) in the dustbin, and a package of five condoms in the night drawer of the second bedroom.

Both Appellants were thereafter arrested.

Other evidence in the case was that Appellant No. 2, after the arrest, was inspected by the district surgeon in prison. He determined that the coloured female had suffered penetration of her vagina by an object. There was evidence of scratches and bleeding in her female parts.

The prosecution also offered an undated letter, sent to Appellant No. 2, allegedly by Appellant No. 1, to meet him at the Company Gardens during the Klopse Carnival, which I find to be circumstantial and inconclusive.

There were only two other testimonies brought in the case (Appellants elected not to give evidence). One was that of a white orderly, Japie van Wyk, from Groote Schuur Hospital. The orderly testified that he had heard Sister Promise Madiba, the owner of the house in question, allege that Appellant No. 2 was a relative of Appellant No. 1. And the second testimony, accepted by the magistrate as fact, was even more dubious. Namely, that, due to police surveillance of Appellant No. 1 and Sister Madiba, a police constable had

allegedly /....

allegedly seen Appellant No. 1 disrobe in front of a coloured female in the mouth of Woodstock Cave on Table Mountain.

The magistrate concludes: "Hence, the only reasonable inference I can draw from the facts is that, at some stage during the course of the evening of October 4, Accused Number 1 and Accused Number 2 had carnal intercourse. I convict them of conspiring to, and the conducting of, carnal intercourse." The magistrate accordingly convicted them of such a conspiracy to intercourse.

Conspiracy to commit a crime requires the sentient agreement of the two or more accused to commit the criminal act (vide. R. v. Solomon, 15 S.C. 107 and R. v. Dhlamini, 1941, O.P.D. 154). Simple intention is insufficient: there must be an actual concurrence of conscious thinking to commit the act in question.

And that concurrence need not be explicit through the spoken word, as the agreement may be arrived at tacitly (vide. e.g., R. v. B., 1956 (3) S.A. 363-365).

Further, where this agreement is inferred from the actions of the conspirators, these inferences must follow the cardinal rules of logic summarised in R. v. Blom, 1939 A.D. pp. 202 & 203, and be consistent with all proven facts as well as exclude all reasonable inferences except for the one sought to be drawn. Further, there is no evidence that actual intercourse took place between the two Appellants. The Magistrate presented evidence that Appellant No. 2's.

vagina /....

vagina had been "penetrated with an object" The inference made was that it was Appellant No. 1 who was the penetrator. But there were no spermatozoa present in Appellant No. 2. The only semen that was found was on the bed sheet, which does not in itself constitute a crime. Hence the damage done to Appellant No. 2 might have been self-inflicted. A condom was found in the dustbin. I have heard of candles, covered with a condom, used by certain females as a means of self-gratification. Which, again, does not constitute a crime.

With all of these considerations, I cannot find it possible to share the magistrate's view that the only reasonable inference from the facts presented is that "at some stage" the two either conspired, or conducted, unlawful carnal intercourse together. This clearly can only be held as speculation on the magistrate's part and thus, in my view, without validity.

That the whole scenario in the house was an unusual one is patently obvious. One might go on to say that this certainly rouses strong suspicion regarding the relationship between the two Appellants. But the offences stipulated under the Immorality Act are specific and cannot be attributed to an accused unless the evidence brought is equally specific and unequivocal. For the reasons given above, the appeal of both Appellants is allowed, and the convictions and sentences are set aside.

Botha J.A.

Justice of the Supreme Court: Cape Provincial
Administration.

Neveling.V.

Registrar of the Supreme Court: Cape Town.

†

CHAPTER 33

The Cape Times Herald
The Paper that Cares.
May 31, 1961

REPUBLIC DAY CELEBRATIONS
By Editors

Despite widespread strikes, boycotts, and calls to stay at home, South Africa declares itself a republic.

Today is the first day of the New Republic of South Africa. To prevent violent protests from spreading across the country, Prime Minister Hendrik Verwoerd has staged the largest peacetime call up of military and police personnel since the War. Saracen tanks patrol townships and police helicopters the air, while meetings have been banned, printing presses seized, and legislation passed in Parliament to permit the police to detain charged prisoners for twelve days without bail...

†

The Cape Times Herald

The Paper that Cares.

May 31, 1961

DUTCH DOCTOR FALLS FROM DEVIL'S PEAK

John Terreblanche

Dr. Willem Jansen, a noted Dutch surgeon at Groote Schuur Hospital, fell to his death while climbing Devil's Peak. Jansen, who was born in Indonesia and had been interned and tortured in a Japanese prisoner of war camp there during the Second World War, had recently been charged under the Immorality Act. He was to appear in the Supreme Court, yesterday, to appeal a sentence of two years of imprisonment. Dr. Jansen has no living family in South Africa and no descendants. He will be buried at the Groote Schuur Hospital Cemetery, tomorrow, at 2 p.m.

†

EPILOGUE

As I think back on how this story has unwound, I am strung up with guilt and a feeling of deep loss. My stringing started when Dr. Willem Jansen didn't arrive for the Supreme Court hearing. I did not know then that Willem had had a misadventure but sensed something dreadful had happened from Promise and Marja's demeanour that day. They were both dressed in black and had taken their usual positions, Promise up in the gallery, Marja in the dock across from where Willem should have sat. Neither would catch my eye but, sensing my querulous look, both stolidly looked down: Promise sucked in her cheeks and glowered; Marja tightened the hold she had on her wrist, an epitome of sorrow. I got the feeling that I was to blame for whatever had prevented Willem from attending.

And then, when an usher came and called me to the waiting telephone call outside, I started sweating; my cravat felt like a noose around my neck, constricting further when my worst fears were confirmed. Willem had fallen from Devil's Peak. I suspected suicide; my feelings of reproach intensified. After all, I had instigated the police raid.

Having heard from the orderly, Japie van Wyk, about the goings-on at Groote Schuur Hospital between Sister Madiba and Dr. Jansen, I had verified the facts by spying on Promise's cottage from my Porsche and so had reported my findings to the police chief at Caledon Square Police Station — launching the raid. I was responsible for Willem's untimely death.

You see, before this tragedy, I thought I was doing the right thing by providing the necessary information to the police, but now I deeply regret what happened. If only I could twist back the clock to unwind my actions. I should have thought further. I should have set aside my wish to make some easy money. I should have known better that prosecutions under the Immorality Act have dire consequences. I should have...

The fact of the matter is that the pursuit of this story changed me. Or, rather, getting to know Promise, Marja and Willem and their loving relationship did.

At first, my upbringing prejudiced me against them. A love triangle between a black woman, a coloured prostitute and fallen Dutch doctor who was in the habit of taking ether for breakfast did not sit well with me. But then my perspective changed. As I attended the Immorality Act court proceedings (and the Taj Mahal dinner) I realised that the colour bar was a nonsense. Love is colour-blind. And so I asked myself the question I ask of you: *can there be anything immoral in human behaviour when it fosters love? Can there? Shouldn't we take love wherever we can find it as they did?*

Accordingly, my mission changed mid-stream.

At first, I was motivated by money — I would write

a book and sell the story so that I could leave my debts behind me and leave the country to start a new life abroad.

But now I needed a guilt salve. I had, unwittingly, engineered the death of a friend, a man who had trusted in me and whom I had failed. Utterly. I needed forgiveness for my role in this tragic loss, by bearing witness to events. Like Shakespeare's Hamlet, who used a play as the means to assuage the guilt he felt for his father's death, I needed to find a means of atonement for my abhorrent act. I needed to keep Willem's memory alive, and the story of Marja and his prosecution under the Immorality Act in the public conscience. It was my journalistic responsibility.

But the problem was whether I was up to it. Was I a good enough writer to bear witness to this heartbreak? After all, I am just a hack reporter working for a little-known newspaper, and an imposter at that. Could I render adequate testimony to these complicated events to get a book published to champion this cause?

I let it all rest for a while — quite a while, I must admit. But then Willem forced my hand so to speak — compelling me from beyond the grave to complete the story.

In November of 1961, I was sitting in my third-floor office at the *Cape Times Herald*, worrying about my inability to secure a passport to leave the country now that Alan Paton, the celebrated author of *Cry the Beloved Country*, had had his withdrawn, when my reverie was suddenly broken by a sharp knock on my door. A brown paper parcel, tied tight with coarse string, was deposited on my desk by the delivery boy. It was addressed to me in black Koki pen. The sender, till today, remains a mystery. But the source not. The parcel contained an envelope crammed with newspaper cuttings (mostly authored by me and included in this book), a photograph album, and Dr. Jansen's seven diaries. A wealth of information that would help authenticate the book.

But, to conclude this history to my satisfaction, I needed to know what had become of Promise and Marja. You see, I never returned to the court room after taking the telephone call that fateful day when they found Willem dead on Devil's Peak, because I could not face the girls' anguish and so could not render a first-hand account of the court proceedings myself — hence I have included the court record in these writings instead.[1]

Unsurprisingly, I lost all contact with the girls despite my earlier efforts to achieve closure with them. I suspected I was persona non grata; the girls felt they had revealed too much to me or worse. My telephone calls to the District Six cottage remained unanswered; Promise was no longer working at the Casualty Unit, and my carefully penned letters of invitation for a rendezvous were returned to sender, address unknown.

But now I was desperate to find them, having received Willem's trove of material, so that I could finish the book and serve as an effective witness to their story. As I sat looking out my office window over the Company Gardens, the fine vista framed by the massive presence of Table Mountain looming beyond, I remembered something, probably from the dinner we had had together at the Taj Mahal in District Six. The girls liked to visit Decca Records on Tennant Street, across the way from the Hanover

---

[1]   *Such a copy has been appended in Chapter 32.*

Building, on Saturdays, to purchase records. I had my plan for a stake-out.

Saturday upon Saturday, I was in and out of Decca Records. My L.P. collection burgeoned, my funds dwindled, all to no avail. I had a favourite booth in the back of the shop. I put on the headphones, closed the glass-paned door and watched, unobserved, the centre record display where customers congregated to peruse the latest collection. Finally, after about three months of wasted Saturdays, I was rewarded. My long-playing record had just finished, so I heard the tinkle-bell that announced yet another customer's entrance.

Marja and Promise manoeuvred a pram through the door, positioned it in front of the Jazz Records section, conveniently in front of my booth, turned their backs on me and continued their conversation while leafing through the sleeved records in front of them.

I was able to surreptitiously observe them, and set the glassed door ajar, so I could clearly hear their conversation. Perfect.

They held hands and took turns folding down the records after examining each carefully and passing comments.

Marja: "That's a nice one. I like Miriam Makebe."

Promise: "Aikona, silly, we have that one already at home. You've heard it playing many times."

Marja: "I suppose I have. I should study the L.P. covers better."

Then, I heard a baby's sniffled cry from the pram, positioned next to Promise, who said, "Marja, it's your turn to pick up our baby."

"Agh, yes, but only you can give Willem breast milk." Marja bent over the pram and picked up the boy, dressed in a little white suit, his pudgy brownish legs writhing as his stubby toes curled.

Marja swung the boy across her saronged hip and turned to face my booth, attempting to hush Willem by gently swaying from side to side. She looked down at the boy with love in her face. "Shush, shush, Willem, shush, shush. Promise, are you ready for milking?" Marja's cheeks rose.

"Oh yes, let me go into a booth with him. It is nice and quiet there." Promise also turned to face my booth. All three must have seen me at precisely the same time, for all three responded.

"Aikona, aikona, hau, what are you doing? Spying on us?" shouted Promise.

"Ag, nee, ag, nee, daai man again, sies," wailed Marja, clutching the baby tighter.

While little Willem balled his heart out, setting up a skreich that I can never forget to this day.

I had opened the booth door further, to escape, but Promise wasn't going to let me get away easily. She put her booted foot against the door, jamming me halfway out of the booth.

As I struggled to extricate myself, and Promise leant into the door, I could smell the sweat broiling out of her. She was incensed, a wild cat protecting her brood. She snarled like one too as I freed myself and scurried for the front door. "Get out. Get out of our lives. You've screwed us up. Just leave us alone," Promise yelled at my receding back. I left Decca Records, feeling ever more guilty and remorseful. And... unredeemed.

THE END

The Cape Times Herald

The Paper that Cares.

May 13, 1963

JOURNALIST JOHN TERREBLANCHE APPREHENDED at S.A. BORDER.

By Special Correspondent

Mr. John Terreblanche, who was until quite recently employed by this newspaper as a political and police reporter, was apprehended on Beit Bridge, at the railway crossing into Rhodesia. Mr. Terreblanche has recently published an acclaimed novel entitled *Immorality Act*, which has been banned in South Africa. The book has been published by The Book Guild Ltd in England and tells the history of a Xhosa sister from Groote Schuur Hospital and of the prosecution of Dr. Willem Jansen and Marja de Koning, under the Immorality Act. The case against them was set aside by the Supreme Court on June 30, 1961. Tragically, Dr. Willem Jansen fell to his death from Devil's Peak the day before the Supreme Court ruling.

John Terreblanche, who is well known to this correspondent, told me before he left that he felt the need to write the novel to "bear witness to Dr. Jansen's wanton death caused by the immoral apartheid legislation that is the Immorality Act". He also told me that, having published the book, he fears for his life if he remains in South Africa.

The Cape Times Herald commits to keeping you up to date on our colleague's fate.

†

ACKNOWLEDGEMENTS

Prime acknowledgement goes to Ulane, my wife. We contrived *Immorality Act* in 2019 after I had attended a fiction writing course at Cambridge University's International Summer Writing Programme, where I learnt that a novel was indeed possible. Ulane has helped shape this story ever since, by providing innumerable ideas for, and critiques of, my writing.

I wrote *Immorality Act* during my enrolment for a master's in fine art degree in creative writing through Carlow University in Pittsburgh, and thus am most thankful for the mentorship I received from Joseph Bathanti, Evelyn Conlon, Carlo Gebler and Niall Williams in support of writing the novel.

Obviously, this historical novel required a great deal of reading to situate Willem's, Marja's, Promise's and John's fictional stories within the historical arc of the time, hence I have been most grateful for the many sources that I have tapped, only a few of which are listed below.

I was born in Indonesia, lived there and grew up as a Dutch national in apartheid South Africa living in Cape

Town for close to 15 years, where I went to medical school at Stellenbosch University and trained as well as practised anaesthesia through the University of Cape Town at the Groote Schuur Hospital, and so ran the many footpaths that criss-cross Table Mountain and Devil's Peak, as Promise and Willem did in the book. (No one should climb the ragged front of Devil's Peak.)

My father was also born in Indonesia and imprisoned in a Japanese concentration camp as a youth, liberated, and returned to Holland to become a doctor and eventually settled in South Africa (as Dr. Willem Jansen does in the novel, but Willem's character in no way resembles my father.) My father has written of his experiences, which has greatly helped inform the novel with respect to Indonesia and Holland.

I accessed many accounts (mostly in Dutch) and several videos: *De Buitenkampers*, for example, which witnessed the 300,000 Indos who were subjected to the violent Indonesian nationalism that prevailed after World War II — one of which informed Marja de Koning's rape, necessitating her repatriation to Holland.

The Surveys of Race Relations in South Africa (1957–1958 & 1959–1960), both compiled by Muriel Horrell for the South African Institute of Race Relations, were an invaluable resource.

The *Reader's Digest Illustrated History of South Africa* (1994), as well as *Long Walk to Freedom* (1994) by Nelson Mandela, *Memoirs of a Geisha* (1997) by Arthur Golden, *The Brotherhoods: Street Gangs and State Control in Cape Town* (1984) by Don Pinnock, *Buckingham Palace District Six* (1986) by Richard Rive, *Sugar Girls and Seamen*

(2008) by Henry Trotter and *The Covenant* (1980) by David Michener deserve special mention, as do my many computer visits to Wikipedia, YouTube and the internet to find historical detail of Cape Town and District Six in the 1950s.

The District Six Museum in Cape Town is another valuable resource that I have visited; the maps and photos on their website were of great help to reconstruct District Six as it was between 1950 and 1961. (The Blue Lagoon is a fictitious night club in the Hanover Building.)

The book has benefitted from the research performed by Joline Young, who was able to find an original court record at the Cape Town Archives of an Immorality Act case brought in 1958 and prosecuted in both the magistrates' and Supreme Courts of Cape Town, allowing me to bring further verisimilitude to the book.

For all those who have not been acknowledged, and have wittingly or unwittingly helped inform this book, thank you.

Berend Mets M.B. Ch.B. Ph.D. M.F.A.

ABOUT THE AUTHOR

Dr. Berend Mets was born in Indonesia of Dutch parents, has lived on four continents, and among other countries grew up in South Africa under apartheid, where he became a doctor, anaesthetist and scientist. He came to writing fiction after a career of medical and scientific writing and has published two books for the lay person: *Waking Up Safer? An Anesthesiologist's Record* and *Leadership in Anaesthesia: Five Pioneers of the Deadly Quest for Surgical Insensibility.*

Berend divides his time between the USA, the Dutch Caribbean and Cape Town, South Africa. *Immorality Act* is his debut novel.

†

Made in United States
Troutdale, OR
03/22/2024